A Heron's Balance

by Cathy Barker

www. HERONSBALANCE .com

206 - 390 - 4990

Copyright © 2007 by Cathy Barker

ISBN 0-7414-3938-7

Scripture excerpts from the New Revised Standard Version Bible, copyright 1989, Division of Christian Education of the National Council of the Churches of Christ in the United States of America. Used by permission. All rights reserved.

Cover: Sketch by Linda Barker, photo by Cathy Barker, design by Scott Ward.

Inside: Photos and sketches by Cathy Barker.

Published by:

PUBLISHING.COM

1094 New DeHaven Street, Suite 100
West Conshohocken, PA 19428-2713
Info@buybooksontheweb.com
www.buybooksontheweb.com
Toll-free (877) BUY BOOK
Local Phone (610) 941-9999
Fax (610) 941-9959

Printed in the United States of America

Printed on Recycled Paper

Published April 2007

Acknowledgments

My deepest gratitude to God for the blessings of all creation, and for the extraordinary people who grace my life.

I am indebted to Patricia Schneider and her Creative Writing class for helping me get a start on this project. Yet this novel would never have been awakened from its dormancy if not for the energies of the Seattle summer creativity group: Kizzie Jones, Maggie Bassetti, Paul Tonnes, and our ingenious leader, artist Scott Ward (scottwardart.com). My deepest thanks to you. I am grateful to Eleanor, Griffin, and Duncan for the use of their names. I have gained deep inspiration from *The Phoenix Affirmations* by Rev. Dr. Eric Elnes, and the influence of this work, especially Affirmation 3, will be evident. My family has provided support and encouragement all along, as have friends and church members. Most of all I thank my husband, Dick Weaver (a fine writer himself) without whom I would never have experienced the Boundary Waters and discovered its healing potency.

The best and safest thing
is to keep a balance in your life,
acknowledge the great powers
around us and in us.

Euripides
(484 BCE – 406 BCE)

Chapter 1

Good sense somehow prevented Jack from tearing up the check. He tore up the compassionate letter instead, and swept the pieces into the trash.

$100,000.00.

How dare they suppose – some distant, faceless insurance company –that $100,000 could pay for the loss of a life? His dear Abby, his wife for ten years, gone. And this check was supposed to make him feel better? The anger welled up again. He hated insurance companies and their forms. He hated drunks, he hated drivers, he hated drunk drivers most of all. He slammed his hand down on the table, making the dirty dishes jump. And then he cradled his throbbing hand.

Jack Freeman was discontented before, but his wife's death had sent him spiraling down. He had been unhappy in his job for years. Teaching English at a Community College was supposed to be a stepping stone, but he had never taken the next step.

He had written his letter of resignation. He'd written at least six of them at various times in the last few years. They were all there in his desk drawer, shoved in with a sigh as the fear of change overwhelmed the desire. The last such letter he had drafted just last night.

This time President Dyrud had made it mandatory that faculty attend the year-end reception for the entire college community—including parents—when what the instructors really wanted to do was skip out. *Hey, students skip classes, why can't we skip this?* But Dyrud had spoken, so the whole cynical bunch trudged in Saturday night, determined to have a bad time.

The reception table, sporting a blue-and-white checked tablecloth, had been laden with baskets of crackers and breads and an amazing array of aromatic cheeses on little matching cutting boards. Punch bowls of lemonade sat demurely beside wine bottles. The faculty had descended on the wine and cheese with more appetite than manners. They had managed to acknowledge proud parents with merely a nod and a cheesy smile, keeping their cheeks so full of food that they never had to speak.

Jack, never more than a social drinker, had given up alcohol entirely after Abby's accident. As a sober spectator he could see the effect of several glasses of wine on his colleagues, and the sight did not endear them to him. He'd retreated to a far corner of the room.

When the instructors had swarmed at the serving table the second time, their laughter was already a little too loud. Much of the conversation had focused on the most unlikely item on the table, a so-called apricot cheese. Those few who had tried it had already expressed the opinion it tasted a lot like old gym socks, as if they knew. Two faculty members from the computer department had decided to have some fun at their colleagues' expense. When Jack had approached the table for a refill of lemonade, they had spotted him as their first victim.

"Have you tried this apricot cheese?" Dwayne Blickenstaff asked earnestly.

"I've never tasted anything quite like it," Liza Hanson gushed. "Try some, Jack!"

Jack had dutifully slathered a lump on a cracker. The pungent smell should have been a clue. When he bit, the cracker shattered and he had to shove the whole thing into his mouth. His face had contorted as his taste buds rebelled. "Miff mff wfll!" was the best commentary he could give. He had headed for the rest room to spit it out privately. As he stumbled off, he had heard Dwayne and Liza cheerfully recommending the apricot cheese to the auto-shop trainers.

I don't belong here with these social morons! I hate this school! Jack had thought as he shot his soggy napkin into the trash. From the restroom he went straight to his office where he had written his most recent letter of resignation. He had read it over twice, admiring his own prose, and stared out the window for a time, thinking about job hunting. He would have to shape up his résumé, and check out the openings at colleges and universities.

Am I good enough? Have to put my best self forward...but I haven't seen my best self around lately. I'm cynical, angry, and hollow inside. I've gained weight and I'm out of shape. I'm a mess. I can just see myself in an interview, trying to dazzle a potential boss with my brilliance and healthy outlook.

With a sigh he had opened the desk drawer, added the latest letter to his collection, and gone home.

Now another plodding, lonely day had gone by, and it was Sunday night. *Only difference is, now I'm rich,* thought Jack bitterly. *Fat lot of good it does me.*

Jack hated to go to bed. It was not so when Abby was alive, but now he dreaded the abject loneliness of their bedroom. Some nights the walls seemed to close in, but tonight the room seemed alarmingly large, too expansive for his small sense of self. He stood in the corner to undress, dreading his trek across the vast wilderness between the dresser and the bed.

A huge quilt in a double-wedding-ring design covered the queen-sized bed. Abby's aunt Keziah had made it for their tenth anniversary, wholeheartedly celebrated less than a year ago. That quilt, dancing with marriage symbols, taunted Jack, challenging him to make the treacherous solo journey to the bed, and daring him to try to sleep.

One step at a time, only five steps really, but it took tremendous effort. Jack flung back the quilt – it billowed for a second, then sank to the floor. Good riddance. He crawled between the cold sheets, lay on his back, and closed his eyes.

Here, where he and Abby had shared their most intimate secrets of mind and body, here where they had filled the room with their love, here, where they had touched skin and souls, here he was, alone. The two of them had become one in this place; now he was barely half.

Jack rolled onto his side, caressing Abby's pillow, still next to his on the bed. He remembered her silky skin, refreshingly cool and smooth compared to his. She would nestle against him, seeking his warmth, and he would bury his face in her voluminous, sweet-smelling hair, kissing her neck if he could find it, gently stroking her breast or thigh. The pillow was a pitiful substitute.

When they had fought, which didn't happen often, the worst possible outcome was to deprive themselves of this closeness, this transfusion of touch. When anger had driven them apart like opposing magnets, each would cling fiercely to their edge of the bed, too stubborn - or perhaps too hopeful - to leave the bed for the couch.

This was the scene Jack dreamed. He was reaching, reaching for Abby, who seemed to be clinging to the edge. Longing for her, he stretched his body across the bed but she was still out of reach, beyond his grasp. For a moment he could feel the softness of her hair with his fingertips but then she was beyond touch, moving away, and he could not free himself from the bedclothes to run, to catch her. She was gone.

Jack awoke to find himself splayed across the bed, sheets and blanket knotted around his feet. It took a moment to realize the mournful cry that woke him was his own.

Monday morning, Jack stared into the mirror. He had a habit of shaving without really looking at himself – just doing the job and moving on. Today he looked himself in the eyes, and he could hardly believe what he saw. His face was doughy and pale, almost gray, and he had dark rings under his eyes. They looked sunken into his head. This was not the face of a healthy man. He thought about his resolutions to exercise and eat right, but that was impossible without Abby.

She made everything good. She motivated him to join her in walking, or skiing, or flying kites. She cooked wonderful food and made mealtimes a delight. Her very presence inspired him. Her absence made life almost unbearable.

After a breakfast of soggy cereal with a Pop Tart for dessert, Jack headed to an appointment with the bland college president. Jack had once told Abby, "If Dyrud were a color, he would be beige."

Glad he asked me to come in – how opportune. I can air my complaints, if I get the courage. Might as well use this ever-present anger to fuel the conversation. He catalogued his points as he drove to the college. *Long hours, lack of vision, dense students...dare I say that?*

Now that classes were out he was less rushed, so he actually arrived fifteen minutes early at the flat brown administration building. He sat in an ancient leather chair to wait, feeling like a chastised kid waiting for the principal. Liza Hanson emerged from Dyrud's door, and her face seemed puckered, with a little red around the eyes. She greeted Jack without any of the sparkle she'd had over the apricot cheese. *Wonder if she's been chastised for that nonsense.*

The portly, pale-skinned Dyrud gestured him into his brown office. On another day the décor might have appeared cozy and inviting, but the summer sun washed the warmth out so the earth-tones looked more like dry dirt. Dyrud seemed to be working at warmth himself as he unbuttoned his out-of-date sport coat and perched against his desk.

"Jack, thank you for coming! I appreciated your presence at the reception on Saturday."

I had a choice in either one of these? Jack flicked a bit of lint from his slacks and slouched back into his chair.

"You're probably wondering why I asked you to come in today." Dyrud rubbed his crew-cut nervously, then hunched his shoulders and relaxed them, making a concerted effort to look casual. "You've been with this school for a lot of years, and you deserve credit for all you have done."

Wonder just how many years it's been, and just what I've done. That's stuff to put on a résumé. Jack's eyes wandered around the room, taking in the framed credentials, hand-shaking photos, and watercolors of ducks. *He must be a member of Ducks Unlimited.* Picturing the paunchy president camouflaged in a duck blind made a half-smile twitch his mouth. He forced his attention back to Dyrud's words.

"This is a big year, 1998, pre-millennium and all that. Change is in the air. With the community colleges becoming part of the state University system, we've all had to make some adjustments. The uncertainty has kept us all on edge." Dyrud circled round his desk and sat in his impressive leather chair. He leaned forward and folded his hands on the blotter in front of him. "Some of us have been fighting to keep our fine institution on an even keel, with no dramatic change of direction."

That's your life work, Dyrud, fighting change. Jack nodded with feigned interest.

"But all the same, changes are coming. In fact, there will be changes in the English department."

Suddenly Jack was not the critical observer, but a participant. He leaned forward. "What changes?" he shot back.

Dyrud cleared his throat and wheezed softly. "I'm afraid...I'm sorry to have to tell you your position is being eliminated here. It has nothing to do with you, Jack—you do excellent work—it's the word from the powers that be."

Jack leaned back again to let the reality wash over him. His stomach knotted. All those perfectly-worded letters of resignation in his desk mocked him. He burped quietly, and tasted apricot cheese.

Dyrud waited for Jack to process the news in his own time. *Dyrud is working from a script – he must have gone to a seminar on Downsizing 101. Same thing must have happened to Liza. Can't even think about this right now. It's too much.* When the president saw Jack's eyes come up from the floor, he began to offer more information.

"We are prepared to offer you a severance package," Dyrud began. *Great, more money for my trouble.* "We'll do whatever we can to make your transition as easy as possible. You can opt for job retraining, so that you can switch to a field with more positions available. Or we will give you assistance in the job search. Or if you are willing to relocate, we may well be able to find you another position within the Minnesota State College and University system."

Jack swallowed, trying to get the repulsive taste out of his mouth.

"You don't have to decide now which option you want to take; think it over, and get back to me within the next couple of weeks. A person of your intelligence and skill, Jack – you have a lot to offer. Think of this as a time of new possibilities. We can talk again when you've had a chance to think it through."

Dyrud was standing and stretching out his hand. Jack struggled to his feet, shook the offered hand, and tried hard to think of something intelligent to say. "OK," he mumbled. "OK," he said again, and then wondered why.

Anything was better than going home to the empty house, so Jack had developed the habit of staying in his school office late into the evening. After finishing up with papers and preparations, he frequently played solitaire on the computer until he couldn't see through the yawns. Free Cell and Spider were undemanding pals, easier company than the loneliness.

This morning he needed to escape from the new reality of Dyrud's revelation, so he sequestered himself in his office and alternated between staring out the small window and losing himself in the computer games. After a few hours he decided to drag himself to his car and then home.

As Jack stepped out of the air-conditioned school, the humidity clapped his face. The heavy city air and his own sweat made a sticky combination on his skin. The day smelled heavy and ripe with exhaust. By the time he got to his car, his hair was wet and his eyes runny. *The Cities in summer is like living in an athlete's armpit.*

The car's air conditioning began to make a difference about the time Jack turned into his starkly angular neighborhood, rolling down the cramped streets of identical two-story buildings with postage-stamp lawns. Pulling into a driveway just like all the others, he punched the garage door opener and parked, a machine among machines.

He dreaded walking into the townhouse these days. When Abby was alive, he had loved arriving home. She would typically greet him with a joyful, reckless hug, often throwing him off balance. He recalled how he tried to brace himself if he saw her coming. She had delighted in catching him off guard, claiming that if she didn't he would become a stodgy old professor.

Well, guess what, Abby, I'm stodgy now. I expect no surprises, and I get no surprises. Snap at my students and chide them for not being creative when I'm the one who's dry as a bone. Life is a desert of ritual actions that take me numbly from one week to the next. Nobody can keep me on my toes like you did. I miss you, Abby, I need you!

Can't give in to those feelings, Jack chided himself. He unlocked the door and slouched through, steeling himself against the silence.

What does a non-drinker do to avoid feeling pain? Caffeine? Chocolate? Fasting? Overeating? Thrills and spills?

First his wife had been ruthlessly killed by a drunk driver. Now he was forced out of his job. He hadn't felt this bad since…well, he'd never felt this bad before. He didn't know how to act, what to do. And he was alone. No children, no close friends, no family nearby, nobody.

Jack's parents had divorced when he was thirteen, and after many years of only sporadic contact, he had finally completely lost track of his father, who had been a school superintendent. Their relationship had been so confusing that he was not inspired to hunt for him. When Jack was seventeen, his mother had married again, a man with most of the traits he detested in his father. Jack had been more or less on his own since he went off to college. Now he visited his mother and her husband in Florida every two or three years, and that was enough.

He had been hopeful that Abby's parents might fill the niche for him, and in fact he had developed a delightful relationship with her father. They joked and punned with each other, and relished the time they spent together. Cancer had taken him, too soon, just three years ago. Abby's mother was now frail, living in a care facility near Abby's sister Alice in Los Angeles.

He sat at the kitchen table and stared at a framed pen-and-ink sketch on the wall, where a Great Blue Heron balanced incredibly on long spindly legs at the edge of a peaceful lake. Its body seemed massive for such minimal support. The legs seemed no more substantial than the reeds in which it stood. *I'm like a heron, perched precariously. I could topple at any moment. Way too much weighing me down for the puny support under me. Abby was my other leg, and she is gone. I can't balance without her. I could be headed for a fall.*

Jack wanted to lay his head down on the table, but with the dirty dishes and the mountain of mail, school memos, and newspapers, there was no room. He shifted from emotional to rational in a twinkling, grateful to escape his sorrow again. *If Abby were here, she'd insist on tidying this up.* At first it had been a perverse pleasure to let it all accumulate, but now the junk was just one more annoyance in his little world. He would rather not deal with what was there.

He would rather not deal with anything. Since Abby's death, Jack's colleagues and acquaintances had been reluctant to bring up the subject of his loss, because Jack never did. He tried to pretend that there had been no change in his life, but the spring had gone out of his step and his cynicism had deepened. He labored hard to keep up the work façade.

Alone at the kitchen table, Jack had to face the desolation. *I miss Abby so much!*

They had married ten years ago after a delightful year of dating and discovery. He had been single so long that he feared marriage; she had been married for a brief time when she was "too young to know better," she said. They had both been so reluctant to make a commitment that their families had doubted there would ever be a wedding. When they finally agreed to get married his world changed, not according to his fears but beyond his hopes.

Abby, the more social of the pair, brought sparkle and laughter to daily life. She lured him away from lethargy to action, ranging from concocting gourmet meals to playing Scrabble to folk dancing.

By career Abby had been a middle school math teacher. Her natural gift with numbers and her adventuresome creativity had made her an extraordinary teacher. She had spiced her lessons with challenges and games that made learning fun. She'd loved her students, especially the malleable ones – in these she could often inspire a love of math and zeal for its disciplines.

Her least love had been grading papers, so frequently she and Jack would sit at the kitchen table in the evening, she with piles of quizzes or equations and he with essays. Working together had made it easier to plow through the work. They'd shared tidbits from their teaching, chuckling over silly incidents and marveling over moments of inspiration. In honor of Jack's discipline of teaching good writing and grammar, she had often hidden a grammatical error in the text of her tests, giving her students extra credit if they spotted it. They had both kept track of the students who caught on.

Abby had matched her diligence at her work with a delight in play. She had always come up with interesting ideas for weekends, and without her Jack had no ideas of what to do for fun.

Right now Jack missed the simple aspects of their life together. Their creative conversations at the kitchen table. Her remarkable ability to find almost anything in the house. Her maddening tendency to be right.

Now he had to think about a new job, and he could use some of her resourcefulness and rightness. He slammed his fist down on the table, making the dirty dishes jump.

The phone rang just as he was getting some aspirin.

"Hello?"

"Jack? This is Pastor Luke. I didn't know if I would catch you at home now. How are you?"

"Fine." He privately acknowledged the lie.

"Jack, you know, it's been six months or so since Abby's memorial service, and I just wanted to check in with you and see how you're doing. I imagine it's still lonely at times."

"Yeah." Jack squinched up his face. His voice was so tight all of a sudden, it didn't seem possible to speak a whole sentence.

"So I was wondering if I could come by and see you this afternoon then, say around 2:00. Are you busy?"

Jack cleared his throat, knowing it wasn't good for many more lies. "Uh, no. Come on over."

"Good! So I'll see you in a while then."

Pastor Luke had that amazing intuition that some clergy possess: he knew when to call. His relaxed style made it possible for people to say yes to his visits, knowing they would find a listening ear, a new perspective, and a healthy sense of humor. A native of rural Minnesota, he padded his conversation with ample "wells" "you knows" and "So...thens," and never fussed with formalities.

Jack and Abby had met when they were in the singles group at Faith United Church of Christ. Jack had attended that church most of his life, since his family had settled in Minnetonka, a suburb of Minneapolis. Abby had been "church shopping" when she moved to Eden Prairie, and because of the singles group she had made Faith UCC her church home.

It was on a trip to the Boundary Waters Canoe Area Wilderness that romance had begun to blossom for Jack and Abby. The singles group had planned for months for this retreat to the magnificent wilderness that stretches for a couple hundred miles along the Canadian border of north-eastern Minnesota. Lakes chained together by portage trails make over a thousand miles of canoe routes possible, through beautiful boreal and transitional forests. Pastor Luke had been eager to share his love of this special place, which he called his "spiritual home."

Jack recalled that they had all been awkwardly inexperienced when they'd started out in the BWCAW, but with Pastor Luke's patient guidance and the joy of the adventure they had each discovered their strengths. Jack had even learned how to carry a canoe over the rocky trails, balancing the portage yoke on his shoulders and keeping his gait smooth. He remembered his heady sense of accomplishment, and the admiration of Abby and others that had made the experience even sweeter. He had felt strong and capable.

Strong and capable. Wish I could feel that way again.

Right on time, Pastor Luke was at the door. Tall and lanky, he had the physique of a runner. His red hair was showing gray at the temples; his beard could be called salt-and-cayenne. The sun had weathered his fair skin, deepening laugh lines and adding character. He was never seen outdoors without a jaunty hat, presumably to protect his skin, and he smelled faintly of coconut sunscreen year round. Friendly without being overbearing, his good nature and intelligence endeared him to young and old alike.

Pastor Luke sat comfortably on the sofa. Jack was glad he had not spread his clutter to the living room of the townhouse yet. As the summer sun shone in the window, he noticed the dust was rather thick, but he felt pretty confident that Pastor Luke would not mind. *Maybe it's time to hire someone to clean.*

Their conversation moved from pleasantries to the present, with Jack keeping his emotions in close check. This had become habit after so many months, and he wasn't even sure how to release them. He heard himself talking rather matter-of-factly about being single again, and how he had not yet regained the rhythm of cooking and cleaning. Pastor Luke, himself a single man, resonated with the challenges of keeping up with everyday chores.

When Jack related his experience of losing his job at the Community College that morning, Pastor Luke frowned and shook his head sadly. "I'm so sorry that happened. You didn't need any more stress, I know."

Jack gave his head a little shake and swallowed hard. He picked up the narrative again. "Dyrud offered me three options: retraining, help in finding another position, or placement elsewhere in the state college system."

"So which one are you leaning toward then?"

"I haven't thought about them very hard yet. My first reaction is that they all sound bad. Retraining would be a lot of work, and I don't want to do anything else. A job search sounds impossibly hard. Going somewhere else in the system might be the easiest, although I might have to move, and that would be – ugh, I don't want to think about it." *I would have to go through all of Abby's things. Should have done it long ago. If I move, I'll have to face that wrenching task.* Jack gave a little shudder.

"Moving sounds ominous?" Pastor Luke had noticed the shudder.

"I would have to do a lot of sorting, cleaning, going through stuff…" Jack's voice trailed off.

"That can be daunting…but it can also be helpful in a way. It can move us along on the journey, if you know what I mean."

Does he know how stuck I've been? Jack took off his glasses and scrubbed his face with his hands.

"I suppose a fresh start can be good," he said finally. Jack had to get off this train of thought, switch gears. "Are you going to the BWCAW this summer?"

Pastor Luke blinked at the sudden change of topic, but went with it. "Matter of fact, I'm getting ready to leave after church this Sunday."

Jack leaned forward, his eyes brighter. "For how long?"

"Just under a week."

Pastor Luke saw the interest in Jack's face and scratched his beard thoughtfully. He made a quick decision. "Say, why don't you come along with me?"

Jack was caught off guard by this possibility. He took some minutes to think. *Why not go back to the Boundary Waters? I have the summer stretching before me with very little to recommend it. Could get away from all this crap, get out of the stifling city, and smell the fresh air again.* He pictured the stillness of the lakes in the morning mist, the breeze in his face while paddling, gazing ahead to the line where green woods meet blue water. He could practically hear the call of a loon echoing in his consciousness. *I could go back.* He sighed. *But would Pastor Luke really want me as a companion?*

Jack's words were slow and measured. "Well, I have the time. But are you sure you want company? I'm not very experienced. It's been ten years." He studied Pastor Luke's face, looking for rejection but seeing none.

"Well, I'd appreciate having you along. And I don't mind a bit helping you to get more experience." Pastor Luke rubbed his hands together eagerly. "I enjoy taking people to the Boundary Waters. It's such a wonderful place for finding your balance, you know."

Buoyed by Pastor Luke's enthusiasm, Jack felt hope infiltrating his despair. "I could use some balance," he admitted to the floor.

"It'll be good for you to get away. We'll leave right after coffee hour on Sunday then," Pastor Luke said with a matter-of-fact nod.

"I'll be ready." Jack was surprised to hear a lift in his voice.

Pastor Luke looked kindly at Jack, waited several seconds and said quietly, "Would you like me to say a prayer before I go?"

Jack considered for just a moment. *What could be the harm? Pastor Luke doesn't know how angry and distant I've been with God.* "Sure," he said.

Pastor Luke leaned forward with his elbows on his thighs, his hands clasped, and Jack did the same. As Pastor Luke prayed, Jack breathed deeply and welcomed the sense of – what was it? – connection. *I'm glad to know Pastor*

14

Luke and glad to check in with God. It's been a while. He let the words wash over him without concentrating on their meaning. He suddenly tuned in to Pastor Luke's voice when he heard,

"Please, Almighty God, lead these two pilgrims north to your healing wilderness of crystal waters, lush forests, and Northern Lights! May your will be done. Amen."

After Pastor Luke left, Jack paced around the living room, talking aloud to himself.

"What have I gone and done? This is either the best idea of the year or the stupidest. I should have taken more time to think! I am not an impulsive person!

"I'm an out of shape city kid – hmph, a middle-aged clod – with no wilderness survival skills. Probably be eaten by a bear. Won't be able to keep a canoe afloat, let alone paddle it – or carry it! These excursions take stamina and courage, neither of which I've got. What am I thinking!

"But…the idea of going to the Boundary Waters captivates me. I want to go! And I need someone like Pastor Luke to help me remember and learn. He'll be great to travel with. Problem is, I'll be a stupid albatross.

"Too bad we'll have less than a week. Shoot, I have a whole summer with nothing I want to do."

Jack plopped down on the sofa and leaned back, stretching his legs out in front of him. Hands behind his head, he stared absently at the top of the window frame. *Hey, what if I stay up there? Nobody here would miss me. Could just lose myself in the wilderness for a while.* Jack squeezed his eyes shut and held his breath. He thought his head would burst with this idea. It seemed daring, even dangerous. His anger fueled the desire to escape, to run away. He shouted to the ceiling, as if winning an argument, "Heck, I could just stay there forever. Nobody would care."

Later in the afternoon, Jack's anger had reduced to a simmer, and he still liked the idea of staying in the Boundary

Waters longer than a week. He thought he'd better let Pastor Luke know. He phoned him at the church office.

"Hey, Pastor Luke, I've been thinking about our trip."

"Not backing out, I hope – now I'm planning on having you along you know." Luke sounded as positive as ever.

"No, I'm definitely going. Thing is, I'm thinking about staying a week or two longer."

Luke was quiet for a beat, then exploded into the phone. "Jack, that's a great idea! Yeah, you betcha, you can go solo for as long as you want. What a perfect way to spend your summer!"

Jack grinned in spite of himself. "So we'll just take two vehicles then, so you can come back when you need to."

"Alrighty then, that'll work fine. I'll have to be back by Saturday night…and I hope you don't mind, but I'll have to work on my sermon during the week."

"No problem." *Maybe I'll even learn something.* After their goodbyes Jack stared at the telephone. *Wonder what 'working on a sermon' means.*

Chapter 2

The Boundary Waters trip went from "idea" to "plan" in the space of one hot afternoon. By evening Jack's head was spinning with all the things he needed to do, and the items he needed to take. He finally resorted to writing a list:

Clean
Deposit insurance check
Pay bills
Buy equipment: canoe! tent, etc.
Stop mail and newspaper

Abby would be proud of me... getting organized!
The notion of time in the northern wilderness so captured his attention that he lay awake for a time that night, picturing himself in the beauty. When sleep came it was gentler and longer than usual, with only a few nightmares toward morning. When he awoke on Tuesday, he felt different. Rather than dreading the day, he found himself interested in how it might unfold.

First he called a maid service, and arranged for someone to come clean the townhouse on Friday. He figured he might as well leave it clean; it needed to be done. He walked around the house, forcing himself to really look at it.

In the entrance hallway he had stacked Abby's periodicals as they came in the mail: "Games" magazine where she got so many of her teaching ideas, state and national math teachers association newsletters and journals, and, oddly, a magazine called "Women Who Rock". He'd piled them all there as they arrived for six months, and they had started to topple in a colorful, slick avalanche. He should have cancelled them, of course, but that would mean admitting she was gone. He clenched his jaw and ground his teeth. *She's gone. Gotta make the calls today.*

The living room looked okay because he rarely used it. He'd moved the television out to the kitchen and closed off the room. The décor reflected his greens and her blues, his dark and her light, his tradition and her free spirit. *Really like that sofa – it's comfortable! Could reclaim this space.*

The bedroom held the most memories. He opened Abby's closet doors and looked at all her clothes, shoes, and treasures. He shook his head sadly. *Still can't face this. I know I need to go through it all but I just can't.* He hung his head, eyes tightly shut, for a few heartbeats. Looking up, he moved closer to the colors and textures before him and ran his hands along the clothes, still on their hangers, laden with the essence of their wearer. Impulsively he buried his face in the fabrics, breathing in, seeking some remnant of her scent. His eyes stung but tears would not fall. He forced himself to turn away.

On her dresser was the blue metal urn with Abby's ashes. Jack hadn't known where to put it, or what to do with it, so here it sat. *I remember the moment the funeral director put this in my hands. A chill in my gut, an emptiness in my chest.* As he touched the urn he felt the internal vacuum again. *I should spread her ashes somewhere special. Have to think about that.* He sighed. *She would not want me to procrastinate like this. She'd say, "Get going, Jack! Make a plan!"* Jack lingered a few minutes more with his eyes on the urn, but he didn't have any good ideas. *I'll think about it. But not now.* He moved on to continue his survey of the house.

The kitchen was a mess because that's where he spent more of his waking hours. The refrigerator teemed with green things better suited to the science lab than a dining table. And the table – such an ominous pile. He decided to start there.

It was like archaeology to work down through the layers of school memos, mail and newspapers. In an hour and a half he had three bags of recycling and one of garbage, and a small pile of important items which were easy enough to file. He put the bothersome insurance check in his wallet.

Then he moved to Abby's periodicals in the hallway. He pulled out one of each and located a customer number. He took a deep breath and dialed the first one. "I'd like to cancel the subscription for Abby Freeman... I don't need a refund... No, I don't want it to just run out... I don't want them... She's dead, don't you understand? Just stop the damn magazine! Thank you. Yes, thank you. I appreciate that. Yeah, bye."

Idiots. This is why I didn't want to do this! Jack stomped around the kitchen in a rage. *But I have to get this done!* He steeled himself and dialed the other numbers, and worked his way through the maze like a determined lab rat. Each time he had to explain her death again, but it got microscopically easier as he went along. Toward the end, some of the customer service people actually sounded genuinely sorry.

He was now determined to get rid of the magazines themselves, so he found a couple of boxes and loaded them up. *They're no good to me, but they might help or at least entertain some other teachers. I'll drop them by her school this afternoon.* He hauled the boxes out to the car in the stifling heat. *Breathe shallowly – don't let the bad air in...it must be a hundred degrees at least today! Thank God for air conditioning.*

The air shimmered with heat and humidity. Jack's shirt stuck to his back uncomfortably, a result of his exertion and hurry. A brown haze hovered over the city and even the traffic moved lethargically. Only those without AC sped along, trying to cool off by sheer velocity. The rest rolled along in their sealed bubbles of artificial comfort. Jack felt the familiar isolation in the crowd.

When he got to Abby's school he hesitated, but made himself go in. Fortunately the office was minimally staffed with a matronly secretary whom he knew only by face. He plopped the boxes on the floor and explained briefly that the magazines were for anyone to use, and they might especially be interesting to the math teachers. She thanked him politely and he turned on his heel and bolted out to his car. *Whew! That's done! Ten points for me!*

Bit by the cleaning bug, Jack headed to his office at the college, stopping on the way for a burger and fries. Once inside the school, he located the janitor who found him some boxes, and Jack began sorting. The recycling bin soon overflowed, and the janitor got into a pattern of stopping by to dump it every fifteen minutes.

Bent over double to clean out the bottom desk drawer, Jack suddenly had the prickly feeling he was being watched. When he straightened up he saw Liza Hanson leaning against the door frame. She was wearing a formerly white tee shirt and black jeans, her hair was stringy, and she had dark circles under her eyes. "You got sacked, too, looks like," she said bitterly.

Not wanting to share any psychological space with Liza, Jack put on a cheerful face. "Yeah," he chirruped. "Best thing that could have happened. I was going to resign anyway, and this way I get severance."

Liza grunted in reply. *Will she buy it? Or is she brighter than I thought?* She surprised him by echoing his fabricated mood. "Yeah, me too. I was dreading the changes when the tech schools joined the Universities. We'll never be treated like equals – we'll always be the 'poor relations,' the embarrassing bumpkins who never measure up to the sophisticated academics." She brandished an elegant hand and tipped her nose up and rolled her eyes. Then her face clouded and she punched the air with a pudgy finger. "I'll bet you anything we'll get hand-me-down computers with dinosaur software. Dwayne thinks it'll catch us up but I think we'll be left eating their dust. So I'm glad to be rid of this place. I've got better things to do with my life." She tossed her head dramatically, looking more pitiful for it.

"So what are you going to do?" Jack was curious in spite of himself.

"I'm not sure yet – go out West maybe. I hear there are jobs in computers in Seattle, and California. This is as good a time as any for a fresh start. How about you?"

Jack's first thought was *Good, I won't ever have to see her again.* "I'm leaving Sunday for the Boundary Waters Canoe Area Wilderness."

Liza's stiff demeanor melted into a sigh. "Oh, I love the Boundary Waters! I went there as a kid in youth group. Aw, lucky you! Lucky, lucky you! Oh, you lucky dog!"

Jack responded to this eloquence with a tight smile, but inside he couldn't deny that he felt lucky indeed. He didn't want to continue this conversation lest some of his luck erode, so he raised a hand in farewell. "Bye, Liza, good luck to you out West."

"Bye, Jack. Uh, have a great time up there." She moseyed off shaking her head, muttering about how some people have all the luck. "Lucky, lucky dog…"

Jack packed up books, files, and other items that seemed worth keeping. Finally he pulled open his center desk drawer, knowing what he would find there: six letters of resignation. He leafed through them. Great prose, but there wasn't much of a market for them. He smiled grimly as he ripped them in half and tossed them into the recycling.

That prompted him to seek out Dyrud. He found him in the coffee room.

"I've made my decision. I'll take a job elsewhere in the University system. Wherever they can find a slot for me, I'll go."

"Well, Jack, that'll be fine then. I've heard there are openings for English instructors in Little Falls and Granite Falls, and there are probably others. I can contact you in a week or two with the particulars…"

"Actually," Jack interrupted, "I will be gone most of the summer and I won't be reachable. Can you just work it out and I'll get in touch in August?"

Dyrud's spindly eyebrows shot into his forehead. "Well, I guess so…"

"Thanks," he interrupted again. "Talk to ya then." He tossed the astonished man his entire college key ring.

Jack loaded his Toyota with nine boxes – the sum of what was worth saving – and felt a sense of liberation. He didn't look back as he drove off from the college, not even in the rear-view mirror.

Now to the bank. He swung into the parking lot. As he set the brake he thought, *Hold it! I don't really know what I'm doing with this money!* He sat back hard. *Abby would have wanted all of it to be invested. She would have known just what to do. But I only have this money because she's gone! Augh!*

He tried to remember anything he had learned about investment from the money programs on Public Radio. *Should probably hire someone to help me. But where to even start? Would be good to get a referral from somebody. Don't want to hassle with that now!*

Need to buy equipment for the Boundary Waters trip. No idea how much that will cost. So I need a bunch in my checking account. And I'll pay my rent for the summer, and utilities. But I should put some of it in savings so it can get some interest. How much? Jack scratched his head. *Maybe I'll go half and half. Then whatever's left over I can put in savings when I get back.*

Jack got out of the car, still debating with himself as he approached the bank. The air shuddered hotly around him and the cicadas sang their electronic hum. *Really should put it all in savings and bag the trip. But I want to make this trip – I think I need to do it. So I'll buy what I need and still have some for saving. Fifty-fifty, that's fair. It's so much money! Plenty to spend and save too.*

Jack found himself at the teller, tongue-tied. "I, uh, I need, uh, I have a check to deposit. I guess I should get a deposit slip. Slips."

The teller looked at him kindly and said, "I can help you with that, sir. Checking or saving?"

"Yes."

"Both. You bet."

Jack nodded and swallowed hard. *Why is this so embarrassing?* He looked up at a sign with the current rates for Certificates of Deposit. *Sounds smart.* "I think I want to get some C.D.'s for the savings part."

"Oh, then, you'll have to go over to that person right there. She can help you with the C.D.'s. Since it's one check, you can do your whole deposit with her. So is there anything else I can help you with then?"

"No, thanks." Jack stumped over to the desk indicated and plopped down. The woman reminded him of one of Abby's teacher friends, but it couldn't be her. The sense of familiarity made him a little more comfortable, though.

"May I help you, sir?"

"I need to deposit this check. Half checking and half savings." Even as he said it the debate started in his mind again. He forced it to the background and cleared his throat as he produced the $100,000 check from his wallet. He laid it in front of the banker and watched her.

The woman's eyes took in the information quickly and to her credit she registered no emotion. "Half checking and half savings?" she asked. "What sort of savings? We have a good rate on long-term Certificates of Deposit right now."

Jack relaxed as the woman's professional narrative led him through the possibilities. By the time he signed the papers he had almost accepted the idea that he had these funds to his name. Walking out of the bank with his handful of C.D.'s and whopping checking account balance, he felt a little giddy.

Done a bunch of difficult things today! All this banking, cleaning out my office, cleaning out at home...Time for a celebration! I should go out to dinner! Been eating way too much fast food lately – when I even remember to eat.

Jack drove down toward Cedar Avenue, then to River-side and parked behind the fortune cookie factory. He took a deep breath of the good smells there, then crossed Riverside, checking out the variety of oddly-named bands playing at the local bar. Today's best was "Red Rubber Band" which brought a smile to his face. *How do they dream these up?* In the middle of the block he opened the door of Odaa, an Ethiopian restaurant that he and Abby had always enjoyed.

A complex array of exotic smells assaulted his senses. He closed his eyes and breathed it in. Memories of good

23

times with Abby started to emerge, and he almost bolted. But now his mouth was watering, so there was no turning back.

The menu, always a good read, was nevertheless unneeded. He ordered the vegetarian sampler, just like always. And just because this was supposed to be a time of celebration, he ordered an enticing mango drink. It was just the thing to occupy him while he waited for his meal. This was the loneliest part of eating out solo.

The veggie sampler arrived, and the waitress dutifully identified each mound of food on the tray. It really didn't matter to him – he loved it all. Before she disappeared she warned him about the hot sauce in the center with the yogurt, and he looked at it with relish. From the accompanying basket he tore off a section of budeena, the spongy "bread," and used it to scoop up some yellow lentils and a little spicy sauce. The contrasting tastes were as delightful as he remembered. Busy with the process of eating without utensils, he didn't feel so conspicuous or lonely.

Why have I deprived myself of all this since Abby died? Need to be nourished by good food. Endorphin rush might have a welcome effect on my mood. He tackled the tray of savory and spicy tastes with enthusiasm. Carrots, lentils, cauliflower, green beans – everything tasted wonderful. When he finished the array of entrees, the waitress asked if he wanted any seconds on anything. It was tempting but he thought better of it. He ate up the budeena that lined the tray – it was well marinated from the entrees. The last bite had the kick of cayenne from the sauce. *Mmmm.*

Now his stomach was full, maybe even a little too full, but that felt unusually good. He paid his bill and stepped out into the warm evening. Further down the street at the Cedar Cultural Center, the marquee boasted a Celtic trio performing that evening. Jack looked at his watch. *Why not? Don't have any other plans.*

Good food and good music had further elevated Jack's mood, and again he slept reasonably well. Wednesday morning, crunching cereal at his now-clean kitchen table, he marveled at his spontaneity the night before. *Yeah, it was lonely eating out and going to a concert alone, but I did it. Music was wonderful, and even though I couldn't share it with Abby, I enjoyed it. In a way it's not a big deal, but in a way it's like I've 'graduated' or something. Interesting.*

He felt alert enough to handle the dreaded finances, so he balanced the checkbook, paid a pile of bills, and updated the checkbook balance. He struggled to enter five digit amounts in the little columns. He shook his head in amazement. It was still unreal to have so much money.

I'll be buying a canoe. And a Duluth pack, and tent, and sleeping bag. It'll add up.

Bills in hand, Jack stopped in at the post office. While waiting in line to get stamps, he absent-mindedly perused the various forms. "Hold mail" caught his eye. *Need to stop my mail while I'm gone! Oh, for dumb, as my students would say!* He took a form and the pen chained to the table and filled out his name and address. As an afterthought he put Abby's name on it too. *Stupid subscriptions won't stop immediately, I'm sure.* When he came to "End Date for Hold" he paused. *What should I say? Three weeks, or four? End of July, or early August?* It was crazy to be so unsure. He swung the pen's chain back and forth, made snaky designs with it, and drew a triangular doodle in each corner of the form.

He finally decided to put the absolute outside date; he could always come back earlier and ask for his mail delivery to resume. Since he would have to prep for the school year in late August, he printed "August 17" on the line, stared at it for a moment, and put the pen down. *OK, then.*

Back at home, he thought again about his bills. *How will I pay for them while I'm gone? What if I do stay away all summer?* He looked again at the checkbook. Abby, ever practical, had arranged for automatic payment on many of them. He wrote another check for the townhouse rent, to cover two more months.

The phone rang. *The phone! Can't let the answering machine run all summer!* He explained to the telemarketer that he did not want another credit card, thank you. That done, he called the telephone company and put his phone "on vacation" starting Monday. "End date?" the woman asked.

Again he paused. "August 17." It was easier this time.

Thursday's project was shopping. Daunted by the enormity of buying a canoe and everything else, Jack let the morning slip away. He lingered over the paper, did the crossword and all the other puzzles, even the ones he didn't really like. Late in the morning he poked through his closet and started a pile of what he wanted to take. After a lunch of toast and jelly, he finally set off.

He drove past a Wilderness Mart billboard every day, so he decided to go there.

The store was almost an entire block long, with the name plastered across the front in man-sized letters. A raging grizzly bear stood sentinel at the entrance. Inside it felt like the air conditioning wasn't working properly; he smelled something musty. But he could see they had everything he needed – the place was crammed floor to ceiling with recreational gear.

Jack took a deep breath. He could see canoes suspended from the ceiling in the distance, so he headed there. Underneath them, craning his neck, he saw differences but had no idea how to evaluate them. He changed his posture and looked every direction for a salesperson, but saw none. There weren't even any customers in this department. He felt lonely.

At a deserted customer service counter in the center of the store he saw a sign saying "Ring Buzzer for Assistance." He pushed the button politely and waited. He hadn't heard any buzz. *Must sound in a back room somewhere.* After a few minutes he rang again, longer this time. Just when he was going to buzz in the rhythm of "I Can't Get No Satisfaction" a breathless young man in a bright red shirt appeared.

"Can I help you?"

"Ahhhh." Now Jack wasn't sure where to start. He took a deep breath. "I'm going to the Boundary Waters, and I need some equipment." His words came out in a rush.

"What exactly do you need?" the young man asked, wrinkling his pimpled brow.

"Everything." Jack was dismayed to see the fellow give a tiny jump of enthusiasm. *Dollar signs in his eyes, that's scary.* A moment's hesitation, then the next question.

"Where do you want to start?"

"Uh, canoes I guess."

Red Shirt started to walk and jabber: cedar-strip—aluminum—vinyl—fiberglass—durability versus weight—keel line with rocker—tumblehome… *What? Did he just say "tumblehome"? What the heck is he talking about? Oh, mercy, I'm over my head.*

They stopped under the watercraft and Red Shirt brightened. "Say, maybe you'd like a kayak instead of a canoe? We have some great deals on kayaks this week. Lots of people prefer them."

Jack felt stunned. *Help! I don't know what I'm doing! Don't know the answer to this question and I think it's important!* He closed his eyes to concentrate. *Picture the Boundary Waters. Picture Pastor Luke… He's in a canoe… Everyone is in a canoe…* "I want a canoe."

"Ooookay. What material do you want?"

"Something lightweight, for portaging. I want one that's easy to paddle. It doesn't have to be big, it's just for me." The snare drum in his gut rattled briefly.

Red Shirt pointed out the solo canoes overhead that worked best for lake touring. Jack looked them over until his neck hurt. He hemmed and hawed, shrugging off another "Sure you don't want to look at kayaks?" and struggling to understand how the differences in shape affected their feel in the water. *Wish I knew more physics.*

He kept coming back to a small red canoe called the Independence. "This one." *May just be the name, but this is the one I like.*

Next he sat on a bench with a measuring stick between his legs, while Red Shirt noted the position of his nose. Somehow this determined the length of paddle he needed. He chose a standard design; the bent ones looked awkward. Red Shirt unnecessarily noted the double kayak paddles. Jack ignored them.

Red Shirt helped him find a reasonably comfortable portage yoke with good pads. This would fit into the canoe as one of the thwarts, or cross braces, and allow him to carry the upside-down canoe on his shoulders on the portage trails between lakes. Jack could remember carrying a heavy aluminum craft on his previous trip, and it took some balance and skill. He chose the yoke carefully.

Jack spotted the Duluth packs nearby, and gaped at the selection taking up ten square feet of wall space. He'd thought they were all the same: a big square frameless canvas bag with heavy-duty straps for carrying. They were much wider than hiking backpacks-they held a ton of gear and sat solidly in a canoe. The first one he tried felt pretty good. *Of course it's comfortable – it's empty! If it had bricks in it I could test it better.* Red Shirt picked up a plastic liner to go with the pack.

They moved on to the life jackets – elegantly called Personal Flotation Devices. He chose a blue-green one. Next Jack got distracted by a display of small packs and chairs. He was intrigued by an under-seat pack that could hold a camera, binoculars, etc. handy while he was in the canoe. *But then I'd have to unfasten it for the portages, or have it dangle there – oh, my old fanny pack will do just fine.* The Crazy Creek chair reminded him of outdoor concerts and Shakespeare in the Park – he had seen people looking pretty comfortable in them. Lightweight and compact, it folded flat – he added it to his armload of purchases.

"Now what?" Jack asked, shifting his awkward burden of paddles, portage yoke, pack, PDF, and chair. *Why isn't he helping me carry this stuff? He's losing interest.*

"I tell you what," Red Shirt said, taking a few strides to an information display. "Here's a Gear List for Canoe

Camping." He pulled out a paper with three columns of checklists. "This might be helpful."

Peeking over his armload, he peered at the paper. "Yeah, this is just the ticket!" Jack blinked back the feeling of overload. It looked like the kayak freak was going to leave him to his own devices, but maybe that was all right.

"I'll just take all these items to the front, and whenever you are finished, you can pay for them all together. And I'll go arrange for your canoe to be ready for you to load, too."

"Sounds great."

Red Shirt staggered a bit and dropped the list as he took all the equipment. "Your name?"

Jack swooped up the paper from the floor. "Jack Freeman."

Red Shirt was off on his mission as Jack called out his thanks.

The Gear List started with the obvious items he'd already covered. Next in line: tent. He and Abby had a four-person tent they had used for car-camping, but he needed something smaller and lighter for this trip. He was painfully aware that it need only be big enough for one person.

A petite young woman with a mouth full of braces greeted him as he swept his gaze across the tents set up on a patch of carpet. He explained that he was going to the Boundary Waters and he needed a small, lightweight tent for himself. Just as he started to examine one, she explained hastily that in the BWCAW, a free-standing tent is best, since the soil is so shallow it's often hard to get the stakes in solidly. This rang a bell – he remembered bending a stake rather badly when he'd tried to drive it into a rock.

That narrowed the tent choices. A bright aqua one with a side opening appealed to Jack. He got in and lay down, and it fit him well – it would be just right for him and his gear. And he could sit up in the middle, in the peak of its arch. As he climbed out he thought this was an easy door for a 5'10" 40-something guy. "Sold!" he announced. She grinned metallically and found one on the shelf. He marveled at how compact it was in its carry bag.

Amused to learn that a tailor-made tarp for his tent was called a "footprint," he got one. The young woman recommended a couple of tent pole repair items, which made sense. She also got him a cart to carry his purchases, and sent him on to the sleeping bag department. One back wheel on the cart wobbled and clattered, but it was better than carrying everything. *I'll get a chance to carry all this stuff soon enough...* He had an absurd mental image of pushing a clattery shopping cart across a portage trail from one lake to another.

He and Abby had two old sleeping bags that they used together, but they were both pretty bulky. Again he winced to remember that he now slept alone. He squelched the emotions that bubbled up and waxed practical. A good-quality goose-down bag would pack compactly. One that would be good to about 30 degrees would be best, since the nights could be cool. He found one that weighed just two pounds twelve ounces, and compressed to seven by fourteen inches, and it had a great name: Blue Kazoo. *Hope it doesn't keep me awake humming.* He nearly choked on a chuckle, and tried to cover with a cough.

Now, a sleeping pad and compression sack. *Wonder how much I'm spending here. Seems so odd to have no concern about the bottom line. But in a way I want to get rid of the insurance money.*

The Canoe Camping list helped Jack to stock up on the smaller items. Remembering Pastor Luke's insistence on purifying all their water on the retreat, he chose a state-of-the-art water filter. A compact camping stove, fuel, and a mess kit, and a splurge on a campfire espresso maker... a collapsible water bottle... a funny folding saw... lots of rope... a plastic trowel... biodegradable soap... first aid kit and/or survival kit... *Yikes, that's sobering. How much help will I need? How clumsy will I be? Hate to even think of getting injured up there!* He chose a well-stocked first aid kit.

Jack worked his way through the list, trying not to get rushed and miss anything. But soon he tired of shopping.

Novelty is wearing off. Wearing...what do I need to wear?
He sighed. *Better look at boots.*

Once he finally got a sales person, Jack tried on some hiking boots and walked around the store to get the feel for his stride and balance. That pair slipped a little on his heel, so he tried another style, trekked around some more, and sat down with satisfaction. Some wool socks and liners were added to his cart. He decided the amphibious sandals he was wearing would work nicely as an alternative to the boots.

He found a waterproof, breathable anorak on sale, but it was purple. *Don't have to buy what's on sale.* He located a green one. In the hat display under a sign claiming "It floats" Jack found a paddle hat. The wide brim would save him from the sun and rain, and a breathable mesh band provided ventilation. *And if I drown, at least the hat will mark the spot...perish the thought...*

A sign reading "Convertible Pants" caught his eye. *What the heck?* These turned out to be long pants whose legs zipped off to make shorts. Perfect for packing light! Jack selected two pair. He found quick-dry underwear and a shirt he liked.

Could he possibly be finished? Jack looked at his watch in amazement. He had spent nearly four hours in this endeavor! *Time to finish up. I'm beat.*

Food was the last thing on his checklist. He gaped at the exotic freeze-dried meals. Tired of making decisions, he just took one of each item. He figured that would last him three or four weeks, and after that he could stock up in Grand Marais if he needed to.

On his way to the checkout area, he passed a display case with compasses, knives, and watches. He quickly picked out a compass, and made a mental note to be sure to pack his waterproof watch and Swiss Army knife. Both had been birthday presents from Abby.

At the checkout he caused a bit of mayhem while salespeople rallied to gather up all his purchases. He pulled out his checkbook and tried to stay calm. The staff seemed disorganized.

"That'll be $3,712.68," the clerk announced distinctly. Heads swiveled and Jack tried to look cool, like this was an everyday thing. He chewed on his tongue as he wrote the check, taking care to write small to get all the words on the line. *Well, that only leaves about $96,000.* A bitter grimace crept across his face.

Out to the hot mega-parking lot, Jack finally found his Toyota and unlocked it. The car had become a solar oven set on broil. Jack waved some of the hottest air out, gulped and climbed in. Every inch of skin responded with sweat. He rolled the windows down and drove to the loading area. Red Shirt helped load the gear in the trunk and back seat, and got the canoe mounted on top, using foam pads to protect the roof and rope to secure the craft. *Little car is bursting at the seams!* As Jack expressed his thanks for the help, Red Shirt reminded him to get a canoe license at the local license bureau. "Right!" Jack said, pretending he had remembered all along.

It was 4:30. He would have to make a run for it, since they presumably closed at five. His hands were sweaty and slick on the steering wheel. Traffic frustrated him, but at least he was able to keep moving. Parking was exasperating with his limited visibility, so it was 4:50 when he dashed in, praying there would not be a line. Just two people waited for one tired agent. Jack had time to get his breathing back to normal before his turn at the window. He got the license, but the sticker would not come in the mail for four to six weeks. Jack's eyebrows shot up, and he explained that he would be leaving in three days. The agent reassured him, saying that as long as he carried the license with him it would be legal. Both men sighed with relief – Jack because he would not be thwarted by a technicality, and the agent because he was finally off shift.

When Jack pulled into the garage, he looked again at the canoe on the little car. *Not a good fit. It looks like the canoe could carry the car. Maybe I need another vehicle.* Abby's car had been totaled in the accident. *Old Toyota has served*

me well for how many years? Eleven? Maybe I need some-
thing more solid, something that would carry a canoe
handily, something that might protect me from a drunk
driver if need be.

He rolled this thought around in his head as he unloaded his purchases. Once he had strewn everything around the living room and admired it a while, he plundered the magazine rack for ads for sport utility vehicles. He admired them as he munched on chips and salsa. *Tomorrow I'll do some test driving.*

Chapter 3

Early Friday morning the cleaning service arrived. Jack felt awkward no matter what he did. His new gear dominated the living room, so he occupied himself there peeling and snipping off tags and tossing all the new-smelling items into the new Duluth pack. One of the maids startled him when she asked in a commanding voice, "When may I clean this room?" He slung the pack onto the sofa and scampered out of her way.

He started into the kitchen, but the other woman warned, "The floor's wet in there!" He had to use the bathroom but decided he'd better wait until they were gone.

"Where can I be?" he finally asked.

"We're done with the bedroom, you can go in there." *Great, my least favorite place to hang out.* He plopped on the bed and stretched out stiffly. He felt like a child, with his mother insisting, "Go to your room and stay there, the house is clean for company." *Wonder if they'll tell me when I can come out.*

His gaze fell on the urn of Abby's ashes. *It's been moved! They touched it! It's not in its exact place!* He launched off the bed and lunged for the urn. Because the dresser had been dusted he couldn't tell exactly where it had been, but he put it where it looked right. *I'm being ridiculous. Really doesn't matter. Should deal with this and let it go.*

The sound of the vacuum reminded him of the others in the house, so he once again postponed making the difficult decision. Instead he stared out the window absently until the authoritative voice said, "We're all finished, sir." He wrote a check and thanked them.

When he closed the door and turned around he caught an unfamiliar whiff. *Guess I'm pine-fresh now!*

Jack put on his new hiking boots to break them in a bit while he ran errands. He set out in his Toyota to the grocery store to pick up sundries like zipper bags that he knew would come in handy. Next he made a stop at the food co-op and bought lots of dried foods, peanut butter, coffee, and a few spices.

The Ford dealership was just coming to life as he pulled in. He wandered into the cool showroom and no one seemed to notice him, so he located the brochure rack and picked up the glossy viewbooks on the two models he wanted to try.

Finally a salesperson approached him. "Are you being helped?" he asked. Jack shook his head. "What can we help you with today?"

"I'm interested in the Explorer and the Expedition. I'm going to the Boundary Waters and I need something to carry my canoe and gear," he stated matter-of-factly. The man smiled, gave a nod, and strode off to get some keys, leaving Jack alone. He almost bolted – the prospect of negotiating for a vehicle seemed more than he wanted to take on today. *If I'm going to do it, I need to do it today – I leave day after tomorrow!* So he stood his ground and resolved to make the most of the experience. *At least for once I have money. Might be fun to write a check for the whole amount. A first for me!*

"Let's look at the Expedition first." They walked up to an imposing red vehicle. The salesman unlocked the door from a distance with a remote device. Jack had never had one of those. He tried not to gawk. Jack clambered up into the driver's seat, a bit of a climb. From the passenger's seat the salesman pointed out the features from four-wheel drive to airbags. Seating for nine sounded absurd to Jack, and he twisted around to see for himself the two rows of seats behind him.

"It's the size of a small house, or at least a dorm room!" he exclaimed.

"118 cubic feet of cargo space, when the back seats are folded down!"

My canoe might even fit inside! Jack test-drove it, but he had already decided it was too large for his needs. He resisted comparing it to a tank, since it actually handled fairly easily.

The salesman had the wrong keys for the Explorer, so he had to run back to the office. It gave Jack a few minutes to read the sticker. He noticed that the gas mileage was a far sight from his little Toyota. *That will take some getting used to.*

"It's open now!" the salesman called out as he approached at a slow jog. *That remote unlocker would be a nifty toy.*

The Explorer felt better than the Expedition, and Jack relished the chance to test drive it. It handled smoothly. It felt safe. *Could see myself owning this.*

The salesman chattered on about the many fine features, which Jack found mildly interesting. The term "puddle lamps" caught his attention, and he had to learn more. Small lights underneath the exterior rear view mirrors would illuminate the ground so you wouldn't step in a puddle. *People are paid to think up these gizmos!*

Jack realized he hadn't broached the subject of price, and it was time to make a move. The process of buying a vehicle reminded him of the mating ritual of certain birds, with all the ceremonial verbal swooping and dancing. "So what're you asking for one of these, then?" he said, leading off.

"It's normally $31,080.00, but today you could have this fine Explorer for $27,548.70."

"That's down to the penny! How about rounding it off to $25,000?" Jack countered.

"This is a very special price; I'm afraid we don't have much negotiating room on such a special sale," the salesman said with exaggerated sadness. They headed back to the showroom. "Let's sit down and get the particulars."

They hashed out the model he wanted and the options, and determined that there was one on the lot that he could have today. The salesman started pulling out the paperwork. "And how would you like to make the payments? Do you have a trade-in?"

"No, I'll just write a check for the full amount." The man studied him for what seemed like a full minute. When he snapped out of it he headed off to the manager's office to consult and do a credit check anyway. *What day did I deposit the check? Will it show up on my credit history? Wonder if they'll wonder where I got the money?*

The salesman came back with a big smile. "No problem," he purred. "Our manager can offer a reduced price of $27,000 since you like round numbers. But he cannot go any lower. Do we have a deal?"

Jack was ready to settle, even though it felt a little rushed. "Sure," he said, and shook the man's hand. It seemed to take an hour to finish the paperwork. Finally he got the keys on their fancy remote control keychain and headed out to the parking lot to claim his new purchase. The color was "Medium Wedgewood" which he would have called blue if anyone asked him. Jack felt empowered in the big rig as he drove it off the lot. The salesman followed in the Toyota to Jack's place, and Jack drove him back to the dealership.

As he pulled the Explorer into the driveway, Jack wondered if he had sold out to peer pressure. About 75% of the townhouse residents drove SUV's. Well, his was to carry his canoe. An Explorer to carry his Independence. *Good symbolism.*

Now, to introduce the Independence to the Explorer. Jack untied all the knots from his new canoe, slipped the rope off, and took a deep breath. He reached over the trunk of the Toyota and grabbed the canoe, sliding it out until he could get under it. *For being so light, it's heavy enough.* He teetered a bit, then tried to set the portage yoke on his shoulders. Tipping his head up to examine the sunny yellow interior of the canoe, he remembered that the yoke was separate. He would have to attach it. A thwart made a poor substitute, causing such a pain in his neck that he promptly carried the craft to the Explorer, and reaching high above him, slid it gently onto the luggage rack. One of the foam pads had dropped off and another was squished against the rack. Jack retrieved the stray and figured out how to use the pads to cushion the new canoe. He took a few steps back to admire it again.

Looked so large a minute ago – now so small! Must have fallen into a rabbit-hole. Alice must be around here somewhere…

A breeze that should've offered relief blew cruelly hot. He looked at his watch. *Lunchtime. Plenty of time to secure the canoe on the Explorer after I have a bite to eat.*

The air conditioning indoors felt good. The clean kitchen table looked unfamiliar, though, like he was in someone else's house. He spread the day's mail out just to feel at home. On the bottom of the pile of junk was the latest issue of his favorite consumer magazine. Jack flipped it open to read while he ate.

He almost choked on his sandwich as he read an article about Sport Utility Vehicles. *Classified as trucks so they don't have to meet such strict safety standards? That stinks! I wanted safety! What have I done!?*

Driving was a huge issue for Jack, with the memory of Abby's totaled car still so vivid. Now he was reading that in case of a crash he would be less safe in his new SUV than he would be in his old Toyota or just about any car.

I want my money back! Wonder if they've cashed my check yet! I'll feel like a fool to go back there but I don't want this vehicle any more. I've only put a few miles on it. What will they think? How humiliating. But I can't live with this bad decision! Oh, I am so stupid, stupid, stupid!

Jack clawed his fingers through his hair and held his head with both hands. A headache started banging around inside, first assaulting his forehead, then the nape of his neck, then his temples. He stomped around the house furiously, but that made the pain worse. He flopped onto the sofa and closed his eyes.

Accept the fact that you are a dolt. Take the Explorer back. You'll probably have to pay something. Be reasonable with them and they will be reasonable with you. Go now before you lose your nerve.

Leaning his red canoe against the Toyota, Jack climbed into the Explorer. He felt a revulsion out of proportion to his circumstances. Behind the wheel, he played out disastrous scenarios: A tree limb falls and dents the hood. Another car sideswipes him and creases the doors. He turns a corner too fast and the whole vehicle flips. *Stop, stop! Just drive from here to there. Watch and be wary.*

Miraculously he arrived at the Ford dealership in one piece. He approached a parking spot right in front, swinging wide to maneuver the Explorer into place without contact with the adjacent vehicles. He turned the key off and let out an enormous sigh of relief.

The salesperson greeted him in the showroom with a tentative smile. "Everything all right?"

"Yeah, uh, no, actually, I've changed my mind about the Explorer. I just – I thought – I… " Jack's words trailed off in his confusion. The headache banged inside like a hammer on the loose. "Will you take it back?"

The salesman's eyes darted across Jack's face, assessing his sanity, perhaps. Jack massaged his left temple. He jiggled the Explorer keys in his hand, desperate to turn them over. "Please?"

"Ah, come with me." The salesman, now eager to get Jack off the sales floor lest his attitude might be contagious, whisked him into a small office and sat him down. "Someone will be right with you."

Jack sat quarantined for what seemed like a small eternity. He used the time to craft some sentences. *I'm seeking a vehicle that will be safe, and I just don't feel safe in the Explorer. It's a fine vehicle, but it's really bigger than what I need. I'm going to have to keep looking. I'm sorry to put you to any trouble, but I just want my money back. I've only driven it about eight miles, you can check the odometer. It's still in mint condition.* Jack fidgeted in his chair, still rattled by fear and failure.

Finally the manager who had handled his paperwork appeared with a file folder and clipboard. "How can I help you, sir?" he crooned.

Jack stammered out his position. It wasn't as eloquent as he had hoped, but he got his point across. The manager didn't seem to need to argue; he just asked Jack to pay a fee and fill out a form about his satisfaction.

Perusing Jack's comments, the manager looked up abruptly. "You know, if safety is important to you, and I see it is, I have a suggestion. We have a late model Volvo station wagon that we got on trade-in last week. Volvos are rated very high for safety in crash tests. I'm sure we could work out a deal. Would that be of interest to you?"

Jack shifted in his chair as he processed this idea. The curtain of despair seemed to lift a few inches. "Can I look at it?" he asked stupidly.

"Of course! I'll have someone bring it around." He picked up the phone, punched one number, and gave instructions. He turned back to Jack with a fatherly tone. "It's a sound car – it may be just what you are looking for. You'll want to drive it to see how it feels to you. It's blue, if I remember correctly."

Driving home in his new/old Volvo, Jack felt like the transaction really couldn't have been much better. Yes, he was shown up for being impulsive, uninformed, and even juvenile, but at least he got a good vehicle and even a warranty out of the deal. He was bruised, but not beaten.

He pulled into the driveway behind his old Toyota with his Independence resting against it. *Next challenge: canoe on car.*

Now how was that tied on? Why didn't I pay more attention? I'm so dumb! I'll never make it in the Boundary Waters. Jack gave in to another moment of despair, then reassured himself that Pastor Luke would be there, and he would be a good coach. *Just have to pay more attention to details.* He jockeyed the canoe to make sure it was centered, then did his best to anchor the rope and secure the craft. He looped the rope and tested the knots over and over, fighting a mental image of the canoe sailing off the car and skidding down the highway, causing a major pileup.

When he was finally satisfied, Jack headed toward the house. At the door he looked back. *Looks like a giant deranged spider tried to capture the canoe in its ropy web. Embarrassing, but I think it'll hold.*

In his living room Jack spread out his gear. *The portage yoke – oh, great. I need to attach that to the canoe!* He examined the clamps and decided he could do it without Pastor Luke's help. *But I'll have to undo the canoe and everything!* He sighed. *How else can I mess up today?*

It took a while to undo the ropy web to get the canoe off the car. Attaching the portage yoke was not difficult but when he lifted the canoe onto his shoulders it took a nose dive and made a divot in the lawn. *Too far back. Try again.* He cleaned the sod off the craft and moved the yoke a few inches toward the center, tightening it down hard on the gunwales. It balanced better when he tried it this time. Once again he lifted the bright red canoe onto the Volvo's roof rack and secured it. His rope technique didn't improve much, so it looked like the deranged arachnid had returned.

Inside Jack tried setting up his tent, following the instructions as a last resort. Then he took it down, and just to be sure he set it up one more time. It looked large in his living room. He crawled in, lay down, and imagined himself in the Boundary Waters, snug in his sleeping bag on a crisp northern morning, listening to the loons. He closed his eyes and drifted into a happy half-sleep. When he woke it was time to go to bed.

After breakfast Saturday morning as Jack went into his bedroom to pack his clothes, a huge clap of thunder startled him. *Whoa! This is not an omen. Just a reminder to take rain gear.* Lightning flashed, followed closely by more thunder. Steely clouds suggested a lingering rain rather than a fleeting squall. Soon big drops hit the window, propelled by wind. Jack turned off the air conditioning.

He laid out what he thought he needed on the bed. He remembered Pastor Luke saying sternly, "Pick out everything you need and then put half of it away. Just take the bare minimum." Jack eliminated almost half. He found a thinner towel that would pack compactly. He hunted for his Swiss Army knife and waterproof watch. He found a small pair of binoculars and a flashlight and added them to the pile. He located his 35mm camera and made a mental note to buy some film. *Think I have a couple of rolls in the fridge but that's not going to be enough.*

In the dresser drawer he saw a blue spiral notebook – Abby's journal. He had not previously touched it, but now he picked it up reverently. His stomach tightened and he squeezed his eyes shut. *Should I read it? If not, what should I do with it? If anyone should read it, it should be me.* As the summer rain sheeted down the bedroom window, he took a deep breath and opened the journal, flipping gently through the pages.

Abby had apparently not been diligent in her journaling. Only about twenty pages of the notebook had been used. The first entries were three years ago, when her father's cancer was diagnosed.

April 23, 1995

I am beside myself, feel like I'm going crazy, don't know which way is up. I just learned that my Dad has pancreatic cancer! It's bad, really bad. He won't live very long. My Dad! I can't stand to think about not having my Daddy!

And Mom is in terrible shape. Dad has been her caregiver, keeping her at home and happy, but now he's not going to be able to do

42

that. She gets around, but slowly, sometimes with a cane. But that's the easier part – her mind is going away and she can't keep track of things. It won't be safe for her to be by herself. She will leave the stove on, or water running, or forget to take her medicine. Oh, what will she do without Dad!?!

And what will I do! He's been like a strong maple tree for me all my life, one I could lean on, and find shelter, tell my worries to. And he has always been full of sweetness too. He's always been there for me and now he won't be there!

The future looks terrible. Daddy will get sicker and sicker. Momma will need more help. Alice is clear out in LA, and I know she'll do what she can...but Jack and I will be the ones who will have to walk this journey with Mom and Dad, because we're the ones who live close. We're going to be burning up the road between here and White Bear Lake. Oh, Jack, he loves Dad – he'll hurt too. This is going to be very hard!

Think of the positives, Abby. That's what you are good at. Turn yourself around. You can do it.

At least they're near. (it would be worse if they were 100 or 200 miles away)

We have good doctors and the Mayo Clinic and everything here in Minnesota

Alice may be a long way away, but she will help as much as possible.

Alice has a good income and that may be helpful too

It's near the end of the school year and I'll have more time in the summer to be with them

Jack will be with me whatever happens

That last one is the most important one.

She had written several pages, then later one page, then several pages more later. Her handwriting, once so ordinary on shopping lists, notes, and birthday cards now seemed incredibly precious. Jack touched a page with a trembling hand and traced the words with one finger.

He sat down on the bed with the journal in his lap. The pages were crinkled from her apparent pressure with the black ballpoint pen. As he slid the pages, skimming the words, he recognized her forthright acknowledgement of her anger and sadness as her father's condition rapidly worsened. They had talked some about these feelings, but clearly she had needed to vent further. Jack felt a little guilty.

On a new page, in blue ink this time, she had written about a month after her father's death:

I miss my Dad so much! Tonight I just laid down on the floor and cried and cried. Jack got down next to me and held me while I sobbed, then went and got a tissue at just the right time. Each time I cry like this I feel a little bit better afterwards, still sad, but like some of the weight has been lifted. I wish it didn't take so many tears. Will I ever get through this?

And my poor Mom, so sad and with so many problems of her own. Thank God Alice is there to take care of her and help her adjust to the assisted living place. I don't know what to do but keep up my weekly calls—at least I'm in touch. And we'll go out to LA to see her in the summer. I have to be positive for her sake.

Jack was suddenly stricken with acute guilt. *Haven't called her mother in months! Got to do that right now.* He closed the journal with a snap and tossed it on the bed in his haste to do a good and positive thing for Abby. *Don't let the apathy win out—just act right now.* He located the number and dialed.

After two rings he hung up. *Can't do it. What if she wants to talk about Abby, what if she can't remember Abby died and I have to tell her all over again? I can still hear her wailing – I can't do it.* He kept his hand on the receiver and hung his head.

I'll call Alice instead. This seemed manageable, and he dialed the number and held his breath. When he heard Abby's sister's voice, so similar to his beloved's, he gasped. As he struggled to say hello, Alice's voice continued, and it finally dawned on him that he'd reached her answering machine.

At the beep he took a deep breath. "This is Jack, Abby's, uh, husband, and I just wanted to touch base. I'm, um, going to be gone a lot this summer, up north, out of contact, and then I may be moving, somewhere in Minnesota but I don't know where yet, so I guess I'll just let you know what becomes of me when I know, I mean, when I have something to report. Oh, sorry I'm rambling. My love to your mom. Bye."

Jack was sweaty from this endeavor. He wiped his brow with his arm. *Good thing I didn't reach her. Just that much was an ordeal. At least I made an effort.*

Jack looked again at Abby's journal. *Take it along. I want to read it but it's going to take me some time.* He added it to the pile of things to pack.

Still have to decide what to do with her ashes, though. He stared out the window at the rain. *Could leave them here and figure out something later.* The snare drum rattled in his gut. *Instead I could take them up to the Boundary Waters and ask Pastor Luke to help me do something meaningful with them. Should maybe talk to him ahead of time about that. I'll call him.*

Jack called Pastor Luke at home first, thinking he was probably packing his gear. Jack watched the rainstorm abate as he listened to the phone ring on the other end. Pastor Luke's answering machine picked up and Jack thought fast: *Can't leave a message about this. He's probably at the church. I'll call him there.* He hung up and dialed the church number. Once again he heard an answering machine message. *I'll just call him later. He's probably out loading his canoe on his car.*

Jack put the urn of Abby's ashes in a large plastic zipper bag, and gently put it into his Duluth pack with the journal next to it. He loaded in his tent and sleeping bag on opposite sides. The unstructured pack kept flopping over so he hurried to fill in the bottom with his cook kit and the rest of his equipment. He laid his clothes on top. Next he took his big bag of freeze-dried food and stuffed it in the top. The bag wouldn't close – the top bulged impossibly. So he took everything out and started over with the tent on the bottom, rolled his clothes the way Pastor Luke had showed them, and squeezed each item in so there was no wasted space. This worked better. He was just barely able to get all the food in and fasten the clasps.

He hefted the pack onto his back, swayed a little, yelped, and then found his balance. He felt like the hunchback of Notre Dame. *Whoa, heavy! Food supply will diminish though.* He adjusted the shoulder straps and the load felt a little better. He hiked up and down the hallway, fantasizing about the beautiful scenery on the portage trails.

Sunday morning the weather was still stormy. Jack got ready for church, wondering how many things he was forgetting for the trip. The canoe was secured on the Volvo, with the paddle, pack and life vest stowed inside the vehicle. By the door was a day pack with some travel clothes, so he could change at church and be all ready to head out.

The nagging feeling of forgetting something continued. He went to the bathroom. *Toilet paper!* He hustled out with a couple of full rolls, thankful that had popped into his head. They wouldn't fit into the bulging pack, so he tossed them onto the seat. Before leaving the house he turned off the air conditioning, took out the garbage, and made sure all the windows were secure.

Pastor Luke greeted Jack with a big grin. "Kinda damp out there yesterday," he teased.

"I don't care if you don't! I won't shrink." Jack responded.

"Sorry I didn't call you...it's been a busy week."

Jack realized he hadn't called Pastor Luke the night before as he had intended. *Just talk to him later.* "Don't worry about it. I meant to call you and didn't do it. We're even."

"Pretty soon we'll be out of the reach of telephones, and you know that will be fine with me!" Pastor Luke shook his head and chuckled.

The worship service revolved around the theme of gratitude. The hymn "Now Thank We All Our God" reminded Jack of Thanksgiving. Pastor Luke spoke of being thankful to God and to each other. He speculated that God is thankful for us, and played with that concept. At the close of the sermon he stepped out of the pulpit and spoke more informally.

"Yesterday we buried a beloved member of our congregation, Ruth Anderson." Jack sat stunned. He had been so absorbed in his preparations that he had not paid any attention – he had not read the paper or been in touch with anyone. Ruth had been one of his Sunday School teachers, served on the Church Council and other boards, and in her later years she had become a real character. Her salty remarks would have been shameful in a younger person, but she got away with it somehow. A ferocious advocate for mission, she was a lively part of any budget discussion, well into her eighties. But her health had begun to fail rapidly in the past year, ever since her eighty-ninth birthday.

"Ruth was a thankful soul," Pastor Luke was saying. "She frequently expressed her gratitude for her church when I visited her in the nursing home. She regretted being 'out of the loop' and you know, she always asked how we were doing on our mission giving.

"I believe God is grateful for Ruth. I know I have been." Pastor Luke continued, his voice slightly hoarse. Jack was surprised to feel his eyes burning. He missed several sentences while he distracted himself to get his feelings in check. *That's why Pastor Luke didn't answer the phone yesterday – he was doing the funeral for Ruth.*

What would Ruth have said about my current predicament? Can just hear her saying, 'You've had a damn tragedy, Jack, but now you've got a chance to do some good. Take that checkbook in your hot little hand and support the mission of the church!'

Well, Ruth, maybe I will. And you know what? I'll do it in memory of you. Jack wrote out a check for $5,000.00 and carefully wrote on the memo line "In mem. of Ruth A.: MISSION." He tore the check out carefully to make minimal noise. When the offering plate was passed and he placed his gift in it reverently, he experienced a heady mixture of sadness and euphoria.

As Pastor Luke's offering prayer closed with "God is good! Amen!" Jack busied himself finding the next hymn in the hymnal. By the Benediction he had placed the lid tightly on his emotions again.

Coffee cups in hand, Jack and Pastor Luke made their plans. They would caravan up to Grand Marais, but just in case they got separated they would meet at the Angry Trout restaurant for supper. "My canoe is on the car – as soon as I've completed my duties here I'm ready to go. All I have to do is change out of my Sunday duds!" Pastor Luke was visibly excited.

"Same here!" Jack said, thankful to have the companionship of this good-natured man.

Sunday traffic was light, so it was easy enough for the two canoe-clad vehicles to stay together as they headed out of the Twin Cities. Interstate 35 would take them 150 miles to Duluth. Once they were clear of the urban/suburban speed limits they each kicked in their cruise controls at 75 miles per hour.

Pastor Luke took the lead in his green Subaru with matching canoe and Jack followed, aware of a different feel behind the wheel. He experimented a little with the various settings of the fan and his seat. He fiddled with the radio, locking in classical music, news, jazz, and oldies. *Suppose I'll have to start investing in music on CD's, now that I have a CD player in the car.*

Pastor Luke had handed him a sack lunch before they left. Jack gingerly opened it with one hand, not wanting to spill anything or interfere with his driving. He found a turkey and cheese sandwich on homemade wheat bread, with lettuce and a spicy mustard that tasted good. *He sure does better than I do at kitchen stuff.* He saved the apple for later, but ate the chocolate crunch cookie after wrestling it out of its plastic wrapper.

The scenery rolled by, reminiscent of so many jigsaw puzzles. Tidy farms with blue silos, lush crops of corn, soybeans, and alfalfa, and the occasional cattle herd alternated with groves of oak, basswood, and maple trees and the inevitable lakes and ponds. Small towns crouched with Sunday afternoon quiet - the picnic scene was stifled by the real possibility of a warm drenching.

The day continued to be dark and overcast, and the further north they got the more real the threat of rain became. The drive seemed to go on forever. Jack squirmed uncomfortably in his seat. Just as the internal clouds seemed to be closing in, Jack came up over the hill and gasped as Lake

Superior's expanse dominated his view. The shadows lifted from his spirit as he absorbed the vast, open feeling of the big water. His eyes darted from the highway to take in the lake on the right and the city of Duluth on the left.

In Duluth they stopped to gas up, just as it started to sprinkle. The air was cool, too cool for June. Both men dove into their packs for jackets.

When Jack paid for the gas he spotted a box of matches that said, "For our matchless friends." *Matches! I don't have any matches!* He was no Eagle Scout – he needed this convenience. He nonchalantly picked up a handful of matchbooks and stuffed them into his jacket pocket.

As they headed out of Duluth on London Road, which became Highway 61, the rain started in earnest. The storm obscured their view of the north woods scenery and driving took extra concentration, with two-way traffic and intermittent rain squalls. After some fumbling with the controls, Jack managed to turn on the heater. *I'm not looking forward to setting up camp in the rain tonight. Wonder how Pastor Luke will take to the idea of an alternative.*

The rain came down in sheets for a while, causing the traffic to slow. The tunnels provided welcome relief from the torrents. The wipers flipped ridiculously under their shelter, then went back to work upon emerging.

On the south edge of Tofte, Pastor Luke signaled a left turn into the Ranger Station, and Jack followed. When they had parked, Pastor Luke called out, "Let's get our permit here – I don't know how late the Grand Marais station is open on Sundays." Jack felt glad for the chance to stretch.

Inside, Pastor Luke took the lead. The Ranger filled out the permit, asking questions as she went along. Luke indicated that they would be entering Clearwater Lake tomorrow, with two watercraft, two people. She asked about the exit date, and Pastor Luke said, "July 2 for me – Jack how about you?"

His hesitation spoke volumes. "I'm not sure."

"It's just an estimate," the Ranger offered. "I'll just put down the 2nd." She turned to consult a computer screen. "I'm afraid Clearwater already has the maximum entries for tomorrow. Do you have a second choice?"

Jack looked at Pastor Luke. He hadn't thought at all about their route – he would defer to Pastor Luke's experience.

"How about East Bearskin then?" Pastor Luke suggested.

A quick check of the screen and she turned back to the pair. "That will be fine." She checked and circled East Bearskin on the permit. "You may only enter the BWCA Wilderness at East Bearskin, but you may exit from any location." Then she looked up with a twinkle in her eye, and added, "Just make sure you note where you leave your vehicle."

Pastor Luke pulled out his wallet to pay the fee, but Jack beat him to it. "Let me get this for both of us," he offered. "I'd like to get some maps of that area of the BWCAW too." He wrote a check, and the Ranger noted the payment on the permit form. "Has there always been a fee?" he asked.

"No, it's relatively new. It gives us more income to work with to take care of the wilderness, and we're better able to serve the public with extended hours at the Ranger Stations." She seemed prepared for a negative response.

"Sounds like a good idea. Ten dollars apiece isn't much to pay for the privilege of visiting such a special place." Jack's agreeable answer brought a nod and smile.

Next she ran a video for them to watch. It highlighted the rules and responsibilities of visiting the Boundary Waters Canoe Area Wilderness. Pastor Luke watched casually, while Jack stared intently at the screen, taking it all in. He would have liked to see it again. He especially wanted to get the part about hanging a bear bag. *But Pastor Luke will coach me.*

The Ranger then asked a series of 14 questions of the two, checking them off as they answered correctly, sometimes helping out with a little extra detail. The questions were based directly on the information in the video. *Video and a quiz – good learning technique for this era.*

The question about glass and metal containers made Jack think. He really hadn't known about the rule prohibiting them, but as he thought about it he had accidentally done the right thing. The only cans he had were fuel for his camp stove, and those were allowed.

The Ranger gave them a plastic garbage bag. "Could I please have another one of those?" Jack asked. She complied. Before asking Pastor Luke to sign the permit, she reiterated, and wrote on the form, "Hang Packs High."

"Have there been problems with bears?" Jack asked her.

"There are always a few. Just take precautions and you should be fine."

Chapter 4

Back at their vehicles, Jack noticed Pastor Luke's fishing pole. "How's the fishing in the Boundary Waters?" he asked. He couldn't remember from their previous trip.

"It's a mixed bag. Some lakes are great, others are duds you know. But the rain may actually make it better."

"Maybe I should get myself a pole."

"You bet, you sure could. If we leave right away, we might make it to the Beaver House in Grand Marais before they close."

Thirty minutes later they pulled up in front of a corner building with an outrageously large trout bursting out of the roof and wall. Jack gaped at the sculpture, and shook his head with a smile.

Inside, the store was crowded with anything an angler might need, including live bait in vats. The rain made everything feel close, and there was a smell only a true sportsman could appreciate – earthy musk overlaid with WD-40, and just a hint of rubber boots.

With the help of Pastor Luke and a salesperson, Jack compiled the equipment he needed to fish the northern lakes. He procured a license and wrote a check for the works. As he and Pastor Luke headed out to load his new fishing gear, Pastor Luke commented casually, "You seem to have lots of spending money."

"I got a big check from Abby's life insurance. In a way, I just want to use it," he confessed. "I'll invest whatever's left," he added, a little defensively.

Pastor Luke said nothing, just put his hand on Jack's shoulder for a moment.

At the Angry Trout restaurant in Grand Marais, Jack and Pastor Luke lamented the rain. Pastor Luke's plan had been to drive up the Gunflint Trail, and camp at the National Forest Campground that night, getting an early start on the water the next morning. Neither wanted to be the first to suggest staying in town, but the rain showed no sign of stopping, and the prospect of setting up camp in soggy conditions was not attractive.

Jack finally broached the subject. "Um, I saw a place on the highway back there, I think it was called Lakeshore Cabins. Maybe we should stay there tonight and head out early in the morning."

"I was thinking the same thing," Pastor Luke admitted. "When I was younger I would have braved the elements no matter what, but now I don't have anything to prove."

Jack picked up the tab, but when he pulled out his checkbook the young man at the cash register shook his head and pointed to a sign that said, "No personal checks."

That stopped Jack short. He hadn't brought much cash. *But wait a minute* –he pawed through his wallet and came up with a debit card from his bank. "Will this work?" Abby used to use hers but he never had. She called him "just an old-fashioned check-writing guy".

The young man peered at the card. "Yeah, sure, this is a MasterCard." He swiped it in a machine and gave Jack a receipt to sign. He wrote his name with relief.

The office of Lakeshore Cabins was a simply-constructed older log home. A boy of about twelve came in along with Jack. While the boy asked for some microwave popcorn and gave the proprietor some coins, Jack took in his surroundings. A counter divided the public from the owners' living quarters, which looked cozy and very inviting. The scent of roast beef pervaded the room. A business card told him the hosts were Elmo and Dottie. On a lower shelf of the counter his eye was drawn to a spoon sitting in a puddle of vanilla ice cream. When the woman's attention shifted to him, he pointed and said, "Someone left their ice cream spoon here."

"Eeuuwww," said Dottie with a grimace. But her face brightened as she picked up the spoon and puddle, which were attached, and showed it to him. "You mean this? My brother-in-law gave it to me and I just love it."

Chagrined, Jack chortled and changed the subject, indicating that they needed a cabin for the night. She described the options and he chose one. "Changed your mind about camping?" she guessed.

"Yeah. We're headed to the Boundary Waters tomorrow."

"It's wise to have a good night's rest tonight," she said cheerfully. "Enjoy your stay."

The little cabin, which went under the unlikely name of "Bob," had two beds, a small oilcloth-covered table with two chairs, a rocker, TV, a bathroom with shower, and a tiny kitchen which sported a hot plate, microwave, percolator, and a sink. It was rustic; adequate for their needs. The TV and microwave were obviously later additions – otherwise it was like stepping back in time. They were grateful for the heater, and cranked it on before they started unloading.

Jack hauled his pack out of the Volvo. He immediately unbalanced. *Heavy!* Pastor Luke saw his stagger as he was unloading and called, "Everything okay?"

"Yeah. Well, no. My Duluth pack is a shade on the heavy side," Jack admitted, lugging it into the cabin.

"What-all have you got in it then?" Pastor Luke banged through the door behind him, carrying his pack with one hand.

"Tent, sleeping bag, clothes, cook kit and all that. The usual stuff. And food – lots of food." Jack opened the pack as he spoke. On top was the fantastic array of all the freeze-dried meals he'd bought.

"Wow, you betcha! You do have a lot of food! So you must be planning to stay a while then!" Pastor Luke gave Jack a probing look.

Jack shifted his weight and avoided Pastor Luke's gaze. "I don't exactly know how long. I have the whole summer free. I thought I'd better stock up." His voice trailed off. "I don't really know what I'm going to do."

Pastor Luke saw the lostness in Jack's posture and expression, a demeanor he'd seen so often since Abby's death. He longed to hear Jack's wit and joie de vivre return. Maybe this guy could move toward healing in this sacred wilderness. "To tell you the truth, Jack, I'm more than a little envious of your adventure. I think your idea to stay is brilliant, and it's a blessing that you can be so flexible with your schedule. It makes sense to me that you stocked up on food."

Jack didn't hear the last part – he was captured by the word 'brilliant.' *Brilliant! Can't remember the last time an idea of mine was called brilliant!* He straightened his spine.

"I tell you what," Pastor Luke was continuing, "I've brought enough food for this week – I had leftovers from my last hiking trip, and I bought some of my favorites. I thought we'd pick up a few fresh things tomorrow morning, too. How about if you leave your cache of food in your car, and when I come out to head home next Saturday you can stock your pack for your journey then?"

Jack thought a minute, liked the convenience of the plan, and nodded his head. "Okay. You're such a generous guy, Pastor Luke. Thanks."

Luke waved his hand dismissively. "Don't mention it. After all, you're my guest this week you know – the least I can do is feed us."

Jack nodded, satisfied that he was not taking advantage of his friend. Pastor Luke gave him a big plastic bag and he scooped the meal packages into it. His hand touched Abby's journal and he felt a rush of intense feelings. *Shouldn't take this – something might happen to it. Keep it in the car.* When he took the journal and bag of food out to the Volvo he had a sudden worry about theft, so he shoved them under the seat on the passenger side where they would be somewhat out of sight. He brought his new fishing equipment in.

Bringing their gear to the cabin through the rain, they seemed to bring the outside in. Everything was a bit damp and quite cold. They turned on the TV to see about the weather. Tornado warnings for Duluth, a rare occurrence this far north. The weatherwoman predicted precipitation all night, with cloudy and rainy conditions throughout the week. Lows in the low forties.

"Uff da! We made the right decision to stay here tonight!" Pastor Luke affirmed.

"I thought this was supposed to be summer!" Jack complained. "Oh well, at least it's not hot and sticky like the Cities."

They spread the Boundary Waters maps out on the table and pored over them, planning two different routes: one if the weather was friendly, one if it was not.

"We can play it by ear. If we want to stay in the same campsite for a couple of nights, we can do that. I've learned through the years that it's good to push yourself some, but since you'll be staying a while you don't have to have the full dose the first week." They planned to paddle the north arm of East Bearskin Lake, portage to Moon, then on to Deer, and finally to Caribou to find a site for Monday night. With one day planned they felt prepared enough.

Jack dug around in his pack and found a small spiral notebook and a pencil. While he entertained Luke with the tale of his Wilderness Mart shopping excursion, he sketched the relevant portion of the map into his notebook. Starting at first to include every contour of Caribou Lake, he then smoothed the shores out for a simpler representation. Following the code of the map, he put in dots for the campsites and dotted lines for the portages, adding the length of the portages, such as "P 115 r" which he assumed meant "Portage 115 rods." Deciding not to get into all the contours of the land, he shaded around the lakes and used his eraser to smooth the background.

"I didn't know you were an artist," Luke commented.

"I'm not. I just doodle a bit. Good to use the other part of my brain, right?"

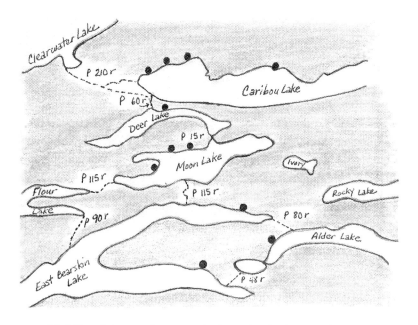

Holding his work at arm's length, Jack noted, "Interesting how many of these lakes have two 'arms,' isn't it? I wonder why that is."

"Probably has to do with the scouring and eroding and all the action that makes this area what it is. You know, I often wonder about the brave souls who located the best portage paths and bushwhacked their way through so we could enjoy all this. I'm grateful to the Voyageurs and all the rest."

Jack nodded and waited for a pause in the conversation. "Pastor Luke, I have something to ask you about. I tried to call you yesterday but didn't get you, and then I forgot." Pastor Luke looked interested. Jack took a deep breath. "I brought Abby's ashes. I wonder if you'll help me to scatter them up here somehow." Jack fidgeted with his notebook and pencil as he spoke.

Pastor Luke looked at Jack intently and nodded his assent. "I'll be honored to do that, Jack."

It rained all night long, noisy on the roof of the little cabin. Jack slept lightly, and every time he woke he was glad they were indoors. *How am I going to survive? How long will I last up there? Is this really a 'brilliant idea?'* He tried not to dwell on the unknown, and he drifted off to sleep again.

Jack awoke with his excitement renewed. He pulled the curtain back to look at the sky. The rain had stopped but the sun was hiding behind clouds, shading the morning in blue. He figured out the shower in the little cabin, but it took both of them to piece together how to run a percolator, all the while humming a catchy tune from an old coffee ad: Bada-BadaBopbop, dabadaBopBop. They threw together a quick breakfast. They packed up in a hurry, wondering if the clouds had played their hand, or if there was more rain to come.

Dodging puddles, Jack jogged up to the office to return the key. A girl of about eight was doing the same, right behind him. As he left, he heard Dottie saying "Eeuuwww," enjoying the spoon trick yet again.

They stopped briefly at the grocery store and picked up some fresh fruit, carrots, cheese, and a small container of milk. They decided on steak for their first night. They put the meat in a zipper bag and wrapped it and the dairy products in several layers of the day's newspaper to keep them cool. The bundle was bulky, but the fresh foods would be welcome for the first day or two. Their cuisine would change soon enough.

Pastor Luke tucked the groceries into his Duluth pack. "When we turn to go up the road called the Gunflint Trail, look to your left back in the trees, and you'll see the cabin where I lived when I was summer pastor here." Jack recalled that Pastor Luke's love affair with the north country began when he served here years ago.

When they made the turn, Pastor Luke slowed down and flailed his arm out the window at the little cabin. Jack worried about the traffic, but he dutifully looked. The cabin was tiny and rustic, just the spot for an adventuresome young seminary student. He felt a surge of envy.

The Gunflint Trail started in residential Grand Marais and led north out of town. Dense woods, rich green in the muted light of the overcast sky, lined both sides of the road. The rain-soaked soil was deep brown. After some miles Pastor Luke, still in the lead, slowed and stretched his arm out and pointed over the roof of his car toward the right-hand side of the road.

Jack soon spotted the reason for the signal: a moose, its early antlers dripping with weeds, stood in a marsh only about 100 yards away. Jack's heart leaped to see the impressive animal. It stood at least five feet tall, even more when it raised its magnificent head. Long blunt nose, massive brown body, skinny legs…Jack thought of Bullwinkle in spite of himself, and laughed. *This is what I've come for – it's a scene totally different from home. Hope I'll have at least one other chance to admire a moose!*

But soon he was reminded of urban life as they slowed and then stopped to wait for construction. *At least construction tie-ups have scenery here.* After a long wait the column of cars began to move. As they passed the construction workers themselves, Jack was amused to note that the personal vehicles parked along the shoulder all had canoes on top.

They turned right onto county road 146. Passing the entrance to Bearskin Lodge and the National Forest Campground, Pastor Luke kept going and Jack followed. They passed little roads poking into the forest toward private cabins, one after another, beckoning like sirens. Finally they came to a dead end. Pastor Luke turned around and shouted out the window sheepishly, "Sorry – my map doesn't have the whole road. The access must have been at the campground back there." Jack shrugged. They retraced their route and found it.

They pulled up their vehicles side by side at the lake access. The view ahead was not picture postcard material: clouds blanketed the sky. The lake was the color of a steel griddle, with no reflections, no sun sparkles, no mirror effect.

The surface rippled slightly in the breeze. Jack felt trepidation, insecurity, and anticipation all at once. Pastor Luke had his canoe down and half in the water while Jack was still fiddling with the multiple knots that held his. Jack took a deep breath, told himself to get a grip, and wrestled the ropes free. He easily lifted the lightweight canoe off and down to the water. Following Pastor Luke's example he pointed it out into the lake, leaving the stern up on the sand. He turned back to the Volvo to get his gear out, and heard Pastor Luke shout, "Come back here, you!"

Fortunately Pastor Luke had carried his paddle in his second load, because now he needed it to retrieve Jack's canoe. It had slid down the sand and quietly drifted off on its own. "Independence – that's aptly named!" Pastor Luke quipped. Jack stood watching with his mouth open until the new canoe was back on the sand. Relieved that Pastor Luke's reaction held no judgment, he resolved to pay attention to how he "parked" the lightweight craft. *If I'm on my own and my canoe leaves me, I'll be – up a creek!*

Once they'd unloaded their fishing gear and packs by the water and secured the canoes, the two men slathered on sunscreen, drove up to the lot, parked side by side, and locked their cars. Pastor Luke duly admired Jack's new Volvo. A quick stop at the outhouse, and they eagerly raced to the canoes. Life preservers and hats on, they were set.

Pastor Luke dragged his canoe half into the water and swung his pack into it. "Mine is a tandem canoe, so to use it solo I ride backwards." Seeing Jack's puzzled expression, he chuckled and explained. "I sit on the bow seat but face the other way, and that equalizes the weight better. The canoe is reversible." Jack pretended to understand. He was reckoning with a fair amount of anxiety about his paddling skills.

"In your slick little solo canoe, you've only got one seat," Pastor Luke continued. "so you'll want to balance your body weight by putting the pack in front of you."

Jack dragged his canoe next to Pastor Luke's and swung his pack in, thankful it was so much lighter than yesterday. "Like here?"

Pastor Luke scratched his jaw. "Looks good for starters. I think you'll just have to experiment to find the best balance." He slid his fishing pole and paddle into his canoe and Jack did the same.

Jack stood up and took a deep breath, suddenly very insecure about the whole endeavor. *Am I really ready for this?*

Pastor Luke offered a casual prayer. "God bless our time here with safety, serenity, and … fun!" Jack relaxed a little. "Ready?"

"Ready as I'll ever be." Pastor Luke pushed off smoothly, like the experienced paddler he was. Jack pushed the Independence further into the water and gingerly put a foot in, reaching for the gunwales.

"Keep your center of gravity low," Pastor Luke advised, and Jack's bend became a crouch. The canoe rocked. His rear plopped onto the seat and he unfolded his legs, grabbing clumsily for the paddle and bonking himself on the head with it. Pastor Luke politely refrained from commenting.

Jack used his paddle to push the canoe off the sandy shore into the water. He released a sigh, only vaguely aware that he had been holding his breath. Pastor Luke had paddled several strokes into the lake, and Jack tried to head in the same direction. But every stroke on his right headed him to the left, and when he tried to correct from the left he headed right. This crazy zigzag was alarming. And the nose of the canoe seemed so high.

Maybe this is the wrong canoe for me. Maybe I'm not up to this. Maybe I should just go back now and save the humiliation. A frown clouded his face.

Pastor Luke had turned to check on Jack and saw his growing frustration. He skimmed over to him, watching the canoe's erratic path, and wondered what to suggest first. "You've got a wild canoe there, Jack. Needs taming."

"We've already noted its name – it sure is 'independent.' What am I doing wrong?"

Pastor Luke studied the craft. "The bow is too high, it looks like to me. What if you move your pack further forward?"

"Suits me – it would give me better leg room too." Jack poked his pack with his paddle and shoved it further from him. He tried paddling again. The equilibrium felt better but he still zigzagged. "Pastor Luke?" he appealed. "Now what?" *If I can't paddle straight I can't do this. Calm down and listen to your teacher.*

"Let me show you the 'Solo C' stroke, it might help. Reach the paddle forward – but don't lunge – and keep your top hand low, below your eyes is best." Jack jerked to correct each action. "I know, it's a lot to remember. Here, I'll demonstrate." Pastor Luke buried the wide part of his paddle into the water about two feet ahead of his body, and about a foot out from the canoe. He pulled back and toward the canoe. "This is the arc of the 'C,' and you actually want to go under the canoe a little. Then thrust it out, not too far back, making the other side of the 'C'. Give it a try."

Jack had been watching intently, but now he looked skeptical. "Do it again," he pleaded.

Pastor Luke complied, repeating the commentary. "OK, just try it. I'll help as much as I can."

Jack's first attempt was slow and deliberate. "Good job," Pastor Luke encouraged. "Now try to speed it up a little, and make sure you tip the blade so you go slightly under the canoe."

While the instructions played in his head, Jack carefully outlined the C in the water once, twice, three times. Each time got a bit easier.

"You're doing great, Jack!" Pastor Luke came up parallel to him. "Before long you won't have to think about it at all. You betcha, you'll be fine."

Wonder when that will be. Right now I have to concentrate like I'm threading a needle.

With Jack still getting a feel for the rhythm of paddling solo, they headed east around a point and bore left around a large wooded headland.

Chapter 5

Motorboats putted by at a respectful distance, reminding them that they were not yet officially in the BWCAW. With their canoes side by side, Pastor Luke explained to Jack in a few sentences about the perennial controversies about where motorized watercraft would be allowed within the boundaries of the Wilderness.

To their left were the cabins whose private entrances they had passed on the road. Each one had a dock, and most had a motorboat or canoe present. *Wonder what it would be like to live there?*.

They paddled in silence most of the time, drinking in the beauty of the forest-rimmed lake. Low clouds moved briskly overhead, but no rain came down. The wind was at their backs.

The peninsula which creates north and south arms of East Bearskin Lake loomed ahead, and Pastor Luke again paddled closer to communicate. "We'll take the north arm. Up here a ways we might spot the marker of the edge of the Boundary Waters. Not far from that is the portage, on the north bank."

Jack needed to concentrate to keep from bumping his canoe into Pastor Luke's. "You go ahead and navigate – I forgot to get my maps out." He could barely remember even though he had sketched the lakes; his brain seemed full. *Need to acquire some good habits as well as skills, I can see that. Pastor Luke will be with me only one week.*

The marker was subtle; Jack almost missed it. He kept his eyes peeled for some sign of a portage, but he didn't see it until Pastor Luke turned and pulled in. He followed him in, wincing as he scraped his new canoe on a rock as he landed. Again he felt clumsy, clambering out of the craft.

First thing, Jack dug out his maps and a zipper bag. He folded the F-14 map to make East Bearskin and their route clearly visible, tucked it into the bag and zipped it shut to keep the map dry. He bent over it and announced, "This portage is 115 rods. How much is a rod again?"

Pastor Luke scratched his head. "It's the length of an average canoe…16 feet or so? If I remember rightly, 160 rods equal half a mile. You'll have to do the math – I'm numerically impaired, you know." He grinned.

"That's enough for me to go on. What do we take first?"

"Let's set our packs, paddles, and poles to the side out of the way, in case someone else wants to land here. First we'll take the canoes across to the next lake, then we'll come back for the rest." Pastor Luke took action as he spoke.

"It seems strange to just leave all our gear unattended here." Worry was written all over Jack's face.

"It does seem strange at first, doesn't it. There's a high code of honor up here, you know. I've never had anything stolen. By a human anyhow."

"We're not in the city any more, are we."

"You noticed?" Pastor Luke teased, stretching his arms out as if to embrace all of nature.

Jack studied Pastor Luke as he smoothly grasped the portage yoke of his canoe, twisted and lifted, and set it gently on his own shoulders. Jack's effort was not nearly as smooth, but it worked. He balanced the craft, adjusted the pads a little, grasped the gunwales, and they set off on their first portage with Pastor Luke bringing up the rear to spot for Jack.

Navigating the path was not too challenging once he got his balance. The trail led uphill for a time, then gradually down. Suddenly he saw what he thought was a cliff ahead, and he slowed abruptly. It was steps going down – about ten of them – made of railroad ties. He tipped the canoe forward to keep from bumping its low end on the ground. He felt a little dizzy as he imagined himself and the canoe tumbling to their destruction so early in his journey. He paused and continued, cautiously turning ninety degrees, gingerly finding his footing on two steep stone steps at the bottom.

"Excellent job! God is good!" came encouragement from above, specifically from Pastor Luke who stood at the top of the steps. Pastor Luke picked his way down until they were standing side by side at the water's edge. Moon Lake rippled in the breeze, looking like a washboard awaiting its entrance in a jug band number.

Pastor Luke rested the tip of his canoe on the ground in front of him, lifted the yoke off his shoulders and flipped the craft upright as he lowered it gently. Jack's attempt at this maneuver was fair, about a C+, he thought. They slid the canoes into a secure spot and went back for the packs. Jack's knees felt like rubber when he ascended the steps. The portage area was still deserted when they got back. They helped each other get their packs on comfortably, grabbed paddles and fishing poles and headed over the portage again. The steps seemed less imposing with this load.

Jack felt happy to see his red canoe again. Moon Lake sparkled as the sun made a brief appearance. "I'd like to take a picture of my canoe and the lake, do you mind?" Jack asked.

"No problem."

"I'm glad I remembered my camera – I have it right here near the top of my pack." Jack pulled out an automatic 35 millimeter camera in a soft case. "This camera is foolproof! I've gotten some great shots with it."

"How much film did you bring?"

The color drained out of Jack's face. "Film!" He could picture the film in a plastic bag in the refrigerator. He hadn't even moved it to the kitchen table to pack it, nor had he remembered to buy extra rolls. "Maybe there's some in the camera?" he asked as he pulled the camera out of its case. He flipped the switch on and saw an "E" flashing in the top window. "Awwww, shoot!"

"Guess you won't be able to shoot much then," Pastor Luke quipped. "I didn't even remember to bring a camera, so I can't help you."

The two men put their canoes in the water and loaded up, first Pastor Luke and then Jack. "Step into the center, and keep your center of gravity low," Pastor Luke reminded Jack when he stepped into his craft too quickly, setting it rocking. "You'll get the feel of it, don't worry."

They soon accomplished the short paddle across Moon Lake to the next portage. On his map, Jack saw the three big red dots indicating campgrounds, but even though he strained his eyes he couldn't spot them. *This will take some learning too.* He found the portage easily, at the point of the lake.

This 15-rod portage was all rocks. "It would be so easy to twist your ankle!" Jack exclaimed.

"Please don't do it," Pastor Luke pleaded. "That's why you need good boots, like the ones you've got. People who wear sneakers take a terrible risk on a portage like this. Once I even saw a kid in flip-flops – that was an accident waiting to happen!" They picked their way carefully up and then down, first with canoes and then packs, paddles, and poles.

They paddled into the wind on Deer Lake. With the sun behind the clouds they felt cool, glad for the added warmth of the life vests. Jack had to pay careful attention to his paddling, to compensate for the wind gusts that wanted to steer him off course. Again he strained to see the camp-ground that was marked on the map. He thought he saw it at last, but it turned out to be the portage.

Landing and disembarking went a little better for him this time. He lifted his canoe and set out while Pastor Luke was still taking a drink from his canteen. "I'll see you at Caribou Lake!" he teased.

This path was broad and grassy like a walk in the park, except that you don't usually wear a canoe for a hat. These and other amusing thoughts danced through Jack's mind as he walked easily along. He experimented with his balance under the canoe, tried holding it with one hand, then no hands briefly, then went back to both hands. *Forgot to look at how long this portage is – don't think it was farther than the first though, and it seems to be taking longer. And it's easier walking on this old road, if that's what it is.* Suddenly he heard his name called from behind him.

He carefully turned the canoe and himself, and saw Pastor Luke, empty-handed, coming his way, pointing over his shoulder. "There was a turnoff to the right back there – you're on the path that leads to Clearwater Lake."

Jack was embarrassed. "I thought it was getting to be kinda far," he mumbled.

"So let me take your canoe, you must be tired then."

Not really, but maybe Pastor Luke wants to try carrying the Independence. He can have a turn.

"Wow, this canoe is nice and light. Well, I got to Caribou and you weren't there, so I left my canoe and came back to look for you. You could actually get to Caribou this way, but you'd have to take a left turn up ahead, and you would go about 210 rods instead of 60."

"Thanks for coming after me. I guess my peripheral vision is limited under the canoe. I'll just be looking at the maps more closely from here on..." Jack took note of the three-way junction when they came to it. He vaguely remembered it from his sketch. He took his canoe from Pastor Luke and hurried down the hill to Caribou as Pastor Luke headed back to Deer Lake to get his pack. Jack hustled back for his own pack, but he never caught up with Pastor Luke.

When Jack finally arrived at Caribou Lake and wearily shrugged out of his pack, Pastor Luke had a late lunch of granola bars and milk ready. It tasted heavenly.

Once on Caribou Lake, the two campers needed to look for a campsite. The map showed three sites, fairly close together, on the north shore across from the portage. Further east was another site, and through a narrows to the eastern end of the lake were two more. They decided to go for one of the further sites.

"Most canoe trippers look for a site around mid-afternoon," Pastor Luke explained. "That way you can get settled, get your firewood, go fishing if you want." When they launched their canoes, moving past the tree cover at the portage, they noticed that they were not alone. Two canoes were visible well ahead of them. Pastor Luke's practiced eye discerned even at a distance that they were loaded with gear, so he surmised that these travelers were also looking for campsites.

"We have competition," he said to Jack, gesturing with his paddle toward the two. "Considering what time it is and their position in the lake," he squinted at the cloudy sky, then looked at his watch, "they are probably heading for the sites east of here. Well maybe we'd better check out the three that are close by then."

They paddled north across the lake. Jack peered at the shore. To the left he saw a bald spot – maybe a rock face, maybe a campsite. To their right he was soon able to make out a spot but he also saw a blue tent back in the trees. "The one on the right is already taken," he said to Pastor Luke, pleased that his perception seemed to be improving. They adjusted their course to the northwest and saw yet another canoe, this one coming from the west. "Busy lake – it must be rush hour!" Jack quipped, and Pastor Luke grinned.

The other paddler slowed at the bald spot, but kept pad-dling. Closer now, they could see that it was indeed a campsite, with the fire ring on a huge rock, more exposed than most. They watched the canoe slow again and Jack saw that he was checking out the second site, this one with more tree cover. But the lone traveler rejected that one too, and paddled on.

"Let's go for that middle one there," Pastor Luke suggested.

Jack noted that Pastor Luke kept staring at the site on their left, even as he steered straight for the other. *I couldn't do that – it takes all my concentration to keep going on a reasonably straight course. I sure admire Pastor Luke's skill.*

The landing was easy on a gentle slope of rock. They stepped out and pulled their canoes up on either side of a large cedar with gnarled, exposed roots.

"God is good!" Pastor Luke spread his arms in delight as he took in the site. "This is a marvelous campsite! Look, there's room for two tents, and a nice big flat rock to use as a kitchen counter. Alrighty! And this is a great grate!"

"Why all the upright stones around it?" Jack asked.

"I think they'll help shield the fire from the wind," Pastor Luke surmised. "Good log benches to sit on around the fire…and someone's left us a little firewood! You betcha, this is perfect!"

They unloaded their gear and began to set up camp. The wind was brisk so they layered on their long-sleeved shirts. Pastor Luke claimed the eastern tent site, and Jack took the westerly one. He tackled his tent with determination, glad that he had practiced at home.

"I'm going to check out the 'stool on the hill'," Pastor Luke announced. He headed up the trail to the seclusion of the box latrine.

Jack got his tent all set up and staked into the rocky ground with some effort. Then he burrowed in the Duluth pack for his sleeping bag and plastic bag of clothing. "Dang!" he exclaimed aloud a he pulled the "footprint" tarp out of his pack. *This was supposed to go under the tent!* He stomped around waving the tarp, angry at his ineptitude. *What do I think I'm doing? I'll never get this right!*

Pastor Luke heard the outburst as he returned. He slowed to let Jack burn off a little steam, then approached him gently. "Hey, it's okay." He put a hand on Jack's shoulder and cocked his head to look him in the eyes. "It's okay," he said again. "How can I help?"

They pulled up the stakes, and Pastor Luke lifted up the little free-standing tent while Jack spread out the tarp. With very little fuss they situated the tent on its 'footprint' and re-staked it. "That was not too hard! Now, want to help me with mine?" Pastor Luke asked. Jack obliged, even though he knew Pastor Luke didn't need the help. It just felt good to work cooperatively.

The steak smelled and tasted delicious, grilled over an open fire. After their fine meal, the two men sat on the log benches, picking their teeth with toothpicks from their Swiss Army knives, gazing out on the lake.

"I'm going fishing! Want to come?" Pastor Luke leaped up and started gathering his fishing gear.

"No, I think I'll stay right here. Have fun." As an after-thought he added, "May I look at your BWCA guide?"

"You bet, I'll get it." With smooth economy of motion Pastor Luke got the book for Jack, collected his gear, and was off.

Jack sat with the dog-eared book in his hands, watching Pastor Luke go. *Need to learn about fishing, too, but not tonight.* He opened the book and read the introduction, which inspired the reader to be a student of the wilderness, open to its spiritual teachings. *Okay, I'll try.* He turned to the section on their route and read several pages. He was interrupted by the haunting call of one loon to another. The sound, and its response, gave him a shiver of joy. The serene lake reflected the opposite shore like a mirror.

A loon landed with a gentle splash, its black and white checked wings folding into its body. As it drifted along Jack admired its elegant black head and beak, white striped collar, and stunning red eyes. Without warning it ducked beneath the water, emerging ten yards away in a twinkling.

It stretched its neck and called again, reared up and flapped its wings triumphantly, then settled back into quiet drifting.

The light was dimming. Alone, in this peaceful place, he almost felt like he could relax. *Been running hard this past week – so much has happened since I decided to come up here to the wilderness. Had to deal with my office, and the house, and the money. Now I'm finally here, away from it all.* He sighed and tipped his head back to look at the early-evening sky. *Clouds, clouds, clouds. Maybe the weather will clear soon, and my mind will clear too.*

Pastor Luke was back. "Look what I caught!" he cried jubilantly from the canoe. He lifted up a Northern Pike, at least four pounds.

Jack lumbered down to the shore, stiff from sitting on a log bench too long. "Wow!" He was really impressed. "Fish for breakfast?"

"You betcha!" Pastor Luke was already heading off again. "I'm going to clean it away from the campsites, so we don't invite unwanted visitors. Be back in a bit." On second thought he said, "Throw me my gloves – my hands are cold. And a zipper bag for the fish." Jack obliged.

Pastor Luke paddled off to the east. Jack decided to gather up the cooking gear and get the bear bag ready. He was still insecure about hanging it. When he picked up the garbage bag they'd gotten at the ranger station, he noticed that it had a slip of paper attached with directions for two different methods of hanging a bear bag, with sketches. *This is handy.*

He studied the pictures a while, then fetched his notebook and pencil. It bugged him that the pack in their sketch was really small, nothing like a big old Duluth pack. So he made his own version, taking careful note of the way the ropes were attached. He would again be a student of Pastor Luke's skill as he learned this important process tonight. He wondered which technique Luke would use.

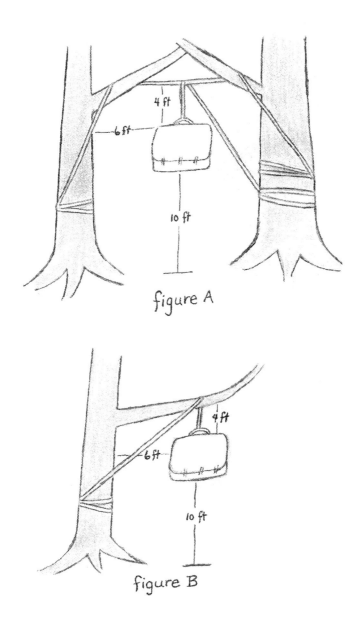

4 ft

6 ft

10 ft

figure A

4 ft

6 ft

10 ft

figure B

I'll just keep this. He slid the paper into his notebook.

Pastor Luke's pack had most of the food in it, so it made sense that it would be their bear bag. Jack gathered up his mosquito repellent, and the dish soap…what else? He thought back to the video and the questions the ranger had asked. *Toothpaste! First filter more water and use it, then include it.*

He took his water filter to the lake along with his water bottle. The rubber tube with the screen went into the lake, with the other one positioned in the bottle. It took a little jockeying to get the bottle stable between his knees so that he could hold the filter with one hand and pump with the other. With the bottle finally full he headed away from the lake to the trees and brushed his teeth, spitting onto the ground and rinsing his toothbrush from the bottle. He was putting his toiletries by Pastor Luke's pack when Luke returned.

They wrapped the zipper bag of fish filets in newspapers and added them to the bear bag, figuring it was cold enough to keep it safe. Pastor Luke washed his hands and rubbed them together to warm them up. He reached for his gloves and, to his dismay, found only one. He checked the canoe and the ground, and came up empty. "Rats!" he said. "Those were new, too."

"Maybe you left it where you cleaned the fish."

"That's probably it. It's too late now to go back. I'll have to check tomorrow."

Pastor Luke carried the rope and a paddle, and searched for an appropriate pair of trees for hanging a bear bag. Jack followed, carrying the heavy pack clumsily in front of him. He was wishing he had put it on his back properly, but he kept thinking they were almost far enough away from the site. Pastor Luke finally settled on two trees, and searched around for a rock that fit in his hand. The rope was all in a tangle, and he struggled to find an end. When he did he tied it once around the rock. Jack dropped the pack on the ground and watched like his life depended on it.

Pastor Luke carefully untangled the rope, and pitched the rock up and over the branch he had his eye on. It went in the direction he wanted, but the rock sailed out of the rope and the end fell uselessly to the ground. He retrieved his rock and tried twice more, with various knots, but to no avail. Next he tried a different rock. Jack untangled the rope for him a few times and marveled at his patience.

At last the rock and rope made it over the appointed branch, and both men gave a little cheer. Pastor Luke secured the end of the rope by wrapping it around the trunk of the tree several times. They threaded the other end of the rope through the straps of the pack, making sure the straps were secure, and Pastor Luke went through the whole rock-and-rope process again to get the end of the rope over the branch of another tree, about twenty feet away. *Ah, Figure A.* This took five more tries, but he persisted and finally got it.

Pastor Luke pulled on the rope while Jack hefted the heavy bag to get it suspended between the two trees. When it rose over Jack's head he used the paddle to push it up, while Pastor Luke tightened the rope. When he was satisfied that it was out of the reach of any bear, he secured the rope around the trunk of the second tree.

They both stood back with their fists on their hips, admiring their work. *Will I be able to do this alone? Will I have the patience to do it right? I'll have to!*

On the way back to camp, Pastor Luke spotted a log suspended across two trees – perfect for hanging a bear bag. "I wish I'd seen that before!" he shook his head. "You know, that reminds me that we don't always perceive the gifts that are provided for us!" They chortled as they walked back to their camp in the fading light.

"Anyway, nice job, Pastor Luke. That process took perseverance."

"Consider the postage stamp, Jack."

"What?"

"It's usefulness is in its ability to stick with one thing until it gets there." Luke paused for Jack's chuckle. "An old humorist by the name of Josh Billings said that."

"You're so full of lore. I used to quote the classic writers in my classes but I'm rusty now."

"OK, let's have a quote-off. We'll pick a topic, like, um…wisdom. Think of everything you can about wisdom."

Jack grinned and thought. "'Early to bed and early to rise, makes a man healthy, wealthy and wise.' Poor Richard. I mean, um, Benjamin Franklin."

"Good one! Let's see if I can get this one right, from the book of Proverbs in the Bible: 'My child,' uh, something something something," Luke scrunched up his face, then relaxed it and nodded. "'Keep sound wisdom and prudence, and they will be life for your soul and adornment for your neck.'" Jack made approving sounds and Luke held up his hand and closed his eyes. "There's more, let me think. 'Then you will walk on your way securely and your foot will not stumble. If you sit down, you will not be afraid; when you lie down, your sleep will be sweet.'"

"Oh, I like that one. Now my turn to think." Jack looked at the ground and pinched the bridge of his nose. At last he raised a finger triumphantly. "'Knowledge comes, but wisdom lingers.' Tennyson."

"Excellent! Aristotle: 'Wisdom is the reward you get for a lifetime of listening when you'd rather have been talking.'"

"Oh, that's to the point. Perhaps I should be wise and stop talking now?"

Luke laughed. "No, this is fun! Keep it up. It can be an ongoing endeavor."

"I'll keep thinking. It's good brain exercise."

They poked the fire to try to warm up before crawling into their tents. "It's sure cool tonight." Jack observed, turning his back to the fire to warm that side.

"You know, I was up here in early June one time and I thought I'd freeze! I wore everything I had to bed and I was still cold. I didn't have a very good sleeping bag then. How's yours?" Pastor Luke asked.

"It's goose down. Should be good. But I haven't tested it yet."

"Tonight will be a good test. I will say this, though: the nice thing about cool weather is that there are no bugs! I hate it when you're almost asleep and you hear the whine of a hungry mosquito by your ear: eeeeeeeeeeeeeeee" he demonstrated, pressing his thumb and index finger together and whirling them around his head. Jack shuddered and agreed.

"I'm glad we're here, Pastor Luke. I've wondered dozens of times if it was a wise decision. Now that I'm here it feels right."

"Here's another quote to sleep on, by Minnie Haskins: 'I said to the man who stood at the gate of the year: "Give me a light that I may tread safely into the unknown." And he replied: "Go out into the darkness and put your hand into the hand of God. That shall be to you better than light and safer than a known way!"' You're going into the unknown, Jack, and it's the right thing to do! God is with you."

"Uh... Amen!" Jack smiled.

They doused the fire, said their goodnights and retired to their tents before they got any colder. Jack made quick work of getting out of his clothes and into his sleeping bag. It was cold at first but his body heat warmed it up in time. He hunkered down and fell asleep promptly.

Chapter 6

"That was quite a storm!" Jack croaked as he emerged from his tent. Pastor Luke already had the bear bag down, coffee on the camp stove, and he was poking at a fire that was better at smoking than burning.

"I didn't sleep as well as I had hoped," Pastor Luke lamented.

"Me neither. I feel more tired now than when I went to bed," Jack growled, his voice low and raspy. He cleared his throat so the next sentence would come out better. "The weather looks, well, like more of the same today," he changed the subject before he was tempted to tell Pastor Luke about his troublesome morning dreams of Abby.

Luke scanned the sky. "We're lucky we didn't get snow. It must have been close to freezing. My feet felt like ice most of the night. But – there were no mosquitoes!" He poured a cup of coffee as it started to sprinkle. "Oh great, more rain."

Pastor Luke and Jack dove into their tents as the rain came down hard. For about fifteen minutes it pounded the fabric of each tent's rain fly. Each man sat alone worrying about the day, and wondering what the other was thinking. Packing a wet tent was undesirable, but it could be done. Paddling in this torrent would be miserable. Portages could get pretty muddy. But they hadn't come to just stay put for a week. What if the weather didn't improve?

Jack began to think – *didn't I buy a rain fly in addition to the one on the tent? Must be at the bottom of the pack. Lot of good it's doing us there. Hope this isn't typical weather up here. Once my jacket is soaked it won't keep me warm enough. Maybe this was a dumb idea after all.*

When the rain let up, two heads popped out of their tent flaps. They chuckled at the symmetry of it. The wind was making whitecaps on the lake and the air was chilly and damp.

"I propose," Pastor Luke said dramatically, "that we stay here and relax today. We can just take it easy, let the storm blow on by, and plan to break camp and head out tomorrow morning. What do you think?"

"Agreed," Jack said. He was frustrated by the weather, and unsure of what to do, so he was thankful that Pastor Luke had a plan. After all, he had a whole summer to spend here if he wanted; it made sense to let Pastor Luke call the shots this week. If he didn't feel like he had to keep moving, that was all right.

"So how about some fish for breakfast then?" Luke was ready for some action.

"Quick, before the next rainstorm!"

The grilled Northern was the best either of them had ever tasted – it melted in the mouth. They savored every bite, and wished for more. "I'll have to try a little fishing later." Jack said with anticipation.

Pastor Luke showed Jack how to work his new camp stove, and they initiated it by boiling water to wash the dishes. Luke filtered some extra water and filled the canteen, while Jack tidied up the campsite. The wind had diminished somewhat, and they got the fire going strong at last with the remainder of the woodpile. They took turns searching for dead trees back in the woods and sawing them up into firewood. Luke even paddled off to find firewood once. The fire required constant tending, and it was persistently smoky, but it gave them warmth, or the illusion of warmth. Short rain squalls could be endured as long as the fire was going.

Pastor Luke produced his F-14 map, and he held the left edge while Jack took the right. Starting on the west he pointed to East Bearskin Lake. "Here's where we started; we went north to Moon, Deer, and now we're here on Caribou."

"Caribou is a long one! We'll have a long paddle tomorrow," Jack commented.

"We won't go quite the full length – see, here's the portage north to Clearwater. Now, we have several choices. If we really push ourselves we can get up to the border chain. There's lots of paddling, not so much portaging. And here between Mountain Lake and Moose Lake we'd follow the Pigeon River, which should be deep enough to paddle this time of year. If not, there are portages, you know. Over here on the east side of our map between North Fowl and John we'd be on the Royal River for a while."

"It looks like a long loop," Jack offered, wondering about his stamina for long paddling days.

"It is. Instead of knocking ourselves out, we could do Plan B, which has more portaging mixed in. It takes us from Clearwater to West Pike to East Pike, then John, Little John, McFarland, and Pine, back to Caribou, Deer, Moon, and East Bearskin." His finger traced the loop as he narrated. "That retraces yesterday's trip, which I usually resist. Which leads me to Plan C, which is the same as B as far as Pine, but then we take this 'little' 232 rod portage from Pine to Canoe, then to Alder and back to East Bearskin."

"Whoa – that portage has *switchbacks!*" Jack looked incredulously from the map to Pastor Luke and back to the map.

"Makes your shoulders hurt, does it?"

"Just thinking about it!"

"Well you know, sometimes we need to challenge ourselves..."

Jack knew this whole adventure would challenge him, so he wasn't sure how to answer.

After a moment's silence, Luke offered, "How about if we take the shorter loop, and see how we do – if we get to Pine and want to tackle the harder route, we can do it. If we want to kick back, we can choose to do that."

"That sounds like a good plan. We can keep our options open."

For lunch they made Pastor Luke's favorite camp meal: oriental noodles in flavored broth. The noodles had been somewhat crushed in the pack, but they still tasted good. Crisp apples rounded out the meal.

The sky was a little lighter after lunch. "I can't decide whether to take a walk or take a nap," Luke said, stretching. "Maybe I'll do both. Nap first."

"There's a trail that takes off from behind my tent," Jack suggested. "I found some firewood that direction, but I didn't go far. Want to explore a little later?"

"Sure, you betcha." Pastor Luke stretched again and headed for his tent. "But first there's a little catnap with my name on it."

A nap sounded like a fine idea, so Jack stretched out on his sleeping bag. He rested, maybe even slept a little. After a while he decided to get up and try his little camping-sized espresso maker. He filled the bottom with filtered water, just to be safe, since it wouldn't boil for long enough to purify. Then he loaded the tiny basket with coffee, surprised that it only took a heaping tablespoon. He positioned the blue enamel demitasse under the curved spout and lit the camp stove with a whoosh. As the heat increased the espresso maker sputtered and gurgled and finally spewed out a stream of rich, dark coffee into the little cup.

The smell brought Luke out of his tent yawning and stretching. Jack made him a cup and they enjoyed sipping them together.

"I've never seen such a darlin' little thang," Pastor Luke drawled, examining the espresso maker. "I gotta get me one of these!"

"I thought of another quote about wisdom! I haven't got it exactly, but Alexander Pope said something about coffee making the politician wise."

"What does that mean, do you suppose?"

"I have no idea!"

Jack came down the path from the biffy and heard the repeating song of a bird, nearby it seemed. Pastor Luke was standing in the middle of the campsite, gazing up into a tree. About half of the birdsongs were coming from him. It seemed to be some sort of conversation. Luke turned toward Jack and reverted to English. "A red-eyed vireo, I think."

Jack looked up but couldn't locate the bird. "Oh, oh, oh, Robert Browning… '…the WISE thrush;'" Jack emphasized the key word as he struck his best poetry-quoting pose and oratory tone. "'He sings each song twice over, / Lest you think he could never recapture / The first fine careless rapture!'"

"Wow, you are really good at this game – I didn't realize I was challenging a master!"

"Well, English is my field, you know – I just have to access the right mental data base and search around. Now that I'm into it bits of things keep bubbling up! There's some Shakespeare I've been trying to piece together, too – I think it's from 'As You Like It' but I could be wrong about that. I had a teacher who had us memorize a lot of quotes but I can't always associate them with the right plays."

"Well, what is it?"

"'The fool doth think he is wise, but the wise man knows himself to be a fool.'"

"That's rich. 'The fool doth think he is wise…'" Luke paused as he memorized the phrase.

"'But the wise man knows himself to be a fool.'"

Luke repeated the quote and nodded with pleasure. "That's splendid, I can use that."

"Nice one. You've memorized a lot, too," Jack commented with admiration.

"I had a grade school teacher who encouraged it, and I discovered I had an aptitude. So I've continued to do it, as a self-discipline. Sometimes a quote comes in really handy to help make a point."

"It shows how wise you are, too!"

"I need all the help I can get in that department! I'm grateful for your endorsement, showing," Luke paused dramatically, setting up the quote: "'The cunning seldom gain their ends; the wise are never without friends.'"

"Well said! By whom?"

"I think that one is from the prolific author known as 'Anonymous.' It's the moral of a story but I'm afraid I've forgotten the story!"

"Oh well! So, are you ready for a little hike?"

"Let's stash our packs under the canoes in case it rains again." Luke acted on his suggestion as he spoke.

The trail was clear, except two spots where they had to detour around fallen trees. Presently the path widened considerably and Jack stopped. To his left and down the hill he saw a fire grate with a circle of log benches around it, and beyond it the lake.

"This is where our group camped ten years ago! We were right here! Our tents were here on this path, and the latrine is up the hill from here, and that was our fire circle! And we climbed on those boulders!" Jack was like a child discovering a favorite playground.

"You are right, my friend. You know, when I looked at this campsite from the lake I thought it looked familiar." Pastor Luke followed Jack down to the fire circle.

"This was the best site, because some of the group could stay up and talk around the fire, and they didn't bother the ones who wanted to go to sleep. I remember Abby and I were up very late one of the nights we were here."

"As I recall, you and Abby really got acquainted on that retreat." Pastor Luke broached the subject gently.

"Yeah." Jack tried to swallow the lump in his throat. "We fell in love here."

"I can tell you miss her terribly, Jack." Pastor Luke's hand rested lightly on Jack's shoulder.

"Yeah." Now his voice was totally unreliable.

"Let's sit down here for a spell." Pastor Luke steered him to the fire circle.

Pastor Luke tenderly recalled Abby's vivacious personality, her zest for adventure, the love she had for Jack. When Jack buried his head in his hands, Pastor Luke's arm supported him around his shoulders. When the sobs came from deep within, Pastor Luke murmured, "Let it come. It's good to cry," and continued to hold him.

Anger, loneliness, and pent-up frustration poured out of Jack's soul. He had not allowed himself to give in to these feelings before; it went against his self-imposed rules. But once the flood of tears started he could not stop it. Pastor Luke offered his clean bandana at just the right time, and reminded him to breathe deeply.

When Jack was finally able to talk, he began tentatively, his voice wavering. "It was so awful, when I saw the car smashed and twisted, and realized it was Abby's. She was in there! They had to bring the Jaws of Life to get her body out. And the other driver just popped out of his car and wobbled around on his drunken legs until the police put him in a car. I'll never forgive that man for snuffing out Abby's life!" At this the sobs began again.

"It must have been horrible to see." Pastor Luke murmured.

"I feel so guilty that I wasn't able to prevent the accident somehow. Maybe I should have driven her to work and back, I don't know. I should have been able to protect her. I feel so bad!"

"Jack, it's not your fault that she died."

Pastor Luke listened with care while Jack went on to talk about his relationship with Abby in a stream of consciousness.

"We had such joy in each other. She made me laugh. She could always think of something interesting to do. Just simple things brought her such delight – like going to feed the ducks at Lake Calhoun. I would never even think of doing that, but she did, and it was fun.

"She loved her work. She took very seriously her job of nurturing young minds and turning them on to math. She wanted to see more women in the field, too, so she watched for girls who showed particular interest. If she'd had more time, she might have really influenced the field of math. Her peers respected her, too. Sometimes I was a little jealous of her career; I didn't like my work as much as she liked hers.

"We argued back and forth about whether to have kids or not. Sometimes I wanted to, just to see what they'd be like. She didn't think that reason was good enough. Sometimes she wanted to, but then I was afraid of how it would tie us down. Now I'm still ambivalent. I wish I had kids because they would carry on Abby's presence for me and for the world, but I'm glad I don't because I wouldn't know what to do with them now. I'd probably be a lousy parent.

"I wonder if I was a good husband. I don't know if I loved Abby enough, or if I told her I loved her enough."

"Jack, it's always been evident to me that you loved Abby deeply. You don't ever need to worry about that." Pastor Luke's sonorous voice comforted Jack.

Pastor Luke's so understanding. I've never felt so broken. It's a little embarrassing, but I know Pastor Luke's OK.

Luke continued to offer little syllables of comfort and understanding as he listened to Jack's pain and reminiscences. They spent a long time deep in conversation.

After a silence Jack said, "The hardest thing was that I never got to say goodbye. She was just gone in an instant. I think about that all the time. If she had just lived for an hour, or a few minutes…if I just could have held her in my arms and kissed her, no matter what she looked like, bloody or anything, and told her I loved her so that she could hear that before she died…I just wish I'd had that chance. It's not fair, it's just not fair!" The sobs began again.

Jack wiped his eyes and nose and found his voice again. "I've never told anyone this: the day Abby was…killed…that morning, our last conversation before she went to work…it was just a normal day, we thought. We had a little argument, something dumb, I can't remember what it was about. We were quiet for a while over breakfast. After a while she said, out of the blue, 'Yesterday I changed three toilet paper rolls – one here at home, and two at work. I wonder if I'll beat that record today.' 'Good luck,' I said. That was it! That was our last conversation! I wish I had another chance so it wouldn't be so stupid!" He rubbed his eyes and tentatively started to chuckle through the tears, and they both laughed wryly at the absurdity of it all.

At last he took a deep breath and said, "Thank you, Pastor Luke. I feel better. I feel...drained."

"You've done some hard work today. Grieving is hard work. Right now it probably feels like you're out of balance, with more pain than anything else." Pastor Luke held his hands out in front of him, palms up, with the left much higher than the right. He lowered the left and raised the right until they were side by side. "In time, as you travel the grief journey, you'll regain your balance."

Jack looked hard at Pastor Luke's hands, memorizing the image. "I'd like to feel balanced again."

"You will, Jack, you will." He paused a few beats. "So are you ready to go back to our campsite then?" Luke took his tiny nod for a yes, and stood up.

"Pastor Luke?" Jack had one more thing to say, so Pastor Luke sat down again. "Ever since Abby's death, I've been really angry with God."

"That's normal, Jack."

"I'm not going crazy, then?"

"No, you're not going crazy. Not at all. Try reading the Psalms – lots of people have felt the way you do. When you're ready, talk to God about it. You'll find a good listener. God is good."

"How come you say that all the time? I'm not so sure God is always good."

"I picked that up from my African American brothers and sisters. In some black churches it's a kind of mantra – one person says 'God is good' and another, or the whole group, responds, 'All the time!' It reminds us that God is good in the good times, and even when life is terribly bad. Our circumstances may change, but God's goodness is everlasting."

"God is good," Jack tried skeptically.

"All the time!" Pastor Luke replied, clapping Jack on the back. "Let's go back to camp."

When they'd walked the short distance back to their site, Jack asked, "Remember I told you I brought Abby's ashes?"

"Yes."

"Could we scatter them here, on this lake?"

"I don't know why not. Do you want to do it now?"

Pastor Luke brought their paddles and Jack brought the blue urn of Abby's ashes. They launched Pastor Luke's canoe into the cove, Jack in the bow and Luke in the stern. They were pleased to see no other traffic on the water. Sunlight broke through the clouds sending shafts of light down to dance in reflections. The rain-washed air smelled fresh to Pastor Luke; Jack's sinuses burned with unwept tears.

In the middle of the lake the breeze rippled the water, causing a gentle slapping of waves against the hull of the canoe. They positioned themselves with the wind at their backs so Jack could hear Pastor Luke speak. They shipped their paddles and let the canoe drift. Jack held the blue urn on his lap and curled his body over it.

"You know Jack, about a week ago I visited Ruth Anderson at the nursing home," Pastor Luke began. "She was dying, and we have both known that for a couple of weeks. She couldn't speak any more. When I arrived Wednesday they had her in her chair, but she was slumped over in sleep. I didn't want to wake her, so I just took her limp hand and prayed. I started to get tearful, as I thought about how fond I am of her, and how I value her perspective. I didn't want her to die; I'll miss her.

"I was thinking all this and praying, with tears filling my eyes, and she woke up. With effort she lifted her head and looked at me, and she scowled! I was so startled!

"I immediately understood what she meant by that look. 'Don't hold me back, Pastor Luke! I can almost see God, and I'm eager to get there! I'm ready - let me go!'

"Abby didn't have preparation time like Ruth did. But just the same as Ruth, she may be saying, 'It's OK to let go of me!' I don't know what to think about 'heaven' really. I don't think it's exclusive and I don't think it's a reward for good behavior. I guess I just want to believe that when we die we'll be closer to God than ever before, or perhaps more aware – although right here on this lake we may be closer than usual to the Divine Presence – and we who remain here maybe shouldn't be selfish about clinging to those we've lost. We can trust Abby to God, who said through the prophet Isaiah, 'I have called you by name, and you are mine…you are precious, and honored, and I love you.'

"That affirmation of God's care applies to Abby, and to you, Jack, and to me. We are all loved by God, and we'll be given the strength that we need to cope with the struggles of this world. God is good, no matter what. Sometimes life's experiences leave a lot to be desired you know, but God is always good. So you can let her go, entrust her to God's hands, and honor her with your good memories."

Jack heard all this without looking at Pastor Luke, letting the hot tears fill his eyes and spill down his cheeks. The canoe rocked a little, like a cradle. After a few minutes of silence he realized it was his turn to say or do something. He lifted his head to the sun, felt warmth that could be interpreted as God's love, and blew out a long, slow breath. "Shall I scatter them now?" he asked Luke in a throaty rasp.

"Now would be a good time," Pastor Luke responded, "or do you want me to pray first?"

"Yeah, pray please."

Pastor Luke's prayer echoed his prior thoughts, and gave Jack more courage. After the prayer they sat in silence for another minute or two.

"Now I suggest that you note the direction of the wind, so the ashes will blow away from us," Pastor Luke said gently. "Just to warn you, there will be some fine ash and some larger bits of bone and such. Don't be shocked by that."

Jack removed the lid from the urn and saw the ash remains for the first time. With nothing there to physically remind him of his beloved Abby, and emboldened by Pastor Luke's words, he felt free to lift the urn and tip it into the wind, letting ashes and all fly and fall. As he twisted his wrist to empty the urn, it fell out of his grip and dropped into the water. He gasped at first and leaned toward it, but it soon sank out of sight. He watched it go, whispering, "Goodbye, Abby."

The urn's lid was still in his lap. He turned it in his hands, felt its smoothness, gripped it tightly and thought about letting go. He relaxed his hands, whispered, "Good-bye, Abby," again and slipped the lid into the water.

"Amen." Pastor Luke said, and Jack echoed the word. He sat very still for a long while looking out over the lake. Finally he reached for his paddle, and only then did Pastor Luke do the same.

Back in camp, Jack worked on getting the fire going while Pastor Luke dug in his pack for the makings of a meal. Jack vigorously sawed away at the firewood, jumped on sticks to break them into kindling, and fed the fire until it reached for the sky like a signal.

Luke, working deftly with his camp stove, soon served up three courses: savory lentil soup, then wild rice and mushroom vegetable pilaf, with cookies for dessert. "I hope you don't mind - we're vegetarians tonight," Pastor Luke said. "I wanted to take a break after having steak last night."

"No problem. This is great stuff." Jack cleaned his plate. "It reminds me of another quote from Shakespeare: 'I am a great eater of beef, and I believe that does harm to my wit.' No idea what play it's from. But vegetarians love it!"

Luke threw his head back and guffawed. Jack couldn't help but join in.

When the lake was calm and the fire had died down, Pastor Luke announced that he was going fishing. "Want to come along tonight then?"

"Hey, we forgot to look for your glove today. Let's do that, then fish."

"Sure enough. Thanks for remembering."

They set out together in Pastor Luke's canoe. With both paddling they glided along smoothly. "Let's move it!" Jack said over his shoulder from the bow. They pulled out all the stops and the canoe sped through the water. Muscles straining, they pushed themselves and saw immediate results in power and speed. In no time at all they were on the point of land where Luke had cleaned the fish the night before. They slowed their paddling, panting from their exertion.

Pastor Luke adeptly steered them in, and there on the rock was his glove. "Eureka!" he announced as Jack snatched the glove and waved it triumphantly overhead.

Luke caught a small Northern and released it, but Jack had only nibbles. Back in camp they prepared the bear bag and hung it on the frame previous campers had prepared. The process went much more smoothly this time.

After their chores were done, Pastor Luke said meaningfully, "It's been a good day, Jack."

"Yeah. Even though I'm now red-eyed like that bird you were talking to. I'm glad we had this day here."

"Me too. See you in the morning then. I'm going to bed."

Jack headed toward his tent, then turned awkwardly back. "Uh, Pastor Luke, did you bring a Bible?"

"Yes I did. I have to work on Sunday's sermon." Pastor Luke ducked into his tent and came out with a small, well-worn Bible in a plastic bag. "This is my travel Bible. It's been a lot of places with me, can you tell?"

"Yeah!"

"You're welcome to use it. Good night."

"Thanks. Good night."

Once inside his tent, Jack considered reading the Bible by flashlight, but set it aside. He shrugged out of his clothes, unzipped his sleeping bag, rolled in, and with some effort, zipped it up again. Lying on his back, he laced his hands behind his head and thought about the day. *I opened the door to my pain, and survived. The abyss was there, all right, but I didn't fall into it. That is notable.*

Jack pondered why he had locked up his feelings. *What makes me act like a glacier when I have such fiery feelings inside? Why am I using so much energy to keep my emotions in check? The effort is exhausting. Even when I'm alone, I guard my feelings. Haven't shed a tear since the week of the memorial service, until today.*

Where did these habits come from? Where do I come from?

"Everything you do or say reflects on your father." His mother had communicated this verbally in a confidential whisper, and nonverbally, with eyebrows that knotted in disapproval at his tale of revenge on the playground, or flew up in horror when he uttered a forbidden phrase.

Over time, the house rule came to be: "No matter what's happening on the inside, don't let it show on the outside."

Appearances were everything. The superintendent's family needed to be a model of decorum for the school and the community. *At what cost*, Jack thought. *At what cost.*

He resolved to continue opening the door, even if only an inch at a time, to see if the pain might subside. *If it means defying my family's house rule, so be it; here in the wilderness I don't have to be a model of decorum for anyone. I can try out a new way of being. If I don't like it, I don't have to stick with it. This wilderness time can be an experiment. Maybe I'll even try reading the Bible again. Maybe tomorrow.*

Chapter 7

Jack awoke slowly. Stretching his stiff body, he wondered if he had slept in the same position all night. Something felt different – he rubbed his eyes, yawned, and considered. *No nightmares! I slept through the night!*

Buoyed by this accomplishment, he crawled out of his tent. The sun was bright – he must have slept late. With a start he realized Pastor Luke's tent was gone. His eyes raked the site. *Deserted! And only one overturned canoe – Pastor Luke left without me!*

Jack took a step back, scratched his head, and thought. They hadn't made a schedule for their departure, so it wasn't like he had held them up by sleeping late. *What would make him pack up and leave? Pastor Luke must have been disgusted at my show of emotion yesterday. That was it. I've driven away the best friend I had.*

I can't blame him. I should have known better than to let my feelings out. Why did I let my guard down? I was taught better.

But I thought Pastor Luke was trustworthy. I hoped I could be myself without judgment, but maybe that was too much to ask from a minister. Maybe Pastor Luke is punishing me now, teaching me a lesson by abandoning me in the wilderness.

Could I make it on my own? That was my goal. I have already gained some skills in our three days out; I might have what it takes. I had hoped for a little more guidance from my mentor, but I might be forced to find my way alone.

As these thoughts buzzed in his head, Jack set about breaking camp. He just crammed everything in, without trying to make them compact or tidy. Just as he was stuffing his tent into the Duluth pack, he heard the scrape of a canoe on the shore. Wheeling around, he saw Pastor Luke step out and pull the craft further up. Jack's heart beat faster and more questions whirled in his head.

Pastor Luke's posture looked different – more slumped than usual. He looked down as he slowly strode to the fire circle and sat on a boulder there. "Morning." he mumbled.

"Morning," Jack replied. He finished his task of bagging his tent and stowed it in his Duluth pack. *What to do? What to say? Should I apologize for yesterday's tears? I clearly made Pastor Luke depressed. Can I salvage our friendship, at least for the rest of the trip? Why did Pastor Luke desert me? Am I so disgusting? Why did he come back?* Jack sat on the stone furthest from Pastor Luke in the fire circle and cleared his throat. "I don't know what to say."

"You don't have to say anything. I'm just glad you're here." Pastor Luke's words didn't make sense to Jack. *What is he glad about, if I am so despicable?* He puzzled over this. An idea occurred to him. *Maybe Pastor Luke came back to get his Bible! It was a much-loved, well-traveled possession. Perhaps he started out and realized that I still had it and came back to get it. But he didn't walk into camp demanding his treasure.* Jack thought about digging into his pack to retrieve the book, but he stayed put.

After a long silence, Pastor Luke sighed and looked up at Jack. He smiled a little. "If you were a cartoon character, you would have question marks all around your head," he said. "Well I guess I owe you an explanation.

"I didn't sleep well last night. I had to deal with some of my own demons, I guess. I stared at the inside of the tent all night, it seemed. When it got light I got up and took the darned thing down to get it out of my sight. I stowed my gear under your canoe and shoved off to drift and think. Sorry I didn't make you any breakfast."

Jack shrugged to indicate that it didn't matter. Of course he had assumed Pastor Luke had left with a loaded canoe. He didn't trust his own thoughts enough to make any comments, so he just listened.

After a raspy sigh, Pastor Luke continued. "Years ago I had a marriage that ended badly. Our conversation yesterday brought back a lot of memories. I still have a lot of guilt and pain." He gazed out at the lake as he spoke. "It's so peaceful here. It's a good place."

Jack's eyes followed Pastor Luke's gaze. The morning sun made the lake shimmer with diamonds. A loon called. Jack let his former assumptions drop away like leaves from an autumn tree. Pastor Luke had not abandoned him. He was a friend who even trusted him enough to share a little of his pain. They both understood pain. That was enough.

"Hungry?" Luke asked.

"Not really," Jack lied.

"Then let's paddle."

The sky once again grew cloudy, but it was not as cold as the day before. The wind was friendlier; it helped propel them eastward. They made good time paddling on Caribou Lake. Jack kept his map and compass handy and referred to them often, trying to match the contours of the land to the contour lines on the map. He admired the ridges to the north and south, covered with trees so dense they looked impermeable. He missed spotting the campsite on their left, but he was able to clearly see the broad peninsula before they came to the narrows. Once through the narrows he stayed closer to the north shore, and he did spot a campsite when he was almost upon it. *Now about the same distance ahead should be the portage.*

In the middle of the lake a brown canoe demanded their attention because its middle passenger was in constant motion. As they got closer Jack and Luke sorted out the scene: a couple with a beautiful medium-sized black and ginger dog between them. The dog, in its enthusiasm, moved constantly to peer around the woman, first over her right shoulder, then her left. This kept the canoe rocking from side to side, and the couple laughed as they tried to compensate with their bodies and paddling.

"I've seen dogs move like that in the back of pickups, but never in a canoe!" Luke exclaimed. "Must be an eternal search for the best view."

"He - or she – is sure excited to be on this adventure!"

The couple headed into the portage, and the dog froze uncharacteristically. When they were still a couple of yards from shore the dog sprung out of the canoe, splashed across the rocks, and bolted barking into the woods.

"FEEEEE – BEEEEEE!" the woman shrieked. The man maneuvered the canoe quickly so they could climb out, clunking against a couple of rocks. "...squirrel..." was the only discernable word from him. The woman bounded to shore and started calling for the dog in a cheerful voice with an undertone of panic. Her partner's voice joined in. Soon the happy beast burst out of the woods, tongue lolling and tail wagging. The woman captured her and snapped a leash on, speaking deliberately in the dog's ear. The man helped her with the Duluth pack, picked up the canoe, and they set out at the dog's rapid pace.

By this time Luke was poised at the portage to watch the show. He headed in and Jack was not far behind. They landed with some effort and secured their packs out of the way, still smiling about the drama they'd just seen. "That was one happy dog – a few minutes of freedom to chase a squirrel made her day!" Jack seemed to have caught the enthusiasm.

"Well I'm just glad it wasn't a bear the dog was after." Luke said ominously. "But - any bear would probably have been put off by her boisterous behavior and turned tail and run!"

The two men began their 200-rod trek with the canoes. The weather was cool enough that they still wore their jackets, but the exertion of the slowly ascending portage made them peel them off before they got to the descent to Clearwater Lake. Luke tied his around his waist by the sleeves, just in case he needed it later, and Jack followed suit. Halfway back to Caribou they donned them again, then shed them again when they got to Clearwater with the packs, paddles, poles, and life vests.

Jack was glad to dump the Duluth pack in to his canoe. In his strange mood that morning he had poked everything in willy-nilly, and now something in there was poking him in the back. He considered repacking it, but he was a little embarrassed about the poor job he had done. He figured he could endure it for the day.

Clearwater Lake, a large one open to motorized water-craft, was normally busy. The two were only passing through the southeastern edge, however. In their short time on the lake they saw only one canoe and heard one motor from a distance. They navigated around two peninsulas and saw a small island off to their left. The portage, at the eastern tip of the lake, was easy to find.

"214 rods to West Pike – our longest portage of this trip, unless we take the Pine-to-Canoe Lake route," Pastor Luke reported. "It's good to have this one in the morning, when we're more energetic."

"Right. Energetic. Keep telling my shoulders that I'm feeling energetic, and maybe they'll believe you!" Jack retorted. "Weren't there canoe rests here and there when we were here before? I remember they made a good excuse for a break."

"They took them all out in 1995." He anticipated Jack's next question: "To make the wilderness more of a wilderness, I guess."

Jack harrumphed as he rotated and massaged his shoulders.

The portage was mostly level at first, with some muddy areas. Jack's new boots didn't look new any more. Presently they began to descend, and the trail met the Border Route Trail. When they had deposited their canoes on the bank of West Pike and turned to hike back, Jack asked Pastor Luke what he knew about the Border Route Trail.

"I don't have any experience with the Border Route. But I've been on the Grand Portage Trail. When I was in semi-nary, I coaxed three of my friends into coming up here.

Actually only two were able to come with me. I had planned a vigorous route, you know. We canoed the border chain: Mountain, Moose, North Fowl, South Fowl – which is a lot of paddling – and then I convinced them to take the Grand Portage Trail, which is about eight and a half miles. We were carrying our canoes and all our gear, of course – and we hadn't eaten up enough food, so we couldn't get it all in one trip, and we had to double back. They were not happy campers! It would be fun to hike that trail with a backpack, but it's a long haul with a canoe on your shoulders. And you don't get to enjoy the scenery so much."

"As I recall, you planned a vigorous route for our retreat group, too. We finally had to revolt to lay over a day on Caribou," Jack teased.

"I'm finally learning to be more flexible with the route. I get into the history and spirit of the voyageurs, who had to cover the land and water in as little time as possible. So I have a tendency to really push a group, and there's merit in that...but sometimes I overestimate what people can actually do. I like to see people stretch their limits you know, yet have a good time doing it."

"And besides, everybody's different."

"Right! It's challenging to plan a route with the right balance. And you also have to allow for weather and other contingencies. Sometimes Mother Nature snatches the pencil away and rewrites the plan."

They paused partway through the ascent to catch their breath. "Now that I'm getting older I've had to become more flexible in my planning," Pastor Luke added. "I still don't want to admit that *I* can do any less you know, but I'm more lenient with others somehow."

"Funny how that works, isn't it?" Jack agreed.

The long portage behind them, the two trippers were pleased to paddle. To their right and left they saw beautiful steep tree-lined hills rising as much as 500 feet above the water of West Pike Lake. The map indicated that the Border Route Trail followed the high ridge, paralleling the shore to the south. Jack pondered if there were people dragging along it, laden with canoes and gear, grumbling about the judgment of their leader. *The view must be spectacular, though. Sometimes we miss the beauty because we are all wrapped up in our other agendas. Hmm, profound.*

Luke paddled near. "How about a little island lunch?" he proposed.

"Sounds great – I'm starved. I see there's a campsite marked on the map," Jack added. "I'll bet it's popular."

"I don't see any other travelers nearby – if it's not occupied by campers we'll stop for a bit. I'm hungry now too."

The men were pleased to find the campsite empty. They landed the canoes and brought Luke's Duluth pack up to the fire circle. They feasted on sharp cheddar cheese, smoked salmon and crackers, with oranges for dessert and some filtered water to wash it down. As they tidied up Jack decided to say the sentence he'd been rehearsing in his mind.

"I'm sorry I cried so much yesterday."

Pastor Luke looked at him with sorrow. "You don't need to apologize to me. You were just expressing your grief in a very normal way."

"I just – I don't – I haven't – I guess I worry about what people will think if I cry."

Pastor Luke's voice was soft. "They might think that you loved your wife."

Jack couldn't answer. He looked down. He felt the familiar pain but another feeling joined it, a feeling of – was it acceptance? *'They might think that you loved your wife.'* He memorized Pastor Luke's sentence. *I want to think about that some more.* "This was the first time I've really talked to anyone about how I feel."

"Here's another quote for you, Jack, from Seneca who lived around the same time as Jesus: 'Light griefs are loquacious, but the great are dumb.' And that doesn't mean dumbstupid, it means silent. The deepest grief is the hardest to talk about, and you did some really hard work yesterday. Good work."

Jack looked down, lost in thought, and Luke gave him some time before his next question. "What was your experience of Abby's memorial service, Jack?"

Jack moaned and covered his face with his hands. He leaned forward with his elbows on his knees and looked at the ground as he spoke slowly and deliberately.

"I was so crazy with grief, it's only snapshots in my mind now – I can't play it like a video. I remember coming early to the church, but not knowing exactly why or what to do. At one point I was the only one in the sanctuary…it must have been before anyone else came…I walked right up to the altar and stood there a long time looking at the urn, and the flowers, and the candles, and the cross. I felt like I was losing touch with reality somehow, so I wanted to touch everything. As I touched the urn the numbness went away and a cold ten-ton weight settled in on my heart."

Jack reached his hand out in front of his face and closed his eyes. "I touched the cross and prayed for help. I touched each flower and thought about love and beauty. Then I heard the organist coming in so I left." Jack dropped his hand and looked up at the sky. "The next thing I remember was holding hands with my mother and Abby's in the parlor when you prayed with us before the service.

"Another picture in my mind is following you into the sanctuary, keeping my focus on the back of your head and the strength you had in your physical presence. I tried to copy your posture." Jack turned his head and looked at Pastor Luke, who met his gaze with love and a fraction of a smile.

"No offense to you, but I don't recall much about what you said. I remember we had talked about the 'mansions' scripture the day before, about how Jesus prepares a place for us. So that caught my ear. But mostly I remember the sound of your voice, and the sense of comfort and strength in every word."

Pastor Luke's silent attentiveness encouraged Jack to continue. "I was glad you suggested Easter music – resurrection music. It lifted me up, and I think any of the old standards would have dragged me under.

"After the service I remember thinking about how many people were wearing black. They all wanted to shake my hand or hug me and I didn't want to fall apart, so I just kept distracting my mind by thinking about how many kinds of black clothes there were." Jack chuckled hollowly.

"Self-preservation," Pastor Luke suggested, nodding.

"Yeah. It worked, to a point. But now I wish I could remember more about who was there and what they said."

"You got the sense of it, though?" Pastor Luke asked.

"I got the sense that lots of people were also hurting." Jack paused and thought. "And they were concerned about me."

"I think that's accurate. What was life like for you in the days after that?"

"Hell." Jack was going to leave it there, but Pastor Luke seemed to want more. "The dead weight in my chest went away, and a hollowness moved in. It felt like a vacuous hunger sometimes, and other times like my muscles were cramping up for dry heaves. I had headaches, and my throat and eyes burned. I did stupid things every day, like setting a place for Abby at the table or locking my keys in the car."

"Did you cry?" Pastor Luke asked softly.

"Very little. I was raised to be stoic, you know."

"I understand. Well, most of us were. I've come to believe that stoicism is more destructive than tears."

Jack looked at Pastor Luke with a frown. "It's not good to be strong?"

"It takes a lot of strength to cry tears of grief. Grieving is not for sissies, you know!"

This brought a wry smile. "So it's okay if I cry a little?"

"It's not just okay, it's essential to your healing."

"Really. That's interesting." Jack again looked up at the sky and rolled the idea around in his mind. *It's acceptable to cry. It would help. It would not be a disgrace. Can I really believe that?*

"Grieving for Abby, tears and all, is a tribute to how much you loved her. If you didn't love her, you wouldn't hurt so much."

"I love her so much." Jack's voice wavered. "I miss her so much."

Pastor Luke's hand on his shoulder spoke volumes. Jack felt the moisture in his eyes and nose, and sniffed. He sighed deeply.

Sensing Jack's need for privacy, Pastor Luke got up and dusted off his pants. "I need to take a walk up the hill. Do you want some tissue for that drippy nose?" Jack nodded and Luke obliged.

Once Pastor Luke was out of earshot Jack opened the gate he had kept bolted and barred for so many months, and the tears rolled down his cheeks. Like yesterday, for a while he cried in huge hiccupping sobs. He dug the heels of his hands into his eyes and told himself again, *it is acceptable to cry. I'm crying because I loved her and she's gone forever. I love her.*

Every time Jack thought he was through crying, the tears started flowing again. He didn't know how much time had passed when he finally moved into a stage of quiet calm. *I'm tired, but some of the tightness is gone. I believe I can make it through another day.*

He turned around at the sound of a footstep behind him. "Thank you for giving me some time to myself. I guess I needed it." He looked at Pastor Luke with admiration. "You sure have good judgment."

"Grieving takes time, some with a listener and some alone. You're doing well with this hard work. But don't give me too much credit, Jack. Nature called!"

Luke yawned and stretched, feeling the effects of his poor night's sleep, but he shook off his drowsiness and they set off paddling again.

The portage from West Pike to East Pike was level but rocky, indicating that it was a former stream bed. Pastor Luke set off first with his canoe on his shoulders, and Jack followed. They walked alongside a small lake, probably a mere pond in the drier seasons. Suddenly Luke stopped short. Jack, lost in thought, noticed just in time to keep from bumping into his canoe. *What is the problem?* Then Jack caught on. Peering out from under his canoe, he saw a cow moose and her calf, twenty yards to their left, standing in the water up to their knobby knees. The mother had a big, brown, wary eye on the pair of canoes-with-legs disturbing their peace. She raised her head and sniffed with her enormous nose. Pastor Luke stood stock still, so Jack did too. She paused her chewing to assess them, perceived no threat, and went back to her meal. Jack relished the wonderful chance to admire the huge animal, and the gangly youngster. He didn't have film for his camera, so it would just have to be a mental picture. Jack tried to memorize the whole scene: the majestic mother, the youthful copy of her, the cloudy sky bringing out the deep green of the foliage.

Pastor Luke finally began to step cautiously forward. They both knew the foolishness of alarming a cow with her calf. Since they were not between the two they were not as threatening, but moose can be unpredictable. So they stepped gingerly as they continued along the path.

Once past the awe-inspiring scene, Luke let out a long breath. "Wow, that was incredible!" he said, wiping the sweat from his brow. "That's as close as I've ever been to moose. I could actually smell them!"

"It was exciting and frightening all at once. And we'll get to go by twice more. I wonder how she'll take that?"

"I guess we'll find out!"

On the return hike along the portage trail, they saw the two moose again, but they had moved further from the human traffic. And when they returned with the packs, they couldn't see them at all. The exhilaration of their earlier encounter still gave them plenty to think and talk about as they completed their jaunt.

East Pike Lake began as a narrow channel, finally widening as they paddled eastward. They saw an older man and a boy in a canoe just drifting along – when they got closer Jack could see that they were fishing.

With three campsites on the lake, they were hopeful of finding one available. The first one they saw immediately, because there was a bright red canoe marking the spot. They kept on, and saw a cooler plopped in an obvious place at the second. The fishermen had reserved that one. They paddled toward the portage and the final campsite, knowing that if that site was taken, they would be portaging again today.

"This one looks open," Jack called back to Pastor Luke. He had sprinted ahead, eager to know the future. He landed his canoe, glanced around, and hollered, "This will work!"

Chapter 8

Setting up camp went somewhat better this time. Jack was slower than Luke, but he finally got the job done. With his tent set up and gear stowed, he smacked his hands together, stepped back, and admired the scene with hands on hips. "I'm getting the hang of this! No leftover parts this time!" he exclaimed.

"You've got what it takes," Pastor Luke responded.

"It's starting to cool off again. Shall I make a fire?" Jack answered his own question by starting the hunt for firewood. Luke sat down on the ground with his back against a smooth stone.

When Jack emerged from the trees with an armload of wood, he found Pastor Luke asleep in the same spot, with his head tipped back and mouth wide open. *Poor guy, he's exhausted from the day's exertion.* He remembered that Luke had slept little the night before, so he tiptoed the best he could in his hiking boots. He moved well away from his snoozing friend to snap and saw the branches into fire-sized chunks. He carefully laid the fire with dry moss and tiny twigs first, then bigger kindling and finally some larger sticks. He dug into his pack for matches, glad he'd remembered those, and thankful he'd transferred them to a plastic bag.

Soon the fire was burning merrily, and Jack added a sizeable log. The change in sound, warmth, and light woke Luke, and he came to with a snort.

"Ummm, guess I nodded off." He stretched his arms up and out and yawned.

"No problem. What's for dinner?"

Pastor Luke rubbed his eyes, struggled to his feet and fumbled in his pack. "We have several choices," he said, reading the labels as he pulled them out. "Chili Tortilla Pie, Turkey Tetrazini, or Chicken Cashew Curry."

"Wow, gourmet fare! That last one sounds like it would hit the spot. Curry is one of my favorites."

"You bet, curry it is. This one is really easy – just boil some water." Luke fanned out some smaller packages like cards. "You like mixed vegetables, green beans amandine, or corn?"

"Any of those – how about corn? I'll filter some water. And let me get my cook stove so I can keep practicing."

Soon Pastor Luke had coached Jack once more on assembling the stove, pumping the fuel, and lighting the burner. They had enough water to fill the biggest pan, and while it was heating they filtered more to use for drinking. When the water finally reached a vigorous boil, Jack opened the foil pouch and carefully poured the steaming water into it. The curry's spicy aroma whetted their appetites. After stirring as well as possible, Luke folded the top down and secured it with the tape on top. They repeated the procedure with the vegetables and waited the prescribed minutes before opening and serving.

The meal was delicious. "Amazing what freeze-drying can do!" Jack exclaimed, scraping his dish clean. "Now, I'll wash the dishes."

Luke had suggested heating a second pan of water while they were eating, so the dishwashing could begin promptly. Half went into a smaller pan for rinsing. Their few dishes were cleaned up quickly. "Will these pouches go into the fire?" Jack asked.

Pastor Luke shook his head. "Nope, they're foil, so we have to pack them out. A small price to pay for such gourmet convenience, eh?"

Jack agreed and added the empty pouches to their garbage bag, fastened it up and put it in Luke's pack with all the other food. After brushing their teeth with filtered water, they added their toilet kits and set out to hang the bear bag.

They found a convenient setup nearby, and Jack helped by lobbing the rope over the two branches. With two of them on the project, the job was accomplished in about fifteen minutes.

Back in camp Pastor Luke yawned and stretched. "I'm fading fast. I'm going to bed."

Jack had hoped for some conversation around the fire, but it was clear Pastor Luke needed to catch up on his sleep. Jack felt a little shy about asking, but he did it anyway: "I still have your Bible. Which Psalm would you say I should read?"

"Oh, you can scan through and see what resonates for you. You might want to look at Psalm 22 for starters. The writer was feeling pretty angry with God, so you might find some common ground." Pastor Luke looked like he had something else to say, but he just added, "I hope you don't mind if I turn in. We can talk more tomorrow."

"Sure. Goodnight, Pastor Luke. Sleep well," he said, really meaning it.

Jack positioned his Crazy Creek chair near the lake so he could enjoy the sunset. He watched a pair of loons diving and re-emerging. Other loons called across the water.

He flopped the Bible open right in the middle, remembering a Sunday School teacher who taught him to find Psalms that way. He flipped through the maddeningly thin pages until he found Psalm 22.

> My God, my God, why have you forsaken me?
> Why are you so far from helping me,
> from the words of my groaning?
> O my God, I cry by day, but you do not answer;
>   and by night, but find no rest.

Shuddering chills went through Jack's body. His eyes burned with tears. The hollow ache in his chest increased. *If I had words for my feelings, they would read like this!* His loneliness for Abby had fueled anger at God for allowing

106

this tragedy to occur. *If God is all-powerful, why did a good person like Abby have to die? What had she done to deserve that horrible death? What did I do to deserve this horrible grief?* His midnight tirades with God had been met with silence. In his time of greatest need, God had deserted him. *My God, my God, why have you forsaken me?* He hadn't said it so poetically, but this was exactly how he'd felt.

He curled over the Bible, straining to read the words again in the fading light. Jack took a deep breath. In an odd way, in this moment he felt less alone. Someone else had felt as he did. *Whoever wrote this Psalm knew the hollow ache, knew my pain!* This writer understood. At this realization his burning eyes released tears.

Not wanting Pastor Luke to hear him, Jack struggled to keep from sobbing audibly. He rocked forward, buried his face in his red bandanna, and gave in to the pain like he had that afternoon. The abyss yawned before him but did not swallow him up. After a time he raised his head and gulped the sweet evening air until he could breathe normally.

He'd heard Pastor Luke say yesterday and again today, "It's good to cry." Three times in two days after seven dry months of grief – now it was like the flood gates had opened. At least he was in the wilderness, with relative privacy. Pastor Luke was OK, but he didn't want anyone else to see him in this vulnerable state.

Stumbling off to bed, Jack realized it must be quite late. Once in his sleeping bag, the exhaustion that comes from emotional catharsis washed over him, and he fell right to sleep. In the hours before waking, he dreamed about Abby as he so often did...but this dream was different. She stood near, not near enough to touch, but near enough that he could see her beautiful eyes. She spoke to him, saying earnestly, "It's all right, Jack. You're going to be all right." He felt that he could believe her.

"I love you!" he said to her.

When Jack awoke, he felt different. He lay in his tent, aware of the difference and searching for words for it.

Lighter, somehow, like a weight had been lifted from his shoulders, or actually, from his heart. He felt quiet. He recalled dreaming of Abby, and he closed his eyes to picture her beautiful face again. She'd said what he needed to hear. Maybe he *would* be all right.

He liked being warm in his sleeping bag. He sat up, hunching the bag around his shoulders. Reaching for his little notebook and pencil, he flipped past his sketches to a blank page. He wrote Tuesday's date, June 30, and the word "tears." Under July 1 he wrote "Psalm 22." Then today's date, the 2nd, and "You're going to be all right." He stared at the words, pondering how simple and complex they were at the same time.

The smells of wood smoke and coffee motivated him to get out of his sleeping bag. He found Pastor Luke tending the fire and getting ready to fry a big Northern. "You've been fishing already!"

"I woke with the sun and felt like catching breakfast instead of re-hydrating it. I left you a note this time." Luke indicated a piece of paper that said in big letters "GONE FISHING." Jack smiled his gratitude. "How are you doing this morning?"

This sounded to Jack like more than a perfunctory greeting. "I feel good. I slept well. I feel better." That was all he could put together at the moment. He wanted to tell Pastor Luke about his dream and his encounter with Psalm 22, but the time didn't seem right. He handed Pastor Luke his Bible in its plastic bag, saying merely, "Thanks."

"Sure." Pastor Luke put the Bible into his tent.

In a companionable silence they prepared the fish, enjoyed it, and cleaned up.

Breaking camp, Jack struggled a little getting his sleeping bag stuffed and compacted. The rest of his packing went more smoothly, until he tackled the tent. The day before, in his angst, he had just wadded it up into his pack. He had all the pieces strewn about on the ground when Luke came over to see if he needed help.

"Looks like you're doing fine here," he commented optimistically.

Jack wasn't so sure. "I can't remember exactly how it all goes into the sack," he muttered. "Or maybe it really doesn't matter."

"My camping mentor taught me to always fold the tent, then put the rain fly on top of it before rolling it up. It's too easy to fold the fly, put it to one side, and forget it," Luke offered. "I also recommend counting the stakes each time to be sure you've got them all."

"Good advice. Now I think I've got it." Once he got his tent rolled up, Jack took some care distributing the weight in the Duluth pack more evenly this time.

They scoured the area for litter or any other evidence of their presence. "What's the mantra for this? Jack asked. "I can't remember even though it was in the video and everything."

"Leave No Trace," Pastor Luke droned dramatically.

"Right, leave no trace." Jack picked up a tiny piece of paper and tucked it into his pocket. "The fire is out cold," Luke observed. "Well, I think we're ready, what do you think?"

"Let's go," Jack agreed.

A very brief paddle brought them to the 180-rod portage to John Lake. Jack decided to take his pack first, to see if it was more comfortable than the day before. Sure enough, he'd fixed the problem. This was like toting a pillow by comparison.

Before putting into John Lake, Jack studied his map to familiarize himself with the day's route. Like West and East Pike, this one was bordered on the south by a high ridge. He noticed that John Lake butted up against the boundary of the BWCAW. Little John and McFarland were actually outside the Boundary Waters. They would return when they entered Pine Lake, it appeared. Looking more closely at John Lake, he searched the map for the portage to Little John. The boundary marking partly obscured the red dotted line. Did that say 10 rods? Short! And the next was 16! He had to check with Pastor Luke about the portage from McFarland to Pine…it looked like 2 rods!

"Am I reading this right?" he asked his pastor. "It looks like a 2-rod portage!"

"Sure enough! Two canoe lengths!"

"Hardly seems worth the trouble, does it."

"We'll see how it looks – depending on the water level we might be able to paddle it."

Wouldn't you know, now that my pack is perfectly balanced and comfortable we have all these short portages. Must be some corollary of Murphy's Law.

The morning went by fast, with the short portages and short paddle on Little John Lake. When they rounded the elbow of McFarland Lake, Pastor Luke pointed to the north shore. Jack followed his gesture and spied several pretty cabins, which intrigued Jack. He remembered that they were outside the BWCAW. He tried to imagine living in this beautiful setting all summer long. *Well, in a sense I might do just that, but not in a cabin. How this adventure will play out still remains a mystery. That is okay; I can live with the certainty that Pastor Luke will be with me this week, and then I will deal with the next week, and try not to freak out about it.*

Thank God for Pastor Luke. What a blessing to have a pastor who could be wilderness mentor, listening ear, and friend as well. Wonder what burdens of his own the guy carries?

At the northwestern end of McFarland Lake, Jack searched for the mini-portage. Luke saw it first, and slowed to drift his canoe into the channel. Sure enough, the water was high enough, but just barely, for them to navigate it in their canoes. Using their paddles as poles, gondola-style, they quickly emerged into Pine Lake. A campsite at the portage was occupied.

Maneuvering alongside Jack's canoe, Pastor Luke proposed lunch at a nearby site. They decided to follow the northern shore but soon they could see that this site was also taken, by diners like themselves. They struck out across the water to a site on a small point at the southeastern end of the lake. This one was open, so they claimed it for their midday meal.

"Nice spot – the point makes you feel closer to the water," Luke observed. "Not like you're very far from water anywhere here!" he added. He knelt carefully to filter some for the canteens. "So much water, so much precious pristine beauty."

As they assembled lunch and ate, Jack brought up a theological question he'd been pondering. "Pastor Luke, I heard a preacher on the radio one time talking about how environmentalists are 'of the devil' because God says in the Bible that we are supposed to 'subdue the earth and have dominion over it.' What do you think about that?"

Luke sighed. "I look at it differently. You have to take the Bible in its context. The ancients were not faced with pollution, or urban sprawl, or diminishing wilderness. Their challenges were more about how to survive in the wild world around them."

"I hadn't thought of that. It's a big difference."

"So when we go into the wilderness, what do we need?"

Jack was amused by the feeling of sitting in the student's chair. He smiled and waved his hand toward their Duluth packs. "Tents, sleeping bags, cook kits, mosquito dope…"

Luke pointed to the water filter he'd just used, and Jack nodded and added that to his list.

"Right! We use these things for protection from the elements, so the rain and cold and bugs don't threaten us. Even though we're very respectful of the wilderness, in our own ways we are 'dominating and subduing' in order to survive."

"So there's no conflict between being a Christian and being an environmentalist?"

"Not in my book, Jack. The whole creation sings of God's presence! Reverence for God and for the earth go hand in hand. We're called to care for the earth."

"That makes sense to me, too, on a gut level. Thanks for putting it in words for me."

"Words are my life, you know!"

Lunch and the stimulating conversation fueled them for the long trip westward on Pine Lake. Each of the men was lost in thought as they paddled into a brisk breeze. Jack felt his muscles stretching, in a somewhat uncomfortable way. He was sweating from his effort. *I'd gotten pretty out of shape. Pastor Luke's being easy on me with this route, I think. Hope I get stronger. Actually today is better than the first day.*

With some canoe-to-canoe consultation they decided to stop early at an available campsite on the northern shore, since from this point they needed to make a decision about the rest of the route.

Clambering out of the canoe, Pastor Luke surveyed the site. Jack joined him and stretched mightily. "Whew!" he exclaimed. "I need a shower!"

"How would you feel about a cold bath instead?" Luke laughed. "There's a big tub right behind us."

"Better sooner than later – the water might chill down a degree or two as evening comes. Okay, I'm game." Jack peeled off his clothes and, before he lost his nerve, he plunged in. "Yikes! It's cold! I mean, 'Come on in, the water's fine!'" he called in mock reassurance to Luke.

More deliberate, Pastor Luke had opened his pack and dug out a few items. He shed his clothes and watch and dropped a towel and sandals close to shore. He strode into the lake until he was waist-deep, dunked under to get wet, then scrubbed his hair and skin in a soapless wash. Another dunk underwater to rinse and then he lay back onto the surface to float. This only lasted a few minutes before he was ready to get out.

Meanwhile Jack swam out a way, feeling invigorated by the clear, cold water. Aware of his tired shoulder muscles, he reached his arms wide as he swam the breast stroke, feeling the benefit of the stretch. The water was too chill for a long swim, though, so he headed back to the shore. After a vigorous shake of his head he strode out. "Ahhh, refreshing!" he exclaimed. "But now where's my towel?" Stepping gingerly and dripping as he went, he extracted his towel with effort and rubbed his body briskly. "This calls for clean clothes."

"Canoe sighting at 50 yards," Pastor Luke warned. Jack, suddenly modest, hopped behind a bush where he finished drying his feet and donned pants and a sweatshirt. He rubbed his stubbly face, pondering whether he should shave. He quickly abandoned the idea when he realized he had a razor, but no mirror. *Pastor Luke might have one, but what does it matter anyway? I'm camping.*

Luke had dressed and now he stretched out full length on the log bench. "I was hoping I could float awhile – that's one of my favorite things. But it's just too cold, darn it! You know, the philosopher Soren Kierkegaard likened faith to floating on deep, deep water. If you struggle, splash around and get all tense, you will sink. But if you trust, and relax, you'll be able to float. Think of Peter walking on the water to Jesus. As soon as he doubted he started to sink. He did fine as long as he trusted."

Jack looked at his pastor with admiration, not sure what to say. He liked these little mini-sermons but he wasn't used to responding directly. He just smiled.

Pastor Luke got up and reached into the food pack. "Want to try the Chili Tortilla Pie tonight? I'm curious about this one."

"I'm game. How do we make it?"

"Got me – guess I'll have to read the directions."

Jack gathered up some firewood, eager to keep his body moving until he felt warm. He flipped the hood of his sweatshirt over his damp hair to keep his body heat in. The fire would feel good. He hastened to get it going.

"Well, this isn't exactly what I thought it was going to be." Luke scratched his head as he analyzed the cooking instructions.

"Don't worry, I'll eat anything someone else cooks."

Luke looked up at Jack. "How are you doing with cooking and eating alone? I remember Abby was a great cook."

Jack swallowed hard before answering. "She…was. I'm lousy. I mostly buy prepared foods, which I know isn't the best. But when I buy fresh vegetables or fruit they just rot. I eat a lot of sandwiches and junk food too. I eat in a hurry because I hate eating alone." He was a little surprised at his long answer.

Pastor Luke did not pass judgment on his bad habits, thank God. He only offered a rueful smile and nod of understanding. "I've had to learn a lot," he commented, and left it there.

The chili pie wasn't quite what they expected, ending up all blended together. The spicy chili tasted okay with the corn tortilla, but they agreed that a nice hearty buttered cornbread would have been better. And even better with honey.

With the dishes washed and the bear bag suspended, Jack and Luke sat down by the fire. Mosquitoes started to bite through their socks, so Luke got up for some repellent and shared it with Jack. Once they were suitably covered, they settled in. They sat in comfortable silence for a while, watching as the blue of lake and sky grew deeper to indigo and the lake surface became more and more like glass, reflecting the trees on the opposite shore.

Presently Luke got up and dropped a birch log into the hottest part of the fire, sending a sparkling shower of light into the sky. Watching the flames lick the new log, Jack cleared his throat.

"I guess I sounded pretty angry with God the other day."

"Yeah. I don't blame you," Pastor Luke responded. "It's okay. God can handle it."

"It's just not fair that Abby had to die." Jack's voice cracked a little and he cleared his throat again.

"You're right Jack, it's not fair."

"So why did God let it happen?"

Pastor Luke let the question hang in the air for a moment. "You know, some folks think that God is in charge of our lives, controlling everything that happens to us based on our good or bad behavior. I've never been able to believe in a puppeteer God." Pastor Luke's hands popped up as if dangling from invisible strings, and Jack smiled a little. "That way of thinking leads one to believe that when a tragedy like yours happens, it must be because you or Abby did something wrong. I don't buy that. I believe God joins you in your tears."

"So Abby's death didn't happen to punish her or me." Jack tried to make it sound like a statement but it was more of a question.

"Exactly. Can you believe it?"

"I'd like to." Jack tried on the thought like a garment. A little of the load lifted from his shoulders as he tried letting go of some guilt. *Maybe I'm not to blame. Maybe it's not my fault.* He liked the feel of this new idea. He could maybe grow into it.

"Guilt is a terrible load to carry. I know," Pastor Luke said.

"But you're such a good person. What could you be guilty about?" Jack blurted out in unabashed surprise.

Pastor Luke took a considered breath before answering. He looked at Jack and saw in the firelight the face of a friend he could trust. His past was not widely known, nor was it a secret. Sharing it might even help Jack.

"When I was a kid," he began, choosing words carefully, "my father drank a lot. When he got drunk, which was most every weekend, he would come home and hit my mother and paddle me. He was terrifying. I tried to do everything right and be good, but he beat us anyway. I kept assuming it was because I was bad, you know.

"In Sunday School I learned that God is our Father and God wants us to be good. Naturally I was terrified of God too.

"As a teenager I rejected everything I had learned in church. I didn't want to be like my dad, you know, so I shunned alcohol. But I ate everything I could get my hands on, to try to fill the emptiness inside. I grew seriously fat, and abysmally unhappy.

"As a young adult I got help with my weight, so I looked better but I still felt unfulfilled. I got married to a wonderful woman. Long story short, a new casino opened up near our home, and I started going there once in a while, then every weekend…" Luke paused and cleared his throat. "…and without realizing what was happening, I became addicted to gambling.

"I started skipping out on work – I was in a sales job where I traveled around the state, and I would detour by casinos, first a couple of times a week, finally every day. Occasionally I won, but mostly I lost money, of course. First I used up all of our savings, and then when my losses got bigger I took out a series of loans. I kept thinking I would get a big win and be able to pay back the savings, pay back the loans, and feel fulfilled, you know. By the time my wife found out I had a gambling addiction I'd wiped out all our savings and put us $50,000 into debt. And of course I lost my job because of my absenteeism.

"Long story short, I reluctantly went to a treatment center called Project Turnabout – actually Project Vanguard was the gambling treatment program. It was the only place with an inpatient program for people like me." Luke had been telling his story to the fire, letting Jack overhear. When his friend spoke he turned and looked at him.

116

"I've never heard of a gambling addiction," Jack admitted.

"It's insidious," Pastor Luke said bitterly. "A drunk can only hide and sneak so much – someone is bound to see, you know? Same with drugs – there are physical effects that can be observed. But gambling doesn't have physical effects. You could – I could – hide the financial losses for a long time, hiding the bank statements and the bills. My wife was so devastated when she found out. We tried to work through it but she just couldn't forgive me. We got a divorce. So I lost her, too. That increased my load of guilt."

"What did you do with all that guilt?" Jack asked, thinking about his own burden.

"It took a lot of work. One very helpful sentence came from the pastor who heard my Fifth Step: 'Forgiveness is giving up hope that the past will change.'" Pastor Luke paused.

"Forgiveness is giving up hope that the past will change," Jack echoed. "Wow. That puts it in a different light."

"It did for me. Over time I was able to forgive myself and accept God's forgiveness."

"So how did you end up being a pastor?" Jack could hardly believe all this, but he knew Pastor Luke wouldn't make it up.

"In treatment I got back in touch with God – my Higher Power – and discovered a love that filled the emptiness inside. A chaplain quoted somebody who said there's a God-shaped space inside each of us that only God can fill. I wanted to learn more but I didn't want to go back to the guilt-ridden theology of my childhood.

"About a year after I got out of treatment, when I was working two jobs and paying my debts and going to Gamblers Anonymous, my aunt died and left me a lot of money. I had to face the temptation to gamble again – thank God for my support people! With that money – it was an ample amount – I was able to pay off my debt and enroll in United Theological Seminary, and the rest is history."

"Do you still feel tempted to gamble?" Jack asked.

"Sure, you betcha. I still go to a 12-step group every week, which helps. We'll figure tonight was a good substitute. It helps to share my story." Pastor Luke paused. "What was that quote you taught me? 'The fool doth think he is wise, but the wise man knows himself to be a fool.' I know myself to be a fool, so I try very hard to be responsible to my recovery. You know, maybe one of the reasons I love the Boundary Waters is that there are no temptations for me here. I can just be in the presence of our loving God and feel at peace." Luke sighed deeply.

"Wow, you've come a long way." Jack looked at Luke with awe.

"You could say that." Luke nodded in agreement.

Chapter 9

When Jack got up Friday morning, Pastor Luke was sitting by a tidy fire with both hands around a coffee cup and his Bible open in his lap. He craned his neck around when he heard Jack emerge from his tent.

"Morning."

"Morning."

Luke smiled. "It certainly is morning, and it will continue to be for a while. We have a firm grasp of the obvious. Any other astounding revelations?"

Jack grinned and waved off this comment. "It's too early for such banter, Pastor Luke. Give me a little time to wake up."

"Okay, you tell me when you're ready for banter. I'll just keep working on my sermon here." Luke returned his attention to his Bible, and Jack set about his morning ablutions.

When they sat down to eat their oatmeal, Jack had to ask. "What's your sermon going to be about?"

"I'm not sure yet. The theme scripture is a lovely one from Isaiah 66: 'As a mother comforts her child, so I will comfort you...' It has great possibilities but I'm not sure where I want to go with it."

"Who is talking? Who is the 'I'?" Jack asked.

"God."

"God is like a mother?"

"Yeah! You know, those of us who had devoted mothers and distant fathers find a comforting, maternal God to be easier to love sometimes. Does that image surprise you?" Pastor Luke looked quizzically at Jack.

"Kinda. I've heard you refer to God as Mother sometimes, and it always catches me off guard. Even though I had a distant father, as you describe. I guess I tend to picture God as an old man with a beard. Like Michelangelo painted him."

"You're in good company – lots of people picture God that way," Pastor Luke nodded. "Not that different from Santa Claus."

"Wait, wait, wait – God is different from Santa Claus!" Jack protested.

A smile quirked at Luke's mouth. "Watches you all the time, checks up on whether you're naughty or nice, teaches goodness and generosity…sounds a lot like God to me!"

Jack wasn't sure how to take this. "Are you messing with me?"

"I guess I can't pull anything over on you, Jack. You'll call me on it every time."

"You bet I will!" Jack shot back and socked him softly on the shoulder.

After breakfast they packed up quickly. Luke admitted that he was feeling a little pressure to get his sermon prepared, so he was eager to cover some ground and settle into a site so he could work on it some more.

"I guess we'll pass up the waterfall then," Jack suggested, with a little regret.

"For today. But I recommend it if you come back this way." Jack made a mental note.

After paddling to the west end of Pine Lake, they headed up a steep trail to Little Caribou. A short paddle led them to a short portage, only 25 rods, and Caribou. Once on this lake, Jack thought back to their two nights there at the beginning of the week, his grief and his tears. He looked at Pastor Luke in the other canoe, grateful for his openness and understanding.

He leaves tomorrow and then I'm on my own. What's that going to be like? I'll miss Pastor Luke's companionship. Think I'll enjoy the solitude, though. Just hope I know enough about what I'm doing to cope with contingencies. Am

I really prepared? Jack's paddling faltered as his confidence flagged. *Concentrate, Jack old boy. Find your balance. You can do it.* He resumed his steady rhythm and felt stronger. *God is with you. Like a mother. Hmmph. Have to think on that!*

Jack noticed that Pastor Luke had slowed his canoe, using his paddle as a brake. Ahead of him on their right a large popple tree had tipped into the lake, where it was now half-submerged. The water played tricks with the angle, making the pale green trunk look jointed. They could clearly see branches with green leaves still attached, so it had been a recent fall. On the sloping lakeshore roots fanned out from the trunk where it had formerly been anchored in the shallow soil. Luke was examining the scene carefully, as though he were memorizing each detail. Jack pulled his canoe near Luke's.

"That must have made a mighty splash," he commented.

Pastor Luke started at his voice and turned to him. "Sorry, I was lost in thought. This may be the sermon illustration I've been looking for."

"This tree?"

"Uh-huh. Let's keep going, and I'll keep thinking." Luke dug his paddle into the water to propel his canoe around the tree, and Jack did the same. Though he thought he was giving it a wide berth, leaves tickled the bottom of his canoe as he passed over the tree.

The rest of their route was familiar: Caribou to Deer to Moon. It was still early enough in the day that they continued to East Gunflint and claimed a campsite there, putting them an easy paddle away from the parking lot and their cars. *Pastor Luke seems antsy. He must be mentally preparing to go back home. Plus he has to write that sermon. I'll do what I can to help him. Although I don't know what that might be.*

"I'll set up the tents, Pastor Luke, while you work on your sermon," Jack offered. "I think I can figure yours out." They were munching on lunch before making camp.

121

"Well, that's a generous offer. If you have any questions, just ask. At this point in the process I'm very interruptable."

Jack managed to set up Pastor Luke's tent without too much trouble. Meanwhile Luke sat straddling a log bench in the fire circle with his weathered Bible and a small notebook in front of him. He alternated leaning back and gazing into the trees with leaning forward and scribbling notes. When Jack sat down Luke welcomed him with a contented grin.

"How's it going?" Jack tried to sound casual, but he intensely wished he could see inside Pastor Luke's brain.

"Spiffy. If only my office at the church had this kind of view. It's totally inspiring." He gazed at the sun-dappled forest, the blues of sky and water, and sighed.

Jack's mind bubbled with curiosity. "How do you usually write a sermon? If you don't mind my asking."

"Ahhh, it varies. Usually I look up the scriptures early in the week and read them carefully, and maybe do some background reading in books or online, so ideas can percolate for several days. I watch for illustrations and stories – art, headlines, whatever – that fit in somehow. Some years you know I've had a Bible study group of other clergy, or lay people, who feed ideas into the mix in my head. I like that kind of dialogue; it's very stimulating. I don't have a group like that now. If I have meetings during the week, I sometimes open with a question related to the week's scriptures, and get some conversation going.

"Then on Friday I sit down to write. Sometimes I fill a sheet of paper with thoughts and ideas first, then see how they might flow into a sequence. I often do some more research and reading. At times I already have an idea of the point I want to make and how I want to work with it. When I'm ready I type it in the form of an outline."

"I saw your outline one Sunday – it was very colorful!"

"Yeah, on Sunday morning early I go over it with four colors of highlighters and dress it up. It makes it easier for me to see key words so I don't have to look at the papers too much."

"How do you get such good ideas week after week?"

"I don't know. Some themes are easier than others, you know, and some texts are easier to work with than others. But God's presence pervades everything; it's a rare week that I can't find inspiration somewhere. And there's no shortage this week!"

"I believe it. So where are you going with the 'mothering, comforting God' theme?"

"Well, I think I'll start with some thoughts about Mother Nature, and how we are familiar with that image. I'll describe the beauty of this place and how profound it is to be so connected with Mother Nature, camping and canoeing and fishing. A lot of people will identify with that, I think. Then I'll move us from Mother Nature to an image of our Creator as a nurturing Mother." Pastor Luke leaned toward Jack, body tense with enthusiasm. "Remember that fallen tree back there in Caribou Lake?"

Jack nodded brightly, encouraging Luke to keep the energy going.

"It was a huge tree, but the roots were remarkably short. They tapered down to skinny, breakable tendrils just three feet from the trunk. But the tree was probably eighty feet high! The way big trees like that remain stable is by intertwining with the roots of other trees, forming a strong interwoven web that anchors them to the soil and to each other. We're like that in the church – we need each other in order to remain strong and rooted in our faith.

"Have you ever heard of a nurse log?" Jack shook his head. "When I visited the rain forest in Olympic National Park in Washington state, I learned another way that trees are interdependent. When a tree crashes to the forest floor, we might think it's a sad thing, especially a Douglas Fir that's hundreds of years old. But in the hundred more years that it takes to decay, it provides a rich environment for the next generation to grow. Saplings sprout right out of the log, so it becomes a kind of nursery for a row of young trees." Pastor Luke gestured and Jack could clearly imagine the long, straight procession of three-inch sprouts.

"Do we have nurse logs here in the BWCA?" Jack wondered aloud.

"Yes, we do, but they might have just one baby, maybe two. The rain forest out there in the Northwest is intensely moist, and the weather is pretty mild, so the phenomenon is much more dramatic. The nurse log provides everything the baby trees need at first, but as they grow larger they have to make contact with Mother Earth themselves you know. So they spread their roots down, embracing the rotting log..." Pastor Luke spread his fingers and ran them down the outsides of the log on which he sat. "...until they reach soil – ahhhh – where they anchor themselves and branch out so they can grow big and strong."

Now his arms raised up as joyful limbs. "The tree grows and grows through the generations. Eventually the nurse log rots away – returns to earth, I should say – and what's left is the most amazing sight: strong roots that remember and hold the shape of the nurse log long after it's gone! In the Hoh Rainforest there are some of these so large I could stand up inside, like being in a small cave."

Pastor Luke paused and Jack felt hungry to hear more. "Go on!" he urged.

"The trees, with their connection to Mother Earth, can teach us about our relationship with our Mother God. We need our ancestors in faith, like those we know from the Bible and church history, as well as our recent forebears who have gone before us. The great cloud of witnesses, my favorite image from the Letter to the Hebrews! They're like the nurse logs. They provide what we need when we are young in our faith, which can be at any age. As we grow we need to establish our own relationship with God, so we embrace them and reach to the source of our comfort and strength – Mother God. When we establish that relationship we also find support from the others on that journey – we interweave our 'roots' with them and grow even stronger.

"But we don't forget the presence of those who have gone before. We continue to hold them in our embrace long after they have returned to Mother Earth." Pastor Luke paused and took a deep breath. "And in God's time, we pray that we may become nurse logs for others."

"Wow, Pastor Luke, that's – that's cool." Jack was enjoying the experience, but he wasn't sure what to say in response to such an intimate delivery.

"So you think that will work on Sunday then?"

"Absolutely."

While Pastor Luke made more notes, Jack filtered water and made two cups of espresso. He now felt comfortable with the camp stove and moved smoothly through the steps. *I can do this. I can.* Luke gratefully accepted the steaming cup.

Soon Pastor Luke rose, picked up his Bible and his notebook and put them into his tent. He returned to the fire circle smacking and rubbing his hands together saying, "There! That's done! I always feel like celebrating when I know I'm ready for Sunday."

"How shall we kick up our heels tonight?" Jack teased.

"Well. Good question. How about a brisk swim, after that enjoying a little catch-and-release fishing, maybe even keeping one or two to feast on for dinner, then relaxing in front of a picturesque campfire?"

"Sure!" Jack responded. "Last one in is a toppled tree!"

The afternoon's fishing yielded a fine walleye for dinner, and with vegetables and cherry cobbler from the pack they had a feast indeed. They had let the fire die down for grilling the fish, but now they stoked it enough to smoke the bugs away.

"I'll hang the bear bag by myself tonight, just to prove I can," Jack suggested. *At least I know that I can call for Pastor Luke's help if I need it. That won't be the case tomorrow.* He felt a pang of sadness that he would be saying goodbye so soon. *Seems like we're just getting to know each other better, and now he'll go away. I don't like it when people leave me!*

Uncomfortable with this feeling, Jack busied himself with the task at hand, and felt a surge of pride when the process went smoothly. He even managed to poke the pack up with his paddle while pulling on the rope at the same time, gaining several crucial inches. He returned to the fire feeling more confident than before.

"Thanks to you, I think I'm ready to go solo," he said gratefully. "I've come a long way in a week, doncha think?"

"You betcha, Jack. You'll do fine."

"I can't even imagine what it will be like – I guess I'll just take a day at a time and make the most of the experience. That sounds trite, doesn't it? Anyway, I hope it works."

"Have you decided how long you're going to stay up here?" Pastor Luke asked pointedly.

Jack thought before he spoke. "No, I'm totally open about that. I think I'll just see what happens and how I feel."

"Follow the Holy Spirit's leading, perhaps?"

"I guess that's another way to put it, Pastor."

"You know, you really don't have to call me Pastor all the time. You can just call me Luke if you want to."

"Oh, I don't know if I could do that…my mother wouldn't like it!" Jack chuckled. He felt honored that Luke would invite him to be more familiar. "I'll give it a try, though."

"I've been meaning to say something before now. It's really fine."

"Thanks, Pas-, I mean Luke. I'll have to practice!"

"So how are you feeling about your next transition, in the fall? Any more thoughts about your career decisions?"

Jack realized that he hadn't updated Luke on this topic. "I told Dyrud I'll take a position somewhere else in the state system. I don't know if it was the right decision, but it was the easiest."

"So where might you end up? Will you still be in the Twin Cities?"

"I have no idea. He mentioned an opening in Little Falls and one in another Falls – I can't remember…"

"International Falls? Way up on the Canadian border? You'd be close to the BWCA!" You know, sometimes I dream of serving the great little UCC church in Grand Marais for that reason…"

Jack shook his head. "No, it's not International Falls…"

"Let's see…Fergus Falls?"

"No…" Jack scratched his head as if to activate the brain cells.

"Granite Falls?"

"Yes! That's it! Granite Falls."

"That's where I was in treatment at Project Vanguard. It's a nice little town on the Minnesota River," Luke smiled.

"How little?"

"About 3,000 I think. Big enough to have some fast food chains and small enough to be folksy."

"What does that mean, 'folksy'?" Jack was puzzled by Luke's description.

"Have you ever lived in a small town?" Luke asked.

"I was born in Cadillac, Michigan. It was maybe 10,000 people, more in the tourist seasons. After my parents divorced, my mom and I moved to Minnetonka. I was in the 8th grade. I remember how different it was."

"How was it different?" Luke switched back to the role of questioner.

"The main thing I remember was a different sense of security. We felt like we had to be on our guard all the time in the Cities, while in Cadillac we felt like we knew most of the people. That was probably a gross exaggeration, but the bottom line was that we felt safer and more relaxed in the small town."

"That's what I mean by folksy," Luke said, and Jack nodded his understanding. "What else was different?" Luke seemed to like the interviewer role.

"Well, the Cities felt more claustrophobic, even though we were actually in a suburb. When we lived in Michigan we used to go for drives in the country all the time. In the fall

127

we'd go on our own little color tour, visit the orchards and buy apples. Oh, the Macintoshes! I haven't tasted a good Mac since! And we went to folk festivals, and camping, and picnicking. When we moved to Minnesota we didn't get out of the Cities much; I don't know why. Maybe because it was just my mom and me; or because it took a lot longer to get out of town; or it might have been partly because I was a teenager and getting involved in school and social events – and spending less time with my mother. Anyway, I missed the open spaces, the fields and orchards, the forests…"

"Tell me more about your life in Cadillac."

Jack grinned, pleased at Luke's interest in him. "I liked living there. My friends and I always had something to do. Lake Cadillac is entirely within the city limits. It's big enough for swimming, boating and water-skiing. It's a vacation destination, of course. In the winter the lake freezes over and you can snowmobile on it. And there's a winter festival with fireworks – they're really vivid in the cold weather! I liked to cross-country ski, and the Vo-Tech had this great trail just five minutes from our house. I could go over after school – it was a lot of fun."

"I have to ask, of course: Did your family go to church when you lived there?"

"Yes, Pas-, Luke, First Congregational U.C.C. Good choir, good pipe organ, good youth group. It was a big brick colonial church with pillars in front, near the downtown area. You'll love this: the story was that when the congregation got the lot, the neighbor across the street, who was not a church member, said she would put up a huge chunk of the construction money if they would build it to look just like her church back east. They agreed and designed it after a picture she provided. But she died before she gave them any money, and her family didn't choose to honor the commitment!"

"Whoa – so they were left holding the bag! And the bag was empty!"

"Right! I don't know for sure if it's factual, but my dad loved to tell that story. The church was beautiful, but rather out of place architecturally, so that would explain it. It had a white domed bell tower that they lighted at night. You could see it from clear over on the other side of the lake."

"Cadillac sounds like an idyllic place to grow up."

"Yeah...I haven't thought about it in a while, but I really did like living in a small town. Cadillac people would call it a small city, but compared to the Twin Cities it was just a burg."

"So do you think you could live in a small town again?" Luke's question was apt.

"Yeah, I do. It's funny, when you live in an urban area you think the whole world revolves around the city. Like no place else has culture, or recreation, or, or...value. But now that I think about it, I might be better suited to a rural area."

"That sounds like a good insight. What might the drawbacks be?"

Jack thought for a few minutes. "Well, loneliness comes to mind. But I've been pretty lonely in the city, too."

"A church is a great place for meeting like-minded people."

"Good point."

"I can't remember who's serving our congregation in Little Falls right now. I've been there and the sanctuary is lovely, with nice natural light and a semi-circular arrangement. Let's see...the U.C.C. minister in Granite Falls is a woman. I don't know her well, but I've met her and my impression is that she's very gifted."

"That's a good recommendation. I think wherever I go I'll seek out a church. It's just part of my life. But I'll never find a minister as good as you!" Jack reached over to give Luke a playful swat.

"Yeah, right!" Luke countered. "I'll miss having you around. Maybe I'll come visit you when I need a rural fix. Or maybe I'll end up in a small town too, you never know."

"You think you might leave Minnetonka sometime soon, Luke?"

"God knows," Luke responded meaningfully. "Only God knows!"

Jack emerged from his tent into a blue-sky morning. He stretched with a 'Salute to the Sun,' or as much of it as he could remember from his yoga class years ago. *I'm so thankful for the sunlight after so many days of clouds. I would welcome the light to break through in my heart, too.* He stood softly, feeling the energy from the earth – Mother Earth – and tipped his face up to the sun.

"Blessed morning." Luke's voice was gentle, matching the moment.

"Same to you," Jack murmured. He opened his eyes to see Luke in a yoga position he did not recognize. He stood on one foot with the other knee raised in front of him at hip level, his free foot dangling in a relaxed way. His arms, out to his sides, resembled wings: elbows bent, wrists up, hands drooping gracefully. "What's that pose?"

"I think this is called 'The Heron,' at least it looks kinda like one. I've also heard it called 'The Crane.' It's my latest favorite."

Jack tried to emulate Luke's posture. He raised one leg and tilted over, stumbling clumsily, tried again with the other leg and had the same problem. "Yikes, I can't do it," he complained. He sat down on a log, elbows on his knees, chin in his hands.

"It takes practice. And breathing. Herons and cranes at times tuck one leg up to keep it warm. It seems incredible that they can balance their big bodies on two skinny legs, never mind one." Jack thought of the sketch in his kitchen back home.

Luke brought his dangling foot down, paused to breathe deeply, and then raised the other leg. He held the pose and continued to speak. "Did you know that herons are especially honored in some Native American traditions? They believe that the souls of wise ones come back in herons, to make journeys that are mysterious to us."

Jack gazed at him with admiration. "There are herons up here in the Boundary Waters, aren't there?"

"Oh yes. Maybe you'll see one. You have to look carefully by the shore – they're well camouflaged." Luke inhaled and gracefully lifted his hands over his head, palms together, and brought them down to his sides with an exhale as he returned his foot to the ground.

"I'll have to work on that pose. I'm not very balanced yet, I guess."

"Give yourself time, Jack."

After breakfast they packed quickly, loaded and launched. Soon they reached the landing where they'd begun their week. Jack unloaded his pack and pulled his canoe high onto the sand, remembering its escape attempt when they were here before. Luke put on his pack and lifted his canoe onto his shoulders.

"Wow, you can carry both at the same time?" Jack gaped.

"Not for very far. Your canoe is lighter, though – you can probably handle both."

"That would sure speed up a person's progress." Jack thought about all the doubling back they had done.

"Give it a try – you're strong enough."

Am I? I can try, anyway, once I'm out there.

Jack plopped his pack on the ground next to the car so he could leave his useless camera and load up food from his cache. Jack tried putting the whole food bag into his Duluth pack, but the resulting bulge on top looked unstable, and the pack wouldn't fasten properly. So he grabbed individual packets of freeze-dried food and shoveled them into the pack, sliding them down the sides and into every possible crevice. This worked better, at least for the time being. He had the pack almost full when he realized that he could be helping Luke load his canoe. Together they positioned the craft and Luke showed Jack a power cinch knot that worked great to make it secure.

As Jack returned from a quick trip to the outhouse, he saw Luke next to the Volvo fastening up Jack's Duluth pack. He looked up from his work and said, "I just put our leftover food in your pack. There's peanut butter, and cracker meal and oil for cooking fish. You might as well use it."

"Oh, thanks, I will."

The two men stood between their vehicles, suddenly aware that this part of the adventure had reached an end. Jack felt a rush of emotions: gratitude, anxiety, anticipation, loneliness. Luke opened his arms to offer a hug, and Jack awkwardly responded, patting his friend's back a few times and then releasing.

"Thank you for coming up here with me, Jack. It's been great."

"Thank you! I couldn't have done this without you."

"I'd better get going – I just realized it's the fourth of July weekend, so the traffic may be crazy you know."

"Oh, yeah, the holiday. Have a safe trip. I'll see you when I get back."

"I'll hold you in prayer while you are on this journey. Remember what Proust wrote: 'We don't receive wisdom; we must discover it for ourselves after a journey that no one can take for us or spare us.'"

Jack nodded silently. Suddenly the words that usually served him so well seemed woefully inadequate. *What can I say to capture what I feel?* Nothing came. He swallowed hard. He would let Proust have the last word this time.

Luke climbed into his car, shut the door and rolled down the window. Jack looked at the canoe, the car, and finally the man. His eyes burned but he didn't want to cry now. *Not a good last impression.* He finally managed to say, "Goodbye, friend."

"Goodbye, friend. God is good." When Jack didn't provide the response, he added quietly, emphatically, "All the time." With this Luke backed out and drove away, his left arm out the window waving farewell.

Jack lunged into his car, closed the door, and let the tears come. The familiar sting of loneliness took over, and this time he leaned into the pain and wept. After a while he wiped his eyes. *Luke is not dead, he's just leaving. Why am I reacting so strongly? Must just be the grief from Abby's* death that still needs attention. *Will I ever get this into balance? Oh God, I hope so.*

Insecurity reared its ugly head, and he had to counter with sentences he'd heard Luke say. *'You're strong enough...this is a brilliant idea...you're a quick study...' Luke would not lie. He believes in me. I can do this. I just need to have take a journey that no one can take for me...or spare me. Maybe then I'll gain some wisdom. Or some balance. Or something.*

Abby's journal, which had been with his food bag, lay on the seat next to him. He held his breath and opened it, turning past the pages he had read back when he was at home. The next entry was written about a month later.

May 25, 1995

Everything is all a-flurry because Dad is so sick and Mom is so sick and it's the end of the school year for Jack and me and the days are going by too fast. Sometimes I can't even feel anything because I'm on overload.

I'm just plodding through the days at school. I worry about Dad all the time. He's actually handling this really well, but I guess I'm not. I'm trying to be strong but sometimes I wonder if that's the right approach. I asked Pastor Luke about that and he said "Being strong is over-rated. Being human is better."

So what does it mean to be human? I guess it means to feel what you feel, rather than stuffing it. Most people I know never let on how they feel. But you know, if I just try to be stoic all the time around Dad, how will he know how much I love him and will miss him? I think

I need to let myself be human a little more. I cry at home (like now), but I haven't allowed myself to cry in his presence.

Jack is so dear. He lets me cry and holds me and listens to me. I haven't seen any tears from him, though... I wonder if he needs to cry?

Things are better since we got someone to stay at the house with Mom. At least I don't have to sleep there now. And next week we'll meet with the Hospice people. I hear they are wonderful with situations like this where someone wants to stay at home in their last months. I hope they will be understanding about Mom's needs too. She does best when everything is predictable and routine, and lately everything has been topsy-turvy with Dad in the hospital off and on. Jack and I are in and out of the house a lot too and that must be confusing to her. But we won't stay away!

I still have quizzes to correct so I have to stop. Sometimes writing like this helps me to catch my breath. I almost need to be reminded to breathe.

Jack felt like his heart would explode with love and sadness. Head spinning, he read the entry again. *I remember this—we were stretched so thin with school and family needs pressing in on us. 'Being strong is overrated. Being human is better.' I can just hear Luke saying that. It's the same thing he's trying to teach me now.*

'Jack is so dear'...I did something right...she wondered if I needed to cry...Probably did and didn't know it...but I'm making up for it now...

A tear plopped on the journal and he watched with blurred vision as it spread out and diluted the ink. He brushed it away lest it alter her words. The smear on the page exasperated him, and he let fly with an angry growl. He pounded his thigh with his fist until that pain shouted louder than his heartache.

It was a while before Jack felt ready to start the next leg of his journey. He tenderly tucked Abby's journal into his bulging pack, fastened and shouldered it, and locked his car. He swayed and caught his balance, unaccustomed to the weight of his load. Lumbering over to the shore, he felt the pang of loneliness to see just one little canoe waiting. His heart ached down to his toes.

So now for the next adventure. He swallowed hard. *Can I do this alone?*

Chapter 10

Now, where am I going? Jack grabbed his F-13 map and realized he really needed F-14 as well, so back into the pack, through the food he burrowed until he found the yellow-and-blue map. He was thinking he would like to go up to the border chain of lakes, so he just had to figure out how to get there from here.

Half an hour later, Jack was finally in his red Independence heading west in the midday sunshine. Almost to the end of East Bearskin lake he found the portage for Aspen lake. The 95 rods seemed interminable without Luke's companionship. He kept thinking of things he would say if Luke had been there, like how danged heavy his pack was with all that food in it. He would try carrying his pack and canoe at the same time when the load was lighter.

Across Aspen, then a long 117 rods and he was on Flour lake. Jack realized from the map that he was not yet back into the Boundary Waters, but it was too far to go today. The only camping option for him seemed to be the Forest Service campground on Flour Lake. It was mid-afternoon – he had little choice.

In the campground, it seemed strange to see vehicles everywhere. *I've only been in the wilderness a week, but my frame of reference has already changed.* He carried his belongings along the campground road, found an amenable site and claimed it. *Picnic table will be a welcome convenience. But neighbors are so close!* He shook his head at his reaction, turned around and stumbled clumsily around the fire pit. He cast a quick glance around to see if anyone had seen him…*apparently not.*

When he'd fetched his canoe and propped it in the site, he wondered briefly about vandalism or theft. His bright red canoe certainly called attention to itself. He took a good look at it and examined its scratches with a sigh – nothing serious, but it didn't look brand new any more. He moved it to a more secluded position on the ground, just in case someone found it tempting.

Oh yeah, public campground, I gotta pay. He walked to the pay station, and noticed a typewritten sign:

HUNGRY BEARS ARE IN THIS AREA.
Place all food and personal items
(soap, toothpaste, etc.)
in your vehicle overnight
and when you are away from your campsite.

But, he didn't <u>have</u> a vehicle here!

So much for the solitary journey. Have to approach some other campers. Or maybe I could hang a bear bag; but the site is so small. Shoot.

On the way back to his site he realized that he had left his pack on the picnic table unguarded, so he ran the rest of the way back. He careened into his site, saw the pack still in its place and no bear in sight, and halted puffing and panting, a little embarrassed at his panic.

Jack set up his tent and tossed in his sleeping bag and clothes for the next day. After a dinner of rich three-cheese lasagna, Jack threw his cooking gear into his Duluth pack, on top of the piles of food and the rest of his belongings. He secured the baggy, lumpy pack and shouldered it. He would have to reorganize it sooner or later, but now he set out on a tiny hike to check out the neighbors. Across the road were 20-somethings much like his students, playing the radio and jabbering happily around the fire. Further along was a busy family with a toddler, two grade-schoolers, and a dog. The next site had two women and across from them were two men. He approached the men, who were comparing their fishing poles.

"Hi, would you mind putting my pack in your truck overnight? I don't have a vehicle and I don't want the bears to have a feast."

They stared at him a moment and he used the time to berate himself for his blunt approach. "Sure, you betcha." came the answer at last. Jack shrugged out of the pack and dropped it by their extended-cab pickup.

"Catching anything?" Jack asked, trying to start over and be friendly.

"Not too much. You?"

"Haven't been out today." Jack couldn't think of anything else to say. "I'll be by in the morning to get the pack. When would be a good time?"

"Anytime," one said. "We'll leave the rig unlocked if we go out fishin'. The bears can't work the handles," the speaker grinned.

"OK then," Jack said, and walked away. *Well, mission accomplished. Wasn't seeking friendship, after all.*

Back at his site he built a fire and stared into it. *Now what? Alone again. Now I miss both Abby and Luke. Worse than before, in a way. Maybe I shouldn't have undertaken this crazy journey. I wanted to escape the pain, but now I'm just as lonely, or more so. Even in a campground with all these people around. And I can't flip on the computer or go to a mall for distraction.*

Jack thought of his little notebook and decided it would be a good time to do some writing. Once he had his head in his tent, though, he realized the notebook was in his pack, shut up in some guys' truck. Crushed, he returned to the fire and resumed staring into it. *This stinks. What good is it to be here anyway? I'm miserably lonesome.*

Then he remembered again that Luke had called his summer plan "brilliant." He pondered that for a while, and considered his options. *I could go back to the Cities. But what would I do there all summer? I don't even know where I'll be or what I'll be teaching. I'd be lonely there too. So would I rather be miserable here or there?* In the end, he resolved to continue the adventure, even though there might be awkward parts. *What was it Luke quoted from Proust? 'We don't receive wisdom; we must discover it for ourselves after a journey that no one can take for us or spare us.' and in church he was always saying 'God promises a safe landing, not a calm passage.' I'm in this now – I've got to follow through.*

The mosquitoes started to bother so Jack let the fire die down, doused it, and went to bed. Music and laughter at the nearby site kept him awake later than he was used to.

Next morning, waking a bit later than he planned, Jack walked up the road to retrieve his pack. He stopped short. The pickup was gone! He looked at the site – vacant!

Jack raked his eyes over the scene. No vehicle, no tent, no other sign of the men's presence. They had left no trace!

He checked to make sure it was the right campsite. He walked a little way up the road and then back toward his site, thinking. *There is a "Campground Host" listed on the board – I could ask them.* He turned on his heel and headed toward the site with the big RV he'd glimpsed on up the road. *What can they do, though?* He reversed his direction again and headed back to his campsite. He felt like a dork, walking up and down the road in his indecision. He just had to sit and think this out.

Back at his site he sat at the picnic table and tried to think of a course of action. *I'm just a lousy judge of character, I guess. But if the guys have stolen my pack, they will be disappointed – it was almost all freeze-dried food. Good stuff, though, and worth something if you're hungry. Which I will be if I don't get it back. I'll have to paddle and portage back to my car, and all my tent and stuff will be loose...what a pain. I could probably buy equipment at an outfitter – heck, I can afford it. It's all replaceable, as far as that goes. Oh, wait, though - Abby's journal is in there!* His throat started to constrict like a massive hand was strangling him. He gripped his head in his hands.

A truck roared by, stopped, and reversed more slowly. "Mornin'!" said a friendly voice.

Jack jerked his head around and saw the missing pickup and one of the men leaning out the window. "Morning!" he echoed as he strode over to them, swallowing hard.

"We almost forgot and took off with your pack. Senior moment, I guess." The fellow hopped out and reached behind the seat for Jack's Duluth pack.

"Thanks for remembering." Relief flooded over him.

In a cloud of dust the men were gone and Jack was on his own again.

Jack was eager to be out of the campground and into his canoe, so he threw his gear in on top of the food, snapped it in and walked out. The portage trail from Flour Lake to Hungry Jack took off from the road, so he had a 162-rod hike before he would experience the peace of paddling. Burdened with the heavy pack in addition to his canoe, he was thankful for the cool cloudiness of the morning.

By the time he got to Hungry Jack Lake with his canoe, he identified with the name. *Wasn't hungry for breakfast, but now it's only midmorning and I'm starved. I am one Hungry Jack!* He regretted his earlier haste as he unloaded most of the pack in order to find some peanut butter and crackers. There was no place to sit at the portage so he just stood around and munched. He spread his map out on the overturned canoe and studied it again.

Halfway across Hungry Jack to a cove, a short portage to Bearskin, then on to Duncan. Or instead I could go to Moss – or is that Moses? no, Moss - then to Duncan...but that means longer portages. Bearskin it is.

Arrival at the portage to Duncan Lake meant that he was once again in the Boundary Waters, and that felt good. Duncan Lake would also mean a return to ample campsites, comfortably distant from neighbors. On the portage trail he thought through all he would need to do: set up the tent, collect firewood, build a fire, make dinner, hang the bear bag. No problem accomplishing this before dark, but the clouds looked increasingly ominous. What would be first priority, setting up the tent or getting the fire started? He missed Luke again – he needed his counsel.

If it really pours I'll be better off in the tent, so that might be most important. But if I don't have dry wood gathered, I'll have no hope for a fire to warm up or dry off tonight or *tomorrow morning. Probably best to set up the tent and rain fly, then dash around for some firewood and stow it where it'll stay dry.*

Duncan Lake was choppy in the wind, and the blue-gray cloud cover made the afternoon seem like evening. Other paddlers on the lake seemed to be hugging the shore on the opposite side from Jack, headed northeast. *They're looking for campsites, too. We all have the same agenda, to get in before this storm hits.*

The first site he came to was occupied. He headed straight for a campsite on a point of land, but a glimpse of blue tent told him that it was taken too. *The other canoes were headed northeast; I'll go southwest.* It was the opposite direction from his route, but there were two possible sites. He leaned into the wind and paddled with long strokes.

The next site had two canoes at the entrance. From here the lake narrowed and curved, so he couldn't see ahead very far. Jack peered at his map. *If this last site is not available, then what? Turn around and check out the other sites, hoping the other canoeists didn't take them? Fat chance. Make my own site? Not really supposed to – don't see any clearings along here anyway. Could paddle back around and portage to Moss Lake – it's a short portage, but there's only one possible site there. There's a portage to Partridge Lake at the end of this channel but it's 230 rods – that'll take a while. But there are three sites on Partridge, better odds. Judging from the sky I'm going to get wet no matter what I do. Wonder where my rain poncho is?*

He thought he saw color ahead – a bad sign. Sure enough, it was a blue canoe at the entrance to the campsite. *This is not my day.*

He was almost to the trail to Partridge, so he decided to keep going. The rain was starting, lightly at first, then giant drops that soaked his shirt quickly. He was eager to get off the lake and under the canoe for the portage.

The visibility was so bad he passed the portage once, but when he saw he was at the point of the lake where it became a river, he doubled back a short way and found it. In his haste to land, he stepped in the water to his right knee. *Crap! Oh well, I'll be wet anyway.*

Laden with the pack, he flipped the canoe over, ducked under, settled the portage yoke on his shoulders and steadied himself. *Strangest umbrella I've ever used. At least I know I can carry both the pack and the canoe. That will speed up my progress considerably. But wow, it's heavy with both. This is going to be hard work.*

Step, squish, step, squish, he labored up a ridge in the rain and prayed for stamina. Step, squish, step, squish, he tried to speed up but slipped enough in the mud to slow his pace again. Step, squish, step, squish, he hoped fervently for an open campsite on Partridge Lake. The rain let up some. He stopped to rest twice, perching the canoe against a tree to ease the load on his shoulders. At last he saw the lake ahead of him. *That felt like a lot more than 230 rods! More like 500! They must have measured wrong!*

Jack put the canoe in the water and slung the pack into the canoe with a THUNK. The map indicated a site directly across the lake from the portage. He climbed in and rotated his shoulders a couple of times before shoving off. He'd forgotten to find his poncho, but hopefully he wouldn't be on the lake very long. The rain was easing up a bit but there were plenty of dark clouds overhead.

There was no canoe at the site, which was a hopeful sign. Jack was glad for his wide-brimmed hat, which kept the rain off his face most of the time, but now the wind was smacking moisture into his face, blurring his glasses and his view. The chin strap of his hat wasn't comfy but at least it kept it on his head. He pulled up to the landing, clunking against the rocks and trying to steady the canoe to get out.

Once out, he pulled the canoe up so it wouldn't drift. He hauled the heavy pack out and plopped it on the muddy ground. He turned to survey the site and his heart sank.

Two tents. And voices.

This is for sure not my day. Damn rain!

Pack back in the canoe, shove off and jump in. *Paddle northeast and pray for a site. Two more chances.*

Still no poncho, Jack hunched over in the canoe, soaked to the skin. The wind was more at his back now, and he needed the help. He was cold, and hungry, and exhausted. He hugged the shore so he wouldn't miss the site. Even so, it almost eluded him.

Jack left the pack in the canoe this time, just in case he had to make another getaway. He saw no signs of life as he approached. *Hallelujah! It's open!*

The tent site, sheltered by trees, was not as wet as the rest of the ground. Jack found a reasonably dry spot to plop his pack and proceeded to extract and set up the tarp and tent. His weariness made him clumsy and inefficient; he had to circle the tent an extra time to reposition the stakes. The rain pattered on him and around him as he worked. Once the tent was up he marched off into the woods, determined to find some dry firewood if he could so he could make a hot fire to dry himself out. *If there's time I'll put up the rain fly next.*

The selection was plentiful, as this lake didn't get as much use as some. In a dense stand of trees he found the ground nearly dry, and ample dead wood. He loaded his left arm with branches, his hand full of twigs, and with his right hand he dragged a downed tree the short distance to his fire circle. He found a dry spot under a cluster of pines and dumped it all. As he did, thunder boomed and the rain started up again in earnest.

He heaved his Duluth pack into the tent and dove in after it as the rain came down in sheets. He kicked off his boots and sighed with relief. Now he could relax!

Hunger set the agenda so he pawed through the food packs to find a "cold prep" meal. Chicken and Almond Salad surfaced as a good possibility. He kept filtered water in his canteen, so he used that to rehydrate the clattering nuggets right in the foil packet. He carefully stirred the stuff with his spoon, folded the top over, found a clothespin to secure it, and set it against his pack. He ate some dried fruit while he waited. *This is probably a no-no in a tent, but I'm tired of being soaked by rain and I have everything I need right here. Just don't spill.*

Jack was so hungry he ate every crumb and licked the spoon and part of the packet. The trash went into his garbage bag. He pulled out his Crazy Creek chair and made himself comfortable as the rain pummeled his tent.

Now what?

Alone again.

A vision of Abby came to his mind. He tried to overcome the thoughts like he used to, but without the usual distractions of life in the Cities it didn't work. He closed his eyes.

I miss you, my love.

His throat felt tight. He could almost feel her with her arm around his shoulders, her hair brushing his face, whispering in his ear. He strained to hear her with every fiber of his being. He could discern no words, only love. Love washed over him, sent a chill down his back. Love warmed him then and filled his heart and mind. Love surrounded him and expanded to the tent, the site, the wilderness. This was greater than even Abby's power to love.

The thunder cracked and he started, opening his eyes. *God.*

I am loved. Even now. I am loved. By Abby. By God. Loved.

Finding his eyes moist and his nose running, Jack reached into his pack for a bandanna. Along the edge he felt an unexpected shape – something in a plastic bag. *What on earth?* He pulled it out – Luke's Bible! With a note. Thunder echoed overhead as he read.

Dear Jack,

This Bible has been my companion on a variety of journeys. Since I have to leave you now, I'm sending it to accompany you as you sojourn in the wilderness. The book itself has no magical powers, but it has been known to lead people to experience God's power. All human experience can be found here: conflict, peace, humiliation, glory, loneliness, community...and on and on. Throughout you'll find the Holy Spirit blowing as an animating breath. May she breathe in you and through you, and may you know firsthand the abundant love of God.

Luke

P.S. Some scriptures you might find interesting:

Ephesians 3: 14-21   Isaiah 41: 10

John 14   Romans 8: 35-39

Isaiah 43: 1-3, 19   Hebrews 12: 1-3, 12-13

Ecclesiastes 3: 1-8   1 John 4: 7-13

Matthew 11: 28-30

Luke's Gospel – all of it! (my name notwithstanding) and John also (your name, right?)

This last part was written across the bottom of the page and up the margin, as though he kept having additional ideas and jotted them down.

Jack sat back, note and Bible in his hands. *What a gift. What a friend.* More thunder boomed, but further away this time. The rain diminished but kept up a light percussion on the tent. Jack pictured Luke writing this note, entrusting his special Bible to him, sliding it surreptitiously into his pack with the leftover food. He smiled.

Curious, he looked up Ephesians 3: 14-21. He had a little trouble locating Ephesians, but he found it tucked in with other letters in the New Testament, or 'Christian Scriptures' as Luke called it. He read:

For this reason I bow my knees before the Father, from whom every family in heaven and on earth takes its name. I pray that, according to the riches of his glory, he may grant that you may be strengthened in your inner being with power through his Spirit, and that Christ may dwell in your hearts through faith, as you are being rooted and grounded in love. I pray that you may have the power to comprehend, with all the saints, what is the breadth and length and height and depth, and to know the love of Christ that surpasses knowledge, so that you may be filled with all the fullness of God.

Now to him who by the power at work within us is able to accomplish abundantly more than all we can ask or imagine, to him be glory in the church and in Christ Jesus to all generations, forever and ever. Amen.

Wow. I think I just experienced 'the love of Christ that surpasses knowledge' a few minutes ago! And I certainly am feeling strengthened in my inner being on this journey. Wow. Jack sat for a long time, rereading the passage and thinking about different parts of it. The sentence construction intrigued him as an English teacher; the language of strength and power and love spoke to his immediate experience; and the final sentence so compelled him that he struggled to memorize it.

When Jack looked up from his captivation with the scripture, he realized he needed to do his evening chores before full darkness descended. The storm had passed. He gathered up his trash from dinner, filtered water, brushed his teeth, separated his gear and hung the bear bag. He built a fire to dry his clothes further.

Sitting by the fire with Luke's Bible, he looked up another of his suggestions: John 14.

Do not let your hearts be troubled...
In my Father's house there are many dwelling places...I go to prepare a place for you...

146

He recognized these words from Abby's funeral. Luke had conveyed such love that day. And the image of Abby in God's house was reassuring. Later in the chapter, he read these words:

> The Spirit of Truth... You know him, because he abides with you and he will be in you.

Jack took a deep breath, remembering what Luke had written about the Holy Spirit's 'animating breath.' He noticed that while the Bible used male pronouns for the Spirit, Luke used female pronouns. *Luke must experience the Spirit as a feminine presence. Interesting.* He read further:

> Peace I leave with you, my peace I give to you. I do not give to you as the world gives. Do not let your hearts be troubled, and do not let them be afraid.

Peace. I pray for peace. Jack closed his eyes and felt a tentative peace.

Chapter 11

Jack's eyes popped open. It was still fully dark, way too early to get up. He'd dreamed of Abby again, and this time the image of her smile stayed with him. In the midst of his longing for her, he noticed a new feeling: gratitude. She seemed happy in this dream, and he found himself to be glad and grateful.

Could it mean she's happy where she is, wherever that is? With Jesus, maybe? In the presence of infinite love? Like Luke, I don't know what to think about 'heaven'... but I like the idea of boundless love and light... Comforted by these thoughts, he drifted back to sleep and woke again a couple of hours later.

He had thought he might stay awhile in this campsite, but as he looked it over in the morning light he changed his mind. *When I find one I really like I'll stay longer.* This one didn't have a good place for sitting, the ground sloped a little in the tent site, and worst of all the branches hung so low on the latrine trail that he was rain-soaked from the secondary showers even though the morning was clear.

Over breakfast he read another entry in Abby's journal.

September 1, 1996

School is starting this week and once again I am awash in conflicting feelings. Maybe if I make some lists I will get some insights.

Good things about teaching
Students, especially bright ones
Good colleagues
Creativity
When a student really 'gets it'
Achieving goals

Bad/Difficult things
Students, especially ones who act out
Low salary, and those danged negotiations
Grading papers
Blank stares
Expectations too high (of myself and others too)

Oh dear, the lists are coming out even. I need to get my head around the good parts and make an upbeat start. Sometimes that makes the whole year go better. If I can just focus on the students who are open to learning, and remind myself that I am really making a difference in some people's lives... At least I think I am. I hope I am.

At least I have good colleagues. Jack complains all the time about the instructors at the college. I wonder where they dig them up. I worry about his work. I wish his job were more rewarding for him. It's hard when I know I can't do anything about it.

Sometimes I wonder what it would be like to pull up stakes and find jobs somewhere else. Jack would probably like the idea of something *new. I'm the one who would stand in the way. I guess I really do like my school and the little bit of teamwork we have. I think there's potential for more this year, too. And some of the students through the years have been truly inspiring to me. One or two might even make a splash in the world of math!*

I guess I'm talking myself into a better attitude for this school year. Maybe next year we'll think about a change.

Jack marveled at Abby's ability to shape her own attitude toward the positive. *She was even willing to think about relocating, so that I would be happier! Now it looks like change is a reality, and she doesn't have to adapt. She would have been able to, though. She could turn a wizened turnip into a gourmet dish. She could make a rainstorm into an exotic body wash. She could make a dull, cynical guy like me seem pretty companionable. That's the biggest miracle of all!*

Returning Abby's journal to his tent, Jack turned his attention to the map. He had already detoured from his plan by coming to Partridge to find a site. *But I am on my own now, with no deadlines and no schedules, so what does it matter anyway?*

He had two choices from here. Three, if he counted hiking the Border Route Trail for 2½ or 3½ miles – but with his present load that was definitely not a possibility. Even catching the South Lake Trail from here would take him about a mile and a half on foot – almost 500 rods – that seemed too long, too. So the most reasonable route would mean retracing his steps over the 230-rod portage back to Duncan Lake. That would be enough. He'd rather have a long paddle than a long portage at this point.

And tomorrow, if all went according to plan, he would take The Long Portage. He had to psych himself for that – it would be a test of his stamina. *Yesterday's storm tested me, too, and I came through. The border route will challenge me with both paddling and portaging, not to mention anything the weather throws my way. Need to prove to myself that I am strong.* Jack took a deep breath. He prayed, *God, give me strength.*

He packed up the gear that was inside the tent, taking special care to replace the Bible in its plastic zipper bag with Luke's note inside. He added Abby's journal to keep it dry too. He pulled up the tent stakes and lifted the rain fly, giving himself an unintentional shower. *Once again it's not my day,* he sighed, shaking his head like a dog. He draped the rain fly over his canoe to dry a little in the sun, and returned to the fire to dry himself. *Wait, think about reshaping that attitude. Abby would find ways to notice the positive instead of branding a day as bad so early.*

Packed up, he patrolled the campsite, and satisfied that he was ready he loaded up the canoe and maneuvered it into the water. The contrast of the weather to yesterday was so great, he felt like he was seeing Partridge Lake for the first time. He breathed in the rain-washed morning air.

Mist rose from the lake, backlit by the morning sun, giving him the feeling that he was in a dream. *I am in a dream, in a way. I've often dreamed of leaving everything behind to return to this haven. I'm living a dream right now.*

Thirty yards away on his right, delicate blue irises, blooming in the shallows by the shore, captured his attention. As he drank in their beauty he saw the Great Blue Heron just beyond them, still as a statue. Jack stopped paddling to drift reverently by. He admired the swooping curve of its neck, its sleek head, and its stable serenity as it balanced on its impossibly slender legs. He honored the bird's silent reverie, entering into it in his own way. The ethereal mist and the silence shared with this elegant creature made the morning a prayer.

Not so long ago I was sitting at my kitchen table, looking at the sketch of a heron on the wall. Such balance didn't seem possible then. Now that I'm looking at a real heron, I can see the serenity that keeps it centered. *I can aspire to that. Maybe the balance will come.*

Jack drifted along, paddling only occasionally. *Maybe this is my day. That heron might have had the spirit of a wise ancestor on a mysterious journey. I'm on a mysterious journey too. The spirit of the heron has blessed me with peace. I can open the door to peace.* He breathed deeply and resumed paddling.

The portage didn't even look familiar, but he found it without any trouble.

The ground was still soggy, but much better than his previous trek on this path. He was grateful for the protection the canoe provided him from wet branches. His boots, which had not fully dried from the storm, collected moisture from the vegetation. Again, 230 rods seemed an underestimate, and he had to stop and rest once.

He entered Duncan Lake at the far western tip, and followed the narrow channel to where the water opened out before him, bright blue and sparkling in the sun. He paddled contentedly, stopping from time to time to rotate his shoulders and stretch his neck. The few others on the lake waved a hand or a paddle in greeting. To the north Duncan tapered to a narrow channel with the portage at its point. Jack didn't know what to expect from the Stairway Portage. His first discovery was the answer to his prayer – the route went downhill! *Maybe this is my day! No stairs so far. They must appear later.* He still had to watch his balance. He was pleased to see an overlook open up to his left just before the stairs, and he decided to stop for lunch.

Once out from under the canoe, he realized that he was in the midst of some of the most dramatic scenery he had seen yet on this trip. He was on a high palisade of rock, looking out over the clear water of Rose Lake. On the opposite shore were the woods of Canada, deep greens separating the blue of sky and water. Jack took a deep breath, closed his eyes, and opened them to drink in the beauty again. He wanted to memorize this view, this gift. *If only I had my camera – and film!*

Another solitary man sat chewing on a sandwich, gazing out at the vista. "This is great, isn't it," Jack offered conversationally.

"Mmm, beautiful," the man agreed. "You heading up or down?"

"Down. You?"

"Up. I've been on Rose for a few days. The smallmouth bass were really biting. I caught some 20-inch 'smallies.' Released them, so you can have a chance at them too."

"Good – I'll have to get out there with my pole this afternoon." Jack readied his lunch and sat where he could continue the conversation. "Where are you from?"

"Fergus Falls. You?"

"The Cities."

"I teach high school science, and when I do the geology chapters I love to talk about this place."

"Like what?" Jack knew almost nothing about geology.

"The last glaciers moved through what is now Minnesota about 12,000 years ago. We're seeing the result here. As they advanced, the glaciers scoured out basins for the lakes and rounded the hills. The smaller lakes are kettles, formed when a block of ice fell off a glacier. The block got buried by the outwash from the glacier. When the earth warmed up, the ice block melted to form what we call a kettle lake. This is what the glaciers left behind – all this beauty."

"Wow. A lot of time has gone by since then."

"Plenty of time for moving water to cut channels, freezing and thawing to sculpt the terrain, and forests to grow." The man stood up and picked up his pack. "I've got to get going. I stayed an extra day on Rose and now I have to beat it back to my car. Nice talking to you."

"Same here. Take care."

"Thanks. Enjoy the waterfall – and the fishing."

As the teacher headed up the trail, Jack got ready to head down. He looked out at the panorama again and said quietly, "Thanks, glaciers," before he set out down the stairway.

The steps, constructed of logs, made a steep grade navigable. He imagined the work crew that built this convenience for him and others, and felt grateful. Even though he was going down the steps, his legs began to tire. Tipping the canoe to the front so it wouldn't hit the steps behind required extra balancing.

Jack could hear the waterfall before he could see it. He was glad to stop for the view; besides, his leg muscles were burning. The narrow cascade tumbled down some 100 feet, framed by cedar trees. Mosses grew in stunning greens where the spray nourished them. Jack breathed in the moist air and felt its misty coolness on his face. He lingered a while, basking in the awe of his third dramatic view of the day, including the heron as the first. He offered silent prayers of thanks.

Rose Lake blossomed in beauty like its namesake. The sun shone brightly and a gentle breeze teased the treetops along the shore. Few canoes dotted the large lake. It was early enough that Jack had his choice of many campsites, so he chose to paddle a while before stopping to camp. He spent the late afternoon fishing; as the geology teacher had promised, the bass were plentiful. He kept one and feasted on a "smallie" that night. He turned in early, anticipating a long hike the next day.

Up early, Jack took time to make coffee on the camp stove, and ate a quick breakfast of peanut butter on crackers with dried apples. He broke camp so quickly that he was on the lake by 7:30. He had a bit of a paddle before the Long Portage, and he was hoping to time the portage so he wasn't there in the hottest part of the day.

Paddling along he noticed fellow voyageurs in their campsites. A plume of smoke to his left he traced to a young couple dousing their fire. He felt a pang of loneliness as he saw the woman, with a full head of brown curls like Abby's, bending over the fire, stirring the ashes with a stick. He fairly snapped his head to the front so they wouldn't see him staring.

Further along, on the right, a large campground opened up to the lake. Two canoes of teenagers were shoving off as a woman ran down to the shore, life vest in hand, shouting, "Mandy, you get back here and put this life vest on! It's camp policy!"

Just as he passed the first canoe, he heard the red-haired girl in the center whine, "But it doesn't match my outfit!" even as her friends turned the canoe back to the site to get the jacket. No pangs of envy here, only gratitude that he was responsible only for himself. That scenario reran in his mind all day, sometimes evoking sympathy for the adult and sometimes, strangely, for the girl. He knew the nuisance of the life vest, how hot and uncomfortable it could become. Yet he remembered a sad story Luke had told about a boy who drowned on a youth group trip. Part of his responsibility to himself was to keep his vest on whenever he was on the water.

Would anyone miss me if I were to drown? Luke would. My cousin in Las Vegas – probably not. Some of the church people maybe. But why am I thinking this way? Some months ago, he'd had thoughts about wanting to die to be with Abby – but his will to live had won out. Now he didn't want to be cut off from this place of beauty, this paradise on earth.

By the time he had paddled the length of Rose Lake, the sun was high in the sky. His legs were cramping in the canoe, his thigh muscles tight from the stairway descent yesterday. As long as he was moving on the water, he had a breeze to cool his face and neck. Once he had landed the canoe and started up the trail, the heat began to feel oppressive. The humidity so typical in the Twin Cities was usually less here in the north country, but this day was sticky. Jack's shirt stuck to him and even in the shade of the canoe his face ran with sweat.

Mosquitoes, lured by his sweaty body, descended upon him with a vengeance as he walked. Jack swung at them with his free hand, sometimes throwing himself off balance on the uneven trail. His legs ached. *Barely started the Long Portage and already I'm miserable. This will be a test of my endurance.*

With each step Jack felt worse. Sweat blurred his vision. He stumbled often. Mosquitoes, heat, and pain dominated every thought. *This is awful. Why did I ever choose this route? I'm not up to this. Probably break my leg out here.* His foot snagged on a root and he pitched forward in an awkward dance to keep upright.

That's it, I've got to rest, even if the bugs eat me alive. He perched the canoe against a tree, ducked out from under it and shrugged out of the pack, which seemed stuck to his back.

Water. A big swig wasn't enough – he realized he may have been on the verge of dehydrating. He used his bandanna to wipe the sweat from his face and neck, then fanned himself with it, feeling momentary relief from the stifling heat. He spread mosquito repellent on every inch of skin, knowing sweat would dilute it but still hoping for some good effect. He stretched his arms overhead, then bent over from the waist and stretched his aching shoulders and legs.

If I'm going to make it to the next lake, I'm going to have to think positively. Jack took a deep breath and struggled into the pack, which still wanted to stick to him. He sighed as he ducked under the canoe and adjusted the portage yoke on his shoulders.

The words of a spiritual from the hymnal came to him:

Guide my feet, while I run this race
Guide my feet, while I run this race
Guide my feet, while I run this race
For I don't want to run this race in vain.

This verse ran through his mind several times before he came up with another verse:

Hold my hand, while I run this race ...

His steps kept time with the rhythm of the song as he navigated the trail. He still had to choose his steps carefully in spots, so he slowed the song accordingly, then picked up the pace again when he hit smooth terrain.

Stand by me, while I run this race…

The juxtaposition of standing and running in this verse always caught Jack off guard. He was so literal sometimes. He concentrated on letting the contrast be, imagining the Holy Spirit with him. *Luke would say, "She doesn't stand, anyway! She breathes, blows, and moves. Don't let it bother you!"*

I'm your child, while I run this race…

Luke had introduced this song to the congregation when he preached on his Ordination scripture, and it had soon become a favorite. *What was that scripture? Hebrews, it's from Hebrews. Luke was always quoting it. "Therefore, since we are surrounded by so great a cloud of witnesses, let us run with perseverance the race that is set before us… looking to Jesus …"* Jack couldn't go further than that, but he was pleased he could remember that much.

Who's in my great cloud of witnesses? Luke of course. Jack pictured each person as he called them to mind. *Pastor Fisher from my childhood. Abby. My parents, her parents, and my grandparents. Imagine all these people surrounding me on this journey! With all that support, I can certainly keep going.*

Indeed, step by step Jack made good progress. He forgot his aching muscles, or they stopped hurting. Using his bandanna made the sweat less of a problem. He took frequent drinks of water. The bugs seemed more tolerable.

Soon Jack came to a fork in the trail. He stopped and consulted his map. He was pretty sure of his route, but it was a good excuse to rest again. The right branch, according to the map, was named "Daniels Spur Trail," and rather than heading directly to Daniels Lake it took a circuitous route. *Curious.* Jack would be bearing to the left, off the edge of his map. He noted with satisfaction that he had come 460 rods, his longest portage yet, and he had "only" 200 rods to go. *Not a bad trail, it's just a hot, buggy day. Gotta remember: God is good, all the time!* He celebrated his accomplishment by pulling out a granola bar, devouring it without ceremony.

Continuing on, Jack discovered that the easy trail was left behind and his route became much more challenging. As he navigated the underused trail, Jack occupied his thoughts with gratitude. He started by thanking God for everything he saw: leaves, trees, rocks, roots, soil, mud, sunshine, his canoe, even bugs. Next he waxed more philosophical, giving thanks for his mind, his ability to string words together, his enjoyment of reading. From there he went back to practical matters, thinking about food and water and shelter. People crowded his thoughts, and he gave thanks for his "great cloud of witnesses" one by one, adding his favorite English teacher and his college advisor.

Wonder what Luke is doing right now. Wonder if he wonders what I'm doing right now. Some time passed as he turned his attention to his whole thought process. *Wonder when I'll stop being so self-absorbed. Maybe that has been part of my grief journey – thinking only about myself. And I'm clearly still doing it. There's food for thought.*

Chapter 12

Jack flipped the canoe into Rove Lake and secured it against a log. Once out of the pack he felt lighter than air, and he jumped around, flapping his arms to celebrate. A stab of pain in his back brought him to an abrupt halt. *Ow!*

The spasm seemed to be under his left shoulder blade. *Carrying that load over the Long Portage took a toll. And now – a Long Paddle.*

Jack linked his thumbs and carefully stretched his arms up over his head, paused half a minute reaching for the sky, then bent over at his waist and slowly folded down, exhaling. He tried to relax his back as he drooped over and let his arms swing limply. After several deep breaths, he rolled upright, one vertebra at a time. He rolled his shoulders forward a few times, then backward.

The yoga got some of the kinks out, but the spasm remained. He tried swinging his arms around, which seemed to loosen it some; hugging himself tightly created a fine stretch in his back, which helped. The dull ache remained, however. He closed his eyes and inhaled and exhaled as deeply as he could, visualizing the pain blowing away on the out-breath. *Guess I'm ready to go.*

Jack opened his eyes and saw, for the first time, that the weather was changing. He had been so absorbed in his physical therapy that he hadn't noticed the dark clouds gathering. The wind was in his face, and he'd expected it to be behind him.

Great. Got to get paddling – have a long way to go yet: Rove to Watap, then a portage to Mountain. And now the humidity is heading toward 100%.

He got out his poncho so it would be handy, loaded the canoe and set out determinedly. *Knew this route would test me. Now I have pain and rain to contend with. Here goes.*

Usually when he made the transition from portaging to paddling, he delighted in the use of different muscles. His legs were tired from the Long Portage, so he was thankful to rest them; but the paddling aggravated the spasm in his back. He experimented with variations on his stroke, trying to find the path of least agony. The spasm hurt less when he paddled on the right, but he was afraid of creating its twin on the other side, so he kept switching.

He'd only been on the water about fifteen minutes when the raindrops started. The sky had changed to steel gray and the sun was only a memory. Splat...splat-splot...splat...

By the time he got his poncho on, his shirt was pretty wet. He had left his hat in the pack because of the wind, figuring he'd use the hood of the poncho if he needed it. The temperature was still high, so he was plenty uncomfortable. Jack remembered how drenched he got on Partridge Lake in that storm, so he decided to opt for the rain protection even if it was hot.

Soon the sweat was running down his back. *I have my own portable sauna. Some people pay for this effect. Think of it as a good thing...*

Rove Lake was narrow enough that he had no navigation issues at all. He wasn't just sure where Rove became Watap – on the map that wasn't clear; there was no portage to mark a boundary. That didn't matter, though; he just had to paddle these skinny lakes until he came to the Watap Portage.

That sounded simple enough, but he couldn't seem to make good progress. The storm made the water choppy. The spasm in his back made his stroke less effective, and the wind was not his friend today. Jack felt like he was slogging through mud. The pain in his back seemed to be spreading as the morning wore on.

His arms so tired he could hardly paddle, Jack resorted to counting to keep going. He counted ten strokes on the right, shifted the paddle and counted backwards from ten to one, then switched again.

Four...three...two...one...switch...
one...two...three...four...

Sweat saturated his clothing and now his shirt stuck to his skin. He felt like a drenched and dripping rag. His glasses had rain on the outside and steam on the inside, and he'd run out of dry surfaces to clean them. He peered ahead uncertainly. Sometimes he lifted his glasses and squinted into the grayness, but that didn't help him feel any more confident about the rain letting up or a campsite miraculously presenting itself.

He knew there were no campsites on Rove or Watap. He just had to keep going.

Now he had a new concern: his stomach was growling. The effort of the Long Portage and this long paddle logically produced hunger. *Should have had a snack before I got in the canoe. But I was worried about the storm. Rightfully so – this is miserable weather: hot and wet. If I open my pack for a snack I'll get it wet inside – best leave it protected. I can manage.*

On and on the rainy lake stretched before him, until he wondered if he could have made some mistake. But his mental version of the map didn't allow for any detours – in fact the route was so obvious that he had tucked the map into the pack for safekeeping. He just had to keep going through the rain and the pain.

Four...three...two...one...switch...
one...two...three...four...

After what seemed like grueling hours, he saw the dark shapes of trees in the grayness ahead, and with a little burst of energy he arrived at the portage. *Finally!*

He scraped the canoe into the landing, absent his usual care. One foot got baptized as he scrambled out. *How much wetter can I get?*

He plopped his pack under a tree and reached in for some food. His hand closed around some jerky. *Perfect!* He ripped the package open with his teeth and tore into it like a savage animal. After a big swig of water he steeled himself to don the pack and canoe. The spasm in his back was worse, of course, after all the paddling. He stretched, sighed, and shouldered his burdens. The 100-rod Watap portage would have been a snap any other day, but Jack had to steel himself to face that distance now. *God is good, all the time,* he growled through clenched teeth.

The canoe plus the pack turned out to be too much. *Going to have to make two trips! Dang!*

Jack left his canoe off to one side, in case anyone else arrived, and set out with just the pack. Compared to his recent double loads this felt remarkably free and easy – wide angle view, arms free from steadying his load, and of course less weight. But he just couldn't get the pack to sit comfortably on his back. He spent the entire walk shifting and adjusting trying to find a more tolerable level of pain. The rain was letting up and the path was level; he gave thanks for these blessings.

At the lake he stowed his pack under a large tree, which promptly dumped rain water all over it, responding to a wind gust. He dug out some dried fruit to eat on the way.

Feeling light as a feather, albeit a muddy, sticky feather, Jack made good time back to the canoe. Its presence on his shoulders brought new reminders of the pain, and again he spent the entire walk twitching, stretching, and adjusting. He resorted to whistling to take his mind off the spasm in his back.

When he arrived at Mountain Lake, he flipped the canoe over into the water. Turning to get his pack, he stopped short. The pack's canvas flap was open, the plastic liner was torn, and various food packets, and remnants of them, were strewn all around the tree. *What on earth! Who's been in here? Where's my food? That's MY food!*

At first Jack just stood there in the drizzle, dumbfounded. Finally he dropped down to a crouch and started gathering up the debris, assessing his loss. Some packets were unharmed, but lots of them were torn or punctured.

Freeze-dried food, scattered on the rain-soaked ground, was beginning to hydrate in the puddles.

Then he noticed the paw-print, *Bear!* Only then did he think beyond his personal loss to the problem of his personal safety. He froze, and looked tentatively around, moving only his eyes. Seeing and hearing nothing moving, he ventured a little movement himself, and surveyed a wider area. His heart pounded in his chest. He tried to remember the rules for bear encounters: *act big, make noise, if that doesn't work play dead...*

A tiny scrap of foil drifted down into Jack's line of vision. *What the heck?* A rustling in the tree above him caused him to look up. A black blotch by the trunk, about ten feet over his head, captured his full attention. As he stared, he could make out a face, staring back at him. *Oh God, there's the bear!*

Jack stretched up tall and announced, loudly and with great authority, "I'm going to take my pack and leave! You can just have this tree! I don't need to stay here!" He spun round to fling his pack into the canoe. As an afterthought he added, speaking rapidly, "Hope you liked the food. Leave No Trace!" He shook his finger at the treed bear before fairly leaping into the canoe.

With speed fueled by adrenalin, Jack pushed off into Mountain Lake. He paddled like fury, putting distance between himself and the bear, wondering all the while whether bears swim and how fast. He could picture them fishing in a stream, but couldn't recall any photo of a brown or black bear actually swimming. He sneaked looks back toward the portage from time to time, and didn't see any black shape coming his way. Finally he slowed his frantic paddling and bent over, panting. *Safe! Thank God!*

Having had enough adventure for one day, Jack started looking for a campsite. Mountain Lake, the largest he'd seen on this trip so far, had widely spaced sites on the south shore. He headed to his right so he could take stock of the availability easily.

The first one he saw was taken, but the next one was open, and he claimed it gratefully. Hungry, wet, and exhausted, and the pesky muscle spasm on top of that, he was feeling lousy. He set up his tent clumsily and threw his sleeping gear inside. He filtered some water, lit his stove and got a pan of water heating. His heart sank as he took a look at his food supply. *Good thing I started out with a lot – I lost some but I won't starve. It wasn't like I'd charted out menus, anyway.*

He found a beef stew packet with minimal damage and stirred hot water into it, folded the top down and set it aside so the food could hydrate. He laid out all the packets and divided them into the ones that were intact, and the ones that were battered but usable, and the ones that had big problems. The problem pile was not as big as he had feared, but he wasn't sure what to do with these. He didn't like to waste food. He had to pack it with him no matter what. He made a subcategory of food that was edible but the packets wouldn't hold water. These he could "cook" in a pan or cup. Since he was so hungry now, he threw a collection of wizened little dried vegetables – he wasn't even sure what they all were - into his small pan and poured hot water over them, and put the lid on.

The rest he threw into his garbage bag. These were most of the desserts that had fruits and powdery batter mixes and the pancake and syrup mixes. *Can live without these easily. I'll just be on a diet! That bear must have had a sweet tooth!*

Thinking of his own sweet tooth, he checked in the bottom of his pack for the granola bars and dried fruits. They were still in their bag, thank goodness. He depended on the convenience of these for quick energy when he didn't want to stop for a meal.

The stew and assorted vegetables tasted wonderful. He drank two cups of filtered water and then made a cup of tea. He carried his cup to the edge of the water and sipped tea while he watched the clouds scuttle across the sky. The warm wind still kept the water active. *Need a swim/bath but maybe I'll wait a while. Don't have the energy at the moment. Besides, it'll be nicer when the water is calmer.*

The Long Portage, a downpour, and a portage bear. What a day! Just wait until I tell Luke about this one! Jack smiled. *I'm living my own adventure now.*

Something about that thought brought him deep joy. He was on his own, and he had coped with adversity effectively. He was still glad to be here, even though it had been a hard day. He felt stronger somehow, stronger than yesterday if that was possible.

He had not obsessed about Abby today. He still missed her but he didn't feel hollow like he had. He missed Luke, but knew he could make it without him. Instead of loneliness in the wilderness, he felt a sense of oneness with it, like he could live with less fear and more joy.

This is why I came here. I belong here.

It rained most of the night. Jack slept well until about 4:30, then tossed and turned in a struggle to get comfortable. The back spasm was still with him. He wanted to stretch but the rain outside the tent discouraged that idea, so he pulled his knees up to his chest for a while, and rolled around a bit, then stretched out as far as the tent would let him, then repeated the whole process a few times. By this time he was wide awake and frustrated. He listened to the rain and yawned, but sleep eluded him for a long time.

Dawn caught him dozing. He awoke to the sound of dripping trees, acutely aware of a need to answer nature's call. *At least I got a little more sleep. What a night.*

It was a wet, wet world outside. The sky was still cloudy. Jack contemplated packing up all his wet gear and decided staying another night in this site would be a good thing. He could hopefully dry out and rest up a bit before continuing on his journey. *Some map study would be good, too. And maybe the fish are biting, after all that rain.*

It rained again while Jack was out in the canoe fishing for breakfast. They were biting, though, so he didn't have to stay out long. Back in camp, he retrieved the bear bag, glad it had been somewhat sheltered. He was also glad he'd thought to put a tarp on the top so everything inside was dry. Despite the drizzle he got the coffee going and fried up the fish on his camp stove.

He found a smooth rock in the site that fit in the palm of his hand just like it was poured there. When it was wet it had red and green highlights. He liked it so much, he set it by the door of his tent. A little yoga stretching felt good, but the rain drove him into the tent where he stretched out on his sleeping bag and rested. *If I could just knead that spasm somehow, to loosen it up, that would help. Hey, maybe that rock I found earlier...* Jack unzipped the tent door and grabbed the rock and zipped himself back in. Placing it correctly under his back took some trial and error, but finally he got it in the right place. He gently rolled onto it, leaned into it, counted to ten, then released the pressure. Inching up, he leaned into it again in a nearby spot. About five of these actions and he was ready to remove the rock and roll his back like he had done in the early morning. *My own version of rock & roll!* He rested a while and did another round of "rock & roll," this time singing "Ba-ba-ba, ba-ba-berann," piecing together as many of the words as he could remember. *I think I'm onto something here. Maybe I could market this!*

The sun came out in the middle of the day, and Jack was glad to be outdoors again. A slightly-mauled packet of chili made a good enough lunch. He ate it standing up by the water, admiring the altitude of the Canadian shore of Mountain Lake. This lake was huge! He wondered whether there were trails that would get him up to a view like he'd had of Rose Lake. There probably were, but he didn't even know where to look.

Exploring the area around his campsite, he gathered up some semi-dry firewood. He found a sunny rock and laid the wood out to dry, took off his wet boots and wool socks and laid them in the sun too.

The wind picked up, and Jack looked for a place to sit a while out of the breeze. He discovered a spot where he could lean up against a tree trunk and stretch out his legs quite comfortably, sheltered by a canopy of branches from several nearby trees. He wiggled his toes. He was content to stay in his leafy sanctuary, watching the wind blow drops from the trees. A speck that was more substantive than a raindrop caught his eye. There, not four feet away, was a spider, swinging from an invisible strand. As he watched, its sway was interrupted as it connected with another strand, and it began constructing a web.

Jack was transfixed. The spider traveled long distances, sometimes faster and sometimes slower, seemingly reinforcing the previous run. The subdued afternoon light was such that Jack could clearly see the spider, but not the web – at times the creature seemed to be suspended in space.

There's one destination point on a nearby branch – but where are the other "guy wires" attached? Must be other anchors, but I can't see them. Like God, I guess – I know the Holy Spirit is there but I can't see her.

The spider's diligence is so impressive. She has a goal, and a system, and the skill to make it happen. When the wind blows her, she hangs on and rides it out. She is undaunted. She is my teacher today.

Jack pulled his little notebook from his pocket, found his pencil, and sketched the spider as he watched. An hour went by, then two. The center of the web became evident, then visible, as the sticky silk built up at the hub. Jack wrote "diligence," "goal," and "find a center." The spider made slow circuits around the center of the web in a kind of dance that Jack admired. The periodic kick of a back leg made him think of a samba, though he knew it was function, not fun, for the web-builder. *Or maybe it's fun – what do I know? Doing what you know and doing it well can be fun.*

The afternoon moved along at the spider's sedate pace, until a sudden gust changed everything. A maple seed, a green propeller four times the length of the spider, smacked into the half-made web and stuck! *Emergency!*

Dealing with this intrusion moved to top priority for the web-spinner, since the invisibility of the web insured its effectiveness. The spider rushed to the scene and examined the intruder.

She's probably thinking, 'Is this lunch?' No, not unless you're a vegetarian spider. She's lifting it off the web! I'll be danged. She must be cutting it free somehow! Clever spider.

Within minutes the seed fluttered to the ground. Jack marveled at the ability of this creature to deal with the impediments to its goal. It stayed working in that spot briefly, and Jack imagined she was making repairs. Then she scooted down to a lower quadrant, where a pine needle was caught. In a similar way she cut it free and sent it down to the ground. After this she resumed her circular samba.

When the web was complete, the spider retired to the center. She seemed to rest there a while, but as the wind blew other bits of flora into her trap, she doggedly detached them.

She's teaching me to take interruptions in stride, deal with them, and move on. So you have some rainy days; the sunny days outnumber them. So a bear dined on your food; you can fish and you probably had too much to start with anyway. Set a goal for yourself, deal with the interruptions constructively, and get back on course. And in the process, keep returning to your center: God.

The sun broke through the clouds again and Jack witnessed the invisible made visible: an elaborate web revealed, with its maker in its center. Jack grinned and applauded, and got up stiffly to go fishing. He dropped his little notebook and bent down to retrieve it. As he stood up a powerful wind gust swayed the trees, showering rain on him. He checked on his spider friend and was dismayed to see her web had collapsed into one narrow belt. She was still on it, swinging like she was when he first saw her.

You poor thing! Your beautiful web is ruined. Jack grieved as he thought of all she'd done to make the it. *I can only hope to be as diligent as you are.*

The next day dawned with more clouds than sun, but Jack, a student of the web-building spider, resolved to take all weather in stride. He packed up and was just about ready to load and go when he got the notion to go back to yesterday's "classroom" and see what was happening. He sat for a moment and looked all around, and sure enough, his spider teacher was back, starting a new web. *Thank you, my dear, I've learned a great deal in your class. Keep up the good work.*

Mountain Lake was a long paddle, and Jack just took it easy and slow. His back felt much better today, and he wanted to keep it that way. He admired the scenery and relished the phenomenon of having the U.S. on his right and Canada on his left.

Here's what we call a permeable boundary. The map shows a big dotted line right through these border lakes, so at any given moment I could be in Canadian waters or U.S. waters. Wonder how they decided just where the line goes.

National borders are so arbitrary in a way. I recall my awe at seeing the pictures of the earth from space. We have been so conditioned by globes crowded with names and political lines, I was astonished to see it all looking so whole, so united.

I remember that Jesus prayed "that they may all be one." I'll have to look up the context of that saying. If Luke were here he would just know, I bet. And he would quote lots more interesting scriptures and quotes. I've learned so much from him, and I have so much to learn.

Consulting his map, Jack noticed a campsite with a portage next to it – with the trail leading to a very small lake called Pemmican Lake. This piqued his curiosity, so he kept an eye out and when he found it, and it was unoccupied, he claimed it for a lunch break. After he ate he decided to pull his gear up into the campsite and hike the portage, just for fun.

The trail led uphill for most of its 62 rods, then down to the lake. It was freeing to hike along with no load, swinging his arms and making good time. With a warm sun and rising humidity, he worked up quite a sweat.

Pemmican Lake was pretty, with cliffs rising up on most sides. It seemed especially small after being on the big water of Mountain Lake all morning. Jack sat by the water to soak up the beauty, feeling the privacy of this lake compared to the others. The only way out was the way in, and there was no campsite to make this a destination. *Must be good for fishing – that would be the only reason for coming here.*

It's so secluded. This is a great place for a swim. Without thinking much more about it, Jack peeled off his clothes and his glasses and jumped in. The cold water took his breath away, as it always did, but once he got used to it he was able to swim the breast stroke across the lake. Tiny fishes darted around him, tickling his sensitized skin. He dogpaddled around happily, communing with the residents. When he started to head back, he squinted his nearsighted eyes but couldn't see any landmarks. It all looked pretty much the same. He swam to the other side, expecting to see the trail open up before him on the bank. But it didn't reveal itself.

Can't picture the map in my mind – Don't know the shape of the lake really. Seems like the trail should be right ahead of me, but it's not! Jack dog-paddled along, a little ways out from the bank, searching for a glimpse of the trail or his pile of clothes.

At last he got out of the water and picked his barefoot way along the edge of the lake. Finally he practically stubbed his toe on his clothing, and he breathed a long sigh of relief. His glasses went on first. *Whew!*

Sure feels good to be 'au natural' here in the warm sun! Maybe I'll just put on my boots to protect my feet and walk around a little more to dry off. Once shod he grabbed his clothes and sauntered along the lake's edge. *Wonder if I've lost some weight...I seem a little less pudgy. It's only been a week and a half, but I've had a lot of exercise.* Jack headed up the slope of the trail with gusto, thinking about getting in shape and regaining that sense of health that he once enjoyed. He felt a little decadent, a little silly, a little naughty hiking along with only his boots on. *This is a kick! Never would have imagined myself doing this a month ago.* He grinned at himself.

Should be getting near the end of the trail soon. Should get my clothes on. At this point the trail sloped straight down to Mountain Lake, and Jack could see water ahead. *After the freedom of being naked, clothes will seem an encumbrance.* His good sense won out, though, and he ducked into the trees and dressed before finishing the hike.

It was well into the afternoon by now, so Jack decided to make this campsite his overnight stop. *Hadn't really intended to stay three nights on Mountain Lake, but as long as my food holds out, I'm okay. I'll get an early start tomorrow and see some new territory.*

An afternoon rain shower intruded on his process of setting up camp, but he responded with patience and calm. *Remember the spider! This is just a seed caught in my web. I can deal with it. Wonder what challenges will come next?*

Chapter 13

Jack's third morning on Mountain Lake dawned partly cloudy, with no promise of clear skies but no thunderheads either. Invigorated, he ate and broke camp quickly and slid his canoe into the lake while the day was still young.

In no time at all, it seemed, he arrived at the first portage of the day.

Soon the little Lily Lakes and the Lesser and Greater Cherry Portages were behind him and he embarked on Moose Lake. With his back pain-free, his arms and shoulders feeling strong, and the bonus of wind at his back, Jack powered along on the waters of Moose Lake with ease. In early afternoon he arrived at the marshy Moose Portage, which accompanied the Pigeon River. With his pack and canoe he bogged down in the mud, so he reluctantly decided to make two trips.

As he returned to the landing for his canoe, he spied the group with the fashion-conscious redhead approaching the portage. He remembered their life jacket incident several days before. He stepped off the trail into the woods to be out of their way while they landed their canoes and piled out. The boys, and one man, tossed Duluth packs and paddles from canoes to land, hopped out, shouldered the canoes and set out. The woman and girls, less businesslike about the excursion, fussed over the packs, choosing their preferred loads. Jack watched with interest as the red-haired girl loudly proclaimed, "I'll carry two packs this time." He melted into the trees to observe.

"Are you sure, Mandy?" the woman asked with some surprise. "Amy, Lizzie, would you help her?" She adjusted her own pack, grabbed some paddles, looked back to check on the girls and followed the boys down the trail.

A tall girl held a pack up behind Mandy to facilitate the project, and she slipped her arms through the straps in practiced form. Another girl held a second pack up in front of her and she clumsily got her arms through the straps. As soon as the girl let go, though, Mandy's arms flew out, she flapped a minute, and toppled, front-pack first, onto the ground. "Help me!" she wailed, "I can't get up!" She flailed her arms and legs, tantrum-like.

The other girls doubled up with laughter. "You look like a turtle!" they shrieked. Jack held his breath and squeezed his eyes shut to keep from giving himself away. Only when their gales of laughter subsided could they help their friend out of the dual packs. They all agreed they were glad the boys had already gone. Jack stood unmoving in the trees until they had reorganized and tromped past him, chattering and giggling and making a pact never to tell the boys.

Jack chortled and stalled a bit so he wouldn't be too near the little party. Soon he lifted the canoe on his shoulders and navigated the Moose Portage, collected his pack and got acquainted with North Fowl Lake. He noticed an island campground on the map, in the waters between North and South Fowl. He set his sights on it, heading south, still following the border chain. He noticed a few cabins – a resort perhaps – on the American side, checked the map and realized that both of these lakes were outside the BWCAW boundary.

Since the "portage turtle incident" he had seen only two craft, a kayak and a canoe; one certainly couldn't say the lake was crowded. Nonetheless, the island campsite was taken. As he passed by he heard a man and woman arguing. He couldn't catch many words, but their voices bristled with irritation, and they kept interrupting each other.

Hearing the couple bicker brought back memories. Until now Jack had only replayed the most wonderful parts of his life with Abby. But like the pair he'd just heard, he and

Abby had squabbled. They'd argued about money: *She was obsessed with saving. But what's the point of having money, if you can't spend it?* In their premarital counseling, Luke had told them that spenders and savers usually marry each other; it's one of the checks and balances of a relationship. He said they'd probably always disagree about money…the important things were to fight fair and not keep secrets.

We lived up to that, as far as I know. Haven't found any surprises in our finances. Wonder what Abby would have thought of all my camping purchases. Probably would have barely tolerated that, but she would've hated the idea of buying a second car on top of everything else. That would have been an argument!

I like the Volvo, though, and I needed a change. Not that I really needed two cars. But I don't want to get rid of the old Toyota just yet – it's like an old pal. Jack felt stubborn, almost like he was in an argument with Abby. He thought about that. *Besides, I can always sell the Volvo if I get tired of it.* He gave a wry chuckle. *I never would have admitted that to Abby!*

He paddled on into South Fowl and set up camp in a site there. The afternoon was so warm and surprisingly sunny that when he finished he wished he had shorts to wear. Then he remembered the "convertible" feature of the pants he'd bought. *How the heck do these things work?* He unzipped one side and the bottom part of the leg fell right off. He unzipped the other. *Voila! Shorts!* They felt a bit odd with the zipper around the edge, but at least he was cooler.

In the late afternoon he enjoyed catching and releasing walleye pike, keeping one for dinner.

In the evening, having finished looking up the list of scriptures Luke had recommended, he started reading the Gospel according to Luke. He was intrigued by the unfamiliar first chapter. He got a big kick out of Zechariah, an old priest who was struck dumb for being incredulous at the news that his aging wife Elizabeth was pregnant. Jack couldn't remember hearing this part of the story in church; he only remembered Mary visiting Elizabeth when they were pregnant with Jesus and John respectively. He wondered how many other surprises lay ahead.

Jack put himself in Zechariah's shoes…sandals. *If I had learned that I would be a father in my grandfather years, I would be astonished too! Speechless! But I can't imagine being mute for the entire nine months of pregnancy. They must have developed an elaborate sign language and mes-sage-writing. Says he wrote on a tablet that the baby's name would be John rather than Zech Jr. so he was definitely literate. I would have been writing all the time. I can just see the stacks and stacks of stone tablets all over the house and yard…*

Jack read on. He smiled as he recognized the Christmas story, but was startled by the jump from Jesus' birth to an incident at age twelve, then to his Baptism as an adult. The parables were especially fun to read – Jack had a deep appreciation for good use of symbolism. He'd never read scripture consecutively, and it shed new light on well-known passages while he discovered texts he'd never heard before. He wished Luke were here to answer questions, though. He had plenty.

Jack was vaguely aware of a rain shower in the night, but awoke to a morning bathed in bright light. The clouds had gone and the morning truly sparkled. Leaves shone with a deep green. The aroma of moist earth was overlaid with sumptuous fresh air. Sunlight danced on the water and the birds sang, inviting Jack into the day's adventures.

Jack saw on the map that his most direct route was to double back north, between two islands, then south into a bay to locate the portage to Royal Lake and River. This turned out to be harder than it looked; the passage between the islands was choked with tall reeds. *Like paddling through a giant toothbrush!* Visibility diminished; he could see only reeds on every side. He felt disoriented. He finally cast aside good sense and decided to stand up in the canoe to get a look ahead. He got his feet under him in a crouch, grasping the gunwales, gingerly released his grip and slowly raised himself up, trying to stay centered in the craft. *Keep centered. Like the heron.* His heart pounded with the effort and risk.

Once standing, Jack could see that the channel eventually opened up, and he just had to bear a little to his left and he'd be on course. Seeing it gave him hope to keep slogging through the marsh. He lowered himself down too fast, lost his balance, set the canoe to rocking and landed ungracefully, but thankfully, in the canoe. He straightened himself into his seat and took a few deep breaths, trying to get his heart to slow to normal. He looked around to see if anyone had observed him, and seeing no one, sighed with relief. "Good job, little Independence," he said, patting the canoe's side fondly.

Eons later, Jack emerged on the other side of the marsh. He still had to maneuver among small islands and into the bay. He searched for the portage. The entry was confusing; he had to land and walk along the rocky shore to find the trail. It seemed peculiar until he realized that this must vary seasonally with the water level.

This route would take him west, away from the border, heading back to East Bearskin and his vehicle. He would inevitably follow the same route he and Luke had taken, but his current plan was to take it in the opposite direction, giving him a different perspective.

"How I Spent My Summer Vacation: I got a different perspective." Jack chuckled at himself. *Already I'm feeling like a different guy. And I like this guy better than the one I was back in Minnetonka.*

Let's see, what day is this? Luke left on a Saturday...then I remember it was Wednesday when I first hit Mountain Lake and I stayed three nights there, Thursday, Friday, out Saturday – this must be ... Monday. Been here two weeks so far, and I'm lovin' it! Wish I could stay forever! The fresh air, the wide sky, the trees and the water...this is a great life!

Jack paddled up the Royal River, which was swampy but not as bad as what he'd just experienced. The map, peppered with marsh symbols, had clued him in so he wasn't surprised. Royal Lake barely qualified as a lake, he thought; more of a puddle in the reeds. *Hardly worthy of such an auspicious name.* The channel was clear enough to navigate though, and he was grateful for that. He passed an open campsite right near where John Lake and the river met, thought a minute and doubled back to claim it. He could easily have continued on further, but the sun was so hot all he could think about was a swim. *Not into making progress today, I guess. Just want to relax. I can do that.*

This campsite did not provide solitude, however. Compared to the Border Chain, this junction saw heavy traffic. Jack started to set up his tent, then paused and stood looking at the lake. Fists on his hips, he contemplated his options.

Canoe after canoe – never seen such a steady stream. And on a Monday, too. Must be because there's public access south of here. I don't want to camp in Grand Central Station. Think I'll paddle on and see what lies ahead. I'll get that swim sometime. If I try it here I might be pummeled by paddles!

Jack begrudgingly repacked his tent and other gear and set out again in his canoe. To his delight, an available site soon appeared on the northern shore. He repeated his process of claiming the site and this time set up the tent, feeling grateful for the second chance.

What was it I was just reading in the Gospel according to Luke about second chances? Jesus told a parable about a fig tree that wasn't producing. The owner wanted to rip it out because it was wasting soil. But the gardener said he'd dig around it and fertilize it and give it another year.

I feel like Jesus is giving me a second chance to bear fruit. Been pretty dormant as I've tried to avoid dealing with my grief. Maybe now that I'm healing emotionally I will do better. Maybe the wilderness is providing my cultivation and fertilizer!

On a hot afternoon, nothing compared to swimming. Lakes in the Boundary Waters never became what you would call warm – but in the late afternoon after the sun had helped it along a little, Jack found the water welcoming.

He swam a few strokes out, flipped over on his back and just floated. With each inhale his chest rose up, more buoyant with his lungs full. With each exhale his body leveled out peacefully. The water cooled him from below, the sun warmed him from above. He felt the support of the water under him, holding him, suspending him. *This is like God's grace, holding me up, supporting me. Like being held in the palm of God's hand.*

A cloud passing in front of the sun caught his attention, changing his sense of light and warmth. Yet his sense of safety and serenity remained. *Nothing can separate us from the love of God,* he remembered. *I am a beloved child of God.*

That evening after dinner, Jack brought out the bag with Luke's Bible and Abby's journal. *Which to read? Both are getting a little easier.*

He chose the journal and opened it to the next entry.

Every once in a while Jack brings up the subject of children again. We are too old now, well almost. Seems like the definition of too old has changed. But my mind hasn't changed. I love teaching, but I only like kids if they're someone else's.

When I think of having children I picture a giant ball and chain. All I can think about is that we would be totally committed to that responsibility for our whole lives. To have a baby totally dependent on us for everything – to have it in my womb totally dependent on me for life itself – I just can't bear the thought. I know I'm selfish but I just don't want to make the sacrifices that would be demanded. And so much is demanded of the mother, more than the father I think.

And when Jack talks about it he says "I just wonder what our kids would turn out to be like." That just seems so trivial and superficial and unconcerned and uninformed and distant and mild. Tonight all I could say was "I don't." I really don't.

I guess I just don't have the drive to parent that most women have. Why else would they take the leap? Maybe it's a hormonal thing that overrides selfishness, and I don't have it. It's a good thing the world isn't filled with people like me – the future of the species would be at risk! I like children OK, but I don't go crazy for them like some women do. And I love teenagers and most people don't. Maybe the world needs just a few people like me.

Thank God for birth control and thank God Jack goes along with me. It would be awful if he felt really strongly about being a parent. I guess I can put up with his idle musing since he doesn't insist on having his way.

He just appeared in the doorway with an amorous look in his eye! Hmmm, wonder what will happen next!

Jack smiled to think about Abby, her adamant view on children and her joy in their lovemaking. They'd argued about kids, but fortunately he hadn't felt a strong need to be a father. He was open, but not insistent. *She was dead-set against – oh, gosh, don't use that term!* Jack cringed at his own terminology. He turned to another page to distract himself.

November 14, 1997

The speaker at today's in-service talked about the stresses and fears middle school kids have in their lives. As he talked about their fears — of failure, not fitting in, not meeting others' expectations, losing loved ones...I couldn't help thinking about my own fears. The only way I could get back to concentrating on the speaker was by promising myself I would journal tonight. I had to dig to find this notebook — haven't written in it in over a year. Guess it's time.

What am I afraid of?
Losing Jack
getting pregnant
doing badly at my job
letting people down
getting old
getting sick
becoming bored or boring
meaninglessness
spiders
undercooked chicken
guns

I could go on and on. Some are silly, like spiders.

And for that matter, it's silly to be afraid of growing old. Of course I'm going to get old! Everyone does. Why waste energy *worrying about it? But I do! I dread having parched, wrinkled skin. I don't want to have that wattle under my chin that older women get. I can already see how gravity is pulling me down all over my body. I'm really going to have to watch what I eat, because fat sticks to me more than ever. I hate it! And I look at my mom, and how her mind and memory are deserting her, and I am terrified of being like that. I don't want to be a burden to Jack or anybody else!*

To be really honest (that's what journals are for, right?) I'm afraid of Jack's aging too. What if his mind leaves him? What if he's in a wheelchair or bedridden? What if he gets really temperamental? I love him, but I don't know if I could be a caregiver. I don't think I have what it takes. I'm not very patient. His brilliant mind is what I love most about him, and if that goes I don't know how I would handle it. It's too scary to think about.

Jack was stunned by this. To think that Abby had felt such a fear of growing old, and now she never would… the horrible irony of it gave him chills. He sat paralyzed, staring out at the lake for a long, long time, listening to the loons call.

It's unfathomable to me that God would take such an admission of fear and make it come true by taking her life. That just doesn't make one bit of sense to me. God loves us! We are beloved children of God – Abby was a beloved child of God! God wouldn't kill her!

Luke said he doesn't believe in a puppeteer God. So that means God is not at the control panel, making everything happen. Abby's death wasn't a punishment and it wasn't a misguided answer to prayer. It just happened. It was an ACCIDENT.

Jack clasped his hands behind his head and pulled his elbows forward, hugging his head with his arms, eyes squeezed shut. "It was an ACCIDENT. It was an ACCIDENT," he repeated aloud until he felt he could believe it.

Unfolding his protective embrace and rubbing his neck, Jack opened his eyes to see a loon flap loudly across the lake's surface. *So where is God in all this? Luke says "God is good...all the time."*

Jack rested a while with this thought. *God provides some goodness even in the midst of – or aftermath of – tragedy. We don't always perceive it, or reach out to receive it.*

So one of the tiny bits of goodness out of her death is that she never had to face growing old. And she didn't have to contend with me growing old. Small blessings, but they are something to hold onto. If she had lived, God would have helped her cope. But she died, and she never had to face that fear.

Wow.

The next day Jack set out to East Pike, on to West Pike, Clearwater, Caribou, and Pine. *Never tire of the beauty of this place. In a way each day's view is the same: water, trees, sky. But each lake has its own charm. It's important to notice the details that set them apart. Will I be able to remember any of them distinctly next year or the year after? No camera, just have to hold the images in my mind.*

Johnson Falls, west of Pine Lake, was a must-see. Luke had recommended it when they were here before; Jack remembered how Luke had been anxious about getting his sermon done so they had passed it by. *Wonder how that sermon went. Such an amazing feeling to hear him share it with me alone.*

Jack left his canoe and pack out of the way of other trippers and hiked in. He spent considerable time near the falls, contemplating the vitality and power of water. *I admire the way it's all involved in such action – moving, splashing, eroding, sculpting – a part of its environment and slowly changing it too. Each tiny drop is part of the whole. Alone a droplet would not be so powerful, but together they are changing the earth!*

Makes me think of some of the great nonviolent movements of the world, like Gandhi, and Martin Luther King, Jr. and the dramatic democratization of eastern Europe in the late 80's. They needed the critical mass of many people to effect change – no one alone could have done it. Like a waterfall, they changed their own society with their persistence and sheer volume. Wonder where in the world the next radical change will occur. Wonder what's happening in the world this summer. These ponderings accompanied him back down the river to Pine Lake and his gear.

Without reservation he took the switchbacks that had been such a controversy when he and Luke had passed this way. Now in the third week of his journey, he knew he was fit enough; his stamina had increased dramatically. *No more "sofa spud" – but not yet what you'd call a "stud!" There's a poem in there somewhere...* He knew he'd lost weight; he was cinching his belt tighter to keep his pants and shorts up. It wasn't only because of all the exercise; for the past week he had been eating lightly because his food supply was dwindling.

The 232 rod portage with its changes of altitude and terrain took concentration, so Jack postponed his decision-making until his next long paddle, which would be Alder. After that he would be on East Bearskin and he would need a plan. It had been too easy to procrastinate.

A short paddle across Canoe Lake and a 22-rod portage brought him to Alder Lake. Before he got into his canoe again, Jack thought it might feel good to stretch. He closed his eyes, raised his arms high over his head, inhaled and stretched up tall like a candle, then keeping his arms and hands stretched out as far as he could, he opened them out to shoulder level. He swung his arms around, twisting at the waist, did a couple of jumping jacks, and finally shook his whole body. He heard the putt-putt of a boat motor coming near.

"Do you need help?" a voice called.

Jack's eyes popped open, and he saw a blond man about his age calling from an old aluminum fishing boat with a 5-horse motor. The boat was heading his way. "No, I'm fine! Just stretching!" *How embarrassing! How totally embarrassing! I'm such a dork!*

The man smiled with amusement, waved and changed direction back into the lake. "Allllllrighty then!" he called over his shoulder.

"Thanks for asking, though!" Jack added as an afterthought. He chuckled. *Luke will love this story!* He laughed and shook his head. As he launched his canoe he laughed further and imagined Luke joining in the joke.

Into the waters of Alder Lake, he forced himself to get serious and focus on his future. *Could get in the car and go back to Minnetonka. Could maybe stop at a motel first, get cleaned up, have a nice dinner and a good night's sleep in a bed, then drive south the next morning. The shower-dinner-bed part sounds good. But then what? Go back to my lonely townhouse, no job—or at least uncertainty about a job—and nothing really to do. Don't even know if I'll be moving to another place to teach. Once I know, if I am relocating, I can start to pack. Suppose I need to clear out Abby's clothes and things.* He felt a sting of dread at this task.

Could get together with Luke and tell him about my adventures. Wait, though – he was going to some big church meeting sometime around now. Have to wait for him to get back. His heart sank and the old familiar loneliness started to creep over him. He shook his head.

Not ready yet. Don't want to go back. Being solitary here is better than being lonely in the city. Still have some demons to confront, some healing to do, some ideas to develop. I need to stay in the Boundary Waters.

That much was decided. Now he needed to figure out the particulars. Luke had mentioned Sawbill Outfitters, on Sawbill Lake. He could drive there and get food and advice, and figure out where to explore next. *Maybe they even have showers.*

Chapter 14

After the serenity of the wilderness, Sawbill Outfitters felt overwhelming. When Jack walked in he felt bowled over by the artificial light, the colorful displays, and the cheerful chatter of staff and patrons. He hadn't really prepared himself for this reentry into the commercial world.

He felt suddenly self-conscious about his scruffy appearance, then realized he wasn't the only one; some of the others looked pretty bedraggled too. He was pleased to see a sign indicating showers and laundry.

Eager to get his questions out on the table, he waited for a staff person. When his turn came, he explained that he had been traveling on a permit for East Bearskin, and now he wanted to go to a different area of the BWCAW. Did he need another permit, and if so, how could he get it?

The answer was better than he had anticipated. Yes, he needed a new permit, but they could do a quick request and have one ready for him in about two hours! Next he inquired about outfitting him with food, and that also was possible within the same time frame. In one Duluth pack they could fit enough for about three weeks. Showers, saunas, and laundry were available here for a modest price, first come first served. They advised getting in line soon because a large group was due in. If he would just fill out these forms...

Jack went out to the screen porch to complete the form for the permit and the menu requests. He handed them in, paid for his shower and towel and got coins and soap for the laundry. The sauna had sounded good at first, but the day was so hot he decided against it. Following the signs outside to a separate building, he happily started some laundry. He had so few clothes along, it was only a small load. He looked down at the shorts and shirt he was wearing and realized they needed washing as much as the rest, if not more so. So he trotted off to the shower building with his pack, located his swimsuit, which he had rarely worn, and put it on. He trotted back to the laundry with his pack, and threw the rest of his clothes into the washer. He couldn't remember what he'd done with the packet of soap, so he searched through the pack and finally found it—why had he thrown it in there? He felt clumsy operating the coin washer. At last he got the load going sudsily.

Back to the shower house – *augh! A horde of teenage boys swarming the place!* This must be the big group he'd been warned about. He felt silly in his swimsuit and fussed around with his pack for something to do. The showers were all going full blast, with steam rolling out. He saw an opening at a mirror, wiped the mist away and saw a stranger looking back at him. Suddenly oblivious to the cacophony around him, he stared at the image in the glass.

He had not seen his face in two and a half weeks. He'd never seen himself bearded. His eyes reflected back his astonishment, then critique, then bemused pleasure. The beard was coming in nicely, salt and pepper which surprised him a little. His moustache needed trimming already. He got out his pocketknife, pulled out the scissors, and gave it a try. This would take some practice, he decided, but so far so good. While he was at it he trimmed the hair over his ears.

Stepping back to look again, Jack could see that his face had slimmed somewhat. His skin was tanned and his eyes sparkled with life. Recalling the image he saw at home before he left, this was definitely an improvement.

Someone was trying to rally the teenagers and hurry them out. Jack noted that these boys were just as fussy as females about their appearance, and this was wilderness! There must be girls in their group, he decided. He still had time to put away his knife and clean the clippings out of the sink before he finally had a chance at a shower.

The warm water cascaded over his body, melting off the grime he'd been unable to swim away. *Ahhhh, this is good. Some amenities I do miss.* He took his time with the soap and shampoo, then dried himself with the fresh rented towel. Back in his swimsuit, he headed back to the laundry, transferred his clothes to the dryer, remembering at the last minute to pull out the quick-dry underwear.

Now what do I do? Another half hour until I have clean clothes to put on...lucky thing it's a hot day. A swimsuit is not altogether out of place. He shouldered his half-empty pack and walked over to the dumpsters to get rid of his trash. Next he strolled to his left, across the road to the campground, where signs pointed to a boat launch on Sawbill Lake. There he sat contentedly on a log, watching the group of teens get organized to begin their journey. Aware of the frustration of the leaders trying to corral their energies, he was thankful his was a solo odyssey.

When the excitement died down with the group's departure, Jack decided to clean out his pack. He unrolled the sleeping bag, unzipped it and shook it out. He considered washing it but decided he didn't want to wait for it to dry. He let it air out a bit while he took everything out of his pack and upended it to let the pine needles and other souvenirs fall out. He'd been careful with washing his cook kit and dishes, so they were fine. He packed everything up again and headed back to the laundry.

Jack rolled his clean clothes the way Luke had taught him, so they fit compactly with his other gear. He did such a good job, the pack was barely half full. *Getting another whole pack full of food too. Maybe I'll equalize them. Not looking forward to having two packs for portaging; that means a lot of doubling back.*

Maybe I'll just find an amenable site and stay there a while. As I recall the limit is two weeks in one place. Might be interesting to stay put for a couple of weeks and see how that feels.

Now fully attired in a clean t-shirt and shorts, Jack ventured into the Outfitter store again. He still had quite a bit of time until his permit and food would be ready. He enjoyed examining all the products available to make the wilderness more homey: a battery-operated fan, a multi-tool with pliers and a magnifying glass, a solar shower, even a collapsible kitchen sink! He was already well outfitted, so he didn't want to acquire too much more. But he did select a small mirror, fuel for his camp stove, and a mosquito net that went over the head and fastened with elastic under the arms. It looked goofy in the picture on the package, but it seemed like it would really do the trick with those evening swarms.

When he paid for his purchases, he greeted an older gentleman sitting on a stool near the cashier. The man looked at Jack's shirt and said, "Pilgrim Point Camp – you been there?"

"Sure, several times. Our church has a retreat every summer, and once I helped out at a work camp."

"I helped secure that property for the church, some 40 years ago."

"Really! It's a beautiful spot. It's great for swimming, and boating. I love to walk out on the point at sunset. That property is worth a pretty penny now."

"Yup."

Jack paid for his items and got out of the way of the next customer. Then as an afterthought, he turned back to the man and said, "Thank you for getting Pilgrim Point so we can enjoy it." He was rewarded with a beaming smile and a gracious nod.

His permit indicated that he would enter on Brule Lake. Jack didn't really care where he went, as long as it was different from where he'd been. He found a map that included Brule. He paid for the food pack and the map, and assured the staffer that he had everything else he needed. She explained a few things, but he was feeling impatient to get going, so she cut the narrative short with "Any questions?"

"No, it looks great. Thank you."

This Duluth pack of food outweighed the one with his gear, so he put the new one on his back and clumsily carried his own by the top handle. Once he had loaded them in the car he consulted the map and drove to Brule Lake on gravel roads, which took longer than he expected. The parking area at Brule was fairly full when he got there; in fact, one might consider it a traffic jam. Just as he parked a group of nine young Boy Scouts and leaders launched in four canoes.

It was late afternoon when he locked the Volvo and prepared to shove off in the Independence, laden with provisions for the weeks ahead. A man and his daughter – maybe 10 years old – came in as he was going out. "Just heading out?" the man asked.

Interesting question. In a way it's obvious that I'm heading out, but I'm not starting my journey. How to answer? Go for simple: "Yup."

"We've just been out four days. It's been great! Have a good time!"

Four days. Try four weeks! Jack just smiled and waved his paddle. "Thanks!"

The scouts had formed a flotilla and the leaders were giving instructions. "Don't stand up in the canoe! That's a sure way to make it tip!"

Ah, Canoeing 101. All of a sudden Jack felt like a seasoned expert. He could paddle a straight line (well, almost straight), and he could do it for hours. He'd learned to navigate well, to find campsites and portages, and how to plan his day. High wind and choppy water didn't alarm him as it once did. He didn't panic in the face of adversity, except for that bear… All in all he felt pretty confident.

Jack consulted his map. Brule Lake showed a myriad of islands, many with campsites. *In a way I want to explore new territory; in another way I want to find a site for an extended stay. This lake is so busy, it may not be the right spot. But island sites always intrigue me. I'm sure riding low in the water with the addition of the food pack. It's late enough in the day; find a site here on Brule. If I don't like it, I can move on tomorrow.*

The map was only somewhat helpful. There were con-siderably more islands than it showed. He located one campsite easily – on a point of an island, it was wide open and he could see a green tent and a brown one. In another he saw someone with an orange shirt through the trees. More paddling around a large crescent-shaped island, and he saw a site. He landed and climbed up the hill hopefully, but heard voices. A man came to greet him and Jack said, "Sorry-just checking to see if it's occupied."

"Our canoe is gone because we forgot the tent poles—my wife went back to get them. Good thing we're local!" The man was wearing a red t-shirt with VOLUNTEER in big letters. He offered, "There's another site east of here, on this island, and it's taken. There's one north that's nice – it might be open."

I must have missed that one – I came that way. What about this one on Brule Island?" he asked, pointing at the map.

"I don't know about that one. I saw a canoe headed that way when we came in."

"Thanks – I'd better get searching." Jack waved and got in his canoe and set off smoothly. He rounded the large island and saw the eastern site the man had mentioned. There was no canoe so he got out and took a peek—but when he saw a blue tent he returned to the water. On to Brule Island; he thought he saw a grassy landing on the south side, but the map clearly indicated that the site was on the north side. The cross wind was making the water choppy, so he was glad when he got to the eastern tip. Round the point he had to paddle into the wind, though, and he found this much harder. Again he thought he saw a landing, but it was mighty rocky. He continued on around another point and saw yet another rocky landing, with a possible clearing above. He clambered out of the canoe and wedged it in the rocks.

The clearing was only a clearing. It might be a lunch spot but there was no fire grate or anything. So back to the canoe. He'd go back to the spot he'd passed by and just see.

This stop bore fruit. The landing was rocky and precarious, but he got the canoe secured and climbed up the steep slope to find a huge campsite with room for several tents. The lake was visible on the opposite side, and sure enough, a grassy "lawn" sloped down to a picture-perfect landing! *That was the first place I saw and passed by!* He didn't feel so expert now.

He plopped his hat at the fire circle to claim the site and climbed back down to the canoe. *Easier to paddle around than cart my two packs and canoe up that slope!* The south side proved an easy entry—in fact the easiest he'd ever seen. He steered right up onto gently sloping sand, stepped out on the "beach" and pulled the canoe onto a grassy lawn. The landing was only a couple of yards wide but ample for the purpose. Evergreens bordered this area on the other three sides, making it feel like a back yard. It even had dandelions and clover mixed with the grass. *I'll call this the 'south lawn'. If I only had a croquet set – although the slope would send all the balls toward the lake!*

The site had a small, sunny meadow in its center, colorful with various grasses, occasional daisies, and two ancient gray stumps. On the south edge of the little meadow the fire circle offered a great view of the lake. Paths led in several directions from the open center. *Can hardly wait to explore! But first things first – set up the tent. And cover my knees – the bugs are biting.* He chose a tent spot on the west edge of the meadow, near the trees. *Perfectly flat, with shade to the west and a view of the lake from the front door – ideal! And are these wild raspberries nearing ripeness? Yes! Right outside my door!*

Tent up, pant legs zipped on, he started to explore further. The wooded path to the east took him a short distance to the point of the island. En route back, a small clearing with a level stump seat delighted him. *Could be a meditation spot!* From the meadow, two northerly paths led to the lake, one of which had been his steep initial entry.

Heading south past the fire circle to the shore, Jack stepped carefully out onto a broad flat boulder jutting into the lake. Hands on his hips, he gazed out over the scene, the silvery blue of the water contrasting with the deep green of the forest on the island opposite. The breeze ruffled his hair. *Beauty, beauty, beauty.*

After a few moments of grateful reverie, Jack continued his examination of his new site. The boulder on which he stood provided excellent access to lake water for filtering. Kneeling here he could set the pan on a smaller rock and do the job easily. He turned back toward the shore and stepped carefully off the boulder. *What is this plant? It looks familiar...* Jack plucked a leaf and looked more carefully. Rubbing it released a refreshing scent: *Mint! Gosh, I have mint here! How amazing! I can garnish my meals! Maybe I can make mint tea!* Jack held onto the leaf and brought it to his nose again as he headed back to the meadow.

The path to the west had a small clearing about the size of a shower stall. Jack craned his neck around and spied something red. *A spigot – a solar shower! Cool!* He'd seen these at the outfitters: a 12" by 6" heavy plastic pouch, black on one side and clear on the other so you could lay it in the sun and warm the water. It was hanging by a hole from a short branch, high enough that the spigot was at shoulder height. A little water remained at the bottom. A big stopper secured the hole for filling. *This is great! A real outdoor shower! I will enjoy this!* Jack chuckled and rubbed his hands with glee as he continued his exploration. The path ultimately led to the biffy, which he could tell hadn't been used in a while. *Shower was left here some time ago. Bet they missed it once they realized it'd been left behind. Or maybe it was left as a gift – that little spot is so perfect for a shower.*

Jack took his camp chair to the "south lawn" and enjoyed his surroundings. He observed a sparrow-sized bird with a speckled body, white chest, and what looked like cocoa spilled under its chin. *Wonder what that is? And here's a bird that spends a lot of time on the ground – I've never seen that before. Whoa – was that a hummingbird? I'm in an aviary!*

This site seemed so domesticated, with its grass, dandelions, mint, clover, and daisies. Jack hadn't seen this kind of vegetation in the Boundary Waters before. *Maybe this was once a cabin site. Maybe someone actually lived here! Could have been a hunting or trapping camp in the old days. That doesn't explain the dandelions, though. Maybe the seeds have come in on our shoes.*

Questions unanswered, Jack started to think about dinner. He had the luxury of some fresh food awaiting him. As he passed the fire circle, he noted that the previous residents had left four fine roasting sticks, one with a double fork. *Could use these for my steak!*

Soon he had a roaring fire in the grate. While he let it die down, he cut the meat in chunks and skewered them on the green sticks. He liked the meat best when it was hot, so he alternated the sticks so he could eat one chunk while grilling the next. It took a long time, but he had plenty of time. He warmed slices of wheat bread and tried wrapping bread around the meat. *Delicious!*

Leaning back in his camp chair by the fire, with a full stomach, watching the lake enter its evening quiet, Jack sighed deeply. *This spot is excellent. Definitely can live here a while.*

The mosquitoes started to come out, and he donned his goofy new mesh hood. *By golly, this thing works! Enjoy the sunsets without being munched by hungry bugs. Blurry view through the net, but I can live with that. So nice to be outside instead of sequestered in the tent or slathered with Deet.* He had to get a jacket, though, to cover his arms. Then the pesky bugs went after his ankles, so he had to tuck his pant legs into his socks. *Every site has its drawbacks –this one has a high population of ravenous mosquitoes.*

He swatted at a mosquito on his hand and remembered Abby.

To celebrate her birthday last summer, they had gone out to dinner at a very nice restaurant recommended by one of her colleagues. It was during Sommerfest, the eclectic celebration of music every July in Minneapolis. They had attended a Symphony concert – he couldn't remember now what they'd heard – but he remembered how beautiful Abby had looked. She had worn a tight black dress with tiny straps. She had piled her hair up on her head in a way that looked casually done, but he knew she'd taken great care until it was just right. Her bare shoulders, rarely seen in public, excited him. She'd worn the opal necklace he'd given her for her birthday. He closed his eyes, and he could see her clearly, almost smell her perfume.

The aesthetic memory disintegrated as he remembered the dopey part of the evening. As they walked out of the Symphony Hall into the hot summer night, they encountered a hubbub of activity, with food booths and their clientele, and a jazz combo playing in the courtyard. Delighted by this abrupt change she compelled him to stay for a glass of wine and to listen to the music. He trudged off to fulfill this wish – he really wanted to go home to their bed – and returned with two glasses of wine. But her delight had changed to frustration: the mosquitoes were biting, and she had red welts on her lovely shoulders, her arms and hands! Mosquitoes loved her as much as he did. Trying to resist scratching was clearly taking a toll on her patience. She drank her wine as quickly as possible (he just left his) and they walked briskly to the car, complaining that the city or county or somebody was supposed to spray for the little beasts.

Why do I remember dumb stuff like this? Wish I could separate the wheat from the chaff and only retain the best parts. Mosquitoes, how mundane. He gave one a good slap for Abby, thankful that at least he wasn't as tasty to them as she was. In fact, he'd teased that he liked being around her because she attracted all the bugs and he was pretty much left alone.

But that birthday night, oh, she was so stunning. That's the image I want to remember forever. Lingering over this mental picture, Jack sighed and closed his eyes again. Suddenly they popped open. *That was her birthday! July 18! What the heck day is it today?*

What was normally a simple question took some calculation on his part. He took a roasting stick, shone his flashlight on the ground, and charted the weeks in the dirt. *Luke and I left on June 28, then I was up on the border route for a week and a half, then down to the outfitters and here today...that would make this...July 18! Would have been her birthday today!*

Happy Birthday, dear Abby! Oh, my dear, dear Abby. He reminded himself again what Luke had said about letting the feelings come. Sure enough, deep breathing gave permission to his tears, and rather than squeezing them back he let them flow. *This gets easier with practice, I guess. If Luke's right, the tears will be cleansing and healing.* At least no one could see him here, while he let the feelings wash over him.

After a day on the island, Jack concluded this site was perfect for a spiritual retreat with a group, because each person could have a private meditation spot. With the whole campsite to himself, he luxuriated in migrating from one area to another. He favored the south lawn for its morning sun; in the heat of the day he found shade and seclusion sitting on the stump in the trees. He discovered a tiny cove west of the south lawn that gave the best sunset view. In the evening light, when the lake was like glass, he could see every beautiful stone on the lake bottom in the shallow cove.

In these conducive times and places Jack sometimes read the Bible or reread parts of Abby's journal, and sometimes he just thought. In the Bible he had finished Luke's Gospel, so he went on to read the Gospel according to John, finding it to be written in a style quite different from Luke. John's use of metaphors for Jesus delighted him. *Light of the World, Living Water, Shepherd...these are great! I should use this text in class, to teach metaphor. But I don't know, maybe the people who take the Bible literally would struggle with that. It's most likely against the separation of church and state anyway. I should learn more about that.*

From John's gospel Jack kept reading, discovering Acts of the Apostles to be a fascinating account of the growth of the early church. *Paul was one crazy guy; he sure did a one-eighty. I have to admire his perseverance. I can't figure out some of his speeches, but he sure drew people together and created community wherever he went. That's probably what kept him going.* Jack read and re-read a short passage in the middle of the 14th chapter:

Certain Jews from Antioch and Iconium came and persuaded the people, who stoned Paul, and assuming he was dead, they dragged him out of the city. The disciples stood around him, and he got up and went into the city; and the next day he left with Barnabas for Derbe.

Paul must have been pretty bad off if they left him for dead. But when his friends gathered around him, he got enough strength to get up. Wow. And then he didn't rest and recover for a few days – the next day they continued their journey! Such determination. Probably safer to 'get outta Dodge' anyway. And there's healing in the journey, as I'm discovering.

After Abby died I really didn't let people gather around me like that, literally or figuratively. It might have helped. Jack thought and prayed about this for a while.

Maybe, after I get back, I can be the kind of person who 'gathers around' other folks who have been through a loss. Like Luke helped me. I can encourage them to do a better job than I did at dealing with the grief. Jack sighed deeply.

This contemplative life had its rewards, but one major drawback: Jack wasn't sleeping well. After such vigorous activity each day for the past two and a half weeks, his body couldn't adapt to the lack of exercise. Feeling wide awake one night, he donned long pants and a jacket and the new mosquito net hood and went out to sit on the log in the fire ring. Even though he felt perfectly lucid, he didn't think clearly or constructively in the wee hours of the morning. He obsessed about what kind of job he might be heading for. He worried about his teaching skills. And of course, he lamented Abby's loss.

Bored with this sleeplessness, he got stern with himself. *This 'poor me' line of thinking is getting old. I miss Abby, and I always will, but I can move on with my life. I have to.* He paused, considering how he would find the strength. *O God, help me to find my way.*

Jack raised his head and gasped. The sky overhead danced with color! Ripples of green blended to waves of red. Shimmering, leaping light showered love on Jack. He yanked off the net hood so he could see better. His eyes wide open to take it all in, he 'oohed' and 'ahhhed' as he would for fireworks. Glancing toward the lake, he rose and walked carefully to the edge, where the quiet water reflected the dazzling Northern Lights. This doubled the beauty, causing joy to bubble in Jack's throat. He'd never seen anything like this before! Creation seemed full of delight, offering this awesome gift for anyone fool enough to be up at this God-filled hour.

After a long time, the colors calmed and faded. Jack wanted to witness every second of it, though his eyes were growing heavy. Feeling drunk on beauty, he crawled back into his tent and settled in, ready for sleep.

The next night he resolved to stay in bed and try to sleep. He focused on the beautiful gift of the Northern Lights and tried to resist the negative thoughts, but they persisted. *What will I do this fall? What if I have to move and I can't find any friends?* He felt himself sliding down the slippery slope of worrying obsessions. *Got to get a grip! Use your mind, Jack! Create something to occupy your imagination in a positive way. Some orderly system to let sleep come.* He tried deep breathing, and counting sheep, but neither worked.

Picture yourself sleeping. Picture yourself at rest in as many places as you can think of. He pictured himself sleeping at the site on Clearwater Lake, with Luke in the next tent. He took a deep breath. He pictured himself sleeping with Abby in St Paul, and tried not to fall into sadness, just appreciate them sleeping curled together. He pictured himself sleeping in Alexandria at a convention center where he attended a seminar once.

Hey, I could add a system to this: the alphabet. A is for Alexandria...B is for...hmmm...Brule Island!...C is for Clearwater Lake...D is for...oh... Denver, where our family went on vacation one time; I still remember the knotty pine motel cabin with the brown plaid bedspread and sharing the bed with my dog ...E is for East Pike Lake...F is for Flour Lake campground...G is for Grand Marais... With each mental image Jack pictured himself as clearly as he could, sleeping soundly, and with each image he took a deep breath in and let it out slowly. He had to think hard about the lakes, picturing his map and the sites he had circled. He knew he would use Mountain later, and have to choose one of the sites there. But he never got to M; he was asleep long before then.

Chapter 15

After a good night's rest, a leisurely breakfast, and some meditation and reading, Jack looked out at the lake and wondered what to do with the rest of his day. He needed firewood, so he set out to explore the island on foot and replenish his supply. Downed wood was fairly plentiful, another sign that this site had been underused of late. He stocked up on twigs for kindling, lots of medium-sized branches, and dragged out a dead tree to cut into logs. Sawing was slow with his compact saw, and his hand hurt from the handle, so he took lots of breaks.

A leafy canopy overhead provided a dry place to position his woodpile. He tucked the kindling into the chinks so it wouldn't blow around if the wind came up. Hands on hips, he admired his morning's work and thought about lunch.

Fresh fruit was a treat beyond compare! Jack reveled in the simple pleasure of his last juicy orange. After lunch he sat in the shade, but the day lacked a breeze and it was just too hot. *I'll take a swim! Suit or no suit? Midday, there could be traffic. Better to err on the side of caution.* He donned his suit and splashed into the bracing water with a gasp. Goosebumps popped out on his skin. Swimming kept his body warmer. *Ironic that I'm too cold in the water and too hot out of it! I'll just keep alternating through the heat of the day.*

He straightened himself up to a standing position and walked gingerly on the rocks back to the grassy south lawn. There he stretched out in the sun until he was dry, then migrated to the shade, back into the water, then repeated the cycle. *Like some kind of amphibian! Abby would have had a field day with that idea. She would have gleefully called me a 'crocogater'* or an *'alladile.'* He chortled to think of it, then his throat caught with grief as he missed Abby's humor.

Kept myself so busy with paddling and portaging before, I haven't let myself feel much of anything but tired. This part of the journey will be different. This is my chance for thinking, healing, for 'finding my strength' as I put it when I first hatched the notion of staying up here. Now I am settled in a site, with lots of time on my hands. It had seemed like a good idea to have an extended stay, but now the time loomed before him like a white page in a typewriter, full of potential but terrifying in its blankness. He lived with that uncomfortable reality through the rest of the afternoon.

After a fine meal of stew that took him hours to meticulously prepare, cook, eat, and clean up, he again wondered what to do. *Maybe should take some notes or keep that journal I started.* He rummaged in his pack for a pencil and his little notebook.

His hand touched his wad of keys. In his normal life these would be in his pocket every day, marking his ownership, or at least access, to power and privilege. Here in the wilderness they were just useless lumps of metal, weighing him down. He thought about the college keys he'd thrown at Dyrud – good riddance. He ticked off the rest*: townhouse, garage, locker at the athletic club, safe deposit box, his old car, his new car, Abby's car...*

Abby's car.

Abby's car didn't exist any more. It was destroyed in the wreck that had destroyed her. He would never drive that car again, just as he would never hold Abby again.

Jack sighed once, then a second time more deeply. The tears started to flow as his grief opened up again. He leaned into the ache and let the tears wash it. When he reached the quiet stage, he realized this crying spell lasted much less time than previous ones. He was moving along the grief journey, as Luke had said he would.

Another sigh, right from his toes. He stood up to get the full effect.

Jack walked to the edge of the lake. The mystical calm of evening had smoothed the waters, making the lake a perfect mirror. Hills and trees on the opposite shore were reflected succinctly at their own feet. The setting sun spread soft orange and gold across the sky. A loon called, and its mate responded.

With effort, Jack twisted Abby's car key off his key ring. He held it tightly for a few moments, gently closing his eyes. He flung his arm back and hurled the key into the air, up, up, up in a graceful arc. Down it fell into the glassy lake, spalloosh. Concentric ripples broke the calm. He watched them a long time, until the light faded.

Jack loved his Brule Island site, but he definitely needed more action. Next morning he spread out the map and studied Brule Lake. *It's a big one, all right. Look at all the islands! Here's one called 'Fishbox Island.' Somebody must've sunk their tackle box there!*

Here's Famine Lake and Poverty Lake. No portages – guess nobody wants to go there. I see there's a portage to Wench Lake, though – now how did that get named?! He scratched his beard. *Maybe I could explore Brule Lake. It was so confusing when I first found this site; I'll take map and compass. Check out all these islands and locate the campsites and the fishing holes. Have lunch at a different site each day. I'll start right now!*

He started to make a lunch, then decided it might be wise to take his entire food pack along. He didn't think there were bears on Brule Island, but what if they could swim? It was easier to take it than to hang it, and besides, he needed the counterweight in the Independence.

Jack soon discovered many more islands than the map indicated. He penciled them in to satisfy himself. *I'll have the most accurate map of Brule Lake in existence today. People will call and request the 'Freeman Map of Brule' and I'll be famous for my explorations. I can hold little map-signings at the outfitters.* He fantasized about his potential notoriety as he paddled.

On his second afternoon of exploration, the wind picked up as he was heading into the broad open water in the center of the lake. Attuned to the signs of coming storms, Jack scanned the sky. The weather could change quickly in the north country, and on this big lake he felt especially vulnerable in his small canoe. *Sure enough, dark clouds on the western horizon. Time to turn around and head back in. Good thing I noticed it now.*

Jack could feel the strength in his shoulders as he leaned into his strokes, battling the waves. *What a difference from even two weeks ago when I was on the Border Chain. Got some power behind the paddle that I didn't have before! Well, that and a tailwind...*

Blue-black clouds moved across the sky like someone was drawing a blanket over the lake. As Jack watched, the wind shifted slightly to the south and the blanket seemed to billow over him. To the north bright sky was still visible, making the contrast starker.

As Jack landed the canoe on Brule Island, thunder boomed in the distance. He pulled his canoe far up onto the south lawn, flipped it over and shoved his life vest and paddle underneath. Next he hurried to secure his stove and cook kit, tossing them in the food pack and shoving both packs under the trees where they would stay dry. As an afterthought he dug back into the clothes pack and found his rain poncho.

Swathed in waterproof nylon, Jack settled on the grass to watch the storm. Huge cumulus clouds towered in the west, sunlit white on top and dark gray nearer the treetops. He read shapes in the clouds – a cartoony dog's face, an exploding mushroom, a buxom opera singer – and watched them morph and change as they moved south. Lightning flashed far to the west.

What if a fire started? Get in the water with the overturned canoe over you. He remembered how to save his life, he thought grimly, but he wouldn't know what to do to help anyone else. *With all this water, what would they do to get it to a fire? Bucket brigade?* He'd never done anything like that, but he had a mental picture. *Where would the buckets come from? Guess anyone could help, but I'd be terrified. Never was any good at emergencies.*

I was useless in the face of Abby's accident. In such shock I just stood there with my arms hanging down. Just a block from home – I heard the crash, but didn't know what it was, heard the sirens but didn't know they were for her. When it finally dawned on me and I ran toward the commotion, and I saw it was her car – I just stood there like a statue while everyone was bustling around, calling for Jaws of Life, and an ambulance, and everything. I just stood there.

Wish I had an ounce of courage. Can't think of a time when I did a brave thing. Unless I consider this summer adventure to be brave. This is a pretty benign wilderness – the occasional bear, the sun and storms – nothing too frightening. At least I am taking some initiative in my life – not bravery exactly but it's something.

The dark clouds spit a few raindrops, but presently the sun won out and the sky was blue again. The next rumble he heard was not the weather, but his stomach. Jack shed his poncho, hauled out all his cooking gear, and selected Tequila Chicken and peas for dinner. He boiled water, measured it into the packets per instructions, fastened them with clothespins, and waited ten minutes for them to "cook."

He ate his dinner thoughtfully. After cleaning up he pulled out Abby's journal. He realized that there were only a few entries left that he hadn't read – most of the pages in the spiral notebook were blank. He turned to a long entry that he'd skipped over previously.

June 30, 1996

This has been a terrible day. A terrible month! I feel empty.

All day I've been eating to feel better, and guess what, I feel gross now. Obviously it wasn't food that I needed. When will I ever learn?

I want to talk to Jack about what's going on with me, but he's not interested. He hasn't asked me about how I feel or what's going on with me in so long.

So I'll write and see if that helps.

I keep searching for words for the feelings I have. Sad, lonely, empty — for starters. I miss my Dad, and my Mom is far away and not able to really have a conversation. I'm hollow. I don't feel loved. I know Jack loves me, and he says so, but he's in his own little world these days. (He's going to be co-teaching a class on Human Sexuality and he and the other instructor are doing lots of prep. I'm happy for him because he's interested and excited about doing something new, but I'm also feeling really left out of his life. Maybe I have some ideas about sexuality, but he doesn't ever ask. He's also just been to a regional event for English teachers in Ames, Iowa, and he talks a lot about that too.)

I don't have a very exciting summer planned this year, so I feel kinda left out. A lot left out, actually. He's got all this stuff going and I am just cleaning the house and doing the laundry. I would be a lousy stay-at-home housewife! I hate this crap. It's easier when Jack helps out, not that he's that great, but it just feels better. Like my mother used to say, "Do you want him to do it or do you want it done *right*?" As usual, there was truth in her teasing.

It's so sad to see Mom deteriorate. Her mind and her body have turned against her, it seems like. The only part that's going strong is her heart, so the doctor said she might live a long time this way. I get tears when I think about her heart — she was so full of love and always so supportive, and now I miss that so much! And Daddy too — he loved me and often told me so. I was spoiled to be loved like that — so many people don't know love or at least not healthy love. Now I really miss them.

I have to stop to bawl a while...
Now I feel a little better. Four tissues later. It seems like Jack doesn't ever want me to cry, so I feel a little guilty. It makes him uncomfortable, I know. But he's not home tonight anyway. I can do what I want and he won't know or care.

He can be so emotionally frozen sometimes. And I have all my feelings hanging out like laundry on a line. What a weird pair we are. It's a good thing we didn't have kids — we would have warped them. Although we might have another source of love around. But there are no guarantees about that, either.

I'm rambling, I'm going to quit. I think I'll put on some classical music and lie on the floor naked and let it surround me. And I won't tell Jack!

'Emotionally frozen.' Ouch. But she was right. Jack pressed the heels of his hands to his forehead. *I'm sorry, I'm sorry, I'm sorry! I didn't mean to hurt you, ever!*

Tears sprang to his eyes and streamed down his face. Sorrow and remorse kept them coming. Gasping for breath, he let the sobs come as he had learned to do. *I'm thawing, Abby. I'm not as frozen as I was before. Got a long way to go but at least I'm on the journey.*

Jack sat still, wrapped in thoughts and feelings, as the gentle night descended around him. He'd felt the sting of his wounds again, but the longer he remained there the more he could feel something else, a warmth, like a healing hand on his heart.

If I'd stayed home I would still be stuck in sadness and self-hatred. I can remember the pain of it, holding myself stiff against the wind of change. Now I've given in to a new kind of pain, but this kind moves me ahead to the kind of person I want to be. Two steps forward, one step back, but I'm making progress.

Luke would say, "Keep up the good work. Fear not. God is good...all the time."

Next morning in the meditation spot in the glade, Jack just sat and listened, watching the webs glisten in the morning sunbeams. Concentrating, he heard three distinct bird songs, and then was startled by the laugh of a loon that reached a crescendo as it neared and faded as it passed him. *What a symphony of sound!*

A subtle rustle of a leaf caught his ear and his eyes followed the sound. A tiny gray mouse, or maybe a vole, was nibbling nearby. Jack hardly breathed as he watched. When he raised a hand to scratch his beard, the rodent met his eyes. It went back to its meal but checked on him twice more before ambling away. "Bye, now," he said softly. "Fear not..."

On his mapping expedition that day, Jack passed two canoes, each with two women. A couple of them looked to be retirement age, he thought. They waved happily at him and he waved back. He admired their sense of adventure. *I wonder if I'll still be coming up here when I'm retired? Hope so!*

He stopped at a campsite in Cone Bay for lunch, finding it nicely secluded from the lake. As he approached the fire ring he stopped short. The site was occupied, not by campers but by a furry critter, eyeing him from underneath one log bench. "Hello there!" Jack said cheerfully. "Mind if I join you for lunch?"

Seeing no objection, Jack settled on another log in the shade to make lunch. He still had some real bread from the outfitter, and he smeared it with peanut butter and raspberry jam from regulation plastic containers.

Munching on his sticky, scrumptious sandwich, Jack noted that his four-legged companion had not budged since he arrived. He observed his little buddy. He was about the size of a house cat, with brown fur tinged with auburn. He had a nice little fuzzy tail. *This all sounds familiar...what is it? I know! It's a woodchuck!*

"Chuck! Glad to meet you! I know a tongue-twister about you: 'How much wood would a woodchuck chuck if a woodchuck could chuck wood? He'd chuck as much wood as a woodchuck could if a woodchuck could chuck wood!' That's one of my easier ones. Want to hear more?" The woodchuck still stared straight ahead. "I'll take that for a 'yes.' 'She sells sea shells by the seashore.' That's a little harder. Here's my hardest one: 'Theophilis Thistle, the thistle-sifter, while sifting thousands of unsifted thistles, thrust thrice three thousand thistles through the thick of his thumb.' How's that?"

The woodchuck seemed unimpressed, so Jack shrugged and got up to explore the site. He visited the biffy and on the way back had a mental image of the woodchuck burrowing into his food pack, so he jogged back to the fire circle only to find that 'Chuck' was right where he left him. "You didn't make yourself a sandwich, eat it, and return to your spot while I was gone, did you?" Jack asked, shaking a finger.

I need some human companionship. I'm starting to go over the edge here.

Back in the canoe Jack continued his exploration a while longer, then headed back to his site. On the way between two small islands, a motion to his right caught his eye. He looked and did a double-take: a squirrel was swimming toward his canoe!

Squirrels swim? I guess so! It must be headed from one island to another. "Pardon me, I'll just get out of your way," he muttered as he propelled his canoe onward. *Squirrels swim. I'll be danged. You learn something new every day.*

Again he passed the four women with their canoes in close proximity, and they stopped their chatter and waved in recognition. They were headed to the open site on a point that he'd noticed when he arrived on Brule Lake. He saw several tents of different styles in the site.

The next morning he set out to explore again, and once again he encountered the four women. This time they paddled toward him and one white-haired woman called out in a clear announcer's voice from the bow, "You must be camping on this lake, too!"

"Yes, I'm on Brule Island."

Pointing over her shoulder, she said, "We're right here on this point," She studied his face. "You look familiar to me. Have you ever been to Pilgrim Point Camp?"

Jack's eyes grew wide with amazement. *Small world - that's twice this week!* "Yes, I have!"

"Why don't you come over for tea and a little lunch this afternoon?" She turned to her companions and they nodded their agreement.

"Sure! I'm just paddling around, exploring this lake. Any particular time?"

"I don't wear my watch during vacations. Let's just say mid-afternoon, and if our canoes aren't back, come later."

"Okay. See you then."

"See you!" The other women echoed the signoff and they went on their way.

Jack continued on his way. He explored the southern shore and had lunch in an unclaimed site. He was surprised how eager he was for afternoon tea. Finally he felt the time was about right and he made his way to their site. Their canoes weren't back so he paddled idly around the point and beyond. He didn't want to wait and appear too eager, even though he was. When he got beyond the view of the point, he goofed around with his paddle, going forward and then backward, making turns and braking. Perhaps fifteen minutes went by, and he ventured around the point again. No canoes.

Jack considered going back to his site to wait, but decided to stall on the water for a while longer. He paddled out into the open water and looped back. He looked off in the direction he thought the women had headed, and squinted his eyes. *Is that two canoes, or just one big one? Two, I think. Better give them some more time.*

He shipped his paddle and drifted, noticing the subtle current of the lake and the effect of the sweet breeze. Little clouds scuttled across the sun and made shadows play across the water. Jack hummed a fragment of a hymn, "For the Beauty of the Earth" but couldn't come up with enough words to satisfy himself. He thought he might want to learn some of those songs better.

After this gentle reverie Jack resumed paddling and returned to the campsite on the point. This time the canoes were "parked" in front, and looking up he could see the women's colorful shirts as they bustled around the point. He landed, secured his canoe, and climbed up. "Halloo!" he called.

"Hello! Come on in! I'm Penny." A willowy African-American woman with a velvety voice and short curly hair waved him up the path and into the campsite. Her shorts showed off her long, strong legs. *A runner maybe, or a dancer. Older than I am, and in much better shape.*

The woman who had invited him turned from the camp stove and extended her hand. "Hi, my name is Eleanor." Jack was drawn to her friendly features and bright eyes. She shone with positive energy and good health. *She'd be a great poster mom for happy retirement.*

"I'm Jack."

Eleanor introduced her friends who extended their hands to Jack. "You just met Penny, and this is Virginia." The latter was a matronly sort, shorter and rounder than Eleanor, wearing a voluminous sweatshirt that said "There's nothing like a Gramma." Her pink lipstick added an unexpected splash, and she smelled like a combination of flowers and repellent. Jack shook each one's hand.

"And here's Valerie." Eleanor turned to the tall, athletic 50-ish woman emerging from one of the tents. Her auburn hair was pulled back into a short pony tail, and she tucked a stray lock behind her ear. "Val, this is Jack."

"Nice to meet you." Jack shook her hand. "Eleanor, Penny, Virginia, and Val." He nodded at each one as he rehearsed their names. He often used this technique when he learned students' names in the fall.

"Have a seat! The tea is almost ready. Do you like Good Earth spice tea?" Eleanor asked.

"I love it. I like the restaurant, too." They sat down on the logs of the fire circle while Virginia checked the water.

Val passed him a plate of crackers and tidy triangles of cheese with a napkin, asking, "You live in the Cities, then? That's where we hail from."

"Yes. Thank you." He remembered that in Minnesota "a little lunch" could mean snacks or it could mean a full meal. *Wonder what I'm in for here. No telling what four women might whip up in the wilderness.* He had visions of tuna noodle hot dish with crumbled potato chips on top, or a nice 13 by 9 inch pan of chocolate chip peanut butter bars.

Eleanor chattered as she cut up a Granny Smith apple into perfectly symmetrical slices and offered him some. "We all used to work together – I coached high school girls' basketball and volleyball, and Val still does but at a different school. Penny has gymnastics and Virginia ran the office until she retired. We're on our eleventh annual trip to the Boundary Waters. We love this place."

"Me too." Jack said emphatically, as Virginia handed him a steaming cup of fragrant spice tea in a metal camp cup. "And you said you'd been to Pilgrim Point camp, Eleanor?"

Penny gave Eleanor's arm a gentle whap and teased, "That's her favorite pick-up line."

"I wondered how you could recognize me – I didn't have long hair or a beard until this summer."

"I always look at the eyes," Eleanor said with a twinkle in hers. After a pause she admitted, "Actually I recognized your shirt."

"Oh, sure," Jack grinned, looking down at the camp's name and logo on his chest. "Well, I helped out at a Work Camp last year, and our congregation has held retreats at Pilgrim Point as well."

"I probably met you at the Work Camp. I love those – such interesting people come. I'm on the Outdoor Ministries Committee for the Minnesota Conference of the United Church of Christ." She rattled off the long name like she'd done it a hundred times. "Have you been there when we've had international students on staff?"

Jack thought a minute. "Yeah, I think I remember a girl from Eastern Europe."

"That was Imola. I was telling the girls about her just the other day. She was ethnic Hungarian, from Romania. What a sweetheart – everyone loved Imola!"

"Is she the one who took the whirlwind bus trips?" asked Penny.

"You bet. She wanted to see more of the United States while she was here. So she went first to the southwest to see the Grand Canyon, then to California, Oregon, Washington, Idaho, Montana, North Dakota I think, and back to Minnesota. She only got off the bus for short layovers to see the sights. She mostly slept on the bus." Virginia shuddered to think of it, and Eleanor smiled. "She was quite the adventurous young lady. On her next trip she went from Minnesota to Chicago, down to Oklahoma City, saw the bombed Murrow Federal Building, rode east to Florida to Disney World, where she only had time to stand in line for one ride, then north, where she saw the U.S. capital by night, and on up to Niagara Falls, and back to Chicago and to Alexandria."

"What extraordinary journeys – she was quite the traveler! She saw more of the country than most Americans do in a lifetime!" Jack exclaimed.

"Her English was pretty good, but we worried about her a little. I remember when she came back from the eastern trip, she was telling about seeing Niagara Falls, and how wet the spray was. She said, 'A nice man gave me his paunch.' Poncho, I think she meant!"

The five of them erupted in laughter. *Feels so good to laugh with people! I've missed it!*

"Speaking of Pilgrim Point, you're not the first one to mention that fine place to me lately. When I was at Sawbill Outfitters, an old-timer saw my shirt and told me that he had helped to procure the property for the church camp."

"Wow, what a coincidence! You should wear that shirt every day!" Valerie teased.

Virginia was up rummaging in their food pack, and produced a zipper bag of homemade chocolate chip cookies, offering them all around. *Aha! Minnesota grandmothers do not disappoint!*

"So what are you enjoying on your canoe trip?" Jack asked, seeking to avoid talking about himself. *Don't want to throw a wet blanket over this party.*

Penny responded in her resonant alto voice. "We're taking day trips to other lakes. It's easiest for us to set up a base camp and then explore without hauling all our gear along every time. We hiked a hard portage trail to Vernon Lake off Brule Bay today. I'm really enjoying the short excursions."

"I like that, too," Virginia chimed in. "I'm not much good at carrying a pack these days. Not that I ever was really."

"You do just fine, Ginny," Val assured her. "Myself, I just love being outdoors – canoeing, walking, cooking, eating, sleeping outdoors. That's my favorite thing in the world."

"I like it all but the sleeping," Eleanor contributed. "I just can't get to sleep when I'm lying on the ground, even on the best air mattress. Of course, I often have trouble falling asleep even in a bed."

Hey, I have something to offer here! Jack leaned forward toward Eleanor. "I have devised a method for falling asleep. Do you want to hear it?"

"You betcha!" Eleanor answered, and the others chimed in.

"It has three aspects that make it work." He ticked them off on his fingers, suddenly the instructor again. "One is deep breathing, another is distracting the mind with an orderly system, and the third is visualization of sleep.

"I use the alphabet for the orderly system, and I think of a place I have slept that starts with an A. I picture myself sleeping there, and take a long breath in and let it out, holding that image. Next I go on to B. So – A is for Alexandria, and I picture sleeping at the conference center there – or you could stretch it and consider the camp to be Alexandria," he looked at Eleanor, who was listening intently. "Breathe in," he took a deep breath and they all followed suit instinctively, "and breathe out. B is for Brule Lake, picturing myself in my tent sleeping, and so on like that."

"That's very ingenious, Jack. I'm going to try it!" Eleanor spoke and the others nodded their assent.

"It works for me – I hope it works for you, too." Jack said, pleased at their response.

The friendly conversation continued, comparing lakes and campsites, evaluating freeze-dried meals, and recounting moose encounters. The snacks and tea circulated regularly. Before the topic could turn to him, Jack rose, rubbed his hands on his shorts, and thanked his hosts profusely. They all accompanied him down the path to the water, still chatting and thanking him again for coming over, and for his sleep technique. They all waved as he pulled away, and he smiled and lifted his paddle in a farewell.

This was just what I needed. I've enjoyed my solitude, but human contact has its benefits. And I won't need dinner tonight – I've had a three-course Minnesota 'little lunch'!

Chapter 16

Jack had been on Brule Island for over a week, of late spending most days on the water exploring. He was now well familiarized with Brule Bay, North Bay, and the unnamed bay that led to the Lily Lake portage. He knew most of the islands by sight, although there were so many it was still possible to mistake one for another. He had fished from one end to another and identified his favorite spots.

These daily excursions he book-ended with quiet meditation in one of the picturesque spots in his retreat-sized site. He had finished his slow reading of Acts and started on Paul's Letter to the Romans, noting his questions and observations so he could ask Pastor Luke about them. The much-anticipated raspberries growing next to his tent blessed his morning meals and sometimes yielded enough for a snack as well. He'd dusted off his skill at skipping stones, learned on Lake Cadillac, and was up to seven skips quite consistently with a personal best of ten.

The sites in his neighborhood of the lake saw a lot of use. He had seen Eleanor and her gang a few more times on the water. Just about the time he had decided to invite them over to his island for coffee and wild raspberries, he noticed that they had moved out and another group had moved in. He was only mildly disappointed; there were only so many raspberries, after all.

One afternoon after charting more islands on the west end, he saw storm clouds brewing and headed in early. By the time he reached his island on the other end of the lake, he was battling high winds and waves, and the sky looked ready to dump rain any second. Sweaty and a little weary from his hard paddle, he pulled his canoe up on the south lawn, grateful for the easy landing. The clouds let loose while he was en route to his tent, dropping pea-sized hailstones that bounced like popcorn in the grass. Jack shot a look out at the lake to see a curtain of white descending on the waves.

He was eager to get into his tent for shelter, but he thought he saw a dark shadow on the water. Curiosity drove him back to the shore. Hailstones were peppering his head, but he had to see what was out there.

Not one, but two dark shapes rocked on the high waves. Jack called out but his voice was lost to the wind. He ran back to his tent, grabbed the brightest thing he could find, plus his jacket. He snagged a loop of rope and darted back to the shore, veering over to the south lawn. Waving his red shorts like a flag he jumped up and down and yelled until the shapes, now close enough to be discerned as canoes, pointed their bows toward his island.

Their change in direction put them perpendicular to the waves, which improved their stability. He knew if they could get over the swells without capsizing, they would find an easy landing on the gently sloping sand at his feet. Each canoe held two people, but huddled as they were he couldn't tell anything else about them. Their paddling seemed disjointed and frantic, and at one point the two craft were so close to each other they whacked paddles. When one surged forward, Jack splashed out, grabbed the bow and pulled it in. He pointed them up to the lawn as they tumbled out, and turned his attention to the second craft. It was riding dangerously low, either because they had a lot of gear or they had taken on water, or possibly both. Twice he thought they were goners, as waves splashed over them. At last they came close enough for him and their companions to haul them in.

Once on the lawn the drenched paddlers peeled off their life vests and grabbed their Duluth packs, which indeed looked very heavy. Jack picked up a pack and all four followed him up to the trees in a crouching run.

The five dropped the packs and stood in a ragged circle on the path, sheltered by the trees and Jack's billowing rain fly. Conversation proved difficult while the storm raged.

Jack observed his guests: two men and two boys, seventeen or eighteen years old by the looks of them. Fathers and sons? The man across from him was ruddy-faced and jowly, with broad shoulders and his jacket stretched tight across a considerable belly. The man standing next to Jack was tall and slim, with sandy hair and a full beard. One of the boys also had sandy hair, but much more of it. The other had dark hair and the faint beginnings of a moustache.

Jack stuck out his hand to the nearest man. "JACK," he hollered.

"PETE," the man hollered back. "AND MY SON BRETT." He turned his face to the boy next to him and Jack saw a split second of emotion, but he wasn't sure what he'd seen. Pride? No. Pain? Maybe. The boy held out his hand and gripped Jack's so tightly his knuckles crunched.

The roar of hail abated but the cool wind rattled the trees as they continued their introductions. The larger man leaned toward Jack with his hand outstretched, and when he said his name, "Hank," Jack caught the full force of whiskey-soaked breath. Alarm bells went off in his head and the snare drum started in his gut. He forced himself to concentrate but he missed the son's name and had to ask the boy.

"Micah," was the reply from the dark-haired boy, accompanied by a sweaty handshake.

Jack swallowed hard and resisted running away. "Welcome to Brule Island," he choked out.

"Thanks for saving us," Pete said. "That storm was way worse than we expected."

Hank spoke up so quickly and loudly everyone swung their heads to him. "Guess the worst of it's over. We'd better be on our way."

"Dad, look at the waves!" Micah pointed at the choppy lake. "I don't think it's a good idea to go back out there."

The boy received a condescending "Who cares what you think" look from his father. Pete calmly intervened, "Hank, my paddling skills aren't as good as yours. I don't think I'm up to fighting those waves again."

Hank sighed with disgust and Jack reeled mentally as the smell of alcohol filled the air again. *Can't stand this. Wish they <u>would</u> leave! It's my island and I don't want them here.* Jack felt a twinge of conscience at his possessiveness but it didn't change how he felt.

Brett looked out at the broad clearing and said hopefully, "Maybe we could stay here tonight."

Hank bristled. "No, we're going home. I've had enough of you boys. This trip is over."

Jack caught the look exchanged by the two boys, full of sadness but not remorse. *What has happened here? This guy's mad at them, controlling and drunk. He's a hazard on the water or on the road. Oh, I see the rock on my right and the hard place on my left...*

"You're welcome to stay here tonight," Jack heard himself say. "There's plenty of room for more tents." *What am I getting myself into?!*

The boys seemed cheered by this invitation and looked to Pete to cinch the deal. "I think that's our best bet," he nodded. "Let's get the tents up before it starts hailing again."

"Awright!" The boys grabbed packs and dashed into the clearing. Hank glowered at Pete and then at the boys.

"You two won't be sharing a tent tonight!" he growled at them. "Which way is the john?" he asked Jack gruffly. Jack jerked his head toward the path and stepped out of the man's way. Hank staggered once, then paused and ran the back of his hand across his brow. He peeled off his wet rain jacket and shook the water off. Pete and Jack watched the broad back of his red plaid shirt as he stomped up the trail.

When he was out of earshot, Pete turned to Jack. "Thank you," he said simply.

"No problem," Jack replied. *Should I ask? This may be my only chance.* He let a moment go by, then asked, "What's with him?"

"Oh, he's upset about his son." Pete paused, staring into the trees as he chose his words. "Brett and Micah are best friends. They wanted to go on this trip by themselves, but I didn't think they should go alone; they've just graduated you know; it's not like they're really adults yet. Hank knows more about the Boundary Waters than any of us, so I thought it would be good to have him along, too. I didn't know him that well. Anyway, we were supposed to be out a week, but after one night he blew up and this morning he announced we were heading back home. I don't really want to take Brett back home early – my ex-wife will assume it's all my fault…" Pete's voice trailed off and they both looked up the trail to see Hank approaching.

"Yeah, the fishing is great in Brule Lake," Jack said a little too loudly. "I've discovered some great spots to catch walleye."

"Hank loves to fish, don't you Hank?" Pete chimed in. They looked to Hank but he just shrugged cynically and pushed past them toward the boys.

"Where's my pack?" he demanded. "Don't you have those tents up yet?"

"Your pack's right here, Dad," Micah offered, eager to please. "We're almost finished with this second tent. Isn't this a great site? Plenty of room for our tents and Jack's too."

"Too big for one person, that's for sure," Hank grumbled, scowling at Jack. He threw his pack into a tent and dove clumsily in after it.

Jack scanned the sky. *No rain now, but still cloudy and stormy. I'm tempted to pack up quickly and leave this site to them. Probably something's open somewhere nearby. Not that I remember seeing an available site today…* That option slipped away as common sense prevailed. *Hang in here, Jack. You can't run away. Just take a deep breath to get your balance back.* Nodding to Pete, he walked over to the south lawn. One of the canoes was right where they'd left it, with a few inches of water inside. He tipped the rain out, pulled all the canoes up further and secured them upside down with the paddles and life vests underneath.

Jack didn't want to sit on the wet grass, so he crouched down and watched the waves crash in. *What do you need of me, God?* He paused to think about what he might do and came up blank. *I've learned how to take care of myself pretty well, but I don't know how to take care of anybody else. And these guys need some help. I've given them a place to camp tonight. Is that enough?* Another pause. *I'm not going to tell them about my raspberries!* The waves kept coming. *Guess I can listen.* Jack's legs started to feel cramped, so he stood up and stretched them out. He remembered the quote from Aristotle that Luke had shared: "Wisdom is what you get from a lifetime of listening when you would rather have been talking."

I'll listen for ways to help. And you, God...help us all... please.

He turned and caught sight of the red "flag" he'd used, snatched up the soggy shorts with a smile and wrung them out. He headed up toward his tent, but detoured to the fire circle where he saw some activity.

Micah was laying a fire in the log cabin style Luke sometimes used. Jack noticed how precisely he balanced each stick, intent on a perfect structure. Pete and Brett were standing nearby with an open pack. They looked up when they saw Jack approach. "We've got tons of food, Jack," Pete said. "Dinner's on us."

"Nice of you. Whatcha got?"

Brett brightened at the question and pawed through the food packets. "Lasagna, Beef Stroganoff, Spaghetti, Hearty Beef Stew... what do you think?" He looked up at Jack expectantly.

"Any of those sound good. What do you like?"

"Dad and I got to pick the food, so I like 'em all. Micah, what do you want?" Brett turned his attention to his friend, who was putting a match to his architectural masterpiece.

"Oh, how about Spaghetti?"

"You betcha!" Brett grabbed the packet and cook kit and snapped into action. "First let's filter the water. Come on, Micah."

Jack pointed to the big flat rock that jutted into the lake. "That's a good place to get water. And I've used this boulder here as a kitchen. Do you need any help?"

"Nope, we're Scouts, we know what we're doing." The boys ran down to the water.

Pete gazed after them. "They love this."

"I can tell," Jack agreed. *Don't say too much. Just listen.* He watched the boys work, heads together, obviously close friends.

"So what do you do, Jack?" Pete sat down on one log bench and Jack sat nearby.

"I teach in the English Department in the Community College system," he answered, pleased with the sentence he'd composed. *Not too vague, not too specific. Not bad!*

"So you're used to being around young adults."

A little surprised at this direction, Jack nodded. "Yeah, I've been at it quite a few years."

"Times have changed, haven't they," Pete said with a sigh.

Jack didn't have time to respond to this cryptic comment, as the boys returned with two full pans of filtered water. *What is he getting at?*

"Let's make a double batch, I'm starving," Brett suggested, and Micah agreed.

"I'd better put my 'emergency flag' in my tent – or hang them up to dry," Jack said with a grin as he shook out his red shorts. He headed off toward his tent.

The storm was visible only on the north horizon, on its way to another lake. The wind now propelled high clouds across the late afternoon sky, but no refreshing breeze blew on the island. Hank emerged for dinner, more inebriated but still functional. He chose to eat standing up, rather than join the group around the fire. This distance spoke of the emotional void between him and the others. Jack continued to puzzle over the issue that divided them. He listened in vain for more clues in the small talk over dinner. The topics ranged from spaghetti dinners they had enjoyed to hailstorms to hunting to Boundary Waters trips. Jack regaled them with his portage bear experience, and they laughed uproariously at his advice that the bear 'Leave No Trace.'

222

Jack thanked them for dinner and offered to clean up. As he was finishing up, Hank announced that he would hang the bear bag in fifteen minutes, so everyone should brush their teeth. He lurched around the fire circle gathering up the trash, and Jack worried a little about a misstep leading to a flaming pant leg or sleeve.

"I'll go get my bear bag ready too," Jack told him. As he was ready to fasten up his pack, he thought of the marshmallows the outfitter had provided. *That might be a nice treat for this crowd, and I'll never eat all of them.* He located the package and took it to the kitchen rock. "Dessert, for later," he mentioned. He went to fetch the paddle from underneath his canoe.

Hank had already disappeared with their pack, apparently looking for a place to hang their bear bag. *Should have told him I have a good setup in place. Now he's probably worrying about finding a good branch.*

Sure enough, Jack found Hank hurling a rope-tied rock into the air. With his impaired judgment he missed his target by a mile. As Jack approached he heard a string of expletives as the rock caught a low skinny branch and whirled around it three times. He cleared his throat to announce his presence. "I've got a pretty good setup over to the north here. You want to try that?"

Hank spun around and caught himself from falling with a back step. "Not many good trees around here. There never are."

"Come check this out. I've already got a rope up." He led Hank to his spot and suggested, "Shall we tie our packs together? I think the tree is plenty strong."

Hank harrumphed and plopped his pack on the ground next to Jack's. Jack snagged one end of the rope he'd left dangling that morning. Hank grabbed it from him and tied the two packs together through their straps. *Stay cool, Jack old boy. Don't let him get to you.* Jack casually took the other end of the rope and flipped it into position so he could pull the load up.

"You give them a boost and I'll pull," Jack suggested. Hank bent over, grabbed the two packs in a clumsy bear-hug and straightened up with a grunt. Jack pulled easily with this assistance. When Hank let go, Jack gave the rope a mighty tug. At about seven feet the knot released and the two packs plummeted towards the ground. Hank lunged for them but missed, landing on top of them. Jack held his breath. *This could be bad.* To his surprise, Hank erupted in laughter, still lying on the two packs. Jack tentatively joined in the jollity, relieved at this response.

When they regained their composure, Jack grabbed the rope and said, "Shall we try that again?"

"You tie the knot this time," Hank insisted.

"I usually use a bowline," Jack explained as he tied the tricky knot.

"That's what I thought I tied," Hank chuckled.

"You push and I'll pull," Jack suggested. He gave the rope a mighty yank and hoisted the two packs up about three feet. Hank grabbed the packs and lifted them as high as he could, then used the paddle to boost them further. He was a little unsteady on his feet and the paddle slipped, causing the packs to sway. He whacked at them to try to stop the motion, but only made it worse.

"Stop, you! Stop!" he bellowed. Jack winced at the volume, but figured it was better to play along and keep Hank in a good mood.

"Stop that dancing!" he admonished the packs as he held on to the rope with all his strength. "Not you, Hank, you're looking good," he added.

Hank laughed and continued to flail the paddle, finally managing to slow the swing of the heavy packs. Jack gave one more heave-ho and tied off the rope.

Hank raked his hand through his crew cut and chuckled. "Well, that's done," he said, and slapped Jack on the back.

Keep cool, play along. "Thanks for your help, Hank. I couldn't have done it without you." Jack smiled to himself. *Actually I could have done it faster alone. But it wouldn't have been as entertaining!*

The boys had the fire blazing, sending sparks up into the darkening sky. They sat close together on one of the log benches, poking at the fire with long sticks. Beyond them Pete stood on a rock silhouetted against the placid lake. Loons called.

Jack slipped onto the boys' bench quietly, but Hank chose to disrupt the scene as he plopped down at a distance. "We got the bear bags hung," he announced, as though expecting applause. "It wasn't easy," he added lamely, still waiting for acclaim. The boys looked up and nodded and poked the fire.

"Nice fire, guys," Jack said softly, wanting to make a contrast with Hank's bombastic style. "You all obviously know what you're doing." He included Hank deliberately.

"Yeah, we were looking forward to a nice long week up here," Micah said sadly. From his sidelong view Jack saw Brett reach his hand up and rub Micah's back in a gesture of tenderness and consolation.

They're sure close. Very close. Ahhh, I think I get it. These two boys are boyfriends, and Hank is uncomfortable with that. That's the conflict. I remember Hank's pronouncement earlier: 'You two won't be sharing a tent tonight.' That's it.

Jack's senses were all heightened as he tried to process his realization and keep attuned to the interactions around him. *Did Hank see Brett's hand on Micah's back? I don't think so. He's still in a fairly good mood but that could change at any moment. Pete seemed to be less bothered earlier; he must be more supportive, or maybe he doesn't know. What did he say to me? Something about working with young adults...and times have changed. Aha. He knows.*

Jack watched carefully as Pete joined the group around the fire. "Gosh, it's beautiful up here," he said, shaking his head with wonder. "I like just looking out at the lake. Did you hear the loons?"

The others murmured their affirmation as Pete took a place on a bench across from Jack and the boys. *We're all here - this is an opportunity to talk. Can I offer anything? Or should I leave well enough alone? What should I do, God?*

Hank popped up, clearly restless like he was at dinner. *Keep them together.* Jack said cheerfully, "Marshmallows, anyone? I left them out of the bear bag so now we have to eat them!" He snagged the package and the green toasting sticks, and distributed them all around. He was glad to see that Hank wanted to participate.

Brett turned down the offer of a stick. "I like to make marshmallow taffy," he explained.

"How do you do that?" Jack asked.

"I'll show you." Brett took two marshmallows and mashed them between his thumbs and index fingers. Then he mashed them together. He kept working them, mashing and pulling, with his thumbs and two fingers until they started to change consistency. Before long they had a silky texture like taffy. "Cool, huh!" he exclaimed, stretching the creamy white confection to about six inches between his hands, then looping it together again. As the group expressed their skeptical awe, he popped the blob in his mouth and grinned close-lipped.

When everyone else was engaged in marshmallow toasting, and Brett had started making more taffy, Pete spoke up. "So, you're up here all by yourself, Jack?"

"Yeah, I'm on a solo trip." He paused, not sure which direction to take the conversation.

"For how long?" Pete continued his questioning.

"Well, what day is it today? I've been in the Boundary Waters since June 29."

"Wow!" Brett exclaimed. "This is July 25…that's almost a month!"

Micah joined in the awe with "So cool!" spoken through a mouthful of marshmallow. Pete and Hank seemed impressed, too.

It was Pete who continued to probe. "What brought you up here for such a long stay?"

Jack paused to compose his sentence. "The Boundary Waters is a place of healing and wholeness for me, and I

226

needed a lot of that this summer." Pete looked at him expectantly and he felt compelled to tell more. "My wife died in a car accident in early December. I'd been walking around mostly numb since, and then at the end of the school year I lost my job."

"Oh, man!" Brett said at once with surprising compassion for one so young.

"That's terrible," Micah chimed in.

"I'm so sorry," said Pete.

Hank was last to respond. "How did she die?" he asked.

Jack swallowed hard. Looking right at Hank, he said evenly, "She was killed by a drunk driver."

Silence fell over the group. *That was a show-stopper. Now what?*

Hank looked into the fire. Pete fussed with a marshmallow. Both boys looked at Hank. Jack decided he needed to say something, so he returned to the subject they could all identify with. "So I decided to come up to the wilderness, first with my pastor for a week, and on my own since. I've been thinking a lot, and enjoying the beauty here, and it's been good for my soul. Already I'm a better person than when I started. There's something about paddling and portaging and camping – it gets you back to what's important."

They all nodded and murmured their agreement. *Wish I didn't sound so cliché. How can I summarize my own transformation? I'm still in it – I don't know how I'm going to turn out. Maybe I should turn the focus back to them...What would Pastor Luke say?*

"I've been up here alone, and that's been a blessing for me. But you've got each other, and that's a blessing too. You're lucky to have each other."

The fathers and sons exchanged glances. Jack watched Hank as he looked at Micah and then at the fire. Night had fallen and the firelight danced on each face. This time the silence felt more comfortable to Jack, so he let the time go by. He stretched out his legs, looked up at the stars and breathed deeply. The boys, at the other end of his log, followed his gaze up to the twinkling sky.

Presently Hank stood up. "I'm going to turn in," he announced.

Pete looked at him and seemed to make a quick decision. "Me too. See you all in the morning."

After the two men left the fire, Jack debated. *Should I stay here and talk with Brett and Micah? Or leave them alone? I guess I'll ask them!*

"Shall I stay, or would you like some time to yourselves?"

The boys looked at each other briefly, then turned to Jack. "Do whatever you want," Micah said, not unkindly.

That wasn't exactly an invitation. I'll leave them alone. He yawned and stretched his arms out at an angle. "I think I'll turn in. Goodnight."

"G'night," Brett said, adding, "Thanks for the marshmallows."

"Yeah, good night," Micah echoed. "Thanks."

"Sleep well, guys."

In his tent for the night, Jack thought back over his experience with his four guests. *They really need more of what the Boundary Waters can offer. Given some time and sacred space they might be able to work things out. It's sure been good for me.* He stretched out in his sleeping bag and lay with his hands behind his head. *This is such a good site for them – plenty of room to get away from each other when they need to, but good communal space too.*

A snore buzzed from the direction of the other tents.

I've enjoyed being here on Brule Island – but I know there are other great sites out there, and oodles of other lakes to explore. Maybe it's time for me to move on. I can encourage them to stay here, instead of going home early.

Jack started to think of all the directions he might go next, but sleep overtook him.

Awake early, Jack stuffed his sleeping bag and gathered together the clothes that were in his tent. He emerged into the dawning light to find Hank already up, making coffee on their camp stove.

"Morning," Jack said quietly, not wanting to disturb the others, and Hank responded with a nod. He looked more grizzled, more thoughtful, and more vulnerable than the day before. He silently poured Jack a cup of coffee and held it out to him.

"Did I hear you say that the fishing is good on Brule?" Hank asked in a husky half-whisper.

"Yeah, it's great. This time of day it's perfect. I'd – " He started to say he'd be out there if he weren't breaking camp this morning, but Hank interrupted.

"Would you show me one of the good spots?"

Jack tried not to show how startled he was by this invitation. He scanned the sky to buy time to think. *Why not? Maybe he needs to talk. Or just time to think. Or maybe I'm overreacting – maybe he just wants some fish for breakfast. Anyway, why not?* "Sure, I'd be glad to. Let's leave a note for the others."

They rounded up their equipment as quietly as they could, left a note by the coffee, and headed for the canoes. "Shall we take one or two?" Jack asked.

"Let's each take one – then we can divide and conquer."

Jack led the way in his Independence and Hank followed, paddling his long canoe much better than the afternoon before. The lake was calm and misty. When they reached the nearest of Jack's favorite spots he shipped his paddle and waved Hank over. Hank expertly used his paddle as a rudder to turn his canoe so the two craft were side by side, the two men facing each other.

"I've had great luck here, both walleyes and northerns." Jack assured Hank as they baited their lines. "I hope they're biting today," he added just to cover himself.

Hank bent over his tackle box, and without looking at Jack he said, "I'm sorry if I was an ass yesterday."

Jack looked at him, suddenly sympathetic. "No problem. I hope today's a better day."

"Yeah. I don't know quite what we should do."

"You mean whether you should stay in the BWCA or go home?"

"That's the first question. The next one is what to do with my son."

Jack was a little taken aback, yet also strangely honored, by the intimacy of Hank's comment. *Does he know I know? What can I say? Be positive.* "Micah seems like a fine young man."

"Yeah, I thought so, but now that I know he's... he says he's..." Hank wrestled with a knot in his line that seemed symbolic of his tangled emotions.

"...gay?" Jack filled in the blank with the word Hank couldn't say.

Hank looked up at Jack for the first time. "How did you know?"

"I teach college. I just picked up on their clues." Jack decided not to joke about "gay-dar" as he had in other settings.

"I don't know what I did wrong." Hank scrubbed his big hand over his stubbly face.

Jack spoke up quickly. "He's not gay because of anything you said or did! It's just who he is."

"You really believe that?" Hank looked dubious.

"Absolutely. I co-taught a class on Human Sexuality and Relationships. Homosexuality is not a choice, it's an orientation." Jack was aware he was sounding professorial. "That's what my church teaches, too," he added, just in case that counted for something.

Hank looked at him with one eyebrow raised, and said nothing.

Jack decided to go for it. "Do you love your son, Hank?"

He answered slowly and deliberately. "Yeah, I do."

"Hasn't he always been your son? He hasn't become anyone different – you just know more about him now. He's still the son you love."

Hank wiped his nose on his arm. "I'll have to think about that. Let's fish awhile."

They let the canoes drift apart and cast their lines into the water. Hank was the first to haul in a nice northern pike, not a trophy but a respectable size.

"One more like that and we'll have breakfast for the whole gang," Jack said, admiring his catch.

"You don't know the appetites on these kids! I think Micah could eat this whole fish!" he joked.

Jack and Hank each caught a walleye, and they decided that would make enough for breakfast. They paddled their canoes over to a rock to clean the fish. Jack had decided to let Hank know that he'd be moving on so they could stay if they wanted to.

"I'm going to break camp this morning and be on my way. If you all want to stay, the site's all yours."

Hank pondered this. "I hope we're not scaring you off," he said.

"Not at all. I've been there almost two weeks, and that's the limit for staying in one site. And I feel the need to explore some more. It's a great site for a group like yours. I recommend it," he said hopefully.

"It is a good site. And there's good fishing."

"Definitely good fishing. I can show you some other good spots on the map, too."

"Very tempting," Hank said thoughtfully as he prepared to paddle back.

Having seen the pensive side of Hank, Jack was surprised when the man locked back into the take-charge dad back at the site. Pete, Brett, and Micah sat around a fire made to die down to coals, clearly anticipating a fish breakfast. Hank hitched up his pants and announced, "We're going to stay here another day or so. Then we'll see what happens."

Brett and Micah broke into grins and high-fived each other. Pete stood up and smiled. "That's great news. Jack, you don't mind if we stay?"

"Actually I'm going to head out after breakfast. I have more lakes to explore! I'm glad to leave this island in good hands." He looked at the boys to include them in this affirmation.

Brett spoke up, pointing to the stringer in Jack's hand. "Looks like you know where to find the fish, too – will you let us in on that?"

"Why not? I'll even tell you about the wild raspberries! I don't see any reason for secrecy," he said, smiling at his own double meaning. *And I'll pray for you all, that you'll find ways to be more open to each other.*

Chapter 17

Jack decided to take the long way to Winchell Lake and see if he could find a nice site there. *I'm spoiled now – I'll be picky. This site has been an island paradise. Except for the mosquitoes. But it's time to move on.*

He packed up carefully and loaded the canoe, making a thorough check of the site to make sure he hadn't left anything. He was taking the solar shower – he had enjoyed it so immensely, and the new residents had their own – but he figured he might leave it at his final site as a treat for someone else to find.

At last he shoved off, with a pang of sadness to bid farewell to this place that had been home base for a week and a half. He waved to Brett and Micah, who had come to the shore to see him off. *God bless you boys!*

He set his sights ahead, to the familiar terrain of Brule Lake, and headed for Cone Bay. He passed the campsite where he'd seen the woodchuck, and wondered if Chuck was still hanging out there.

On the map the portage looked like a channel that he might be able to navigate by canoe. As he approached Cone Bay a young couple in a blue canoe emerged. "Is the channel canoe-able?" he called, grateful to have someone to ask.

The shirtless man looked hard at the Independence with its two packs and one man. "You can do it. The next one up may be passable too."

This will be an adventure. As he headed into the cove further he could hear the rapids. The closer he got, the more rocks he saw in the channel – and the more skeptical he became. *Maybe early in the season when the water is high...but this is late July...and I don't need a hole in my canoe!*

He backpaddled and turned around, disappointed. Looking for the portage, he spotted a landing and headed for it. But once he had shouldered his own Duluth pack, paddle and pole in hand, and headed up the hill he stopped short. *This is a campsite!*

Where once he would have berated himself for his stupidity, now Jack just shrugged his shoulders, turned on his heel and headed back down to his canoe. Back on the water, he discovered the portage, right where he had turned around.

He was able to take the food pack and canoe together with some effort, and then retraced the 30 rods for his Duluth pack. *These rocky, rooty corduroy portages are real ankle-twisters.* He stepped carefully.

Out of the channel and a short distance across the west end of South Cone Lake, he again found himself in a channel. Once again the rapids were too shallow for his loaded canoe, so he portaged the rocky 25 rods.

Arriving in Middle Cone Lake, he first saw an abandoned aluminum paddle, then looked up to see four teenage boys in two canoes fishing nearby. One turned back toward the portage and Jack heard, "That's just The Geek being an idiot." As he arrived with his second load they were just paddling up at the portage, and he tipped his canoe into the water, then handed them the paddle. "Did you just come in from Brule?" the older boy asked.

"Uh-huh."

"We came in yesterday. But one of our guys got, like, really sick to his stomach, so two went back in today."

"Oh, that's too bad."

"It happens." The boy shrugged. "Have a good trip!"

They seem adaptable. Wish I could be that easygoing. Wonder if they were drinking. What would it be like to get sick out here? Ugh, that would be terrible. I hope I can continue to stay healthy. Never neglect to boil or filter the water, he admonished himself.

Continuing in a channel to North Cone, Jack hoped he could navigate the rapids this time. The map showed the portage as only five rods. When he got there it was also too shallow – but he got the idea to walk his loaded canoe through. One foot was already wet from the earlier portage. So he steadied the craft by a rock and stepped gingerly out. The water was cold but not freezing. He kept one hand possessively on the canoe and used the other for balance as he picked his way through the slippery rocks. One tipped and his foot scooted off, dunking half his body with a splash before he could recover. *Whoo! Refreshing!*

Once into the canoe he carefully lifted one foot onto the gunwale and let the water dribble out the top of his boot. Wiggling his toes made the rivulet a stream and he laughed. He leaned back on his pack and let both boots return water to the lake.

At North Cone Lake he pointed the Independence east. He decided he would press on to Winchell Lake to find a site. If he liked it he would stay a while. The 160-rod portage to Cliff Lake was demanding, and by the time he'd made his first trip his sweat was running and the mosquitoes were on the attack. He pawed in his pack for the repellent, promising himself a snack from the food pack later. Making it over a downed tree had been manageable with just his pack, but with the food pack and canoe combination it would be harder. On the way back he tried to move the tree, but it was too big for his abilities. He was glad for his long legs – at least he could step over it, with effort. A child or a short person would be at a definite disadvantage. It was tricky with his load, but he accomplished it.

Two skinny lakes and two short portages later, he arrived at Winchell Lake. His first glimpse of a campsite turned out to be a disappointment. It was either a former site or one that had been "unofficially" used. There were more possibilities to the east, so he paddled on and soon landed on a small granite point. *This will do!*

This campsite was beautiful. He entered a small cove and landed easily on a tiny sand beach about six feet wide. A shady, level tent spot nestled in the trees straight ahead. Through a break in the bushes to the right he entered the other half of the site, where domes of huge boulders dominated the point and the fire/cooking area. From the rocks he had a 180 degree view of the lake.

He moved his gear in and set up his tent. He placed the door facing the little beach and bay. He liked the protected tent site and the view. He could keep an eye on his canoe. He could wade in the sandy shallows there and swim in the cove.

The benefits were obvious. The drawbacks soon presented themselves, however. The flies were thick, and some bit him. Small squirrels persistently approached his food pack and he hadn't even opened it yet. A structure for the bear bag had been carefully constructed – a plus – but it was too close to the site. *And I'll bet the squirrels know all about it.*

Is this the right spot for another extended stay? Winchell is a nice, quiet lake compared to Brule, and this is a great site in so many ways. The bugs are unavoidable this time of the summer. The loons and squirrels actually provide some company. This can be home until I'm ready for another change.

From the moment Jack opened his food pack, he had constant visitors. Several of the small squirrels, much smaller than the backyard variety in Minnetonka, scampered over the 'kitchen rock' and the fire circle, checking the scene. He imagined their high-pitched barrage of questions: "Who are you? What's for supper? Did you bring anything for us? Aren't we cute?"

"You sure are cute," he said aloud, "but I don't think I should feed you. I'll bet someone has in the past."

When he returned to the kitchen rock with two pans of filtered lake water for cooking, two squirrels were on his pack, almost inside. "Hey!" he hollered, "that's not for you!" He laughed and shook his head as they scampered a short distance away, then popped their heads up to check on him again.

"I think your name is Billy," he said to the nearest squirrel, who sat up on his haunches in response. "And you must be Toots," he addressed the one on the cold fire grate. He wasn't actually sure how many there were, they were so omnipresent. He decided to call them all either Billy or Toots.

By the time his dinner was ready he'd grown weary of their persistence. His tone had changed to a surly, "Get out of here!" whenever they came too near. They always retreated, but only for a few minutes, and then they were back. He tried waving his fork threateningly, lobbing pine cones at them, and yelling, and still they returned to see if he'd had a change of heart.

God must have taught them to be so dogged. God has certainly been persistent with me, loving me when I'm unlovable and angry. He watched the squirrels race across the rock while he washed up his dishes. *They're omnipresent like God, too.* He felt a little odd, comparing God to Billy, Toots, and company; but then he shrugged. *God has a sense of humor, I hope!*

Hanging the bear bag was easy. Someone had gone to a lot of trouble to lash a sawn log high up between two sturdy pines. As he hauled the bag over, the squirrels bolted up the tree and one sat on the crossbeam. "Over here!" he could hear her say, "hang it here and we'll take good care of it for ya!"

Jack paused but couldn't think of any way to prevent the agile critters' access to his pack. He'd already seen them hanging upside down from a branch nibbling on pine nuts. "Okay, here you go!" he muttered as he hauled the pack high on its rope. "Just leave me some coffee for breakfast." He chuckled as he imagined finding a skinny pack and six fat squirrels in the morning.

There's still enough light for some reading. Anything left in Abby's journal that I haven't read? Jack flipped through the pages, skimming through now-familiar phrases. The last entry she had written in early December, not long before she died. Jack steeled himself and began to read.

December 4, 1997

Last time I wrote I got all wrapped up in my fears about getting old, and Jack getting old. Tonight I'm overcome with fear about losing Jack. I don't know why these feelings come over me sometimes. This is a bad night. Jack is at a faculty meeting and he said it might run long. The wind is howling and there's snow predicted. The wind is giving me the creeps. Jack's meeting is in the conference room and there are no windows, so they won't even know if this blows into a blizzard. There's no phone in there, either. I keep thinking we should get one of those cellular phones to use for emergencies. It would sure ease my mind just to know I could be in touch with him.

My dear Jack! When Dad was so sick, I thought about what it would be like if Jack got cancer or something and died. I could hardly bear the thought of life without him. I would be so lonely! I would think about him all the time.

If I lost Jack, would I ever find another partner who would bring such calm, such a sense of safety to my life? And such intellectual stimulation? Probably not. Dang, there's another fear.

If I were to get sick and die, I would definitely want Jack to find someone else to love. I think he needs a partner to get his energy flowing. He deserves that.

Why am I even thinking these things? It's all about fears. Fear is so paralyzing. When I feel so afraid, I can't do my work, let alone be creative about it. And thinking about one fear just leads me to another. I've got to get a grip.

Yesterday in church Pastor Luke read the scripture about the angel appearing to Mary. He said, "Do not be afraid." I'm not sure that someone just saying that could make it so - although maybe an angel has that power. Maybe I need an angel who will help me to feel less afraid.

Jack's car just pulled up! Yay!

Abby's affirmation of him in this entry felt wonderful, especially as he remembered the earlier phrase "emotionally frozen." He read it all again, and this time another part leaped out at him: "I would definitely want Jack to find someone else to love. I think he needs a partner to get his energy flowing. He deserves that."

These three sentences spoke volumes. *Not everyone gets permission to love another. Maybe some couples have those conversations, but we never did. Wow.*

She perceived that I need someone to 'get my energy flowing.' After she died, I had no energy at all for months and months. I'm starting to get some back now, with help from Luke...and God.

She felt that I 'deserved' a partner. 'Deserved.' Wonder what that means.

Am I open to another relationship? His gut lurched. *Don't feel ready for another marriage at all. But I wouldn't mind having a few more friends. And I could see myself maybe dating again once I get back to the Cities. Or wherever I end up. Just to explore possibilities.* He shuddered to think of entering the dating market again. *Cross that bridge when I get to it. No hurry.*

The sun was nearing the tree-lined horizon. Jack put Abby's journal away, donned his bug-proof hood, and crossed two domes of rock to the boulder that sloped down to the water. Sitting in a hollow of the rock, he faced south across the narrow lake where the green tree-covered ridge was reflected in the calm water. To his right gold-rimmed clouds moved between him and the sun. To his left the water took on a butterscotch hue, sparkling in the slanting light.

Two loons flew in and splashed to a landing across the lake from him. Further to his left a gang of loons laughed raucously, flapping and strutting and preening. *Juveniles, I'd say.* The two loons nearby responded to the hubbub with their own laughing calls. Jack smiled and leaned his head back in prayerful gratitude.

A stiff breeze came up and kept the biting bugs at bay, so Jack stayed out on the rock later than he might have otherwise. The wind blew the clouds away, and with the fingernail moon hanging low, the starry night was captivating. Jack leaned back so he could take it all in.

Such beauty overhead! In the wilderness no human-made light interfered, so the heavenly lights reigned. Bright stars – planets too – shone on a backdrop of tiny dazzling lights. The Milky Way looked spatter-painted across the entire canopy. As he watched, Jack saw movement – *too far away for a plane - satellite!* He followed its steady flight, wondering what it looked like.

A shooting star evoked a gasp from Jack. Excitement bubbled up in him. *A shooting star! Am I supposed to make a wish, or something?* Another bright arc of light caught his eye. *Two shooting stars!* He kept alert for movement as he wished for more. He prayed wordlessly, in awe.

By the time sleep clouded his eyes, Jack had counted three satellites and five shooting stars. He felt blessed with peace and ready for rest.

Thank you for this beautiful place, with its amazing collection of creatures and view of the cosmos. Thank you for the glaciers that scoured out these lake beds, tumbled these stones, and sculpted this land. Thank you for this time to enjoy this sacred space.

When he retrieved his pack in the morning he was dismayed yet not too surprised to find that the squirrels had crawled under the canvas flap of his pack and nibbled holes in the next layer. They hadn't infiltrated the plastic liner yet, though, so the food was intact. "Needed more time, eh Billy?" he queried. "I'll fool you – I'll put a tarp on top tonight!"

The squirrels were not as annoying this morning somehow. In an odd way he appreciated their company. While he sat meditating in the trees that morning, he saw a brown rabbit sitting quietly in the shade. *So that's what I heard this morning: bunny hops around the tent.* In contrast to the myriad birds at his Island Paradise, this Boulder Dome site specialized in four-legged creatures. *Sometime I'll graduate to living among two-leggeds again, but not quite yet. I'm getting to where that sounds possible, anyway.*

Daily laughter returned to Jack's life at the Boulder Dome site. The squirrels started it; their perky presence invited script-writing on his part. "What's up, Jack?" he could imagine them saying each morning in a high, squeaky voice. "Did we get you up too early?" He continued to put words in their little mouths and carried on silly conversations in falsetto, laughing and laughing at them, and at himself. They chattered happily with him.

Laughing felt a little strange, after living without it for so long. *Is it like an unused muscle that needs exercise? Or is it like riding a bike, you never forget?* The more he laughed, the more he felt comfortable laughing out loud at loons, at his own silly thoughts or actions, at the sheer joy of living this rarefied life.

One evening Jack settled himself into his special hollow of the rock, and surveyed the lake. An osprey circled over the water, plunged straight down in a black W and swooped up again. Jack couldn't see if it had a fish or not. Soon it was trying again, so it must have failed the first time. Persistence seemed to be his lesson here, and the osprey and squirrels were his teachers. On the third try the osprey emerged with a fish in its talons, flying in a wide circle and gaining altitude. But out of the blue came an eagle in pursuit! Jack watched the chase until the two were out of sight, never knowing the outcome.

Eagles are just darn scavengers. Fine symbol for our country. I'm rooting for the osprey this time – I know what it's like to come up empty. He deserves the reward for his persistence.

Here's that theme of persistence again. In what aspects of my life do I need to be more persistent? Being a good teacher, that would be one...Could do better at hanging in there with the borderline students. Making friends would be another. Could take more initiative in getting together with people I like. Could try more kindness in general. Loons called to each other across the water. The one nearest him flapped vigorously and splashed across the water, finally lifting clear of the lake. Jack could hear the wind in its wings as it sped to its partners. *Sure takes them a long time to lift off. It's taking me a long time to get back into circulation. Loons are my teachers, too.*

Winchell Lake, long and skinny, didn't ask to be explored like Brule had. The south shore's cliffs made for beauty but poor accessibility. The north shore held all the campsites. Fishing was fair, especially in the evening, so Jack entertained himself in this way and had the benefit of late dinners of fresh fish.

One muggy morning he followed a nearby finger of the lake north and portaged over toward Omega Lake just to check it out. He took only his food pack, which was getting lighter all the time, and his fishing gear.

When he could see Omega Lake was near, he encountered a family in crisis. The dad, tall and blonde, carried a pack and a beautiful long cedar strip canoe, 18 feet Jack guessed. The pony-tailed young mother, with a Duluth pack on her back, carried two bent-shaft paddles. The conflict centered around two mirror-image tow-headed boys, about 5 years old, who were sitting on the trail refusing to move.

"Neither of us can carry you. You're going to have to walk." the mother stated with forced patience.

"I'm tired!" whined one of the boys, and he shrugged out of his little daypack and lay down on the path, using the pack as a pillow. His cheeks were unnaturally bright and rosy, and his nose was running. He sniffed.

"Me too!" echoed his twin, although he remained in a sitting position with his pack on, legs stretched straight out in front of him.

Their father spoke sternly. "I guess we'll just have to leave you here then, Griffin."

"Noooooooo," the seated boy wailed. He scrambled to his feet and tugged at his brother. "C'mon, Griff, let's go home. Let's go home to Chicago."

"I'm hot." the recalcitrant boy complained. He wiped his runny nose on his arm.

"We're all hot, sweetie," his mother empathized. "The sooner we get going, the sooner we'll get home."

Jack cleared his throat and asked, "Anything I can do to help?"

All eyes turned to him, some noticing him for the first time. The boy called Griff whined plaintively, "Carry me, Daddy."

Jack thought a second, turned to the man and said, "I could carry your canoe and pack." The boys' parents exchanged a look and Jack didn't give them time to protest. "Just let me stow my gear." There was no clearing at hand, so he carefully picked his way around the boys, then past the mom and dad with their loads, and flipped his canoe down, slid out of his pack and stowed it with his paddle and pole underneath.

"My name is Jack, and I have a strong back," he quipped. The parents murmured their names, clearly embarrassed by the whole scenario, but the man walked out from under his canoe and shrugged out of his pack. Meanwhile Jack tried to look like he did this every day. "You're Griff," he took the little hand of the rosy-cheeked boy, helping him sit up. "And what's your name?" he asked, reaching his hand out to the other.

"I'm Duncan."

"Glad to meetcha, Duncan. OK if I carry your family's canoe?"

"I guess so."

Jack put on the pack, commenting that it wasn't as heavy as his (even though it felt about the same) and eyed the canoe. It was about a yard longer than his, and it was a beauty; he would have to be very careful not to bump it. He got under it and experimented with the balance. *It's heavier than mine, too.* He reached out a hand toward the woman. "Let me take the paddles, too. Then you can offer a hand to Duncan if he needs it." She reluctantly held them out without a word.

Griff reached his hands up to his father like a toddler would. *This little guy does not feel good, I can tell. I can't help them all the way home, but I can at least give the boy a break. Which may help the parents too.*

"How about piggyback, Griffin?" the man asked. He turned his back to the boy and crouched down. Griff flung his arms around his dad's neck. The man hooked the boy's legs with his elbows, leaned their weight forward and stood up. He jerked his head toward the path. "You go ahead," he said to Jack.

Jack set out down the portage trail back to Winchell Lake. Behind him he heard the dad's encouraging, "Okay, Tiger, let's go," and the mom's call to Duncan, accompanied by the scamper of the little boy's feet.

Conversation, always a challenge on the portage trail, did not seem to flow from this group. Jack concentrated on balancing the long canoe and wiping the sweat from his face with his bandana. When they had accomplished the 44 rods, Jack flipped the canoe into the best spot for loading and launching, and shrugged out of the pack. His back was drenched with sweat.

The woman gave him a sidelong look, and murmured, "Thank you." She turned away and busied herself with getting life vests on the twins, tossing their packs into the canoe and lifting them in.

The man, plucking at his sweaty shirt, nodded with a curt 'Thanks' and loaded the packs. In a moment they were ready to launch.

"Glad I could help. Have a good trip," Jack waved. "God bless," he added, as he watched them pull away, twin towheads in the middle between the packs each with a hand on the gunwale, mother in the bow and father in the stern.

Taciturn couple. They'll need God's blessing to get home without another meltdown. Got a lot of pluck, bringing those little guys up here. But I can see why they'd want to – in a way I wish my family had brought me on adventures when I was little. Then I would have been better prepared for this trip. He turned to retrace the portage back to his gear and on to Omega Lake.

Yet part of the adventure of this journey has been the discovery of what I can do, so many things I never even tried before. I've changed. Even this little encounter – in the past I would have tried to avoid getting involved. Like the priest and the Pharisee in the Good Samaritan story – I would have tried to walk by on the other side. Today I got involved and even though they didn't fall all over me with gratitude, it was worth it. I don't recall a "Thank you" in the Good Samaritan story, anyway.

Chapter 18

The afternoon was hot. Jack filled his solar shower with water and set it out on a rock to warm up. He strung a rope clothesline between the trees in a sunny spot. In a few hours he took the hot bag into his "grove" down behind his tent and hung it on the cedar branch he used for showering. He washed his few clothes, including what he was wearing, and draped them on the clothesline. When he ran out of room on the line, he laid the rest out on the warm boulders to dry.

Abby would not approve of me walking around naked like this. He sighed the guilt away. *But Abby's not here, so some things are different. Guess that's okay. Feels good in the heat of the day.*

Wearing only sandals, carrying his towel, Jack strolled down to his canoe. The cove looked inviting. *It's fairly secluded. Haven't seen a canoe for days. Sun is so hot, a cold dip will be refreshing.*

He waded in, then decided to leave his sandals behind and tossed them onto the little "beach" near his towel and glasses.

Tiny fish fled at his presence. The bottom was uncharacteristically sandy – he enjoyed the sensation in his toes. Wildflowers bloomed to his left where the boulders rose up out of the water. Further to his left the cove opened out to the lake and bigger water; to his right the shore curved around in a perfect arc.

Jack waded in gradually, enjoying the dramatic difference between his overheated body and the bracing water. He stood with his hands on his hips, just up to his thighs in the lake when he heard the 'thunk' of a paddle against a canoe.

His knees bent quickly to protect his modesty, and his nearsighted gaze swept the water.

The canoe wasn't as close as he had thought; sound traveled so well over water. He could make out the yellow canoe heading east with a diminutive solo paddler wearing a pale pink shirt. Squinting, he saw her long blonde hair lifted by the breeze. He waved tentatively, not wanting to call attention to himself if she hadn't noticed him. She lifted a paddle in greeting, then shifted her gaze ahead in an apparent search for a site.

Jack felt a sudden twitch of attraction, and looked down at himself in surprise. *Whoa! Haven't felt that in a long time!* He swam out into the mouth of the cove and dogpaddled, watching her progress along the shore. *She's looking for a site for the night. Maybe she will be my neighbor!* With mingled excitement and chagrin, Jack swam back to his tiny beach and waded ashore. He put on his glasses and sandals quickly and wrapped his towel around his waist. He trotted up to the rocky point of his site and saw the yellow canoe continuing east. His skin dried in the hot sun as he watched until she was a tiny blur, landing in a site two coves away. At this distance he could really only make out the small rectangle of bright yellow, even with his glasses on.

She's a neighbor now! Maybe we'll meet! He tried to imagine "stopping by" but he couldn't quite picture it. People just didn't go calling on their neighbors any more like they did when he was a kid. He could remember his mother taking a plate of homemade cookies to any new neighbor to get acquainted. He smiled at the mental image of himself with a tin plate of Oreos, knocking on her canoe like it was a door.

As he ate dinner he imagined eating with her and showing off his skill with freeze-dried dinners. *Could share my knowledge of the loons' four distinct calls, and we could joke about what the loons were saying. We could admire the stunning view from my boulder site. The breeze would stir her beautiful blonde hair and I might want to kiss her...*

But what about Abby? He thought a long time that evening, and wept for her again. *Our vows were 'until death parts us' and that's exactly what happened. I'll never love anyone the way I loved Abby. She was so right for me.*

But she said I need a partner to 'get my energy flowing.' She said I deserve that. Maybe I will love someone else someday. I'm changing this summer. I'm not so 'emotionally frozen' any more. Maybe there's someone else out there who could love me and accept me. Maybe.

The next day Jack continued to think about his lovely neighbor. He noticed her yellow canoe was still at the site across the water.

When he was out fishing he thought about them paddling together, and wondered if her canoe was big enough, since his wasn't.

Back in camp, he noticed one of the pine trees in his site had a branch from its neighbor tree entwined around its trunk.

He wondered which of his resident squirrels were mates. He asked them, but Billy and Toots didn't give him any clues about their relationships.

He pondered whether she might enjoy skinny-dipping.

Using his mirror and the scissors on his Swiss army knife, he trimmed his hair and shaped up his beard.

That night Jack went to bed early, feeling particularly weary even though he hadn't done much all day. He dreamed that he paddled over to the neighbor's campsite and invited her over for pizza and beer. She was as beautiful as he had imagined, like a young model with a slim figure and beautiful long blonde hair. She said she'd love to come thank you, and they took her canoe, which in the dream was aluminum and very heavy, back to his site, which had become a pizza parlor. They talked and laughed and spoke without words. They left the pizza parlor and he invited her to his tent. They lay snuggling and giggling together in his sleeping bag. And then he woke up.

He awoke with his head aching, his throat raw and his sinuses full. *Can't be getting a cold up here! No-no-no!* He tossed and turned miserably until dawn.

By morning he found himself in the throes of a full-blown cold. *Must have caught it from little Griff. Hope he's okay, poor little guy. At least I'm strong and healthy – hope I can shake it off quickly.*

The gray skies reflected his foul mood. He didn't feel like fishing, or swimming, or anything but sitting by a fire. Raucous sneezes bounced him out of his seat, and his bandana saw constant use as a handkerchief. The wood smoke irritated his throat, so he let the fire die down. He drank cup after cup of water, trying to flush the cold out of his system. He wished for some herbal tea to soothe his throat; coffee didn't help.

The next day he sneezed much less and his sinuses were better, but his throat hurt and he coughed frequently. The coughing scraped his sore throat and brought a wince and a moan every time. *I've always been susceptible to coughs – colds always go right into my chest. Then it takes me a week or more to get over it. This is rotten luck!*

He rummaged through his first aid kit, but couldn't find any cough drops. He took a couple of Ibuprofen tablets to see if that would help him feel any better, but he couldn't detect any benefit. *At least I'm in a settled campsite, not on the trek like I was at first. I'm reasonably comfortable here and I don't have to push myself.*

The cough indeed lasted days. He 'barked' all day long and through the night, and took no joy in either one.

One night Jack had gone to bed early, well before full dark, hoping for a much-needed good night's rest. He dropped off to sleep thinking about his neighbor with the yellow canoe, but woke soon after coughing uncontrollably. He thought he heard a voice, but thought it might just be the echo of his own cough ricocheting around the cove.

"Hello? Excuse me?" It was a voice, a woman's voice.

Maybe it is my lovely neighbor! Maybe she is coming to meet me! And here I am sick! "Hello? Yes?" Jack put on his glasses and stuck his head out of his tent.

There she was, the petite woman he had admired from a distance. But her long braids were silver, not blonde, and her youth was long since past. Jack blinked hard and shook his head to clear it. She was attractive, yes, but in a grandmotherly sort of way. Her face was creased with multiple laugh lines and her button eyes sparkled.

"I've heard you coughing the past few days. You must be miserable." Her face exuded compassion. "I've brought you some herbal tea." She held up a thermos.

Jack didn't know what to think. Even as his fantasies evaporated, he felt some pleasant feelings toward this woman who came over to help him out. He tried to speak and coughed again, holding up his hand in a "just a moment" gesture. He ducked back into his tent, pulled on some pants and a shirt, ran his fingers through his hair and emerged. As he put on his sandals he said with a raspy voice, "You're so kind! I've been longing for some tea that would soothe this throat."

As he led her to the fire circle she explained, "I make my own blend of slippery elm bark and other herbs. I hope it helps."

Jack pulled out his cup from the pile of dishes and held it out. She poured steaming liquid from the thermos. "The aromas are good for you, too, so breathe deeply as you drink." Jack trusted her implicitly. Her kindly eyes, her generosity, and her Earth Mother wisdom drew him in.

"May I rekindle the fire?" she asked.

"Sure," Jack agreed, feeling the evening chill and grateful for her offer. "My throat feels better already."

"I should introduce myself. I'm called Starshine."

"Starshine?"

"Yes, Starshine. I used to have another name a long time ago, but now I'm just Starshine."

"Uh, I'm Jack. I've always been Jack."

"I'm pleased to meet you, Jack." Her warm tone took away his discomfort in having a nonmusical name. "More tea?"

"Yes, please. This is the best thing that's happened to me all week." She filled his cup. "I'm sorry if my 'barking' disturbed you."

"Only because I knew you were miserable. I've been enjoying my stay on this lovely lake."

"How long are you here?"

"Oh, a week or two. My time is my own, so I can come and go as I please. I love to come on solo trips because I can travel at my own pace and stay a while on a lake I particularly enjoy."

"Do you come to the Boundary Waters often?"

"I've been up here almost every summer of my life. I live in Grand Marais now so usually I'm up here several times a year."

"Wow. This is just my second trip."

"And you are traveling solo on your second trip? You are adventurous!"

Jack laughed. "I spent one week with a friend who coached me well. Then he went back home and I set off on my own. This is my..." Jack drummed his fingers on his knee as he counted. "...sixth week now."

"Very impressive! Where have you been?"

Jack recounted his routes to the best of his memory. He told her about the rainstorm and portage bear, and the beautiful site on Brule Island, and the companionable squirrels in this site. She listened with recognition and appreciation, familiar with everything he described.

"This is great fun, Jack, but I'd better get back to my site and let you rest. Oh yes, I have some herbal cough drops for you here, too." Starshine dug in her pocket and pulled out a handful of drops.

Jack, reluctant to end the conversation, asked plaintively, "Will you visit again? This tea is great – I haven't coughed once since I started drinking it. And it's fun to have someone to talk to."

"Certainly I'll visit again. I'll leave this thermos here with you, and I'll bring some more herbs over tomorrow afternoon. In fact, I'll bring dinner. Do you like pizza?"

Jack smiled to remember his arousing dream. To cover his private mirth, he asked, "They deliver up here?"

Starshine crinkled her weathered face in laughter and said, "Yeah, you just have to know who to call."

Jack smiled as he watched her paddle away in the moonlight and starshine.

A good night's sleep and more herbal tea did wonders for Jack's health. He coughed considerably less and felt stronger in general. He sucked on a cough drop as he filled the solar shower and laid it on a boulder in the morning sun, tidying up the campsite and stocking up on wood while it heated, then took a welcome shower. He warmed up the last of the tea from the thermos on his camp stove, and looked out at Starshine's site as he drank it.

Just as well she's not a sweet young thing. But I learned that I am capable of thinking about affection for someone besides Abby. That door has opened just a crack, and it's okay. Don't have to test it just yet.

I'm really relishing conversation with Starshine. Maybe I'm reaching the end of this solitary journey, ready to be among people again.

Not looking forward to the bustle of the Twin Cities, though. I'd like to live in a smaller, quieter place, like Grand Marais or even smaller. Get back to my rural roots.

Wonder what Dyrud is finding for me. I'll just make the best of whatever comes. Hope there's a good pastor like Luke there, though.

Starshine's second visit exceeded Jack's expectations. They continued getting acquainted, and enjoyed each other's Boundary Waters tales as they sat around a small afternoon fire.

"My favorite season in the BWCA is autumn. I like to come up for a few nights in early October, when the crowds are really light and the colors are spectacular. I usually see more animals that time of year, too."

"Like what?" Jack asked.

"Moose, beaver, bear, mink. One time I didn't remember to tip my canoe up under the trees – I left it right where I pulled it out of the water. A moose and her calf walked right out of the woods and through my camp. I kept backing away, trying to get out of their way and not call attention to myself or look like any kind of threat. But to my dismay they headed right toward my canoe! It was in their way! Kevlar is strong, but a moose is stronger. I was spinning out scenarios of a smashed canoe, and how I would have to flag down other paddlers to hitch a ride back to my rig… it was not pretty. I felt totally helpless watching those huge beasts approach my yellow wonder. But miraculously, they picked their way around it. I was fortunate!"

"Wow, yeah. That makes me realize that I've been fortunate, too. I didn't think of getting my canoe out of the potential path of a moose!" Jack glanced over at his red canoe.

"We should start cooking soon. There are some perfect coals for baking over on this side of the fire. I brought this 'Pesto Pizza' packet I've been wanting to try – but it serves two. And leftovers are such a nuisance up here-no fridge, no microwave!"

"Pizza sounds great to me."

While Starshine took a trip up the hill to the biffy, Jack filtered water for washing and cooking. As he thought about her moose story, he dashed over to his canoe and pulled it in under the trees out of the way. He noted that she had stowed hers properly when she arrived.

"Here's the Kitchen Boulder," Jack gestured to the flat stone surface. "It's very handy except there's no place to sit conveniently."

Starshine shrugged good-naturedly, washed her hands and set out her packet, a large pot, and camp stove. "I wasn't sure what you had, so I brought everything," she explained, setting her small pack aside. "Thanks for filtering the water. It's tiresome, isn't it."

"Yeah, but important. If you don't mind, I'll keep my cold germs to myself and let you cook."

"Sounds like a good plan." Starshine pulled out her Swiss Army knife and cut the tops of the packages off. She added water and a tiny vial of olive oil to the dried green pesto to make the sauce and set it aside to hydrate. She sprinkled the yeast over the crust mix and stirred it around with a fork. She eyeballed the package and the instructions and decided to dump the flour mixture into the pan to mix the water in. Once it was incorporated she used her hand to mix and knead it thoroughly. "Now it rises for 10 minutes," she explained.

She leaned against the rock. "I haven't tried this kind of meal before. It's made for a certain kind of camping oven that I don't have, but I think I can adapt it for us."

"Necessity is the mother of invention," Jack commented. "I have some peach cobbler mix – would you like to make that for dessert?"

"Sounds yummy."

Jack produced the packet and she whipped it up while the pizza dough was rising. It smelled wonderful. She uncovered the dough and tried to stretch it into a circle. This proved difficult, as holes kept appearing. She persevered until she had a circle twice as big as the pot, and she draped it over the pot like a cover. She squeezed the pesto mixture onto the center of the dough and spread it around, then eased the pizza into the pot, letting the excess dough flop over to form a top crust. After fussing with this a bit she pronounced it ready for baking. She smeared the outside of the pan with dish soap to make cleanup easier, and nestled the pan into the hot coals, using a stick to bank the coals halfway up the sides. "About 20 minutes, I'd say," she announced.

While the pizza baked they settled back into their conversation. Starshine had been a school librarian before her retirement some years ago. Jack mentioned that he was an English instructor, so they talked about writers they loved, like Maya Angelou and Wendell Berry. Starshine shared her favorite Shakespeare quote, from Julius Caesar:

"Let me have men about me who are fat,
Sleek-headed men and such as sleep o' nights.
Yon Cassius has a lean and hungry look.
He thinks too much; such men are dangerous."

Jack applauded with delight. He dazzled her with "I am a great eater of beef, and I believe that does harm to my wit." She hadn't heard it but she loved it, and had him repeat it three times so she could remember it.

Soon the smell of garlic wafted over them. The pizza looked odd but tasted wonderful, and they feasted. The cobbler topped off the meal perfectly.

After they'd finished the few dishes and settled back at the fire, Starshine looked intently at Jack and asked, "What brought you to the Boundary Waters?"

Jack sighed, wondering how much to say. Trusting her integrity, he began, "My wife Abby was killed in a car accident in December. It's been really tough for me since then – I'd just been going through the motions of living. Then I lost my job, so the summer opened up before me. So I got the idea to come up here and see if I could find peace."

"You brought your woundedness to the wilderness, like so many of us."

"Exactly."

"And how has it been, Jack? What have you learned?"

Jack spoke slowly and deliberately. "I learned that it's all right to cry – and how to cry. I've learned that I am capable and resourceful on my own, as a single person. I'm working on patience and perseverance. And I'm stronger and healthier than I've been in a long time. Except for this cold, of course."

"I can tell that you are a strong person. And you seem to have a source of strength beyond yourself. Are you a person of faith?"

Surprised by her observation and her question, Jack wasn't sure how to answer. "Yes. I've grown closer to God here, too."

"I know what you mean. This is the most sacred cathedral I've ever frequented," Starshine said as she waved her arm to include all of their surroundings. "Many of us find our souls are fed in this holy wilderness."

Jack nodded his agreement.

"How long ago did you say Abby died?" Starshine asked tenderly.

"This is August…about nine months."

"The same span as labor. You've been laboring all this time, and a new birth is about to happen." Starshine gazed up at the sky as she spoke. "Just how many days have you been on this wilderness adventure?"

"I got the idea around June 21 I think…"

"The summer solstice, time of blossoming…"

"…and we left a week later, June 28. We arrived here in the Boundary Waters on the 29th." Jack made marks in the dirt. "Two days of June, plus thirty-one days of July, that's thirty-three. What day is today?" he asked.

"August 6."

"Plus five is thirty-nine days. Almost forty days in the wilderness, like Jesus when he was tempted," Jack said thoughtfully.

"Akin to the forty years the Hebrew people spent in the wilderness seeking their Promised Land."

"Maybe it's almost time for me to come out of the wilderness. I am feeling like I'm almost ready." Jack looked fondly around his campsite, then shrugged. "And my food supply is getting low."

"I sense that forty days and nights will be just the right metaphor for you. And my intuition is often right."

Jack had a lot to think about after Starshine paddled away in her 'yellow wonder.' *She pointed out some uncanny coincidences about my timing. Is it time for me to go back to civilization? I was just thinking about that today. Maybe it is*

time. Maybe I've learned what I need to learn, and now it's
time to apply it.

With more questions than answers, Jack watched the dying fire and retired for the night.

Chapter 19

Jack woke early and broke camp efficiently so he could be on the water in the slanting rays of the morning sun. Each task carried extra meaning today. *This is the last time I'll do this for a while. I'm leaving the wilderness. Life will change. I've already changed.*

He consolidated his two packs into one, pleased that this was possible. It would certainly make portages easier. A last tour of the Boulder Dome yielded no forgotten belongings, but left him strangely wistful. The solar shower he left deliberately in its spot in the trees, hoping a new tenant would enjoy it as much as he had. He toted the bulky pack to his canoe, flipped the craft upright, positioned it in the water and swung his pack in, thounk. He put on his life vest, stepped into the loaded canoe carefully and smoothly shoved off. He looked back at the site, and then out to the lake, and started to paddle. Once out of his cove, he sent a smile and deep gratitude toward Starshine's camp.

He crossed Winchell Lake to the south portage and accomplished it easily. This time he went straight south down Wanihigan Lake to the 200-rod portage to Grassy Lake. That "grassy" name was a clue that he might have a marshy paddle, which he enjoyed in a way. But the hike along Grassy would likely be full of mosquitoes, so he took time at the portage to slather himself with repellent before shouldering his pack and canoe.

First the mud threatened to suck his boots off, then he splashed through puddles, and picked his way among the rocks. This portage did not seem well used, and he could see why. Presently he saw Grassy Lake on his right, which matched the map. It seemed he would parallel the lake for the final third of the way. At one point he thought he heard a voice; he stopped a moment to listen and realized it was the "gallurmp" of frogs conversing in the marsh. The mosquitoes buzzed in his ears, and as his sweat washed the repellent away they took advantage and bit his neck. With paddle and pole in one hand, he swatted with the other. He slogged on, eager to be done with this agonizing portage.

Then he really did hear voices – a cry of a woman, or a bird? – and some calling back and forth and excited chatter. He picked up his pace and came upon a group of girls in a cluster. No passage here, so he lifted his canoe off his shoulders and onto the trail. As it bumped a tree, the 'clunk' drew the attention of the little crowd. One girl jumped and pointed at him, and they all started talking shrilly, mostly to each other. Jack strained to hear but couldn't make out a cogent word.

"What's happening?" Jack asked authoritatively.

"Claudia fell and hurt her ankle," he heard from several kids at once. It was evident who Claudia was – a petite, attractive woman sat askew on a steep, rooty section of trail, her hands clutching her ankle and pain all over her face. The five young people with Duluth packs filled the scene, concerned and confused. One lanky boy hovered protectively near her.

Claudia looked up at Jack. "I heard it snap," she said hoarsely. A lock of brown hair fell out of her pony tail and across her face and she tried to blow it back in place.

Jack felt an adrenalin surge of energy and ideas. "We've got to get you to a doctor," he stated, "but first we need to immobilize your ankle." He turned to a girl near him. "Could you find me some strong sticks? They should be almost the size of your wrist. Green – still growing. Do you have a saw?"

The kids stared at him blankly, so he shrugged out of his pack and dug around for his folding saw, and rope, and his first aid kit.

"It's our first day out, we just started our trip," another girl offered with a glazed look. Jack expected her to burst into tears any minute.

The smallest girl stepped toward him. "I'll help find some sticks. And I know how to use a saw." He handed his saw to her, grateful for a volunteer. She started down the path, then turned back to ask, "How long do you want them to be?"

"About a foot, foot and a half, as straight as possible," Jack gestured with his hands. "Be very careful!" Another girl scooted past him to join the volunteer and they were off.

He pulled a tarp out of his pack and laid it on a level part of the muddy path. This would have been easier with help but the remaining kids stood by uselessly. He flashed back to himself at the scene of Abby's crash, immobilized with fear. Shaking his head to clear away that image, he took a deep breath.

He approached the woman and said, "Hi, my name is Jack. Could you just put your arm around my neck, and I'll move you over there so we can rig up a splint?" He felt that didn't come out quite right, but she complied with a nod. He tentatively put one arm under her knees, the other securely around her waist. He lifted her smoothly, turned, stepped carefully down the hill, and sat her gently on the tarp. The teens accommodated the new arrangement on the crowded path.

"This must hurt like heck," Jack said, looking at her eyes. *Beautiful brown eyes.*

"Yeah," she said weakly. "I – I have some Ibuprofen in the pack. Travis, where's our medicine pack?"

"Right here, Mom." The tall boy shrugged out of his pack and had a small zippered bag to her in short order.

"Good idea. Take about four – it won't hurt you. Anyone got a canteen?" Jack asked.

A girl stepped forward with a water bottle for Claudia. Two appeared with sticks and Jack's saw. "We brought four sticks," they said helpfully.

"That's great, thanks!" Claudia took off her shoe and rolled up her pant leg. *Should have been wearing boots...oh well, no use being judgmental.* Jack set to work fashioning a splint with the sticks and his softest rope, padding it with her sock as best he could. *Keep the kids engaged.* "Tell me about your group."

"We just started today from, um, Brule Lake. We have four days. Our other leader had to go back one portage because we forgot a pack there. She should be along soon. Now we'll all have to go back. Oh, this is terrible!"

"I'm sorry," Claudia practically wailed. "I don't want to spoil our trip!"

"Don't worry," Jack reassured her as he finished the crude splint. "I'm on my way back to my car anyway. I can help get you out to a doctor, and the rest of your group can go on and finish your trip."

"I'll go with you, Mom," Travis added quickly. "I can help, too."

"Thanks, Trav," Claudia said, wincing. "This is my son, Travis." Jack and the boy acknowledged the introduction.

"I just have a solo canoe," Jack was thinking aloud. "How about if your group takes it, and Travis, Claudia and I take one of your bigger ones? Travis and I can paddle and Claudia, you can ride in the middle."

Claudia took this in with a furrowed brow. "But what about the portages?"

"We'll figure out something so you can stay off your ankle. We'd better take your pack, and Travis can carry it, right?" he indicated Claudia and Travis' Duluth pack, and Travis nodded eagerly. "We'll send most of my gear with the rest of you, if that's okay." Jack didn't wait for a response. "May I put a few of my things in your pack, Travis?"

"Sure," the boy said, indicating that there was extra room. Jack opened his pack and pulled out his fanny-pack with compass, map, knife, car keys, and wallet, and snapped it around his waist. He laid his first aid kit in the top of the open pack. He threw in the sunscreen and repellant and his water-filter bottle. He thought a moment and dug out the bag with Luke's Bible and Abby's journal. He didn't want to make a big deal out of it, but he wanted to keep them with him. He felt self-conscious with the kids watching his every move.

"Life vests?" he asked, unzipping his from his canoe thwart.

"They're with the canoes back at the beginning of this portage," one of the girls said.

At this moment another woman, pack on back, appeared above them on the trail. "What's going on?" she asked loudly as her eyes raked the scene. She was tall and strong in a Scandinavian sort of way, with blonde hair sticking out from under a green bucket hat.

Everyone started talking at once. She halted the cacophony with her hand and looked at the woman on the tarp with her makeshift birch-and-rope splint. Claudia said quietly, "I broke my ankle on that hill. This wonderful man is helping us. He and Travis are going to take me to our car so I can get to a doctor. You and the girls can go on."

"Hi, I'm Jack." Jack waved, since the woman was too far away to shake hands.

She looked at him in awe, still taking it all in. "Jeannie Marie," was all she said.

Travis jumped into the conversation. "We're going to trade canoes so we have room for three of us, and you can take Jack's small one. And his gear."

Jack was again aware of Claudia's pain. "I hate to be impolite, but I'd like to get started. How can we get word to you so when you come out you'll know what's up? Did you work through an outfitter?"

"Yes, Sawbill," Jeannie Marie answered, studying Jack's face as if assessing his trustworthiness.

Jack thought a minute. "We can leave word with them. When are you going to be back there?"

"Monday morning sometime, barring other emergencies." Jeannie Marie looked pointedly at the four girls now in her charge. They looked at each other, avoiding her gaze.

"Great, that'll work," Jack said. "You all have a safe and fun time, and don't worry about Claudia and Travis. We'll leave word at Sawbill for you, or we'll meet you there."

"OK," Jeannie Marie said, sounding only slightly more confident. "We'll see you guys later, then."

With much ado, they got the pack situated on Travis' back, and Claudia consented to try riding on Jack's. Her arms circled his neck from the back, and he grabbed her knees. She was small enough that she must have weighed about the same as the canoe and loaded pack, but this piggyback arrangement required a different sense of balance. Furthermore, the splint added weight to one side. Jack and Travis each took the utmost care going up the steep slope where Claudia had fallen, while the group held their collective breath. Only when the trail leveled out did they turn carefully and exchange farewells with the group. Jack looked at his canoe with a twinge of sadness to leave it behind. *Hope they take good care of the ol' girl. Gosh, I didn't know I cared so much...*

Concentrating on their balance and footing kept Jack and Travis preoccupied at first. Conversation was limited to quick checks on how Claudia was doing, to which she responded with a similar question of Jack. Neither let on any discomfort.

Jack observed that Travis was a gangly teenager with enormous feet, but he handled the hiking with energy if not grace. He was wearing baggy shorts and a t-shirt with an apparent rock band on it. His brown hair stuck out oddly under a black ball cap. Where Claudia's face was round, almost pixie-ish, Travis had a long narrow face that hadn't filled out yet. His eyes had the same intensity, though, as he turned to check on his mom frequently, with evident concern. Jack admired their relationship, based on these initial minutes.

When they reached the three canoes, Jack saw Grassy Lake would be a new challenge, with its thick marsh grass and indistinct channels. Bending his knees, he let Claudia slide to the ground with her weight on her good leg. She reached out to grab a tree for support before she let go of him.

Jack was glad to see Travis put his life vest on. He offered one to Claudia and she followed suit. He swung the pack into the canoe nearest the water and jockeyed it into position to be a backrest for Claudia. He put his life vest down in front of it to be a softer seat for her.

"Now, he said confidently, "Travis, you get in the bow – the front seat, and steady the canoe." Travis held a tree and reached out one skinny leg with a huge shoe. "Step right into the middle, and keep your center of gravity low." Jack held the canoe still while Travis did his best not to rock it as he folded into his seat. "Use your paddle to steady us so the canoe doesn't drift away."

Jack smiled at Claudia when he turned to her, and was rewarded with a smile in return. "Are you ready?" he asked.

"Ready for anything," she replied gamely, trying to hide an anxious exhale.

He lifted her carefully as he had on the trail, and set her into the center of the craft with only a small bump. "Elevate your ankle if you can," he suggested, and she shifted herself around against the pack, using both hands to lift her bulky splint onto the gunwale. "How's the pain?"

"It's easing some," Claudia said, as Jack smoothly stepped in and gave the canoe a little push.

"I wish we could ice your ankle somehow," Jack wondered aloud. "It'd keep the swelling down."

"The lake water is cold. Maybe you could put your foot in the water, Mom," Travis said over his shoulder.

"But I'm afraid the splint would drag my leg down too much," Claudia said. "It'd be like an anchor."

Jack had been thinking as he listened. "How about taking a shirt or something and wetting it in the lake – then it would be cold at least for a while."

Claudia twisted around to reach their pack. "That we could do! I'll just use a t-shirt." With effort she yanked a red shirt out from the middle of the pack, dunked it in the water, gave it a squeeze and laid it on her ankle. "Oooh, that feels good! Good and cold!" She leaned back against the pack and adjusted her seating arrangement.

Grassy Lake was indeed a challenge as Jack adjusted to a longer, heavier craft and having a paddle partner. The channel zigged and zagged, so they were constantly slamming into the marsh grass, making slow going.

"Sorry this is such a bumpy ride," Jack apologized.

"We didn't do any better coming in," Travis assured him.

"We thought it was a lot like bumper cars at the fair," Claudia chuckled.

"Does this channel open up at all?" Jack grunted as he forced the paddle against the thick grasses.

Travis replied over his shoulder, "Yeah, it gets a little better right up here."

Soon they were able to make a straighter course, and they reached the portage at the southern tip of the lake.

Getting Claudia out of the canoe was their most difficult task so far. Jack resigned himself to stepping into the water with one foot, just to get closer to the canoe and work around the submerged logs. Once on land Claudia tried to stand on one foot, but the birch splint threw her off balance. Travis handed her a paddle and she used that to steady her stance.

"Hey, maybe I can use the paddle as a crutch!" she ventured. But after a mere three steps she determined that the handle was too long to fit under her arm, and the slim edge of the paddle gave her little stability. "Sorry, Jack – I tried. I guess I'll be your backpack again."

"No problem, Claudia. The rest of the portages are pretty short, and I really don't mind carrying you." *Really, really don't mind! I feel strong enough, and you're beautiful, and I'm glad to do this for you.*

They pulled the canoe up out of the way and left it with the vests and paddles for a second trip. After drinks of water all round, Travis took the pack and Jack crouched so Claudia could put her arms around his neck. Aware that she was still hurting and Travis was worried about her, Jack resolved to put them both at ease with conversation.

"Where are you two from?" he asked.

"Montevideo."

"Argentina? Really?!"

"Noooo, MonteVIDeo, Minnesota!" Travis laughed. "But MonteviDEo is our sister city!"

"I didn't know Minnesota had such a place. Where is it?"

"On US Highway 212, on the Minnesota River, about 130 miles west of the Twin Cities." Claudia rattled this off like she had said it before.

Something connected in Jack's mind. *Where have I heard of the Minnesota River lately? From Luke – that town where he was in treatment.* "Is that anywhere near a town called 'Something' Falls?"

"Yeah, Granite Falls is, like, twelve miles away."

Jack's mind was racing. *Is that one of the places with a position open?* He tried to stay focused on the conversation. "How long have you lived in Montevideo?"

"Oh, pretty much forever," Claudia responded.

"Definitely forever," Travis chimed in.

"Do you like it?"

Claudia paused. "It's home. We have a good school and a good church, and good friends."

"I wish it was closer to the Cities," Travis said wistfully. "There's not that much for kids to do."

"No megamall, huh?"

"Right." Travis sent a grin over his shoulder to Jack.

"Where's the nearest mall?"

"Willmar. That's about 40 miles away." Travis brightened. "Now that I'm 16, and have my license, I can go to Willmar on my own or with friends. Now I can get out of Monte when I want to!"

"When your mother lets you…" Claudia cautioned.

"Well, yeah, right."

"Congratulations on getting your license, Travis," Jack remembered what a milestone that was for him as a teenager.

"Thanks. Now I just need my own car."

"In your dreams, kiddo." Claudia teased.

"What is the car of your dreams, Travis?"

"I either want a little red sports car or a big black pickup. I can't decide."

Talk of cars and trucks passed the time until they reached Mulligan Lake. "You two stay here – I'll go get the canoe." Jack said. Claudia sat leaning against a rock and Travis stretched his long arms as Jack headed back up the trail.

This is a fine development – when I woke up this morning I had no idea the day would be unfolding this way! Glad I'm physically able to do this. At the beginning of the summer I could barely carry my own pack! I've come a long way. This is good.

We'll need to get her to the hospital in Grand Marais. I think I know where it is. We should be able to get there by sometime this afternoon, I would think. We'll have to have a quick lunch, maybe after the next portage. Hope they have some food! Mine's in my pack!

I think this is my last day in the Boundary Waters. I think I'm ready to join society again. It's actually nice to be with people and make conversation.

Carrying the larger, heavier canoe took some getting used to. Jack bumped some trees and stumbled more than usual, feeling clumsy. He slowed his pace a little and adapted better. Typically, the portage seemed longer the second time. Finally he came upon the mother and son, small and tall, chatting and throwing stones in the lake.

"Sorry to interrupt," Jack said, amused at their playfulness. "Ready for another paddle?"

"Ready when you are, Jack!" Claudia smiled in spite of her discomfort.

Hearing a woman say my name like that – wow, gives me goosebumps! Jack grinned and flipped the canoe into the water.

"Cool!" Travis said, admiring the maneuver. "You really know what you're doing, don't you! Do you do this for a living?"

"No," Jack chuckled. "But it'd be fun if I could."

Once they were all settled in the canoe and shoving off, Claudia asked, "What do you do for a living, Jack?"

"I teach English in the Community College system," Jack replied.

"Where?" Travis wondered.

"That's a good question. I was in the Twin Cities, but I got downsized last spring, and I opted to take a position anywhere else in the system they have a slot open. I'll have to call and see where that might be. I could be going any-where in the state." Jack heard himself sounding fairly comfortable with that uncertainty.

"So do you spend all your summers up here?" Travis asked.

"No, but this one I have. I've been here about seven weeks now."

"No kidding! How did you survive?" Travis looked over his shoulder with admiration.

"Cattail roots and berries, mostly. Just kidding! I'm a freeze-dried gourmet! I've had a wonderful wilderness experience." Jack thought a moment. "You're helping me re-enter civilization. I've been basically alone except the first week."

"Who was with you the first week?" Travis had no end of questions now.

"My minister and friend, Pastor Luke."

"Cool. It would be so cool to be here the whole sum-mer!"

"It has been, Travis! I've seen such beauty, and had some good adventures. But I'm ready to be around people again." Jack leaned forward and put a hand on Claudia's shoulder. "You're being quiet, Claudia. Are you OK?"

"Yeah. The Ibuprofen is helping with the pain. I was ac-tually relaxing a little here."

"So tell me, what's your work?"

"CPA."

"CPA! My wife was a Math teacher. Junior High."

"Was?"

"She died ... nine months ago." Jack noticed that he didn't have a giant lump in his throat, just a small one.

"Oh, I'm sorry. That must have been very hard for you."

"Yeah, it was. But I'm doing better now. This time in the wilderness has been very healing." He wasn't sure what else he could say about that, so he directed a question back to her. "Are you married?"

"Divorced, ten years ago. He died four years ago. That was surprisingly hard."

"I imagine."

Their arrival at the portage pre-empted further conversation. The disembarking procedure worked better here, and soon they were organizing for their hike. Jack's stomach growled so he asked the obvious question: "Do you have any food in your pack?"

"We have snacks – fruit and nuts and cheese crackers. Want some?"

"How about when we get to Lily Lake? I can munch on something as I head back for the canoe, and you can have a little picnic at the portage. I don't want to take too much time."

"Sounds good. I'm hungry, too," Travis rubbed his belly.

"You're always hungry, kiddo!" Claudia chuckled.

On the portage trail, Jack thought a bit, then outlined a plan for their journey. "You can stretch out your foot in the back seat of my car pretty comfortably, I think. It'll take a while to get to Grand Marais, maybe an hour or so. I'll have to look at the map."

"Our car is on Brule Lake, in the parking lot near the launch. It's a Honda Civic," Claudia mentioned.

Jack thought a minute. "Can Travis drive it?"

"Yes, I can! I can drive it!" Travis lit up and executed a happy little dance on the trail. "I can follow you."

"I don't know, Trav…"

"I'll be careful, Mom. Don't worry!"

"OK. It'll be better to have our car there, since Jack will want to be on his way."

In the silence that followed, Jack began to put together a further plan. *She's probably not going to want Travis to drive all the way home to southern Minnesota. Could take them home but we have two vehicles. They need to link up with their group on Monday, and so do I, to get my canoe and pack. That means we all need to stay in the Grand Marais area for a few days. What's the name of that inn that Abby and I looked into? Indian name, the name of a gentle spirit. Nan…Nani…Naniboujou!*

At Lily Lake Claudia dug into their pack and produced apples, smoked almonds, and cheese crackers that were remarkably whole in their snug plastic packs. They loaded Jack up with goodies for his walk back to the canoe.

As he walked and munched, he thought more about this friendly pair. He enjoyed their company. Even with the pain that Claudia must be experiencing, she had a good sense of humor and an uplifting spirit. She and Travis shared a wonderful rapport. Travis seemed like a good-natured boy. Jack replayed their conversations so far.

I'd like to get to know them better. Maybe we can all go to Naniboujou and stay there a few days until it's time to meet the other folks on Monday. That would be great if it works.

When he arrived at Lily Lake with the canoe, Travis and Claudia looked up at him with bright smiles. Before he could say anything, they both gestured to a butterfly that had lighted on Claudia's shoulder. He smiled in response, and watched as it fluttered away. "Wow, that was an extraordinary blessing!" he exclaimed. Claudia beamed.

Jack thanked them for the fine lunch, and when he flipped the canoe into the water, he said with a flourish, "Your chariot awaits, my lady!"

Claudia laughed and clapped her hands. "I feel like Cleopatra, treated like royalty."

"Good, my lady!" Jack bowed low, and commented, "Gee, that feels good to stretch my back. I wonder if that's how that bowing tradition got started!"

Lily Lake lived up to its name. Lilies floated everywhere around the perimeter. Yellow bullhead lilies sported a flower that looked for all the world like a golf ball sitting on a tee. Dragonflies buzzed and hovered around them. "It's so beautiful!" Claudia exclaimed.

"Indeed!" Jack agreed. He kept his eyes out for herons, and spotted one in the shadows by the shore. He gently tapped Claudia on the shoulder and pointed his paddle silently. She let out an appreciative sigh and gestured for Travis to see, too. They rested their paddles and savored the moment. Jack looked at the bird with new joy, as he identified with its calm balance, and its ability to see beneath the surface.

When they had moved on and begun to paddle again, Jack decided to venture his idea. "Have you ever heard of a place called Naniboujou?" he asked.

"No, what is it?" Claudia responded.

"It's a historic inn on the north shore of Lake Superior, north of Grand Marais. My wife and I had researched it, and we'd always planned to come spend some time there. It has a fascinating history."

"Sounds interesting, go on," Claudia urged.

"It was built in the late 1920's I think. It was meant to be an ultra-exclusive club for the likes of Ring Lardner, Jack Dempsey, and Babe Ruth."

"Hey, I love Babe Ruth candy bars!" Travis teased from the bow.

"This is the baseball hero, I think, Trav," Claudia corrected gently.

"These folks had a great dream, but it evaporated when the market crashed, and construction came to a screeching halt. After sitting dormant for years, I don't know how many, the lodge was given new life as an inn. I hear the restaurant gets rave reviews. And they serve high tea in the afternoons."

"Sounds wonderful, Jack." Claudia shifted her leg as they approached the portage.

"You can think about this…but I was just thinking…I don't know what the availability is, and it's a weekend and all, but…that would be a great place to stay until your group comes out." Jack wondered why he was stammering this way. "It could be my treat," he added.

"I don't know…" Claudia began. "You've done so much for us already. We can pay for our own motel."

"You just give Naniboujou some thought though. I'm thinking I'll go there anyway. It would be more friendly if you two were there too." Jack had to busy himself with landing the canoe and helping Claudia out, so he left the subject there.

On the portage trail he left some silence so they could all think about their next steps. They chatted a little about the cars again, and Claudia seemed to feel more comfortable about Travis driving the Civic. Jack reminded them that he needed to wait until Monday for their group anyway, to reclaim his canoe and pack. The Naniboujou idea was really growing on him.

As they resituated in the canoe for the last paddle, Claudia said tentatively, "Uh, Jack, I hate to ask it, but I need a potty break pretty soon."

"No problem. We're now on Brule Lake, which I know like the back of my hand. There's a campsite on our left not far from here, and two more ahead on an island. We can probably stop at one of those whether or not they're occupied."

"I don't want to bother anyone," Claudia said, wrinkling her brow, "any more than I already have."

"If you're referring to me, well, just banish that thought," Jack scolded gently. "Let's just look here…oh yes, I remember this one. It's quite a climb up to the site. Let's go on to the island. If it wasn't so much out of our way, I'd take you to Brule Island, where I stayed for a week and a half. I still think of it as "my island." It's a little slice of paradise." Jack described the picturesque island and wondered aloud how the raspberry crop was doing.

Travis spotted the easy access to a nearby site and slowed his paddling. "This will work great, Mom. I gotta go, too." Jack carried Claudia up the trail, waited at a respectful distance and carried her back down to the canoe. Travis joined them in a few moments and they embarked again. Jack deftly navigated around the islands to the access area and parking lot, thankful for his familiarity with this lake. They landed the canoe smoothly, with a satisfying sense of teamwork.

Jack carried Claudia to the Volvo and set her down gently so she could balance on one leg. He extracted his keys from his fanny pack and opened the doors. Waves of heat smacked them in the face, so he insisted they open it all up and let it air out before he would lift her in. Meanwhile he mounted the canoe on top and concentrated hard to remember the knot Luke had taught him.

This is no time to have the canoe slide off - we have to get Claudia to the hospital! Once assured that the craft was secure, he helped her into the back seat so she could stretch out her splinted leg and still buckle the seat belt. The Duluth pack served as a useful prop.

Travis hopped into the Civic and started it with a loud VROOOM, causing Claudia to close her eyes and shake her head. "That boy…" she started.

"He's a fine boy!" Jack interrupted. "It's clear that you're a wonderful parent for him."

"Well, I don't know about that, but thank you."

Jack drove at a sedate pace on the dirt roads, Travis following. "It's going to take us a while to get there. If you want to doze, feel free." Jack had seen Claudia's weariness.

"I may just rest my eyes," she murmured, and they spent the rest of the trip in silence.

Chapter 20

Jack and Travis pulled into the Emergency entrance of the hospital in Grand Marais. Jack watched as Travis hopped out of the car and started to close the door, then lunged in and set the emergency brake. *He's learning. Disaster averted.*

"You stay here, I'll get a wheelchair," Jack told Claudia, who was rubbing her eyes. "You had a good little nap."

"Yeah, that was helpful. I'm glad we're here. The pain is back full force." She dug in the pack for her wallet.

"We'll get you taken care of, don't worry." Jack jogged into the ER and came back with a wheelchair and a staff person in green scrubs.

Travis hovered protectively and the nurse pushed the chair. Jack suddenly felt superfluous. Once inside Claudia and Travis started filling out forms. Jack was pleased to see that the ER was quiet, so he felt confident that they would get prompt attention. A nurse was already elevating Claudia's ankle and gently placing an ice pack on it.

"Claudia, Travis, I'm going to go call Naniboujou to see if they have rooms for us. I'll be right back." He didn't give them time to protest.

He returned from the pay phone with a big grin. "They just had a cancellation, so we got in! Two rooms on the main floor for you and one upstairs for me. And I made a reservation for high tea at 4:45. I hope we can make it, if not I'll just cancel the tea."

Claudia sat back in her wheelchair and beamed a three-star smile at Jack. "You are taking such good care of us! You're our Good Samaritan!"

"It's my pleasure, as I've said before." Jack sat down and immediately bounced back up again. "I don't have my pack! I have to go pick up a toothbrush and a few clothes! Are you OK here without me?"

"Oh, of course. Travis is here. In fact, you can go ahead to the inn and we can come when we're done. That way you won't have to wait around here. Just give us the directions."

Jack thought about this. "Well, OK. You just head east on highway 61 out of Grand Marais twelve miles, the lady said on the phone. You'll see the sign on the right."

"Highway 61. Sounds easy enough. Got it, Travis? I guess we'll see you there whenever we get done here."

"Your pack is in my car – I'll just take it to the inn, if that's OK."

Claudia thought for a moment and looked at Travis. "I can't think of anything we'll need here – I've got my wallet so I have my insurance card and everything... Yeah, go ahead and take it. Travis will have his hands full with a mom hopping on one leg." She grinned at her son and he returned the look.

Jack left through the automatic doors and then spun round and headed back in before they'd even closed. He almost ran into the second set as they reversed direction.

"Here's the phone number of Naniboujou." Jack dug in his pocket and handed her a slip of paper. "You're sure you're all right?" Jack felt reluctant to leave her somehow.

"Sure. Go ahead and we'll meet you for tea."

A nurse appeared with a clipboard. "Claudia? Let's get you into an examining room." She looked at the sticks and rope stabilizing the swollen ankle. "Quite an elaborate apparatus you have there. Boundary Waters injury? Someone's been taking good care of you, I can tell." As the nurse started wheeling her chair toward the double doors, Claudia looked over her shoulder and this time gave Jack a four-star smile.

Something went 'twang' in his chest.

Leaving the hospital, Jack stopped at Ben Franklin for a toothbrush and other sundries. He was pleased to find that he could buy clothing there too. He'd actually changed sizes, so after some trial and error he bought several changes of clothes to get him through the coming days.

From Grand Marais Jack followed the highway east along the shore of Lake Superior. Fog teased at the treetops and merged the water and sky. When his odometer told him he'd come twelve miles, he slowed. On the left he glimpsed a sign for Judge C. R. Magney State Park. Jack turned right into the parking lot of Naniboujou Lodge.

His first impression was one of welcome space – the town of Grand Marais had seemed a little claustrophobic after being in the wilderness so long. Here, broad lawns with huge trees surrounded the arrow-shaped cedar-shake building. A flag flew overhead. Lake Superior stretched expansively not far from the lodge. *This is perfect.*

Jack received a warm welcome at the desk, and soon he was checked in. He made clear that Claudia and Travis would be arriving in a while, and paid for three nights in advance so there would be no quibbling. At the mention of mealtimes Jack remembered high tea and confirmed his reservation for three people at 4:45 in the solarium. "What time is it now?" he asked.

"Ten till four."

Good, I have time for a shower. I need it!

Jack peeked into the dining room before heading to his room. The ceiling and walls dazzled him with their red, orange, blue, yellow, and green geometric shapes. The woman at the desk saw him take it all in and explained, "It's Cree Indian design. Step in and take a look at the fireplace. It's all native stone."

The massive fireplace dominated the far end of the room. Smooth stones of varying sizes and shapes created a mandala above the mantel and continued on up to the ceiling. Two small sofas on the wide stone hearth looked inviting. Relaxing piano music wafted through the room. Jack sighed. *This is good.*

After the best shower of his life, Jack took a good look at himself in the mirror. His eyes sparkled in his tanned face. *I like the beard! It only has a little gray. It needs some shaping, and my hair needs a trim, but it's not too bad this long. My shoulders look stronger and I'm not flabby any more! I look like a new man!*

Folks at home will hardly recognize me. I've changed inside and out.

Suddenly curious about where he would be teaching next year, Jack looked around the room. He soon realized that part of the inn's charm was a lack of telephones in the rooms. He dressed quickly in his new duds and trotted downstairs to the pay phone near the registration area. Digging out his calling card, he closed his eyes to bring to mind the number of the Community College. In a moment he had Dyrud on the line.

"Jack! You just caught me on the way out of my office. How are you?"

"I'm great!" Jack heard himself say. "I won't keep you – I'm just wondering if you found a spot for me to teach this fall."

"Of course. Let me check here." Papers rustled and Jack felt suspense but not fear. "Here it is. Minnesota West Community and Technical College in Granite Falls. Do you know where that is? In the southwestern part of the state?"

"Yes, I know about Granite Falls! When do I need to be there?"

"Faculty report August 20. You've got two weeks, it looks like."

"Sounds great. I'll get back to you next week. And thank you, sir, you've done a wonderful thing."

After a stunned silence, Dyrud stammered his goodbye.

Jack walked out of the lodge and gazed at Lake Superior. It seemed wild and vast compared with the lakes that had been so much a part of his life this summer. He traversed the lawn to the shore and considered occupying a wooden chair, but instead chose to walk by the water. He picked up rocks and tossed them in, examined a curious piece of driftwood, and watched the waves foam at his feet. A glance at his watch sent him back across the broad lawn at an angle, still keeping an eye on the lake as he approached the lodge.

He settled into a comfortable chair in the solarium to await tea. *Granite Falls. Near Montevideo and my new friends. Where Luke got his new lease on life. He mentioned a good church there, too. A fresh start for me. It's like I've been reborn.*

Promptly at 4:45 a server brought a silver tray with a pot of tea, three china cups and saucers, sugar and cream, and a plate loaded with tantalizing delights. She pointed out for him the cucumber-cream cheese sandwiches, salmon salad sandwiches, fresh currant scones, chocolate mint bundt cake, and chocolate-dipped shortbread cookies. Fresh strawberries in the center needed no introduction.

Jack poured a cup of tea and sipped it as he looked out at the big lake. The sun splashed the lawn and trees with light and brightened the dark Superior waters. He turned toward a sound behind him. There stood Claudia, balanced on crutches, sporting a fancy blue splint with her pink toes peeking out. Travis stood beside her, and both wore five-star smiles.

He stood and bowed suavely, perfectly balancing his teacup throughout. "Your tea is served, my lady, my lord."

Life is good. God is good.